GREAT ENGLISH SHORT STORIES

DOVER THRIFT EDITIONS

Edited by
Paul Negri

DOVER PUBLICATIONS, INC.
MINEOLA, NEW YORK

DOVER THRIFT EDITIONS

GENERAL EDITOR: MARY CAROLYN WALDREP
EDITOR OF THIS VOLUME: JANET BAINE KOPITO

Bibliographical Note

This Dover edition, first published in 2005, is a new selection of stories reprinted from standard texts. A new introductory Note has been specially prepared for this edition.

Library of Congress Cataloging-in-Publication Data

Great English short stories / edited by Paul Negri.
    p. cm. — (Dover thrift editions)
    Contents: The haunted house / Charles Dickens — The fiddler of the reels / Thomas Hardy — The parson's daughter of Oxney Colne / Anthony Trollope — The Prussian officer / D. H. Lawrence — The phantom rickshaw / Rudyard Kipling — Under the knife / H. G. Wells — The dead hand / Wilkie Collins — Tobermory / Saki —A lodging for the night / Robert Louis Stevenson — "Oh, whistle, and I'll come to you, my lad" / M.R. James — The broken boot / John Galsworthy — The house of cobwebs / George Gissing — The lifted veil / George Eliot.
    ISBN-13: 978-0-486-44090-3
    ISBN-10: 0-486-44090-7 (pbk.)
    1. Short stories, English. I. Negri, Paul. II. Series.

PR1309.S5G74 2005
823'.010808—dc22

                                                                    2005043293

Manufactured in the United States by LSC Communications
44090706   2019
www.doverpublications.com

Note

Among the vast riches of English literature are masterpieces of that most challenging of literary forms—the short story. To develop character, plot, and other requisite elements within the brief space allotted requires a focus of purpose far different from that of a longer work. The reader must learn enough about the characters to care about their fate, and the story must be sufficiently complex to establish the conflict and its resolution. This anthology will leave no doubt that many of literature's greatest novelists, such as Dickens, Hardy, George Eliot, Lawrence, Trollope, Galsworthy, and Wells—to name just a few—produced short works that satisfy these demands.

This collection of thirteen stories spans approximately sixty-five years, from the publication of Collins' "The Dead Hand" in 1857 to the appearance of Galsworthy's "The Broken Boot" in 1923. The historical milieu is that of the Victorian, Edwardian, and Georgian periods in England. Short fiction was a mainstay of periodicals in the latter part of the nineteenth century (it is still included in some contemporary magazines), and many writers capitalized on this popularity to supplement their income. Several of the stories in this collection first appeared in periodicals, including "The Parson's Daughter of Oxney Colne" (*The London Review,* 2, 1861), "The Fiddler of the Reels" (*Scribner's Magazine,* 1893), and "A Lodging for the Night" (*Temple Bar,* 1877).

Many of the late nineteenth- and early twentieth-century works in this compilation reflect the influence of Gothic fiction: the use of supernatural events ("The Haunted House," "Under the Knife," "The Phantom 'Rickshaw," "The Lifted Veil," " 'Oh, Whistle, and I'll Come to You, My Lad,' "); the creation of an atmosphere of terror ("The Dead Hand," "The House of Cobwebs"); and the portrayal of the oppressiveness of madness ("The Lifted Veil"). The supernatural is also invoked in the comical situation of a cat verbally sniping at the British upper class after it learns to speak like a human in "Tobermory." It is interesting to note how these works use the chaotic effects of superstition, the fear of the unknown, and a belief in ghosts to refute the prevailing Victorian notions of progress, science, and rationalism. The Crystal Palace, the great Victorian exhibition of 1851 that presented "modern" technology in all its glory, is mentioned in "The Fiddler of the Reels." Hardy describes the time as one of "great hope and activity among the nations and industries," and yet his story is colored by words such as "weird," "wizardly," "peculiar," "devil's tunes," "wild desire," "abandonment," and "witchery," implying that the advance of technology has done little to tame human nature—or explain the inexplicable.

The use of local color does much to establish the setting of a brief tale. In these works, the great city of London predominates. It provides a means of escape from the scrutiny of the village for characters in "The Fiddler of the Reels," "The Parson's Daughter of Oxney Colne," and "The House of Cobwebs." In the Gissing story, the wages of progress are commented upon by the narrator, who remarks that "the neighborhood was undergoing change such as in our time destroys the picturesque in all London suburbs."

Rounding out this highly entertaining selection are works by Trollope, Lawrence, and Galsworthy. In "The Parson's Daughter of Oxney Colne," social strictures clash with romantic love. "The Prussian Officer," Lawrence's shocking examination of the explosive nature of repressed feelings, is perhaps the most "modern" of the tales. "The Broken Boot" succinctly uncovers the last shreds of pride of a down-on-his-luck actor. All three stories examine the gap between social classes in expert, dramatic fashion.

Ultimately, the true success of any work of fiction occurs when the reader "inhabits" the story and loses touch with his or her surroundings. Without a doubt, this collection of thirteen short stories by writers as diverse as D. H. Lawrence and John Galsworthy will quickly transport the reader to that remarkable realm.

Contents

THE HAUNTED HOUSE

Charles Dickens

THE MORTALS IN THE HOUSE

UNDER NONE of the accredited ghostly circumstances, and environed by none of the conventional ghostly surroundings, did I first make acquaintance with the house which is the subject of this Christmas piece. I saw it in the daylight, with the sun upon it. There was no wind, no rain, no lightning, no thunder, no awful or unwonted circumstance, of any kind, to heighten its effect. More than that: I had come to it direct from a railway station: it was not more than a mile distant from the railway station; and, as I stood outside the house, looking back upon the way I had come, I could see the goods train running smoothly along the embankment in the valley. I will not say that everything was utterly commonplace, because I doubt if anything can be that, except to utterly commonplace people—and there my vanity steps in; but, I will take it on myself to say that anybody might see the house as I saw it, any fine autumn morning.

The manner of my lighting on it was this.

I was travelling towards London out of the North, intending to stop by the way, to look at the house. My health required a temporary residence in the country; and a friend of mine who knew that, and who had happened to drive past the house, had written to me to suggest it as a likely place. I had got into the train at midnight, and had fallen asleep, and had woke up and had sat looking out of window at the brilliant Northern Lights in the sky, and had fallen asleep again, and had woke up again to find the night gone, with the usual discontented conviction on me that I hadn't been to sleep at all;—upon which question, in the first imbecility of that condition, I am ashamed to believe that I would have done wager by battle with the man who sat opposite me. That opposite man had had, through the night— as that opposite man always has—several legs too many, and all of them too long. In addition to this unreasonable conduct (which was only to be

1

↳ of the house

↳ passing by the house

↳ man w/ >2 legs of absurd length

expected of him), he had had a pencil and a pocket-book, and had been perpetually listening and taking notes. It had appeared to me that these aggravating notes related to the jolts and bumps of the carriage, and I should have resigned myself to his taking them, under a general supposition that he was in the civil-engineering way of life, if he had not sat staring straight over my head whenever he listened. He was a goggle-eyed gentleman of a per-plexed aspect, and his demeanour became unbearable.

It was a cold, dead morning (the sun not being up yet), and when I had out-watched the paling light of the fires of the iron country, and the curtain of heavy smoke that hung at once between me and the stars and between me and the day, I turned to my fellow-traveller and said:

"I *beg* your pardon, Sir, but do you observe anything particular in me?" For, really, he appeared to be taking down, either my travelling-cap or my hair, with a minuteness that was a liberty.

The goggle-eyed gentleman withdrew his eyes from behind me, as if the back of the carriage were a hundred miles off, and said, with a lofty look of compassion for my insignificance:

"In you, Sir?—B."

"B, Sir?" said I, growing warm.

"I have nothing to do with you, sir," returned the gentleman; "pray let me listen—O."

He enunciated this vowel after a pause, and noted it down.

At first I was alarmed, for an Express lunatic and no communication with the guard, is a serious position. The thought came to my relief that the gentleman might be what is popularly called a Rapper: one of a sect for (some of) whom I have the highest respect, but whom I don't believe in. I was going to ask him the question, when he took the bread out of my mouth.

"You will excuse me," said the gentleman contemptuously, "if I am too much in advance of common humanity to trouble myself at all about it. I have passed the night—as indeed I pass the whole of my time now—in spiritual intercourse."

"O!" said I, somewhat snappishly.

"The conferences of the night began," continued the gentleman, turning several leaves of his note-book, "with this message: 'Evil com-munications corrupt good manners.'"

"Sound," said I; "but, absolutely new?"

"New from spirits," returned the gentleman.

I could only repeat my rather snappish "O!" and ask if I might be favoured with the last communication.

"'A bird in the hand,'" said the gentleman, reading his last entry with great solemnity, "'is worth two in the Bosh.'"

"Truly I am of the same opinion," said I; "but shouldn't it be Bush?"

"It came to me, Bosh," returned the gentleman.

The gentleman then informed me that the spirit of Socrates had delivered this special revelation in the course of the night, "My friend, I hope you are pretty well. There are two in this railway carriage. How do you do? There are seventeen thousand four hundred and seventy-nine spirits here, but you cannot see them. Pythagoras is here. He is not at liberty to mention it, but hopes you like travelling." Galileo likewise had dropped in, with this scientific intelligence. "I am glad to see you, *amico. Come sta?* Water will freeze when it is cold enough. *Addio!*" In the course of the night, also, the following phenomena had occurred. Bishop Butler had insisted on spelling his name, "Bubler," for which offence against orthography and good manners he had been dismissed as out of temper. John Milton (suspected of wilful mystification) had repudiated the authorship of Paradise Lost, and had introduced, as joint authors of that poem, two Unknown gentlemen, respectively named Grungers and Scadgingtone. And Prince Arthur, nephew of King John of England, had described himself as tolerably comfortable in the seventh circle, where he was learning to paint on velvet, under the direction of Mrs. Trimmer and Mary Queen of Scots.

If this should meet the eye of the gentleman who favoured me with these disclosures, I trust he will excuse my confessing that the sight of the rising sun, and the contemplation of the magnificent Order of the vast Universe, made me impatient of them. In a word, I was so impatient of them, that I was mightily glad to get out at the next station, and to exchange these clouds and vapours for the free air of Heaven.

By that time it was a beautiful morning. As I walked away among such leaves as had already fallen from the golden, brown, and russet trees; and as I looked around me on the wonders of Creation, and thought of the steady, unchanging, and harmonious laws by which they are sustained; the gentleman's spiritual intercourse seemed to me as poor a piece of journey-work as ever this world saw. In which heathen state of mind, I came within view of the house, and stopped to examine it attentively.

It was a solitary house, standing in a sadly neglected garden: a pretty even square of some two acres. It was a house of about the time of George the Second; as stiff, as cold, as formal, and in as bad taste, as could possibly be desired by the most loyal admirer of the whole quartet of Georges. It was uninhabited, but had, within a year or two, been cheaply repaired to render it habitable; I say cheaply, because the work had been done in a surface manner, and was already decaying as to the paint and plaster, though the colours were fresh. A lop-sided board drooped over the garden wall, announcing that it was "to let on very reasonable terms, well furnished." It was much too closely and heavily shadowed by trees, and, in particular, there were six tall poplars before the front windows, which were excessively melancholy, and the site of which had been extremely ill chosen.

It was easy to see that it was an avoided house—a house that was shunned by the village, to which my eye was guided by a church spire some half a mile off—a house that nobody would take. And the natural inference was, that it had the reputation of being a haunted house.

No period within the four-and-twenty hours of day and night is so solemn to me, as the early morning. In the summertime, I often rise very early, and repair to my room to do a day's work before breakfast, and I am always on those occasions deeply impressed by the stillness and solitude around me. Besides that there is something awful in the being surrounded by familiar faces asleep—in the knowledge that those who are dearest to us and to whom we are dearest, are profoundly unconscious of us, in an impassive state, anticipative of that mysterious condition to which we are all tending—the stopped life, the broken threads of yesterday, the deserted seat, the closed book, the unfinished but abandoned occupation, all are images of Death. The tranquillity of the hour is the tranquillity of Death. The colour and the chill have the same association. Even a certain air that familiar household objects take upon them when they first emerge from the shadows of the night into the morning, of being newer, and as they used to be long ago, has its counterpart in the subsidence of the worn face of maturity or age, in death, into the old youthful look. Moreover, I once saw the apparition of my father, at this hour. He was alive and well, and nothing ever came of it, but I saw him in the daylight, sitting with his back towards me, on a seat that stood beside my bed. His head was resting on his hand, and whether he was slumbering or grieving, I could not discern. Amazed to see him there, I sat up, moved my position, leaned out of bed, and watched him. As he did not move then, I became alarmed and laid my hand upon his shoulder, as I thought—and there was no such thing.

For all these reasons, and for others less easily and briefly statable, I find the early morning to be my most ghostly time. Any house would be more or less haunted, to me, in the early morning; and a haunted house could scarcely address me to greater advantage than then.

I walked on into the village, with the desertion of this house upon my mind, and I found the landlord of the little inn, sanding his doorstep. I bespoke breakfast, and broached the subject of the house.

"Is it haunted?" I asked.

The landlord looked at me, shook his head, and answered, "I say nothing."

"Then it is haunted?"

"Well!" cried the landlord, in an outburst of frankness that had the appearance of desperation—"I wouldn't sleep in it."

"Why not?"

"If I wanted to have all the bells in a house ring, with nobody to ring 'em; and all the doors in a house bang, with nobody to bang 'em; and all sorts of feet treading about, with no feet there; why, then," said the landlord, "I'd sleep in that house."

"Is anything seen there?"

The landlord looked at me again, and then, with his former appearance of desperation, called down his stable-yard for "Ikey!"

The call produced a high-shouldered young fellow, with a round red face, a short crop of sandy hair, a very broad humorous mouth, a turned-up nose, and a great sleeved waistcoat of purple bars, with mother-of-pearl buttons, that seemed to be growing upon him, and to be in a fair way—if it were not pruned—of covering his head and overrunning his boots.

"This gentleman wants to know," said the landlord, "if anything's seen at the Poplars." → house owners?

"'Ooded woman with a howl," said Ikey, in a state of great freshness.

"Do you mean a cry?"

"I mean a bird, sir."

"A hooded woman with an owl. Dear me! Did you ever see her?"

"I seen the howl."

"Never the woman?"

"Not so plain as the howl, but they always keeps together."

"Has anybody ever seen the woman as plainly as the owl?"

"Lord bless you, sir! Lots."

"Who?" Seen @ haunted house?

"Lord bless you, sir! Lots."

"The general-dealer opposite, for instance, who is opening his shop?"

"Perkins? Bless you, Perkins wouldn't go a-nigh the place. No!" observed the young man, with considerable feeling; "he an't over wise, an't Perkins, but he an't such a fool as *that*."

(Here, the landlord murmured his confidence in Perkins's knowing better.)

"Who is—or who was—the hooded woman with the owl? Do you know?"

"Well!" said Ikey, holding up his cap with one hand while he scratched his head with the other, "they say, in general, that she was murdered, and the howl he 'ooted the while."

This very concise summary of the facts was all I could learn, except that a young man, as hearty and likely a young man as ever I see, had been took with fits and held down in 'em, after seeing the hooded woman. Also, that a personage, dimly described as "a hold chap, a sort of one-eyed tramp, answering to the name of Joby, unless you challenged him as

Greenwood, and then he said, 'Why not? and even if so, mind your own business,'" had encountered the hooded woman, a matter of five or six times: But, I was not materially assisted by these witnesses: inasmuch as the first was in California, and the last was, as Ikey said (and he was confirmed by the landlord), Anywheres.

Now, although I regard with a hushed and solemn fear, the mysteries, between which and this state of existence is interposed the barrier of the great trial and change that fall on all the things that live; and although I have not the audacity to pretend that I know anything of them; I can no more reconcile the mere banging of doors, ringing of bells, creaking of boards, and such-like insignificances, with the majestic beauty and pervading analogy of all the Divine rules that I am permitted to understand, than I had been able, a little while before, to yoke the spiritual intercourse of my fellow-traveller to the chariot of the rising sun. Moreover, I had lived in two haunted houses—both abroad. In one of these, an old Italian palace, which bore the reputation of being twice abandoned on that account, I lived eight months, most tranquilly and pleasantly: notwithstanding that the house had a score of mysterious bedrooms, which were never used, and possessed, in one large room in which I sat reading, times out of number at all hours, and next to which I slept, a haunted chamber of the first pretensions. I gently hinted these considerations to the landlord. And as to this particular house having a bad name, I reasoned with him, Why, how many things had bad names undeservedly, and how easy it was to give bad names, and did he not think that if he and I were persistently to whisper in the village that any weird-looking old drunken tinker of the neighbourhood had sold himself to the Devil, he would come in time to be suspected, of that commercial venture! All this wise talk was perfectly ineffective with the landlord, I am bound to confess, and was as dead a failure as ever I made in my life.

To cut this part of the story short, I was piqued about the haunted house, and was already half resolved to take it. So, after breakfast, I got the keys from Perkins's brother-in-law (a whip and harness maker, who keeps the Post Office, and is under submission to a most rigorous wife of the Doubly Seceding Little Emmanuel persuasion), and went up to the house, attended by my landlord and by Ikey.

Within, I found it, as I had expected, transcendently dismal. The slowly changing shadows waved on it from the heavy trees, were doleful in the last degree; the house was ill-placed, ill-built, ill-planned, and ill-fitted. It was damp, it was not free from dry rot, there was a flavour of rats in it, and it was the gloomy victim of that indescribable decay which settles on all the work of man's hands whenever it is not turned to man's account. The kitchens and offices were too large, and too remote from each other. Above stairs and below, waste tracts of passage intervened between patches of fertility represented by rooms; and there was a mouldy old well with a green growth upon it, hiding like a murderous trap, near the bottom of the back stairs, under the double row of bells. One of these bells was labelled, on a black ground in faded white letters, MASTER B. This, they told me, was the bell that rang the most.

"Who was Master B.?" I asked. "Is it known what he did while the owl hooted?"

"Rang the bell," said Ikey.

I was rather struck by the prompt dexterity with which this young man pitched his fur cap at the bell, and rang it himself. It was a loud, unpleasant bell, and made a very disagreeable sound. The other bells were inscribed according to the names of the rooms to which their wires were conducted: as "Picture Room," "Double Room," "Clock Room," and the like. Following Master B.'s bell to its source, I found that young gentleman to have had but indifferent third-class accommodation in a triangular cabin under the cock-loft, with a corner fireplace which Master B. must have been exceedingly small if he were ever able to warm himself at, and a corner chimneypiece like a pyramidal staircase to the ceiling for Tom Thumb. The papering of one side of the room had dropped down bodily, with fragments of plaster adhering to it, and almost blocked up the door. It appeared that Master B., in his spiritual condition, always made a point of pulling the paper down. Neither the landlord nor Ikey could suggest why he made such a fool of himself.

Except that the house had an immensely large rambling loft at top, I made no other discoveries. It was moderately well furnished, but sparely. Some of the furniture—say, a third—was as old as the house; the rest was of various periods within the last half-century. I was referred to a cornchandler in the market-place of the country town to treat for the house. I went that day, and I took it for six months.

It was just the middle of October when I moved in with my maiden sister (I venture to call her eight-and-thirty, she is so very handsome, sensible, and engaging). We took with us, a deaf stable-man, my bloodhound Turk, two women servants, and a young person called an Odd Girl. I have reason to record of the attendant last enumerated, who was one of the Saint Lawrence's Union Female Orphans, that she was a fatal mistake and a disastrous engagement.

The year was dying early, the leaves were falling fast, it was a raw cold day when we took possession, and the gloom of the house was most depressing. The cook (an amiable woman, but of a weak turn of intellect) burst into tears on beholding the kitchen, and requested that her silver watch might be delivered over to her sister (2 Tuppintock's Gardens, Liggs's Walk, Clapham Rise), in the event of anything happening to her from the damp. Streaker, the housemaid, feigned cheerfulness, but was the greater martyr. The Odd Girl, who had never been in the country, alone was pleased and made arrangements for sowing an acorn in the garden outside the scullery window, and rearing an oak.

We went, before dark, through all the natural—as opposed to super-natural—miseries incidental to our state. Dispiriting reports ascended (like the smoke) from the basement in volumes, and descended from the upper rooms. There was no rolling-pin, there was no salamander (which failed to surprise me, for I don't know what it is), there was nothing in the house, what there was, was broken, the last people must have lived like pigs, what could the meaning of the landlord be? Through these distresses, the Odd Girl was cheerful and exemplary. But within four hours after dark we had got into a supernatural groove, and the Odd Girl had seen "Eyes," and was in hysterics.

My sister and I had agreed to keep the haunting strictly to ourselves, and my impression was, and still is, that I had not left Ikey, when he helped to unload the cart, alone with the woman, or any one of them, for one minute. Nevertheless, as I say, the Odd Girl had "seen Eyes" (no other explanation could ever be drawn from her), before nine, and by ten o'clock had had as much vinegar applied to her as would pickle a handsome salmon.

I leave a discerning public to judge of my feelings, when, under these untoward circumstances, at about half-past ten o'clock Master B.'s bell began to ring in a most infuriated manner, and Turk howled until the house resounded with his lamentations!

I hope I may never again be in a state of mind so unchristian as the mental frame in which I lived for some weeks, respecting the memory of Master B. Whether his bell was rung by rats, or mice, or bats, or wind, or what other accidental vibration or sometimes by one cause, sometimes another, and sometimes by collusion, I don't know; but, certain it is, that it did ring two nights out of three, until I conceived the happy idea of twisting Master B.'s neck—in other words, breaking his bell short off—and silencing that young gentleman, as to my experience and belief, for ever.

But, by that time, the Odd Girl had developed such improving powers of catalepsy, that she had become a shining example of that very inconvenient disorder. She would stiffen, like a Guy Fawkes endowed with unreason, on the most irrelevant occasions. I would address the servants in a lucid manner, pointing out to them that I had painted Master B.'s room and balked the paper, and taken Master B.'s bell away and balked the ringing, and if they could suppose that that confounded boy had lived and died, to clothe himself with no better behaviour than would most unquestionably have brought him and the sharpest particles of a birch-broom into close acquaintance in the present imperfect state of existence, could they also suppose a mere poor human being, such as I was, capable by those contemptible means of counteracting and limiting the powers of the disembodied spirits of the dead, or of any spirits?—I say I would become emphatic and cogent, not to say rather complacent, in such an address, when it would all go for nothing by reason of the Odd Girl's suddenly stiffening from the toes upward, and glaring among us like a parochial petrifaction. *⌐haunted by Master B?*

Streaker, the housemaid, too, had an attribute of a most discomfiting nature. I am unable to say whether she was of an unusually lymphatic temperament, or what else was the matter with her, but this young woman became a mere Distillery for the production of the largest and most transparent tears I ever met with. Combined with these characteristics, was a peculiar tenacity of hold in those specimens, so that they didn't fall, but hung upon her face and nose. In this condition, and mildly and deplorably shaking her head, her silence would throw me more heavily than the Admirable Crichton could have done in a verbal disputation for a purse of money. Cook, likewise, always covered me with confusion as with a garment, by neatly winding up the session with the protest that the Ouse was wearing her out, and by meekly repeating her last wishes regarding her silver watch.

As to our nightly life, the contagion of suspicion and fear was among us, and there is no such contagion under the sky. *Hooded woman?* According to the accounts, we were in a perfect Convent of hooded women. Noises? With that contagion downstairs, I myself have sat in the dismal parlour, listening, until I have heard so many and such strange noises, that they would have chilled my blood if I had not warmed it by dashing out to make discoveries. Try this in bed, in the dead of the night; try this at your own comfortable fireside, in the life of the night. You can fill any house with noises, if you will, until you have a noise for every nerve in your nervous system. *← you can think yourself into fear*

I repeat; the contagion of suspicion and fear was among us, and there is no such contagion under the sky. The women (their noses in a chronic state of excoriation from smelling-salts) were always primed and loaded for a swoon, and ready to go off with hair-triggers. The two elder detached the Odd Girl on all expeditions that were considered doubly hazardous, and she always established the reputation of such adventures by coming back cataleptic. If Cook or Streaker went overhead after dark, we knew we should presently hear a bump on the ceiling; and this took place so constantly, that it was as if a fighting man were engaged to go about the house, administering a touch of his art which I believe is called The Auctioneer, to every domestic he met with.

It was in vain to do anything. It was in vain to be frightened, for the moment in one's own person, by a real owl, and then to show the owl. It

SUSPICION. FEAR.

was in vain to discover, by striking an accidental discord on the piano, that Turk always howled at particular notes and combinations. It was in vain to be a Rhadamanthus with the bells, and if an unfortunate bell rang without leave, to have it down inexorably and silence it. It was in vain to fire up chimneys, let torches down the well, charge furiously into suspected rooms and recesses. We changed servants, and it was no better. The new set ran away, and a third set came, and it was no better. At last, our comfortable housekeeping got to be so disorganised and wretched, that I one night dejectedly said to my sister: "Patty, I begin to despair of our getting people to go on with us here, and I think we must give this up."

My sister, who is a woman of immense spirit, replied, "No, John, don't give it up. Don't be beaten, John. There is another way."

"And what is that?" said I.

"John," returned my sister, "if we are not to be driven out of this house, and that for no reason whatever, that is apparent to you or me, we must help ourselves and take the house wholly and solely into our own hands."

"But, the servants," said I.

"Have no servants," said my sister, boldly.

Like most people in my grade of life, I had never thought of the possibility of going on without those faithful obstructions. The notion was so new to me when suggested, that I looked very doubtful.

"We know they come here to be frightened and infect one another, and we know they are frightened and do infect one another," said my sister.

"With the exception of Bottles," I observed, in a meditative tone.

(The deaf stable-man. I kept him in my service, and still keep him, as a phenomenon of moroseness not to be matched in England.)

"To be sure, John," assented my sister; "except Bottles. And what does that go to prove? Bottles talks to nobody, and hears nobody unless he is absolutely roared at, and what alarm has Bottles ever given, or taken? None."

This was perfectly true; the individual in question having retired, every night at ten o'clock, to his bed over the coach-house, with no other company than a pitchfork and a pail of water. That the pail of water would have been over me, and the pitchfork through me, if I had put myself without announcement in Bottles's way after that minute, I had deposited in my own mind as a fact worth remembering. Neither had Bottles ever taken the least notice of any of our many uproars. An imperturbable and speechless man, he had sat at his supper, with Streaker present in a swoon, and the Odd Girl marble, and had only put another potato in his cheek, or profited by the general misery to help himself to beefsteak pie.

"And so," continued my sister, "I exempt Bottles. And considering, John, that the house is too large, and perhaps too lonely, to be kept well in hand by Bottles, you, and me, I propose that we cast about among our friends for a certain selected number of the most reliable and willing— form a Society here for three months—wait upon ourselves and one another—live cheerfully and socially—and see what happens."

I was so charmed with my sister, that I embraced her on the spot, and went into her plan with the greatest ardour.

We were then in the third week of November; but, we took our measures so vigorously, and were so well seconded by the friends in whom we confided, that there was still a week of the month unexpired, when our party all came down together merrily, and mustered in the haunted house.

I will mention, in this place, two small changes that I made while my sister and I were yet alone. It occurring to me as not improbable that Turk howled in the house at night, partly because he wanted to get out of it, I stationed him in his kennel outside, but unchained; and I seriously warned the village that any man who came in his way must not expect to leave him without a rip in his own throat. I then casually asked Ikey if he were a judge of a gun? On his saying, "Yes, Sir, I knows a good gun when I sees her," I begged the favour of his stepping up to the house and looking at mine.

"*She's* a true one, sir," said Ikey, after inspecting a double-barrelled rifle that I bought in New York a few years ago. "No mistake about *her*, Sir."

"Ikey," said I, "don't mention it; I have seen something in this house."

"No, Sir?" he whispered, greedily opening his eyes. "'Ooded lady, Sir?"

"Don't be frightened," said I. "It was a figure rather like you."

"Lord, Sir?"

"Ikey!" said I, shaking hands with him warmly: I may say affectionately; "if there is any truth in these ghost-stories, the greatest service I can do you, is, to fire at that figure. And I promise you, by Heaven and earth, I will do it with this gun if I see it again!"

The young man thanked me, and took his leave with some little precipitation, after declining a glass of liquor. I imparted my secret to him, because I had never quite forgotten his throwing his cap at the bell; because I had, on another occasion, noticed something very like a fur cap, lying not far from the bell, one night when it had burst out ringing; and because I had remarked that we were at our ghostliest whenever he came up in the evening to comfort the servants. Let me do Ikey no injustice. He was afraid of the house, and believed in its being haunted; and yet he would play false on the haunting side, so surely as he got an opportunity. The Odd Girl's case was exactly similar. She went about the house

in a state of real terror, and yet lied monstrously and wilfully, and invented
many of the alarms she spread, and made many of the sounds we heard.
I had had my eye on the two, and I know it. It is not necessary for me,
here to account for this preposterous state of mind; I content myself with
remarking that it is familiarly known to every intelligent man who has
had fair medical, legal, or other watchful experience; that it is as well
established and as common a state of mind as any with which observers
are acquainted; and that it is one of the first elements, above all others,
rationally to be suspected in, and strictly looked for, and separated from,
any question of this kind.

To return to our party. The first thing we did when we were all assembled, was, to draw lots for bedrooms. That done, and every bedroom, and,
indeed, the whole house, having been minutely examined by the whole
body, we allotted the various household duties, as if we had been on a
gipsy party, or a yachting party, or a hunting party, or were shipwrecked.
I then recounted the floating rumours concerning the hooded lady, the
owl, and Master B.: with others, still more filmy, which had floated about
during our occupation, relative to some ridiculous old ghost of the
female gender who went up and down, carrying the ghost of a round
table; and also to an impalpable Jackass, whom nobody was ever able to
catch. Some of these ideas I really believe our people below had com-
municated to one another in some diseased way, without conveying them
in words. We then gravely called one another to witness, that we were
not there to be deceived, or to deceive—which we considered pretty
much the same thing—and that, with a serious sense of responsibility, we
would be strictly true to one another, and would strictly follow out the
truth. The understanding was established, that any one who heard
unusual noises in the night, and who wished to trace them, should knock
at my door; lastly, that on Twelfth Night, the last night of holy Christmas,
all our individual experiences since that then present hour of our coming together in the haunted house, should be brought to light for the
good of all; and that we would hold our peace on the subject till then,
unless on some remarkable provocation to break silence.

We were, in number and in character, as follows:

First—to get my sister and myself out of the way—there were we
two. In the drawing of lots, my sister drew her own room, and I drew
Master B.'s. Next, there was our first cousin John Herschel, so called
after the great astronomer: than whom I suppose a better man at a tele-
scope does not breathe. With him, was his wife: a charming creature to
whom he had been married in the previous spring. I thought him
(under the circumstances) rather imprudent to bring her, because there
is no knowing what even a false alarm may do at such a time; but I suppose he knew his own business best, and I must say that if she had been

my wife, I never could have left her endearing and bright face behind. They drew the Clock Room. Alfred Starling, an uncommonly agreeable young fellow of eight-and-twenty for whom I have the greatest liking, was in the Double Room; mine, usually, and designated by that name from having a dressing-room within it, with two large and cumbersome windows, which no wedges I was ever able to make, would keep from shaking, in any weather, wind or no wind. Alfred is a young fellow who pretends to be "fast" (another word for loose, as I understand the term), but who is much too good and sensible for that nonsense, and who would have distinguished himself before now, if his father had not unfortunately left him a small independence of two hundred a year, on the strength of which his only occupation in life has been to spend six. I am in hopes, however, that his Banker may break, or that he may enter into some speculation guaranteed to pay twenty per cent.; for, I am convinced that if he could only be ruined, his fortune is made. Belinda Bates, bosom friend of my sister, and a most intellectual, amiable, and delightful girl, got the Picture Room. She has a fine genius for poetry, combined with real business earnestness, and "goes in"—to use an expression of Alfred's—for Woman's mission, Woman's rights, Woman's wrongs, and everything that is woman's with a capital W, or is not and ought to be, or is and ought not to be. "Most praiseworthy, my dear, and Heaven prosper yet!" I whispered to her on the first night of my taking leave of her at the Picture-Room door, "but don't overdo it. And in respect of the great necessity there is, my darling, for more employments being within the reach of Woman than our civilisation has as yet assigned to her, don't fly at the unfortunate men, even those men who are at first sight in your way, as if they were the natural oppressors of your sex; for, trust me, Belinda, they do sometimes spend their wages among wives and daughters, sisters, mothers, aunts, and grandmothers; and the play is, really, not *all* Wolf and Red Riding-Hood, but has other parts in it." However, I digress.

Belinda, as I have mentioned, occupied the Picture Room. We had but three other chambers: the Corner Room, the Cupboard Room, and the Garden Room. My old friend, Jack Governor, "slung his hammock," as he called it, in the Corner Room. I have always regarded Jack as the finest-looking sailor that ever sailed. He is gray now, but as handsome as he was a quarter of a century ago—nay, handsomer. A portly, cheery, well-built figure of a broad-shouldered man, with a frank smile, a brilliant dark eye, and a rich dark eyebrow. I remember those under darker hair, and they look all the better for their silver setting. He has been wherever his Union namesake flies, has Jack, and I have met old shipmates of his, away in the Mediterranean and on the other side of the Atlantic, who have beamed and brightened at the casual mention of his

name, and have cried, "You know Jack Governor? Then you know a
prince of men!" That he is! And so unmistakably a naval officer, that if
you were to meet him coming out of an Esquimaux snow-hut in seal's
skins, you would be vaguely persuaded he was in full naval uniform.

Jack once had that bright clear eye of his on my sister; but, it fell out
that he married another lady and took her to South America, where she
died. This was a dozen years ago or more. He brought down with him
to our haunted house a little cask of salt beef; for, he is always convinced
that all salt beef not of his own pickling, is mere carrion, and invariably,
when he goes to London, packs a piece in his portmanteau. He had also
volunteered to bring with him one "Nat Beaver," an old comrade of his,
captain of a merchantman. Mr. Beaver, with a thick-set wooden face and
figure, and apparently as hard as a block all over, proved to be an intelligent man, with a world of watery experiences in him, and great practical knowledge. At times, there was a curious nervousness about him,
apparently the lingering result of some old illness; but, it seldom lasted
many minutes. He got the Cupboard Room, and lay there next to Mr.
Undery, my friend and solicitor: who came down, in an amateur capacity, "to go through with it," as he said, and who plays whist better than
the whole Law List, from the red cover at the beginning to the red cover
at the end.

I never was happier in my life, and I believe it was the universal feeling among us. Jack Governor, always a man of wonderful resources, was
Chief Cook, and made some of the best dishes I ever ate, including unap-
proachable curries. My sister was pastrycook and confectioner. Starling
and I were Cook's Mate, turn and turn about, and on special occasions
the chief cook "pressed" Mr. Beaver. We had a great deal of out-door
sport and exercise, but nothing was neglected within, and there was no
ill-humour or misunderstanding among us, and our evenings were so
delightful that we had at least one good reason for being reluctant to go
to bed.

We had a few night alarms in the beginning. On the first night, I was
knocked up by Jack with a most wonderful ship's lantern in his hand, like
the gills of some monster of the deep, who informed me that he "was
going aloft to the main truck," to have the weathercock down. It was a
stormy night, and I remonstrated; but Jack called my attention to its making a sound like a cry of despair, and said somebody would be "hailing a
ghost" presently, if it wasn't done. So, up to the top of the house, where I
could hardly stand for the wind, we went, accompanied by Mr. Beaver;
and there Jack, lantern and all, with Mr. Beaver after him, swarmed up to
the top of a cupola, some two dozen feet above the chimneys, and stood
upon nothing particular, coolly knocking the weathercock off, until they
both got into such good spirits with the wind and the height, that I

thought they would never come down. Another night, they turned out again, and had a chimney-cowl off. Another night, they cut a sobbing and gulping water-pipe away. Another night, they found out something else. On several occasions, they both, in the coolest manner, simultaneously dropped out of their respective bedroom windows, hand over hand by their counterpanes, to "overhaul" something mysterious in the garden.

The engagement among us was faithfully kept, and nobody revealed anything. All we knew was, if any one's room were haunted, no one looked the worse for it.

THE GHOST IN MASTER B.'S ROOM

When I established myself in the triangular garret which had gained so distinguished a reputation, my thoughts naturally turned to Master B. My speculations about him were uneasy and manifold. Whether his Christian name was Benjamin, Bissextile (from his having been born in Leap Year), Bartholomew, or Bill. Whether the initial letter belonged to his family name, and that was Baxter, Black, Brown, Barker, Buggins, Baker, or Bird. Whether he was a foundling, and had been baptized B. Whether he was a lion-hearted boy, and B. was short for Briton, or for Bull. Whether he could possibly have been kith and kin to an illustrious lady who brightened my own childhood, and had come of the blood of the brilliant Mother Bunch?

With these profitless meditations I tormented myself much. I also carried the mysterious letter into the appearance and pursuits of the deceased; wondering whether he dressed in Blue, wore Boots (he couldn't have been Bald), was a boy of Brains, liked Books, was good at Bowling, had any skill as a Boxer, even in his Buoyant Boyhood Bathed from a Bathing-machine at Bognor, Bangor, Bournemouth, Brighton, or Broadstairs, like a Bounding Billiard Ball?

So, from the first, I was haunted by the letter B.

It was not long before I remarked that I never by any hazard had a dream of Master B., or of anything belonging to him. But, the instant I awoke from sleep, at whatever hour of the night, my thoughts took him up, and roamed away, trying to attach his initial letter to something that would fit it and keep it quiet.

For six nights, I had been worried thus in Master B.'s room, when I began to perceive that things were going wrong.

The first appearance that presented itself was early in the morning when it was but just daylight and no more. I was standing shaving at my glass, when I suddenly discovered, to my consternation and amazement, that I was shaving—not myself—I am fifty—but a boy. Apparently Master B.!

I trembled and looked over my shoulder; nothing there. I looked again in the glass, and distinctly saw the features and expression of a boy, who was shaving, not to get rid of a beard, but to get one. Extremely troubled in my mind, I took a few turns in the room, and went back to the looking-glass, resolved to steady my hand and complete the operation in which I had been disturbed. Opening my eyes, which I had shut while recovering my firmness, I now met in the glass, looking straight at me, the eyes of a young man of four or five and twenty. Terrified by this new ghost, I closed my eyes, and made a strong effort to recover myself. Opening them again, I saw, shaving his cheek in the glass, my father, who has long been dead. Nay, I even saw my grandfather too, whom I never did see in my life.

Although naturally much affected by these remarkable visitations, I determined to keep my secret, until the time agreed upon for the present general disclosure. Agitated by a multitude of curious thoughts, I retired to my room, that night, prepared to encounter some new experience of a spectral character. Nor was my preparation needless, for, waking from an uneasy sleep at exactly two o'clock in the morning, what were my feelings to find that I was sharing my bed with the skeleton of Master B.!

I sprang up, and the skeleton sprang up also. I then heard a plaintive voice saying, "Where am I? What is become of me?" and, looking hard in that direction, perceived the ghost of Master B.

The young spectre was dressed in an obsolete fashion: or rather, was not so much dressed as put into a case of inferior pepper-and-salt cloth, made horrible by means of shining buttons. I observed that these buttons went, in a double row, over each shoulder of the young ghost, and appeared to descend his back. He wore a frill round his neck. His right hand (which I distinctly noticed to be inky) was laid upon his stomach; connecting this action with some feeble pimples on his countenance, and his general air of nausea, I concluded this ghost to be the ghost of a boy who had habitually taken a great deal too much medicine.

"Where am I?" said the little spectre, in a pathetic voice. "And why was I born in the Calomel days, and why did I have all that Calomel given me?"

I replied, with sincere earnestness, that upon my soul I couldn't tell him.

"Where is my little sister," said the ghost, "and where my angelic little wife, and where is the boy I went to school with?"

I entreated the phantom to be comforted, and above all things to take heart respecting the loss of the boy he went to school with. I represented to him that probably that boy never did, within human experience, come out well, when discovered. I urged that I myself had, in later life, turned up several boys whom I went to school with, and none of them had at all answered. I expressed my humble belief that the boy never did answer. I represented that he was a mythic character, a delusion, and a snare. I recounted how, the last time I found him, I found him at a dinner party behind a wall of white cravat, with an inconclusive opinion on every possible subject, and a power of silent boredom absolutely Titanic. I related how, on the strength of our having been together at "Old Doylance's," he had asked himself to breakfast with me (a social offence of the largest magnitude); how, fanning my weak embers of belief in Doylance's boys, I had let him in; and how he had proved to be a fearful wanderer about the earth, pursuing the race of Adam with inexplicable notions concerning the currency, and with a proposition that the Bank of England should, on pain of being abolished, instantly strike off and circulate, God knows how many thousand millions of ten-and-sixpenny notes.

The ghost heard me in silence, and with a fixed stare. "Barber!" it apostrophised me when I had finished.

"Barber?" I repeated—for I am not of that profession.

"Condemned," said the ghost, "to shave a constant change of customers—now, me—now, a young man—now, thyself as thou art—now, thy father—now, thy grandfather; condemned, too, to lie down with a skeleton every night, and to rise with it every morning—"

(I shuddered on hearing this dismal announcement.)

"Barber! Pursue me!"

I had felt, even before the words were uttered, that I was under a spell to pursue the phantom. I immediately did so, and was in Master B.'s room no longer.

Most people know what long and fatiguing night journeys had been forced upon the witches who used to confess, and who, no doubt, told the exact truth—particularly as they were always assisted with leading questions, and the Torture was always ready. I asseverate that, during my occupation of Master B.'s room, I was taken by the ghost that haunted it, on expeditions fully as long and wild as any of those. Assuredly, I was presented to no shabby old man with a goat's horns and tail (something between Pan and an old clothesman), holding conventional receptions, as stupid as those of real life and less decent; but, I came upon other things which appeared to me to have more meaning.

Confident that I speak the truth and shall be believed, I declare without hesitation that I followed the ghost, in the first instance on a broomstick, and afterwards on a rocking-horse. The very smell of the animal's paint—especially when I brought it out, by making him warm—I am ready to swear to. I followed the ghost, afterwards, in a hackney coach; an institution with the peculiar smell of which, the present generation is unacquainted, but to which I am again ready to swear as a combination of stable, dog with the mange, and very old bellows. (In this, I appeal to previous generations to confirm or refute me.) I pursued the phantom, on a headless donkey: at least, upon a donkey who was so interested in the state of his stomach that his head was always down there, investigating it; on ponies, expressly born to kick up behind; on roundabouts and swings, from fairs; in the first cab—another forgotten institution where the fare regularly got into bed, and was tucked up with the driver.

Not to trouble you with a detailed account of all my travels in pursuit of the ghost of Master B., which were longer and more wonderful than those of Sinbad the Sailor, I will confine myself to one experience from which you may judge of many.

I was marvellously changed. I was myself, yet not myself. I was conscious of something within me, which has been the same all through my life, and which I have always recognised under all its phases and varieties as never altering, and yet I was not the I who had gone to bed in Master B.'s room. I had the smoothest of faces and the shortest of legs, and I had taken another creature like myself, also with the smoothest of faces and the shortest of legs, behind a door, and was confiding to him a proposition of the most astounding nature.

This proposition was, that we should have a Seraglio.

The other creature assented warmly. He had no notion of respectability, neither had I. It was the custom of the East, it was the way of the good Caliph Haroun Alraschid (let me have the corrupted name again for once, it is so scented with sweet memories!), the usage was highly laudable, and most worthy of imitation. "O, yes! Let us," said the other creature with a jump, "have a Seraglio."

It was not because we entertained the faintest doubts of the meritorious character of the Oriental establishment we proposed to import, that we perceived it must be kept a secret from Miss Griffin. It was because we knew Miss Griffin to be bereft of human sympathies, and incapable of appreciating the greatness of the great Haroun. Mystery impenetrably shrouded from Miss Griffin then, let us entrust it to Miss Bule.

We were ten in Miss Griffin's establishment by Hampstead Ponds; eight ladies and two gentlemen. Miss Bule, whom I judged to have attained the ripe age of eight or nine, took the lead in society. I opened the subject to her in the course of the day, and proposed that she should become the Favourite.

Miss Bule, after struggling with the diffidence so natural to, and charming in, her adorable sex, expressed herself as flattered by the idea, but wished to know how it was proposed to provide for Miss Pipson? Miss Bule—who was understood to have vowed towards that young lady, a friendship, halves, and no secrets, until death, on the Church Service and Lessons complete in two volumes with case and lock—Miss Bule said she could not, as the friend of Pipson, disguise from herself, or me, that Pipson was not one of the common.

Now, Miss Pipson, having curly light hair and blue eyes (which was my idea of anything mortal and feminine that was called Fair), I promptly replied that I regarded Miss Pipson in the light of a Fair Circassian.

"And what then?" Miss Bule pensively asked.

I replied that she must be inveigled by a Merchant, brought to me veiled, and purchased as a slave.

(The other creature had already fallen into the second male place in the State, and was set apart for Grand Vizier. He afterwards resisted this disposal of events, but had his hair pulled until he yielded.)

"Shall I not be jealous?" Miss Bule inquired, casting down her eyes.

"Zobeide, no," I replied; "you will ever be the favourite Sultana; the first place in my heart, and on my throne, will be ever yours."

Miss Bule, upon that assurance, consented to propound the idea to her seven beautiful companions. It occurring to me, in the course of the same day, that we knew we could trust a grinning and good-natured soul called Tabby, who was the serving drudge of the house, and had no more figure than one of the beds, and upon whose face there was always more or less black-lead, I slipped into Miss Bule's hand after supper, a little note to that effect: dwelling on the black-lead as being in a manner deposited by the finger of Providence, pointing Tabby out for Mesrour, the celebrated chief of the Blacks of the Hareem.

There were difficulties in the formation of the desired institution, as there are in all combinations. The other creature showed himself of a low character, and, when defeated in aspiring to the throne, pretended to have conscientious scruples about prostrating himself before the Caliph; wouldn't call him Commander of the Faithful; spoke of him slightingly and inconsistently as a mere "chap"; said he, the other creature, "wouldn't play"—Play! and was otherwise coarse and offensive. This meanness of disposition was, however, put down by the general indignation of an united Seraglio, and I became blessed in the smiles of eight of the fairest of the daughters of men. Aroused?

The smiles could only be bestowed when Miss Griffin was looking another way, and only then in a very wary manner, for there was a legend among the followers of the Prophet that she saw with a little round ornament in the middle of the pattern on the back of her shawl. But every day after dinner, for an hour, we were all together, and then the Favourite and the rest of the Royal Hareem competed who should most beguile the leisure of the Serene Haroun reposing from the cares of State—which were generally, as in most affairs of State, of an arithmetical character, the Commander of the Faithful being a fearful boggler at a sum.

On these occasions, the devoted Mesrour, chief of the Blacks of the Hareem, was always in attendance (Miss Griffin usually ringing for that officer, at the same time, with great vehemence), but never acquitted himself in a manner worthy of his historical reputation. In the first place, his bringing a broom into the Divan of the Caliph, even when Haroun wore on his shoulders the red robe of anger (Miss Pipson's pelisse), though it might be got over for the moment, was never to be quite satisfactorily accounted for. In the second place, his breaking out into grinning exclamations of "Lork you pretties!" was neither Eastern nor respectful. In the third place, when specially instructed to say "Bismillah!" he always said "Hallelujah!" This officer, unlike his class, was too good-humoured altogether, kept his mouth open far too wide, expressed approbation to an incongruous extent, and even once—it was on the occasion of the purchase of the Fair Circassian for five hundred thousand purses of gold, and cheap, too—embraced the Slave, the Favourite, and the Caliph, all round. (Parenthetically let me say God bless Mesrour, and may there have been sons and daughters on that tender bosom, softening many a hard day since!)

Miss Griffin was a model of propriety, and I am at a loss to imagine what the feelings of the virtuous woman would have been, if she had known, when she paraded us down the Hampstead-road two and two, that she was walking with a stately step at the head of Polygamy and Mahomedanism. I believe that a mysterious and terrible joy with which the contemplation of Miss Griffin, in this unconscious state, inspired us, and a grim sense prevalent among us that there was a dreadful power in our knowledge of what Miss Griffin (who knew all things that could be learnt out of book) didn't know, were the mainspring of the preservation of our secret. It was wonderfully kept, but was once upon the verge of self-betrayal. The danger and escape occurred upon a Sunday. We were all ten ranged in a conspicuous part of the gallery at church, with Miss Griffin at our head—as we were every Sunday—advertising the establishment in an unsecular sort of way—when the description of Solomon in his domestic glory happened to be read. The moment that monarch was thus referred to, conscience whispered me, "Thou, too, Haroun!" The officiating minister had a cast in his eye, and it assisted conscience by giving him the appearance of reading personally at me. A crimson blush, attended by a fearful perspiration, suffused my features. The Grand Vizier became more dead than alive, and the whole Seraglio reddened as if the sunset of Bagdad shone direct upon their lovely faces. At this portentous time the awful Griffin rose, and balefully surveyed the children of Islam. My own impression was, that Church and State had entered into a conspiracy with Miss Griffin to expose us, and that we should all be put into white sheets, and exhibited in the centre aisle. But, so Westerly—if I may be allowed the expression as opposite to Eastern

associations—was Miss Griffin's sense of rectitude, that she merely suspected Apples, and we were saved.

I have called the Seraglio, united. Upon the question, solely, whether
the Commander of the Faithful durst exercise a right of kissing in that
sanctuary of the palace, were its peerless inmates divided. Zobeide
asserted a counter-right in the Favourite to scratch, and the fair
Circassian put her face, for refuge, into a green baize bag, originally
designed for books. On the other hand, a young antelope of transcen-
dent beauty from the fruitful plains of Camdentown (whence she had
been brought, by traders, in the half-yearly caravan that crossed the intermediate desert after the holidays), held more liberal opinions, but stipu-
lated for limiting the benefit of them to that dog, and son of a dog, the
Grand Vizier—who had no rights, and was not in question. At length, the
difficulty was compromised by the installation of a very youthful slave as
Deputy. She, raised upon a stool, officially received upon her cheeks the
salutes intended by the gracious Haroun for other Sultanas, and was privately rewarded from the coffers of the Ladies of the Hareem.

And now it was, at the full height of enjoyment of my bliss, that I
became heavily troubled. I began to think of my mother, and what she
would say to my taking home at midsummer eight of the most beautiful
of the daughters of men, but all unexpected. I thought of the number of
beds we made up at our house, of my father's income, and of the baker,
and my despondency redoubled. The Seraglio and malicious Vizier,
divining the cause of their Lord's unhappiness, did their utmost to aug-
ment it. They professed unbounded fidelity, and declared that they would
live and die with him. Reduced to the utmost wretchedness by these
protestations of attachment, I lay awake, for hours at a time, ruminating
on my frightful lot. In my despair, I think I might have taken an early
opportunity of falling on my knees before Miss Griffin, avowing my
resemblance to Solomon, and praying to be dealt with according to the
outraged laws of my country, if an unthought-of means of escape had not
opened before me.

One day, we were out walking, two and two—on which occasion the
Vizier had his usual instructions to take note of the boy at the turnpike,
and if he profanely gazed (which he always did) at the beauties of the
Hareem, to have him bow-strung in the course of the night—and it happened that our hearts were veiled in gloom. An unaccountable action on
the part of the antelope had plunged the State into disgrace. That
charmer, on the representation that the previous day was her birthday,
and that vast treasures had been sent in a hamper for its celebration (both
baseless assertions), had secretly but most pressingly invited thirty-five
neighbouring princes and princesses to a ball and supper: with a special
stipulation that they were "not to be fetched till twelve." This wander-

ing of the antelope's fancy, led to the surprising arrival at Miss Griffin's
door, in divers equipages and under various escorts, of a great company
in full dress, who were deposited on the top step in a flush of high
expectancy, and who were dismissed in tears. At the beginning of the
double knocks attendant on these ceremonies, the antelope had retired
to a back attic, and bolted herself in; and at every new arrival Miss Griffin
had gone so much more and more distracted, that at last she had been
seen to tear her front. Ultimate capitulation on the part of the offender,
had been followed by solitude in the linen-closet, bread and water and a
lecture to all, of vindictive length, in which Miss Griffin had used expressions: firstly, "I believe you all of you knew of it"; secondly, "Every one
of you is as wicked as another"; thirdly, "A pack of little wretches."

Under these circumstances, we were walking drearily along; and I
especially, with my Moosulmaun responsibilities heavy on me, was in a
very low state of mind; when a strange man accosted Miss Griffin, and,
after walking on at her side for a little while and talking with her, looked
at me. Supposing him to be a minion of the law, and that my hour was
come, I instantly ran away, with the general purpose of making for Egypt.

The whole Seraglio cried out, when they saw me making off as fast as
my legs would carry me (I had an impression that the first turning on the
left, and round by the public-house, would be the shortest way to the
Pyramids), Miss Griffin screamed after me, the faithless Vizier ran after
me, and the boy at the turnpike dodged me into a corner, like a sheep,
and cut me off. Nobody scolded me when I was taken and brought back;
Miss Griffin only said, with a stunning gentleness, This was very curious!
Why had I run away when the gentleman looked at me?

If I had had any breath to answer with, I dare say I should have made
no answer; having no breath, I certainly made none. Miss Griffin and the
strange man took me between them, and walked me back to the palace
in a sort of state; but not at all (as I couldn't help feeling, with astonishment) in culprit state.

When we got there, we went into a room by ourselves, and Miss
Griffin called in to her assistance, Mesrour, chief of the dusky guards of
the Hareem. Mesrour, on being whispered to, began to shed tears.

"Bless you, my precious!" said that officer, turning to me, "your pa's
took bitter bad!"

I asked, with a fluttered heart, "Is he very ill?"

"Lord temper the wind to you, my lamb!" said the good Mesrour,
kneeling down, that I might have a comforting shoulder for my head to
rest on, "your pa's dead!"

Haroun Alraschid took to flight at the words; the Seraglio vanished;
from that moment, I never again saw one of the eight of the fairest of the
daughters of men.

I was taken home, and there was Debt at home as well as Death, and we had a sale there. My own little bed was so superciliously looked upon by a Power unknown to me, hazily called "The Trade," that a brass coal-scuttle, a roasting-jack, and a birdcage, were obliged to be put into it to make a Lot of it, and then it went for a song. So I heard mentioned and I wondered what song, and thought what a dismal song it must have been to sing!

Then, I was sent to a great, cold, bare, school of big boys; where everything to eat and wear was thick and clumpy, without being enough; where everybody, large and small, was cruel; where the boys knew all about the sale, before I got there, and asked me what I had fetched, and who had bought me, and hooted at me. "Going, going, gone!" I never whispered in that wretched place that I had been Haroun or had had a Seraglio: for, I knew that if I mentioned my reverses, I should be so worried, that I should have to drown myself in the muddy pond near the playground, which looked like the beer. → kept quiet

Ah me, ah me! No other ghost has haunted the boy's room, my friends, since I have occupied it, than the ghost of my own childhood, the ghost of my own innocence, the ghost of my own airy belief. Many a time have I pursued the phantom: never with this man's stride of mine to come up with it, never with these man's hands of mine to touch it, never more to this man's heart of mine to hold it in its purity. And here you see me working out, as cheerfully and thankfully as I may, my doom of shaving in the glass a constant change of customers, and of lying down and rising up with the skeleton allotted to me for my mortal companion.

1859 → reliving his childhood up until his father's death?

THE FIDDLER OF THE REELS

Thomas Hardy

"TALKING OF Exhibitions, World's Fairs, and what not," said the old gentleman, "I would not go round the corner to see a dozen of them nowadays. The only exhibition that ever made, or ever will make, any impression upon my imagination was the first of the series, the parent of them all, and now a thing of old times—the Great Exhibition of 1851, in Hyde Park, London. None of the younger generation can realize the sense of novelty it produced in us who were then in our prime. A noun substantive went so far as to become an adjective in honor of the occasion. It was "exhibition" hat, "exhibition" razor-strop, "exhibition" watch; nay, even "exhibition" weather, "exhibition" spirits, sweethearts, babies, wives—for the time.

"For South Wessex, the year formed in many ways an extraordinary chronological frontier or transit-line, at which there occurred what one might call a precipice in Time. As in a geological "fault," we had presented to us a sudden bringing of ancient and modern into absolute contact, such as probably in no other single year since the Conquest was ever witnessed in this part of the country."

These observations led us onward to talk of the different personages, gentle and simple, who lived and moved within our narrow and peaceful horizon at that time; and of three people in particular, whose queer little history was oddly touched at points by the Exhibition, more concerned with it than that of anybody else who dwelt in those outlying shades of the world, Stickleford, Mellstock, and Egdon. First prominence among these three came Wat Ollamoor—if that were his real name—whom the seniors in our party had known well.

He was a woman's man, they said,—supremely so—externally little else. To men he was not attractive; perhaps a little repulsive at times. Musician, dandy, and company-man in practice; veterinary surgeon in theory, he lodged awhile in Mellstock village, coming from nobody knew where; though some said his first appearance in this neighbourhood had been as fiddle-player in a show at Greenhill Fair.

Many a worthy villager envied him his power over unsophisticated maidenhood—a power which seemed sometimes to have a touch of the weird and wizardly in it. Personally he was not ill-favoured, though rather un-English, his complexion being a rich olive, his rank hair dark and rather clammy—made still clammier by secret ointments, which, when he came fresh to a party, caused him to smell like "boys'-love"(southern-wood) steeped in lamp-oil. On occasion he wore curls— a double row—running almost horizontally around his head. But as these were sometimes noticeably absent, it was concluded that they were not altogether of Nature's making. By girls whose love for him had turned to hatred he had been nicknamed "Mop," from this abundance of hair, which was long enough to rest upon his shoulders; as time passed the name more and more prevailed.

His fiddling possibly had the most to do with the fascination he exercised, for, to speak fairly, it could claim for itself a most peculiar and personal quality, like that in a moving preacher. There were tones in it which bred the immediate conviction that indolence and averseness to systematic application were all that lay between "Mop" and the career of a second Paganini.

While playing he invariably closed his eyes; using no notes, and, as it were, allowing the violin to wander on at will into the most plaintive passages ever heard by rustic man. There was a certain lingual character in the supplicatory expressions he produced, which would well-nigh have drawn an ache from the heart of a gate-post. He could make any child in the parish, who was at all sensitive to music, burst into tears in a few minutes by simply fiddling one of the old dance-tunes he almost entirely affected—country jigs, reels, and "Favorite Quick Steps" of the last century—some mutilated remains of which even now reappear as nameless phantoms in new quadrilles and gallops, where they are recognized only by the curious, or by such old-fashioned and far-between people as have been thrown with men like Wat Ollamoor in their early life.

His date was a little later than that of the old Mellstock quire-band which comprised the Dewys, Mail, and the rest—in fact, he did not rise above the horizon thereabout till those well-known musicians were disbanded as ecclesiastical functionaries. In their honest love of thoroughness they despised the new man's style. Theophilus Dewy (Reuben the tranter's younger brother) used to say there was no "plumness" in it—no bowing, no solidity—it was all fantastical. And probably this was true. Anyhow, Mop had, very obviously, never bowed a note of church-music from his birth; he never once sat in the gallery of Mellstock church where the others had tuned their venerable psalmody so many hundreds of times; he never, in all likelihood, entered a church at all. All were devil's tunes in his repertory. "He could no more play the Wold Hundredth to his true time than he could play the brazen serpent," the tranter would say. (The brazen serpent was supposed in Mellstock to be a musical instrument particularly hard to blow.)

Occasionally Mop could produce the aforesaid moving effect upon the souls of grown-up persons, especially young women of fragile and responsive organization. Such an one was Car'line Aspent. Though she was already engaged to be married before she met him, Car'line, of them all, was the most influenced by Mop Ollamoor's heart-stealing melodies, to her discomfort, nay, positive pain and ultimate injury. She was a pretty, invocating, weak-mouthed girl, whose chief defect as a companion with her sex was a tendency to peevishness now and then. At this time she was not a resident in Mellstock parish where Mop lodged, but lived some miles off at Stickleford, further down the river.

How and where she first made acquaintance with him and his fiddling is not truly known, but the story was that it either began or was developed on one spring evening, when, in passing through Lower Mellstock, she chanced to pause on the bridge near his house to rest herself, and languidly leaned over the parapet. Mop was standing on his door-step, as was his custom, spinning the insidious thread of semi- and demi-semiquavers from the E string of his fiddle for the benefit of passers-by, and laughing as the tears rolled down the cheeks of the little children hanging around him. Car'line pretended to be engrossed with the rippling of the stream under the arches, but in reality she was listening, as he knew. Presently the aching of the heart seized her simultaneously with a wild desire to glide airily in the mazes of an infinite dance. To shake off the fascination she resolved to go on, although it would be necessary to pass him as he played. On stealthily glancing ahead at the performer, she found to her relief that his eyes were closed in abandonment to instrumentation, and she strode on boldly. But when closer her step grew timid, her tread convulsed itself more and more accordantly with the time of the melody, till she very nearly danced along. Gaining another glance at him when immediately opposite, she saw that *one* of his eyes was open, quizzing her as he smiled at her emotional state. Her gait could not divest itself of its compelled capers till she had gone a long way past the house; and Car'line was unable to shake off the strange infatuation for hours.

After that day, whenever there was to be in the neighbourhood a dance to which she could get an invitation, and where Mop Ollamoor was to be the musician, Car'line contrived to be present, though it sometimes involved a walk of several miles; for he did not play so often in Stickleford as elsewhere.

The next evidences of his influence over her were singular enough, and it would require a neurologist to fully explain them. She would be sitting quietly, any evening after dark, in the house of her father, the parish clerk, which stood in the middle of Stickleford village street, this being the highroad between Lower Mellstock and Moreford, five miles eastward. Here, without a moment's warning, and in the midst of a general conversation between her father, sister, and the young man before alluded to, who devotedly wooed her in ignorance of her infatuation, she would start from her seat in the chimney-corner as if she had received a galvanic shock, and spring convulsively towards the ceiling; then she would burst into tears, and it was not till some half-hour had passed that she grew calm as usual. Her father, knowing her hysterical tendencies, was always excessively anxious about this trait in his youngest girl, and feared the attack to be a species of epileptic fit. Not so her sister Julia. Julia had found out what was the cause. At the moment before the jumping, only an exceptionally sensitive ear situated in the chimney-nook could have caught down the flue the beat of a man's footstep along the highway without. But it was in that footfall, for which she had been waiting, that the origin of Car'line's involuntary springing lay. The pedestrian was Mop Ollamoor, as the girl well knew; but his business that way was not to visit her; he sought another woman whom he spoke of as his Intended, and who lived at Moreford, two miles further on. On one, and only one, occasion did it happen that Car'line could not control her utterance; it was when her sister alone chanced to be present. "O—O—O—!" she cried. "He's going to *her*, and not coming to *me!*"

To do the fiddler justice he had not at first thought greatly of, or spoken much to, this girl of impressionable mould. But he had soon found out her secret, and could not resist a little by-play with her too easily hurt heart, as an interlude between his more serious lovemakings at Moreford. The two became well acquainted, though only by stealth, hardly a soul in Stickleford except her sister, and her lover Ned Hipcroft, being aware of the attachment. Her father disapproved of her coldness to Ned; her sister, too, hoped she might get over this nervous passion for a man of whom so little was known. The ultimate result was that Car'line's manly and simple wooer Edward found his suit becoming practically hopeless. He was a respectable mechanic, in a far sounder position than Mop the nominal horse-doctor; but when, before leaving her, Ned put his flat and final question, would she marry him, then and there, now or never, it was with little expectation of obtaining more than the negative she gave him. Though her father supported him and her sister supported him, he could not play the fiddle so as to draw your soul out of your body like a spider's thread, as Mop did, till you felt as limp as withywind and yearned for something to cling to. Indeed, Hipcroft had not the slightest ear for music; could not sing two notes in tune, much less play them.

The No he had expected and got from her, in spite of a preliminary encouragement, gave Ned a new start in life. It had been uttered in such a tone of sad entreaty that he resolved to persecute her no more; she should not even be distressed by a sight of his form in the distant perspective of the street and lane. He left the place, and his natural course was to London.

The railway to South Wessex was in process of construction, but it was not as yet opened for traffic; and Hipcroft reached the capital by a six days' trudge on foot, as many a better man had done before him. He was one of the last of the artisan class who used that now extinct method of travel to the great centres of labor, so customary then from time immemorial.

In London he lived and worked regularly at his trade. More fortunate than many, his disinterested willingness recommended him from the first. During the ensuing four years he was never out of employment. He neither advanced nor receded in the modern sense; he improved as a workman, but he did not shift one jot in social position. About his love for Car'line he maintained a rigid silence. No doubt he often thought of her; but being always occupied, and having no relations at Stickleford, he held no communication with that part of the country, and showed no desire to return. In his quiet lodging in Lambeth he moved about after working-hours with the facility of a woman, doing his own cooking, attending to his stocking-heels, and shaping himself by degrees to a lifelong bachelorhood. For this conduct one is bound to advance the canonical reason that time could not efface from his heart the image of little Car'line Aspent—and it may be in part true; but there was also the inference that his was a nature not greatly dependent upon the ministrations of the other sex for its comforts.

The fourth year of his residence as a mechanic in London was the year of the Hyde-Park Exhibition already mentioned, and at the construction of this huge glass-house, then unexampled in the world's history, he worked daily. It was an era of great hope and activity among the nations and industries. Though Hipcroft was, in his small way, a central man in the movement, he plodded on with his usual outward placidity. Yet for him, too, the year was destined to have its surprises, for when the bustle of getting the building ready for the opening day was past, the ceremonies had been witnessed, and people were flocking thither from all parts of the globe, he received a letter from Car'line. Till that day the silence of four years between himself and Stickleford had never been broken.

She informed her old lover, in an uncertain penmanship, which suggested a trembling hand, of the trouble she had been put to in ascertaining his address, and then broached the subject which had prompted her to write. Four years ago, she said with the greatest delicacy of which she was capable, she had been so foolish as to refuse him. Her wilful wrong-headedness had since been a grief to her many times, and of late particularly. As for Mr. Ollamoor, he had been absent almost as long as Ned—she did not know where. She would gladly marry Ned now if he were to ask her again, and be a tender little wife to him till her life's end.

A tide of warm feeling must have surged through Ned Hipcroft's frame on receipt of this news, if we may judge by the issue. Unquestionably he loved her still, even if not to exclusion of every other happiness. This from his Car'line, she who had been dead to him these many years, alive to him again as of old, was in itself a pleasant, gratifying thing. Ned had grown so resigned to, or satisfied with, his lonely lot, that he probably would not have shown much jubilation at anything. Still, a certain ardour of preoccupation, after his first surprise, revealed how deeply her confession of faith in him had stirred him. Measured and methodical in his ways, he did not answer the letter that day, nor the next, nor the next. He was having "a good think." When he did answer it, there was a great deal of sound reasoning mixed in with the unmistakable tenderness of his reply; but the tenderness itself was sufficient to reveal that he was pleased with her straightforward frankness; that the anchorage she had once obtained in his heart was renewable, if it had not been continuously firm.

He told her—and as he wrote his lips twitched humorously over the few gentle words of raillery he indited among the rest of his sentences—that it was all very well for her to come round at this time of day. Why wouldn't she have him when he wanted her? She had no doubt learned that he was not married, but suppose his affections had since been fixed on another? She ought to beg his pardon. Still, he was not the man to forget her. But considering how he had been used, and what he had suffered, she could not quite expect him to go down to Stickleford and fetch her. But if she would come to him, and say she was sorry, as was only fair; why, yes, he would marry her, knowing what a good little woman she was at the core. He added that the request for her to come to him was a less one to make than it would have been when he first left Stickleford, or even a few months ago; for the new railway into South Wessex was now open, and there had just begun to be run wonderfully contrived special trains, called excursion-trains, on account of the Great Exhibition; so that she could come up easily alone.

She said in her reply how good it was of him to treat her so generously, after her hot and cold treatment of him; that though she felt frightened at the magnitude of the journey, and was never as yet in a railway-train, having only seen one pass at a distance, she embraced his offer with all her heart; and would, indeed, own to him how sorry she was, and beg his pardon, and try to be a good wife always, and make up for lost time.

The remaining details of when and where were soon settled, Car'line informing him, for her ready identification in the crowd, that she would be wearing "my new sprigged-laylock cotton gown," and Ned gaily responding that, having married her the morning after her arrival, he would make a day of it by taking her to the Exhibition. One early summer afternoon, accordingly, he came from his place of work, and hastened toward Waterloo Station to meet her. It was as wet and chilly as an English June day can occasionally be, but as he waited on the platform in the drizzle he glowed inwardly, and seemed to have something to live for again.

The "excursion-train"—an absolutely new departure in the history of travel—was still a novelty on the Wessex line, and probably everywhere. Crowds of people had flocked to all the stations on the way up to witness the unwonted sight of so long a train's passage, even where they did not take advantage of the opportunity it offered. The seats for the humbler class of travellers in these early experiments in steam-locomotion, were open trucks, without any protection whatever from the wind and rain; and damp weather having set in with the afternoon, the unfortunate occupants of these vehicles were, on the train drawing up at the London terminus, found to be in a pitiable condition from their long journey; blue-faced, stiff-necked, sneezing, rain-beaten, chilled to the marrow, many of the men being hatless; in fact, they resembled people who had been out all night in an open boat on a rough sea, rather than inland excursionists for pleasure. The women had in some degree protected themselves by turning up the skirts of their gowns over their heads, but as by this arrangement they were additionally exposed about the hips, they were all more or less in a sorry plight.

In the bustle and crush of alighting forms of both sexes which followed the entry of the huge concatenation into the station, Ned Hipcroft soon discerned the slim little figure his eye was in search of, in the sprigged lilac, as described. She came up to him with a frightened smile—still pretty, though so damp, weather-beaten, and shivering from long exposure to the wind.

"O, Ned!" she sputtered, "I—I——" He clasped her in his arms and kissed her, whereupon she burst into a flood of tears.

"You are wet, my poor dear! I hope you'll not get cold," he said. And surveying her and her multifarious surrounding packages, he noticed that by the hand she led a toddling child—a little girl of three or so—whose hood was as clammy and tender face as blue as those of the other travellers.

"Who is this—somebody you know?" asked Ned curiously.

"Yes, Ned. She's mine."

"Yours?"

"Yes—my own."

"Your own child?"

"Yes!"

"But who's the father?"

"The young man I had after you courted me."

"Well—as God's in——"

"Ned, I didn't name it in my letter, because, you see, it would have been so hard to explain! I thought that when we met I could tell you how she happened to be born, so much better than in writing! I hope you'll excuse it this once, dear Ned, and not scold me, now I've come so many, many miles!"

"This means Mr. Mop Ollamoor, I reckon!" said Hipcroft, gazing palely at them from the distance of the yard or two to which he had withdrawn with a start.

Car'line gasped. "But he's been gone away for years!" she supplicated. "And I never had a young man before! And I was so onlucky to be catched the first time he took advantage o' me, though some of the girls down there go on like anything!"

Ned remained in silence, pondering.

"You'll forgive me, dear Ned?" she added, beginning to sob outright. "I haven't taken 'ee in after all, because—because you can pack us back again, if you want to; though 'tis hundreds o' miles, and so wet, and night a-coming on, and I with no money!"

"What the devil can I do!" Hipcroft groaned.

A more pitiable picture than the pair of helpless creatures presented was never seen on a rainy day, as they stood on the great, gaunt, puddled platform, a whiff of drizzle blowing under the roof upon them now and then; the pretty attire in which they had started from Stickleford in the early morning bemuddled and sodden, weariness on their faces, and fear of him in their eyes; for the child began to look as if she thought she too had done some wrong, remaining in an appalled silence till the tears rolled down her chubby cheeks.

"What's the matter, my little maid?" said Ned mechanically.

"I do want to go home!" she let out, in tones that told of a bursting heart. "And my totties be cold, an' I shan't have no bread an' butter no-more!"

"I don't know what to say to it all!" declared Ned, his own eye moist as he turned and walked a few steps with his head down; then regarded them again point-blank. From the child escaped troubled breaths and silently welling tears.

"Want some bread and butter, do 'ee?" he said, with factitious hardness.

"Ye—e—s!"

"Well, I dare say I can get 'ee a bit! Naturally, you must want some. And you, too, for that matter, Car'line."

"I do feel a little hungered. But I can keep it off," she murmured.

"Folk shouldn't do that," he said gruffly. . . . "There, come along!" He caught up the child, as he added, "You must bide here to-night, anyhow, I s'pose! What can you do otherwise? I'll get 'ee some tea and victuals; and as for this job, I'm sure I don't know what to say! This is the way out."

They pursued their way, without speaking, to Ned's lodgings, which were not far off. There he dried them and made them comfortable, and prepared tea; they thankfully sat down. The ready-made household of which he suddenly found himself the head imparted a cosy aspect to his room, and a paternal one to himself. Presently he turned to the child and kissed her now blooming cheeks; and, looking wistfully at Car'line, kissed her also.

"I don't see how I can send you back all them miles," he growled, "now you've come all the way o' purpose to join me. But you must trust me, Car'line, and show you've real faith in me. Well, do you feel better now, my little woman?"

The child nodded beamingly, her mouth being otherwise occupied.

"I did trust you, Ned, in coming; and I shall always!"

Thus, without any definite agreement to forgive her, he tacitly acquiesced in the fate that Heaven had sent him; and on the day of their marriage (which was not quite so soon as he had expected it could be, on account of the time necessary for banns) he took her to the Exhibition when they came back from church, as he had promised. While standing near a large mirror in one of the courts devoted to furniture, Car'line started, for in the glass appeared the reflection of a form exactly resembling Mop Ollamoor's—so exactly, that it seemed impossible to believe anybody but that artist in person to be the original. On passing round the objects which hemmed in Ned, her, and the child from a direct view, no Mop was to be seen. Whether he were really in London or not at that time was never known; and Car'line always stoutly denied that her readiness to go and meet Ned in town arose from any rumor that Mop had also gone thither; which denial there was no reasonable ground for doubting.

And then the year glided away, and the Exhibition folded itself up and became a thing of the past. The park trees that had been enclosed for six months were again exposed to the winds and storms, and the sod grew green anew. Ned found that Car'line resolved herself into a very good wife and companion, though she had made herself what is called cheap to him; but in that she was like another domestic article, a cheap tea-pot, which often brews better tea than a dear one. One autumn Hipcroft found himself with but little work to do, and a prospect of less for the winter. Both being country born and bred, they fancied they would like to live again in their natural atmosphere. It was accordingly decided between them that they should leave the pent-up London lodging, and that Ned should seek out employment near his native place, his wife and her daughter staying with Car'line's father during the search for occupation and an abode of their own.

Tinglings of pride pervaded Car'line's spasmodic little frame as she journeyed down with Ned to the place she had left two or three years before, in silence and under a cloud. To return to where she had once been despised, a smiling London wife with a distinct London accent, was a triumph which the world did not witness every day.

The train did not stop at the petty roadside station that lay nearest to Stickleford, and the trio went on to Casterbridge. Ned thought it a good opportunity to make a few preliminary inquiries for employment at workshops in the borough where he had been known; and feeling cold from her journey, and it being dry underfoot and only dusk as yet, with a moon on the point of rising, Car'line and her little girl walked on toward Stickleford, leaving Ned to follow at a quicker pace, and pick her up at a certain half-way house, widely known as an inn.

The woman and child pursued the well-remembered way comfortably enough, though they were both becoming wearied. In the course of three miles they had passed Heedless-William's Pond, the familiar landmark by Bloom's End, and were drawing near the Quiet Woman, a lone roadside hostel on the lower verge of the Egdon Heath, since and for many years abolished. In stepping up toward it Car'line heard more voices within than had formerly been customary at such an hour, and she learned that an auction of fat stock had been held near the spot that afternoon. The child would be the better for a rest as well as herself, she thought, and she entered.

The guests and customers overflowed into the passage, and Car'line had no sooner crossed the threshold than a man whom she remembered by sight came forward with a glass and mug in his hands towards a friend leaning against the wall; but, seeing her, very gallantly offered her a drink of the liquor, which was gin-and-beer hot, pouring her out a tumblerful and saying, in a moment or two: "Surely, 'tis little Car'line Aspent that was—down at Stickleford?"

She assented, and, though she did not exactly want this beverage, she drank it since it was offered, and her entertainer begged her to come in further and sit down. Once within the room she found that all the persons present were seated close against the walls, and there being a chair vacant she did the same. An explanation of their position occurred the next moment. In the opposite corner stood Mop, rosining his bow and looking just the same as ever. The company had cleared the middle of the room for dancing, and they were about to dance again. As she wore a veil to keep off the wind she did not think he had recognized her, or could possibly guess the identity of the child; and to her satisfied surprise she found that she could confront him quite calmly—mistress of herself in the dignity her London life had given her. Before she had quite emptied her glass the dance was called, the dancers formed in two lines, the music sounded, and the figure began.

Then matters changed for Car'line. A tremor quickened itself to life in her, and her hand so shook that she could hardly set down her glass. It was not the dance nor the dancers, but the notes of that old violin which thrilled the London wife, these having still all the witchery that she had so well known of yore, and under which she had used to lose her power of independent will. How it all came back! There was the fiddling figure against the wall; the large, oily, moplike head of him, and beneath the mop the face with closed eyes.

After the first moments of paralyzed reverie the familiar tune in the familiar rendering made her laugh and shed tears simultaneously. Then a man at the bottom of the dance, whose partner had dropped away, stretched out his hand and beckoned to her to take the place. She did not want to dance; she entreated by signs to be left where she was, but she was entreating of the tune and its player rather than of the dancing man. The saltatory tendency which the fiddler and his cunning instrument had ever been able to start in her was seizing Car'line just as it had done in earlier years, possibly assisted by the gin-and-beer hot. Tired as she was she grasped her little girl by the hand, and plunging in at the bottom of the figure, whirled about with the rest. She found that her companions were mostly people of the neighbouring hamlets and farms—Bloom's End, Mellstock, Lewgate, and elsewhere; and by degrees she was recognized as she convulsively danced on, wishing that Mop would cease and let her heart rest from the aching he caused, and her feet also.

After long and many minutes the dance ended, when she was urged to fortify herself with more gin-and-beer; which she did, feeling very weak and overpowered with hysteric emotion. She refrained from unveiling, to keep Mop in ignorance of her presence, if possible. Several of the guests having left, Car'line hastily wiped her lips and also turned to go; but, according to the account of some who remained, at that very moment a five-handed reel was proposed, in which two or three begged her to join.

She declined on the plea of being tired and having to walk to

Stickleford, when Mop began aggressively tweedling "My Fancy-Lad," in D major, as the air to which the reel was to be footed. He must have recognized her, though she did not know it, for it was the strain of all seductive strains which she was least able to resist—the one he had played when she was leaning over the bridge at the date of their first acquaintance. Car'line stepped despairingly into the middle of the room with the other four.

Reels were resorted to hereabouts at this time by the more robust spirits, for the reduction of superfluous energy which the ordinary figure-dances were not powerful enough to exhaust. As everybody knows, or does not know, the five reelers stood in the form of a cross, the reel being performed by each line of three alternately, the persons who successively came to the middle place dancing in both directions. Car'line soon found herself in this place, the axis of the whole performance, and could not get out of it, the tune turning into the first part without giving her opportunity. And now she began to suspect that Mop did know her, and was doing this on purpose, though whenever she stole a glance at him his closed eyes betokened obliviousness to everything outside his own brain. She continued to wend her way through the figure of 8 that was formed by her course, the fiddler introducing into his notes the wild and agonizing sweetness of a living voice in one too highly wrought; its pathos running high and running low in endless variation, projecting through her nerves excruciating spasms, a sort of blissful torture. The room swam, the tune was endless; and in about a quarter of an hour the only other woman in the figure dropped out exhausted, and sank panting on a bench.

The reel instantly resolved itself into a four-handed one. Car'line would have given anything to leave off; but she had, or fancied she had, no power, while Mop played such tunes; and thus another ten minutes slipped by, a haze of dust now clouding the candles, the floor being of stone, sanded. Then another dancer fell out—one of the men—and went into the passage in a frantic search for liquor. To turn the figure into a three-handed reel was the work of a second, Mop modulating at the same time into "The Fairy Dance," as better suited to the contracted movement, and no less one of those foods of love which, as manufactured by his bow, had always intoxicated her.

In a reel for three there was no rest whatever, and four or five minutes were enough to make her remaining two partners, now thoroughly blown, stamp their last bar, and, like their predecessors, limp off into the next room to get something to drink. Car'line, half-stifled inside her veil, was left dancing alone, the apartment now being empty of everybody save herself, Mop, and their little girl.

She flung up the veil, and cast her eyes upon him, as if imploring him to withdraw himself and his acoustic magnetism from the atmosphere. Mop opened one of his own orbs, as though for the first time, fixed it peeringly upon her, and smiling dreamily, threw into his strains the reserve of expression which he could not afford to waste on a big and noisy dance. Crowds of little chromatic subtleties, capable of drawing tears from a statue, proceeded straightway from the ancient fiddle, as if it were dying of the emotion which had been pent up within it ever since its banishment from some Italian or German city where it first took shape and sound. There was that in the look of Mop's one dark eye which said: "You cannot leave off, dear, whether you would or no!" and it bred in her a paroxysm of desperation that defied him to tire her down.

She thus continued to dance alone, defiantly as she thought, but in truth slavishly and abjectly, subject to every wave of the melody, and probed by the gimlet-like gaze of her fascinator's open eye; keeping up at the same time a feeble smile in his face, as a feint to signify it was still her own pleasure which led her on. A terrified embarrassment as to what she could say to him if she were to leave off, had its unrecognized share in keeping her going. The child, who was beginning to be distressed by the strange situation, came up and whimpered: "Stop, mother, stop, and let's go home!" as she seized Car'line's hand.

Suddenly Car'line sank staggering to the floor, and rolling over on her face, prone she remained. Mop's fiddle thereupon emitted an elfin shriek of finality; stepping quickly down from the nine-gallon beer-cask which had formed his rostrum, he went to the little girl, who disconsolately bent over her mother.

The guests who had gone into the back room for liquor and change of air, hearing something unusual, trooped back hitherward, where they endeavoured to revive poor, weak Car'line by blowing her with the bellows and opening the window. Ned, her husband, who had been detained in Casterbridge, as aforesaid, came along the road at this juncture, and hearing excited voices through the open casement, and to his great surprise, the mention of his wife's name, he entered amid the rest upon the scene. Car'line was now in convulsions, weeping violently, and for a long time nothing could be done with her. While he was sending for a cart to take her onward to Stickleford Hipcroft anxiously inquired how it had all happened; and then the assembly explained that a fiddler formerly known in the locality had lately visited his old haunts, and had taken upon himself without invitation to play that evening at the inn and raise a dance.

Ned demanded the fiddler's name, and they said Ollamoor.

"Ah!" exclaimed Ned, looking round him. "Where is he, and where— where's my little girl?"

Ollamoor had disappeared, and so had the child. Hipcroft was in ordinary a quiet and tractable fellow, but a determination which was to be feared settled in his face now. "Blast him!" he cried. "I'll beat his skull in for'n, if I swing for it to-morrow!"

He had rushed to the poker which lay on the hearth, and hastened down the passage, the people following. Outside the house, on the other side of the highway, a mass of dark heath-land rose sullenly upward to its not easily accessible interior, a ravined plateau, whereon jutted into the sky, at the distance of a couple of miles, the fir-woods of Mistover backed by the Yalbury coppices—a place of Dantesque gloom at this hour, which would have afforded secure hiding for a battery of artillery, much less a man and a child.

Some other men plunged thitherward with him, and more went along the road. They were gone about twenty minutes altogether, returning without result to the inn. Ned sat down in the settle, and clasped his forehead with his hands.

"Well—what a fool the man is, and hev been all these years, if he thinks the child his, as a' do seem to!" they whispered. "And everybody else knowing otherwise!"

"No, I don't think 'tis mine!" cried Ned hoarsely, as he looked up from his hands. "But she *is* mine, all the same! Ha'n't I nussed her? Ha'n't I fed her and teached her? Ha'n't I played wi' her? O, little Carry—gone with that rogue—gone!"

"You ha'n't lost your mis'ess, anyhow," they said to console him. "She's throwed up the sperrits, and she is feeling better, and she's more to 'ee than a child that isn't yours."

"She isn't! She's not so particular much to me, especially now she's lost the little maid! But Carry's the whole world to me!"

"Well, ver' like you'll find her tomorrow."

"Ah—but shall I? Yet he *can't* hurt her—surely he can't! Well—how's Car'line now? I am ready. Is the cart here?"

She was lifted into the vehicle, and they sadly lumbered on toward Stickleford. Next day she was calmer; but the fits were still upon her, and her will seemed shattered. For the child she appeared to show singularly little anxiety, though Ned was nearly distracted by his passionate paternal love for a child not his own. It was nevertheless quite expected that the impish Mop would restore the lost one after a freak of a day or two; but time went on, and neither he nor she could be heard of, and Hipcroft murmured that perhaps he was exercising upon her some unholy musical charm, as he had done upon Car'line herself. Weeks passed, and still they could obtain no clue either to the fiddler's whereabouts or to the girl's; and how he could have induced her to go with him remained a mystery.

Then Ned, who had obtained only temporary employment in the neighbourhood, took a sudden hatred toward his native district, and a rumour reaching his ears through the police that a somewhat similar man and child had been seen at a fair near London, he playing a violin, she dancing on stilts, a new interest in the capital took possession of Hipcroft with an intensity which would scarcely allow him time to pack before returning thither. He did not, however, find the lost one, though he made it the entire business of his over-hours to stand about in by-streets in the hope of discovering her, and would start up in the night, saying, "That rascal's torturing her to maintain him!" To which his wife would answer peevishly, "Don't 'ee raft yourself so, Ned! You prevent my getting a bit o' rest! He won't hurt her!" and fall asleep again.

That Carry and her father had emigrated to America was the general opinion; Mop, no doubt, finding the girl a highly desirable companion when he had trained her to keep him by her earnings as a dancer. There, for that matter, they may be performing in some capacity now, though he must be an old scamp verging on three-score-and-ten, and she a woman of four-and-forty.

May 1893.

THE PARSON'S DAUGHTER
OF OXNEY COLNE

Anthony Trollope

THE PRETTIEST scenery in all England—and if I am contradicted in that assertion, I will say in all Europe—is in Devonshire, on the southern and south-eastern skirts of Dartmoor, where the rivers Dart, and Avon, and Teign form themselves, and where the broken moor is half cultivated, and the wild-looking upland fields are half moor. In making this assertion I am often met with much doubt, but it is by persons who do not really know the locality. Men and women talk to me on the matter, who have travelled down the line of railway from Exeter to Plymouth, who have spent a fortnight at Torquay, and perhaps made an excursion from Tavistock to the convict prison on Dartmoor. But who knows the glories of Chagford? Who has walked through the parish of Manaton? Who is conversant with Lustleigh Cleeves and Withycombe in the moor? Who has explored Holne Chase? Gentle reader, believe me that you will be rash in contradicting me, unless you have done these things.

There or thereabouts—I will not say by the waters of which little river it is washed—is the parish of Oxney Colne. And for those who would wish to see all the beauties of this lovely country, a sojourn in Oxney Colne would be most desirable, seeing that the sojourner would then be brought nearer to all that he would wish to visit, than at any other spot in the country. But there is an objection to any such arrangement. There are only two decent houses in the whole parish, and these are—or were when I knew the locality—small and fully occupied by their possessors. The larger and better is the parsonage, in which lived the parson and his daughter; and the smaller is the freehold residence of a certain Miss Le Smyrger, who owned a farm of a hundred acres, which was rented by one Farmer Cloysey, and who also possessed some thirty acres round her own house, which she managed herself, regarding herself to be quite as great in cream as Mr. Cloysey, and altogether superior to him in the article of cider. "But yeu has to pay no rent, Miss," Farmer Cloysey would say, when Miss Le Smyrger expressed this opinion of her art in a manner too defiant. "Yeu pays no rent, or yeu couldn't do it." Miss Le Smyrger was an old maid, with a pedigree and blood of her own, a hundred and thirty acres of fee-simple land on the borders of Dartmoor, fifty years of age, a constitution of iron, and an opinion of her own on every subject under the sun.

And now for the parson and his daughter. The parson's name was Woolsworthy—or Woolathy as it was pronounced by all those who lived around him—the Rev. Saul Woolsworthy; and his daughter was Patience Woolsworthy, or Miss Patty, as she was known to the Devonshire world of those parts. That name of Patience had not been well chosen for her, for she was a hot-tempered damsel, warm in her convictions, and inclined to express them freely. She had but two closely intimate friends in the world, and by both of them this freedom of expression had now been fully permitted to her since she was a child. Miss Le Smyrger and her father were well accustomed to her ways, and on the whole well satisfied with them. The former was equally free and equally warm-tempered as herself, and as Mr. Woolsworthy was allowed by his daughter to be quite paramount on his own subject—for he had a subject—he did not object to his daughter being paramount on all others. A pretty girl was Patience Woolsworthy at the time of which I am writing, and one who possessed much that was worthy of remark and admiration, had she lived where beauty meets with admiration, or where force of character is remarked. But at Oxney Colne, on the borders of Dartmoor, there were few to appreciate her, and it seemed as though she herself had but little idea of carrying her talent further afield, so that it might not remain for ever wrapped in a blanket.

She was a pretty girl, tall and slender, with dark eyes and black hair. Her eyes were perhaps too round for regular beauty, and her hair was perhaps too crisp; her mouth was large and expressive; her nose was finely formed, though a critic in female form might have declared it to be somewhat broad. But her countenance altogether was wonderfully attractive—if only it might be seen without that resolution for dominion which occasionally marred it, though sometimes it even added to her attractions.

It must be confessed on behalf of Patience Woolsworthy, that the circumstances of her life had peremptorily called upon her to exercise dominion. She had lost her mother when she was sixteen, and had had neither brother nor sister. She had no neighbours near her fit either from education or rank to interfere in the conduct of her life, excepting always Miss Le Smyrger. Miss Le Smyrger would have done anything for her, including the whole management of her morals and of the parsonage household, had Patience been content with such an arrangement. But much as Patience had ever loved Miss Le Smyrger, she was not content with this, and therefore she had been called on to put forth a strong hand of her own. She had put forth this strong hand early, and hence had come the character which I am attempting to describe. But I must say on behalf of this girl, that it was not only over others that she thus exercised dominion. In acquiring that power she had also acquired the much greater power of exercising rule over herself.

But why should her father have been ignored in these family arrangements? Perhaps it may almost suffice to say, that of all living men her father was the man best conversant with the antiquities of the county in which he lived. He was the Jonathan Oldbuck of Devonshire, and especially of Dartmoor, without that decision of character which enabled Oldbuck to keep his womenkind in some kind of subjection, and probably enabled him also to see that his weekly bills did not pass their proper limits. Our Mr. Oldbuck, of Oxney Colne, was sadly deficient in these. As a parish pastor with but a small cure, he did his duty with sufficient energy to keep him, at any rate, from reproach. He was kind and charitable to the poor, punctual in his services, forbearing with the farmers around him, mild with his brother clergymen, and indifferent to aught that bishop or archdeacon might think or say of him. I do not name this latter attribute as a virtue, but as a fact. But all these points were as nothing in the known character of Mr. Woolsworthy, of Oxney Colne. He was the antiquarian of Dartmoor. That was his line of life. It was in that capacity that he was known to the Devonshire world; it was as such that he journeyed about with his humble carpet-bag, staying away from his parsonage a night or two at a time; it was in that character that he received now and again stray visitors in the single spare bedroom—not friends asked to see him and his girl because of their friendship—but men who knew something as to this buried stone, or that old land-mark. In all these things his daughter let him have his own way, assisting and encouraging him. That was his line of life, and therefore she respected it. But in all other matters she chose to be paramount at the parsonage.

Mr. Woolsworthy was a little man, who always wore, except on Sundays, grey clothes—clothes of so light a grey that they would hardly have been regarded as clerical in a district less remote. He had now reached a goodly age, being full seventy years old; but still he was wiry and active, and shewed but few symptoms of decay. His head was bald, and the few remaining locks that surrounded it were nearly white. But there was a look of energy about his mouth, and a humour in his light grey eye, which forbade those who knew him to regard him altogether as an old man. As it was, he could walk from Oxney Colne to Priestown, fifteen long Devonshire miles across the moor; and he who could do that could hardly be regarded as too old for work.

But our present story will have more to do with his daughter than with him. A pretty girl, I have said, was Patience Woolsworthy; and one, too, in many ways remarkable. She had taken her outlook into life, weighing the things which she had and those which she had not, in a manner very unusual, and, as a rule, not always desirable for a young lady. The things which she had not were very many. She had not society; she had not a fortune; she had not any assurance of future means of livelihood; she had not high hope of procuring for herself a position in life by marriage; she had not that excitement and pleasure in life which she read of in such books as found their way down to Oxney Colne Parsonage. It would be easy to add to the list of the things which she had not; and this list against herself she made out with the utmost vigour. The things which she had, or those rather which she assured herself of having, were much more easily counted. She had the birth and education of a lady, the strength of a healthy woman, and a will of her own. Such was the list as she made it out for herself, and I protest that I assert no more than the truth in saying that she never added to it either beauty, wit, or talent.

I began these descriptions by saying that Oxney Colne would, of all places, be the best spot from which a tourist could visit those parts of Devonshire, but for the fact that he could obtain there none of the accommodation which tourists require. A brother antiquarian might, perhaps, in those days have done so, seeing that there was, as I have said, a spare bedroom at the parsonage. Any intimate friend of Miss Le Smyrger's might be as fortunate, for she was equally well provided at Oxney Combe, by which name her house was known. But Miss Le Smyrger was not given to extensive hospitality, and it was only to those who were bound to her, either by ties of blood or of very old friendship, that she delighted to open her doors. As her old friends were very few in number, as those few lived at a distance, and as her nearest relations were higher in the world than she was, and were said by herself to look down upon her, the visits made to Oxney Combe were few and far between.

But now, at the period of which I am writing, such a visit was about to be made. Miss Le Smyrger had a younger sister, who had inherited a property in the parish of Oxney Colne equal to that of the lady who now lived there; but this the younger sister had inherited beauty also, and she therefore, in early life, had found sundry lovers, one of whom became her husband. She had married a man even then well to do in the world, but now rich and almost mighty; a Member of Parliament, a Lord of this and that board, a man who had a house in Eaton-square, and a park in the north of England; and in this way her course of life had been very much divided from that of our Miss Le Smyrger. But the Lord of the Government Board had been blessed with various children; and perhaps it was now thought expedient to look after Aunt Penelope's Devonshire acres. Aunt Penelope was empowered to leave them to whom she pleased; and though it was thought in Eaton-square that she must, as a matter of course, leave them to one of the family, nevertheless a little cousinly intercourse might make the thing more certain. I will not say that this was the sole cause for such a visit, but in these days a visit was to be made by Captain Broughton to his aunt. Now Captain John Broughton was the second son of Alfonso Broughton, of Clapham Park and Eaton-square, Member of Parliament, and Lord of the aforesaid Government Board.

"And what do you mean to do with him?" Patience Woolsworthy asked of Miss Le Smyrger when that lady walked over from the Combe to say that her nephew John was to arrive on the following morning.

"Do with him? Why I shall bring him over here to talk to your father."

"He'll be too fashionable for that, and papa won't trouble his head about him if he finds that he doesn't care for Dartmoor."

"Then he may fall in love with you, my dear."

"Well, yes; there's that resource at any rate, and for your sake I dare say I should be more civil to him than papa. But he'll soon get tired of making love, and what you'll do then I cannot imagine."

That Miss Woolsworthy felt no interest in the coming of the Captain I will not pretend to say. The advent of any stranger with whom she would be called on to associate must be matter of interest to her in that secluded place; and she was not so absolutely unlike other young ladies that the arrival of an unmarried young man would be the same to her as the advent of some patriarchal paterfamilias. In taking that outlook into life of which I have spoken she had never said to herself that she despised those things from which other girls received the excitement, the joys, and the disappointment of their lives. She had simply given herself to understand that very little of such things would come her way, and that it behoved her to live—to live happily if such might be possible—without experiencing the need of them. She had heard, when there was no thought of any such visit to Oxney Colne, that John Broughton was a handsome, clever man—one who thought much of himself, and was thought much of by others—that there had been some talk of his marrying a great heiress, which marriage, however, had not taken place through unwillingness on his part, and that he was on the whole a man of more mark in the world than the ordinary captain of ordinary regiments.

Captain Broughton came to Oxney Combe, stayed there a fortnight,—the intended period for his projected visit having been fixed at three or four days—and then went his way. He went his way back to his London haunts, the time of the year then being the close of the Easter holydays; but as he did so he told his aunt that he should assuredly return to her in the autumn.

"And assuredly I shall be happy to see you, John—if you come with a certain purpose. If you have no such purpose, you had better remain away."

"I shall assuredly come," the Captain had replied, and then he had gone on his journey.

The summer passed rapidly by, and very little was said between Miss Le Smyrger and Miss Woolsworthy about Captain Broughton. In many respects—nay, I may say, as to all ordinary matters, no two women could well be more intimate with each other than they were,—and more than that, they had the courage each to talk to the other with absolute truth as to things concerning themselves—a courage in which dear friends often fail. But, nevertheless, very little was said between them about Captain John Broughton. All that was said may be here repeated.

"John says that he shall return here in August," Miss Le Smyrger said, as Patience was sitting with her in the parlour at Oxney Combe, on the morning after that gentleman's departure.

"He told me so himself," said Patience; and as she spoke her round dark eyes assumed a look of more than ordinary self-will. If Miss Le Smyrger had intended to carry the conversation any further, she changed her mind as she looked at her companion. Then, as I said, the summer ran by, and towards the close of the warm days of July, Miss Le Smyrger, sitting in the same chair in the same room, again took up the conversation.

"I got a letter from John this morning. He says that he shall be here on the third."

"Does he?"

"He is very punctual to the time he named."

"Yes; I fancy that he is a punctual man," said Patience.

"I hope that you will be glad to see him," said Miss Le Smyrger.

"Very glad to see him," said Patience, with a bold clear voice; and then the conversation was again dropped, and nothing further was said till after Captain Broughton's second arrival in the parish.

Four months had then passed since his departure, and during that time Miss Woolsworthy had performed all her usual daily duties in their accustomed course. No one could discover that she had been less careful in her household matters than had been her wont, less willing to go among her poor neighbours, or less assiduous in her attentions to her father. But not the less was there a feeling in the minds of those around her that some great change had come upon her. She would sit during the long summer evenings on a certain spot outside the parsonage orchard, at the top of a small sloping field in which their solitary cow was always pastured, with a book on her knees before her, but rarely reading. There she would sit, with the beautiful view down to the winding river below her, watching the setting sun, and thinking, thinking, thinking—thinking of something of which she had never spoken. Often would Miss Le Smyrger come upon her there, and sometimes would pass by her even without a word; but never—never once did she dare to ask her of the matter of her thoughts. But she knew the matter well enough. No confession was necessary to inform her that Patience Woolsworthy was in love with John Broughton—ay, in love, to the full and entire loss of her whole heart.

On one evening she was so sitting till the July sun had fallen and hidden himself for the night, when her father came upon her as he returned from one of his rambles on the moor. "Patty," he said, "you are always sitting there now. Is it not late? Will you not be cold?"

"No, papa," said she, "I shall not be cold."

"But won't you come to the house? I miss you when you come in so late that there's no time to say a word before we go to bed."

She got up and followed him into the parsonage, and when they were in the sitting-room together, and the door was closed, she came up to him and kissed him. "Papa," she said, "would it make you very unhappy if I were to leave you?"

"Leave me!" he said, startled by the serious and almost solemn tone of her voice. "Do you mean for always?"

"If I were to marry, papa?"

"Oh, marry! No; that would not make me unhappy. It would make me very happy, Patty, to see you married to a man you would love—very, very happy; though my days would be desolate without you."

"That is it, papa. What would you do if I went from you?"

"What would it matter, Patty? I should be free, at any rate, from a load which often presses heavy on me now. What will you do when I shall leave you? A few more years and all will be over with me. But who is it, love? Has anybody said anything to you?"

"It was only an idea, papa. I don't often think of such a thing; but I did think of it then." And so the subject was allowed to pass by. This had happened before the day of the second arrival had been absolutely fixed and made known to Miss Woolsworthy.

And then that second arrival took place. The reader may have understood from the words with which Miss Le Smyrger authorised her nephew to make his second visit to Oxney Combe that Miss Woolsworthy's passion was not altogether unauthorised. Captain Broughton had been told that he was not to come unless he came with a certain purpose; and having been so told, he still persisted in coming. There can be no doubt but that he well understood the purport to which his aunt alluded. "I shall assuredly come," he had said. And true to his word, he was now there.

Patience knew exactly the hour at which he must arrive at the station at Newton Abbot, and the time also which it would take to travel over those twelve uphill miles from the station to Oxney. It need hardly be said that she paid no visit to Miss Le Smyrger's house on that afternoon; but she might have known something of Captain Broughton's approach without going thither. His road to the Combe passed by the parsonage-gate, and had Patience sat even at her bedroom window she must have seen him. But on such a morning she would not sit at her bedroom window—she would do nothing which would force her to accuse herself of a restless longing for her lover's coming. It was for him to seek her. If he chose to do so, he knew the way to the parsonage.

Miss Le Smyrger—good, dear, honest, hearty Miss Le Smyrger, was in a fever of anxiety on behalf of her friend. It was not that she wished her nephew to marry Patience—or rather that she had entertained any such wish when he first came among them. She was not given to match-making, and moreover thought, or had thought within herself, that they of Oxney Colne could do very well without any admixture from Eaton-square. Her plan of life had been that, when old Mr. Woolsworthy was taken away from Dartmoor, Patience should live with her; and that when she also shuffled off her coil, then Patience Woolsworthy should be the maiden mistress of Oxney Combe—of Oxney Combe and Mr. Cloysey's farm—to the utter detriment of all the Broughtons. Such had been her plan before nephew John had come among them—a plan not to be spoken of till the coming of that dark day which should make Patience an orphan. But now her nephew had been there, and all was to be altered. Miss Le Smyrger's plan would have provided a companion for her old age; but that had not been her chief object. She had thought more of Patience than of herself, and now it seemed that a prospect of a higher happiness was opening for her friend.

"John," she said, as soon as the first greetings were over, "do you remember the last words that I said to you before you went away?" Now, for myself, I much admire Miss Le Smyrger's heartiness, but I do not think much of her discretion. It would have been better, perhaps, had she allowed things to take their course.

"I can't say that I do," said the Captain. At the same time the Captain did remember very well what those last words had been.

"I am so glad to see you, so delighted to see you, if—if—if—," and then she paused, for with all her courage she hardly dared to ask her nephew whether he had come there with the express purpose of asking Miss Woolsworthy to marry him.

To tell the truth—for there is no room for mystery within the limits of this short story,—to tell, I say, at a word the plain and simple truth, Captain Broughton had already asked that question. On the day before he left Oxney Colne, he had in set terms proposed to the parson's daughter, and indeed the words, the hot and frequent words, which previously to that had fallen like sweetest honey into the ears of Patience Woolsworthy, had made it imperative on him to do so. When a man in such a place as that has talked to a girl of love day after day, must not he talk of it to some definite purpose on the day on which he leaves her? Or if he do not, must he not submit to be regarded as false, selfish, and almost fraudulent? Captain Broughton, however, had asked the question honestly and truly. He had done so honestly and truly, but in words, or, perhaps, simply with a tone, that had hardly sufficed to satisfy the proud spirit of the girl he loved. She by that time had confessed to herself that she loved him with all her heart; but she had made no such confession to him. To him she had spoken no word, granted no favour, that any lover might rightfully regard as a token of love returned. She had listened to him as he spoke, and bade him keep such sayings for the drawing-rooms of his fashionable friends. Then he had spoken out and had asked for that hand,—not, perhaps, as a suitor tremulous with hope,—but as a rich man who knows that he can command that which he desires to purchase.

"You should think more of this," she had said to him at last. "If you would really have me for your wife, it will not be much to you to return here again when time for thinking of it shall have passed by." With these words she had dismissed him, and now he had again come back to Oxney Colne. But still she would not place herself at the window to look for him, nor dress herself in other than her simple morning country dress, nor omit one item of her daily work. If he wished to take her at all, he should wish to take her as she really was, in her plain country life, but he should take her also with full observance of all those privileges which maidens are allowed to claim from their lovers. He should contract no ceremonious observance because she was the daughter of a poor country parson who would come to him without a shilling, whereas he stood high in the world's books. He had asked her to give him all that she had, and that all she was ready to give, without stint. But the gift must be valued before it could be given or received. He also was to give her as much, and she would accept it as being beyond all price. But she would not allow that that which was offered to her was in any degree the more precious because of his outward worldly standing.

She would not pretend to herself that she thought he would come to her that day, and therefore she busied herself in the kitchen and about the house, giving directions to her two maids as though the afternoon would pass as all other days did pass in that household. They usually dined at four, and she rarely, in these summer months, went far from the house before that hour. At four precisely she sat down with her father, and then said that she was going up as far as Helpholme after dinner. Helpholme was a solitary farmhouse in another parish, on the border of the moor, and Mr. Woolsworthy asked her whether he should accompany her.

"Do, papa," she said, "if you are not too tired." And yet she had thought how probable it might be that she should meet John Broughton on her walk. And so it was arranged; but, just as dinner was over, Mr. Woolsworthy remembered himself.

"Gracious me," he said, "how my memory is going. Gribbles, from Ivybridge, and old John Poulter, from Bovey, are coming to meet here by appointment. You can't put Helpholme off till to-morrow?"

Patience, however, never put off anything, and therefore at six o'clock, when her father had finished his slender modicum of toddy, she tied on her hat and went on her walk. She started forth with a quick step, and left no word to say by which route she would go. As she passed up along the little lane which led towards Oxney Combe, she would not even look to see if he was coming towards her; and when she left the road, passing over a stone stile into a little path which ran first through the upland fields, and then across the moor ground towards Helpholme, she did not look back once, or listen for his coming step.

She paid her visit, remaining upwards of an hour with the old bed-ridden mother of the tenant of Helpholme. "God bless you, my darling!" said the old woman as she left her; "and send you some one to make your own path bright and happy through the world." These words were still ringing in her ears with all their significance as she saw John Broughton waiting for her at the first stile which she had to pass after leaving the farmer's haggard.

"Patty," he said, as he took her hand, and held it close within both his own, "what a chase I have had after you!"

"And who asked you, Captain Broughton?" she answered, smiling. "If the journey was too much for your poor London strength, could you not have waited till to-morrow morning, when you would have found me at the parsonage?" But she did not draw her hand away from him, or in any way pretend that he had not a right to accost her as a lover.

"No, I could not wait. I am more eager to see those I love than you seem to be."

"How do you know whom I love, or how eager I might be to see them? There is an old woman there whom I love, and I have thought nothing of this walk with the object of seeing her." And now, slowly drawing her hand away from him, she pointed to the farmhouse which she had left.

"Patty," he said, after a minute's pause, during which she had looked full into his face with all the force of her bright eyes; "I have come from London to-day, straight down here to Oxney, and from my aunt's house close upon your footsteps after you, to ask you that one question. Do you love me?"

"What a Hercules!" she said, again laughing. "Do you really mean that you left London only this morning? Why, you must have been five hours in a railway carriage and two in a postchaise, not to talk of the walk afterwards. You ought to take more care of yourself, Captain Broughton!"

He would have been angry with her—for he did not like to be quizzed—had she not put her hand on his arm as she spoke, and the softness of her touch had redeemed the offence of her words.

"All that I have done," said he, "that I may hear one word from you."

"That any word of mine should have such potency! But let us walk on, or my father will take us for some of the standing stones of the moor. How have you found your aunt? If you only knew the cares that have sat on her dear shoulders for the last week past, in order that your high mightiness might have a sufficiency to eat and drink in these desolate half-starved regions."

"She might have saved herself such anxiety. No one can care less for such things than I do."

"And yet I think I have heard you boast of the cook of your club." And then again there was silence for a minute or two.

"Patty," said he, stopping again in the path; "answer my question. I have a right to demand an answer. Do you love me?"

"And what if I do? What if I have been so silly as to allow your perfections to be too many for my weak heart? What then, Captain Broughton?"

"It cannot be that you love me, or you would not joke now."

"Perhaps not, indeed," she said. It seemed as though she were resolved not to yield an inch in her own humour. And then again they walked on.

"Patty," he said once more, "I shall get an answer from you to-night,—this evening; now, during this walk, or I shall return to-morrow, and never revisit this spot again."

"Oh, Captain Broughton, how should we ever manage to live without you?"

"Very well," he said; "up to the end of this walk I can bear it all;—and one word spoken then will mend it all."

During the whole of this time she felt that she was ill-using him. She knew that she loved him with all her heart; that it would nearly kill her to part with him; that she had heard his renewed offer with an ecstacy of joy. She acknowledged to herself that he was giving proof of his devotion as strong as any which a girl could receive from her lover. And yet she could hardly bring herself to say the word he longed to hear. That word once said, and then she knew that she must succumb to her love for ever! That word once said, and there would be nothing for her but to spoil him with her idolatry! That word once said, and she must continue to repeat it into his ears, till perhaps he might be tired of hearing it! And now he had threatened her, and how could she speak it after that? She certainly would not speak it unless he asked her again without such threat. And so they walked on again in silence.

"Patty," he said at last. "By the heavens above us you shall answer me. Do you love me?"

She now stood still, and almost trembled as she looked up into his face. She stood opposite to him for a moment, and then placing her two hands on his shoulders, she answered him. "I do, I do, I do," she said, "with all my heart; with all my heart—with all my heart and strength." And then her head fell upon his breast.

Captain Broughton was almost as much surprised as delighted by the warmth of the acknowledgment made by the eager-hearted passionate girl whom he now held within his arms. She had said it now; the words had been spoken; and there was nothing for her but to swear to him over and over again with her sweetest oaths, that those words were true—true as her soul. And very sweet was the walk down from thence to the parsonage gate. He spoke no more of the distance of the ground, or the length of his day's journey. But he stopped her at every turn that he might press her arm the closer to his own, that he might look into the brightness of her eyes, and prolong his hour of delight. There were no more gibes now on her tongue, no raillery at his London finery, no laughing comments on his coming and going. With downright honesty she told him everything: how she had loved him before her heart was warranted in such a passion; how, with much thinking, she had resolved that it would be unwise to take him at his first word, and had thought it better that he should return to London, and then think over it; how she had almost repented of her courage when she had feared, during those long summer days, that he would forget her; and how her heart had leapt for joy when her old friend had told her that he was coming.

"And yet," said he, "you were not glad to see me!"

"Oh, was I not glad? You cannot understand the feelings of a girl who has lived secluded as I have done. Glad is no word for the joy I felt. But it was not seeing you that I cared for so much. It was the knowledge that you were near me once again. I almost wish now that I had not seen you till to-morrow." But as she spoke she pressed his arm, and this caress gave the lie to her last words.

"No, do not come in to-night," she said, when she reached the little wicket that led up to the parsonage. "Indeed, you shall not. I could not behave myself properly if you did."

"But I don't want you to behave properly."

"Oh! I am to keep that for London, am I? But, nevertheless, Captain Broughton, I will not invite you either to tea or to supper to-night."

"Surely I may shake hands with your father."

"Not to-night—not till—. John, I may tell him, may I not? I must tell him at once."

"Certainly," said he.

"And then you shall see him to-morrow. Let me see—at what hour shall I bid you come?"

"To breakfast."

"No, indeed. What on earth would your aunt do with her broiled turkey and the cold pie? I have got no cold pie for you."

"I hate cold pie."

"What a pity! But, John, I should be forced to leave you directly after breakfast. Come down—come down at two, or three; and then I will go back with you to Aunt Penelope. I must see her to-morrow"; and so at last the matter was settled, and the happy Captain, as he left her, was hardly resisted in his attempt to press her lips to his own.

When she entered the parlour in which her father was sitting, there still were Gribbles and Poulter discussing some knotty point of Devon lore. So Patience took off her hat, and sat herself down, waiting till they should go. For full an hour she had to wait, and then Gribbles and Poulter did go. But it was not in such matters as this that Patience Woolsworthy was impatient. She could wait, and wait, and wait, curbing herself for weeks and months, while the thing waited for was in her eyes good; but she could not curb her hot thoughts or her hot words when things came to be discussed which she did not think to be good.

"Papa," she said, when Gribbles' long-drawn last word had been spoken at the door. "Do you remember how I asked you the other day what you would say if I were to leave you?"

"Yes, surely," he replied, looking up at her in astonishment.

"I am going to leave you now," she said. "Dear, dearest father, how am I to go from you?"

"Going to leave me," said he, thinking of her visit to Helpholme, and thinking of nothing else.

Now, there had been a story about Helpholme. That bed-ridden old lady there had a stalwart son, who was now the owner of the Helpholme pastures. But though owner in fee of all those wild acres, and of the cattle which they supported, he was not much above the farmers around him, either in manners or education. He had his merits, however; for he was honest, well-to-do in the world, and modest withal. How strong love had grown up, springing from neighbourly kindness, between our Patience and his mother, it needs not here to tell; but rising from it had come another love—or an ambition which might have grown to love. The young man, after much thought, had not dared to speak to Miss Woolsworthy, but he had sent a message by Miss Le Smyrger. If there could be any hope for him, he would present himself as a suitor—on trial. He did not owe a shilling in the world, and had money by him— saved. He wouldn't ask the parson for a shilling of fortune. Such had been the tenor of his message, and Miss Le Smyrger had delivered it faithfully. "He does not mean it," Patience had said with her stern voice. "Indeed he does, my dear. You may be sure he is in earnest," Miss Le Smyrger had replied; "and there is not an honester man in these parts."

"Tell him," said Patience, not attending to the latter portion of her friend's last speech, "that it cannot be—make him understand, you know—and tell him also that the matter shall be thought of no more." The matter had, at any rate, been spoken of no more, but the young farmer still remained a bachelor, and Helpholme still wanted a mistress. But all this came back upon the parson's mind when his daughter told him that she was about to leave him.

"Yes, dearest," she said; and as she spoke she now knelt at his knees. "I have been asked in marriage, and I have given myself away."

"Well, my love, if you will be happy—"

"I hope I shall; I think I shall. But you, papa?"

"You will not be far from us."

"Oh, yes; in London."

"In London?"

"Captain Broughton lives in London generally."

"And has Captain Broughton asked you to marry him?"

"Yes, papa—who else? Is he not good? Will you not love him? Oh, papa, do not say that I am wrong to love him?"

He never told her his mistake, or explained to her that he had not thought it possible that the high-placed son of the London great man should have fallen in love with his undowered daughter; but he embraced her, and told her, with all his enthusiasm, that he rejoiced in her joy, and would be happy in her happiness. "My own Patty," he said, "I have ever known that you were too good for this life of ours here." And then the evening wore away into the night, with many tears, but still with much happiness.

Captain Broughton, as he walked back to Oxney Combe, made up his mind that he would say nothing on the matter to his aunt till the next morning. He wanted to think over it all, and to think it over, if possible, by himself. He had taken a step in life, the most important that a man is ever called on to take, and he had to reflect whether or no he had taken it with wisdom.

"Have you seen her?" said Miss Le Smyrger, very anxiously, when he came into the drawing-room.

"Miss Woolsworthy you mean," said he. "Yes, I've seen her. As I found her out, I took a long walk, and happened to meet her. Do you know, aunt, I think I'll go to bed; I was up at five this morning, and have been on the move ever since."

Miss Le Smyrger perceived that she was to hear nothing that evening, so she handed him his candle-stick and allowed him to go to his room.

But Captain Broughton did not immediately retire to bed, nor when he did so was he able to sleep at once. Had this step that he had taken been a wise one? He was not a man who, in worldly matters, had allowed things to arrange themselves for him, as is the case with so many men. He had formed views for himself, and had a theory of life. Money for money's sake he had declared to himself to be bad. Money, as a concomitant to things which were in themselves good, he had declared to himself to be good also. That concomitant in this affair of his marriage, he had now missed. Well; he had made up his mind to that, and would put up with the loss. He had means of living of his own, the means not so extensive as might have been desirable. That it would be well for him to become a married man, looking merely to the state of life as opposed to his present state, he had fully resolved. On that point, therefore, there was nothing to repent. That Patty Woolsworthy was good, affectionate, clever, and beautiful he was sufficiently satisfied. It would be odd indeed if he were not so satisfied now, seeing that for the last four months he had so declared to himself daily with many inward asseverations. And yet though, he repeated, now again that he was satisfied, I do not think that he was so fully satisfied of it as he had been throughout the whole of those four months. It is sad to say so, but I fear—I fear that such was the case. When you have your plaything, how much of the anticipated pleasure vanishes, especially if it be won easily.

He had told none of his family what were his intentions in this second visit to Devonshire, and now he had to bethink himself whether they would be satisfied. What would his sister say, she who had married the Honourable Augustus Gumbleton, gold-stick-in-waiting to Her Majesty's Privy Council? Would she receive Patience with open arms, and make much of her about London? And then how far would London suit Patience, or would Patience suit London? There would be much for him to do in teaching her, and it would be well for him to set about the lesson without loss of time. So far he got that night, but when the morning came he went a step further, and began mentally to criticise her manner to himself. It had been very sweet, that warm, that full, that ready declaration of love. Yes; it had been very sweet; but—but—; when, after her little jokes, she did confess her love, had she not been a little too free for feminine excellence? A man likes to be told that he is loved, but he hardly wishes that the girl he is to marry should fling herself at his head!

Ah me! yes; it was thus he argued to himself as on that morning he went through the arrangements of his toilet. "Then he was a brute," you say, my pretty reader. I have never said that he was not a brute. But this I remark, that many such brutes are to be met with in the beaten paths of the world's highway. When Patience Woolsworthy had answered him coldly, bidding him go back to London and think over his love; while it seemed from her manner that at any rate as yet she did not care for him; while he was absent from her, and, therefore, longing for her, the possession of her charms, her talent and bright honesty of purpose had seemed to him a thing most desirable. Now they were his own. They had, in fact, been his own from the first. The heart of this country-bred girl had fallen at the first word from his mouth. Had she not so confessed to him? She was very nice—very nice indeed. He loved her dearly. But had he not sold himself too cheaply?

I by no means say that he was not a brute. But whether brute or no he was an honest man, and had no remotest dream, either then, on that morning, or during the following days on which such thoughts pressed more quickly on his mind—of breaking away from his pledged word. At breakfast on that morning he told all to Miss Le Smyrger, and that lady, with warm and gracious intentions, confided to him her purpose regarding her property. "I have always regarded Patience as my heir," she said, "and shall do so still."

"Oh, indeed," said Captain Broughton.

"But it is a great, great pleasure to me to think that she will give back the little property to my sister's child. You will have your mother's, and thus it will all come together again."

"Ah!" said Captain Broughton. He had his own ideas about property, and did not, even under existing circumstances, like to hear that his aunt considered herself at liberty to leave the acres away to one who was by blood quite a stranger to the family.

"Does Patience know of this?" he asked.

"Not a word," said Miss Le Smyrger. And then nothing more was said upon the subject.

On that afternoon he went down and received the parson's benediction and congratulations with a good grace. Patience said very little on the occasion, and indeed was absent during the greater part of the interview. The two lovers then walked up to Oxney Combe, and there were more benedictions and more congratulations. "All went merry as a marriage bell," at any rate as far as Patience was concerned. Not a word had yet fallen from that dear mouth, not a look had yet come over that handsome face, which tended in any way to mar her bliss. Her first day of acknowledged love was a day altogether happy, and when she prayed for him as she knelt beside her bed there was no feeling in her mind that any fear need disturb her joy.

I will pass over the next three or four days very quickly, merely saying that Patience did not find them so pleasant as that first day after her engagement. There was something in her lover's manner—something which at first she could not define—which by degrees seemed to grate against her feelings. He was sufficiently affectionate, that being a matter on which she did not require much demonstration; but joined to his affection there seemed to be—; she hardly liked to suggest to herself a harsh word, but could it be possible that he was beginning to think that she was not good enough for him? And then she asked herself the question—was she good enough for him? If there were doubt about that, the match should be broken off, though she tore her own heart out in the struggle. The truth, however, was this—that he had begun that teaching which he had already found to be so necessary. Now, had any one essayed to teach Patience German or mathematics, with that young lady's free consent, I believe that she would have been found a meek scholar. But it was not probable that she would be meek when she found a self-appointed tutor teaching her manners and conduct without her consent.

So matters went on for four or five days, and on the evening of the fifth day, Captain Broughton and his aunt drank tea at the parsonage. Nothing very especial occurred; but as the parson and Miss Le Smyrger insisted on playing backgammon with devoted perseverance during the whole evening, Broughton had a good opportunity of saying a word or two about those changes in his lady-love which a life in London would require—and some word he said also—some single slight word as to the higher station in life to which he would exalt his bride. Patience bore it—for her father and Miss Le Smyrger were in the room—she bore it well, speaking no syllable of anger, and enduring, for the moment, the implied scorn of the old parsonage. Then the evening broke up, and Captain Broughton walked back to Oxney Combe with his aunt. "Patty," her father said to her before they went to bed, "he seems to me to be a most excellent young man." "Dear papa," she answered, kissing him. "And terribly deep in love," said Mr. Woolsworthy. "Oh, I don't know about that," she answered, as she left him with her sweetest smile. But though she could thus smile at her father's joke, she had already made up her mind that there was still something to be learned as to her promised husband before she could place herself altogether in his hands. She would ask him whether he thought himself liable to injury from this proposed marriage; and though he should deny any such thought, she would know from the manner of his denial what his true feelings were.

And he, too, on that night, during his silent walk with Miss Le

Smyrger, had entertained some similar thoughts. "I fear she is obstinate," he had said to himself, and then he had half accused her of being sullen also. "If that be her temper, what a life of misery I have before me!"

"Have you fixed a day yet?" his aunt asked him as they came near to her house.

"No, not yet: I don't know whether it will suit me to fix it before I leave."

"Why, it was but the other day you were in such a hurry."

"Ah—yes—I have thought more about it since then."

"I should have imagined that this would depend on what Patty thinks," said Miss Le Smyrger, stand-up for the privileges of her sex. "It is presumed that the gentleman is always ready as soon as the lady will consent."

"Yes, in ordinary cases it is so; but when a girl is taken out of her own sphere—"

"Her own sphere! Let me caution you, Master John, not to talk to Patty about her own sphere."

"Aunt Penelope, as Patience is to be my wife and not yours, I must claim permission to speak to her on such subjects as may seem suitable to me." And then they parted—not in the best humour with each other.

On the following day Captain Broughton and Miss Woolsworthy did not meet till the evening. She had said, before those few ill-omened words had passed her lover's lips, that she would probably be at Miss Le Smyrger's house on the following morning. Those ill-omened words did pass her lover's lips, and then she remained at home. This did not come from sullenness, nor even from anger, but from a conviction that it would be well that she should think much before she met him again. Nor was he anxious to hurry a meeting. His thought—his base thought—was this; that she would be sure to come up to the Combe after him; but she did not come, and therefore in the evening he went down to her, and asked her to walk with him.

They went away by the path that led to Helpholme, and little was said between them till they had walked some mile together. Patience, as she went along the path, remembered almost to the letter the sweet words which had greeted her ears as she came down that way with him on the night of his arrival; but he remembered nothing of that sweetness then. Had he not made an ass of himself during these last six months? That was the thought which very much had possession of his mind.

"Patience," he said at last, having hitherto spoken only an indifferent word now and again since they had left the parsonage, "Patience, I hope you realise the importance of the step which you and I are about to take?"

"Of course I do," she answered. "What an odd question that is for you to ask!"

"Because," said he, "sometimes I almost doubt it. It seems to me as though you thought you could remove yourself from here to your new home with no more trouble than when you go from home up to the Combe."

"Is that meant for a reproach, John?"

"No, not for a reproach, but for advice. Certainly not for a reproach."

"I am glad of that."

"But I should wish to make you think how great is the leap in the world which you are about to take." Then again they walked on for many steps before she answered him.

"Tell me then, John," she said, when she had sufficiently considered what words she should speak; and as she spoke a bright colour suffused her face, and her eyes flashed almost with anger. "What leap do you mean? Do you mean a leap upwards?"

"Well, yes; I hope it will be so."

"In one sense, certainly, it would be a leap upwards. To be the wife of the man I loved; to have the privilege of holding his happiness in my hand; to know that I was his own—the companion whom he had chosen out of all the world—that would, indeed, be a leap upwards; a leap almost to heaven, if all that were so. But if you mean upwards in any other sense—"

"I was thinking of the social scale."

"Then, Captain Broughton, your thoughts were doing me dishonour."

"Doing you dishonour!"

"Yes, doing me dishonour. That your father is, in the world's esteem, a greater man than mine is doubtless true enough. That you, as a man, are richer than I am as a woman, is doubtless also true. But you dishonour me, and yourself also, if these things can weigh with you now."

"Patience,—I think you can hardly know what words you are saying to me."

"Pardon me, but I think I do. Nothing that you can give me—no gifts of that description—can weigh aught against that which I am giving you. If you had all the wealth and rank of the greatest lord in the land, it would count as nothing in such a scale. If—as I have not doubted—if in return for my heart you have given me yours, then—then—then you have paid me fully. But when gifts such as those are going, nothing else can count even as a make-weight."

"I do not quite understand you," he answered, after a pause. "I fear you are a little high-flown." And then, while the evening was still early, they walked back to the parsonage almost without another word.

Captain Broughton at this time had only one full day more to remain at Oxney Colne. On the afternoon following that he was to go as far as Exeter, and thence return to London. Of course, it was to be expected that the wedding day would be fixed before he went, and much had been said about it during the first day or two of his engagement. Then he had pressed for an early time, and Patience, with a girl's usual diffidence, had asked for some little delay. But now nothing was said on the subject; and how was it probable that such a matter could be settled after such a conversation as that which I have related? That evening, Miss Le Smyrger asked whether the day had been fixed. "No," said Captain Broughton harshly; "nothing has been fixed." "But it will be arranged before you go." "Probably not," he said; and then the subject was dropped for the time.

"John," she said, just before she went to bed, "if there be anything wrong between you and Patience, I conjure you to tell me."

"You had better ask her," he replied. "I can tell you nothing."

On the following morning he was much surprised by seeing Patience on the gravel path before Miss Le Smyrger's gate immediately after breakfast. He went to the door to open it for her, and she, as she gave him her hand, told him that she came up to speak to him. There was no hesitation in her manner, nor any look of anger in her face. But there was in her gait and form, in her voice and countenance, a fixedness of purpose which he had never seen before, or at any rate had never acknowledged.

"Certainly," said he. "Shall I come out with you, or will you come up stairs?"

"We can sit down in the summer-house," she said; and thither they both went.

"Captain Broughton," she said—and she began her task the moment that they were both seated—"You and I have engaged ourselves as man and wife, but perhaps we have been over rash."

"How so?" said he.

"It may be—and indeed I will say more—it is the case that we have made this engagement without knowing enough of each other's character."

"I have not thought so."

"The time will perhaps come when you will so think, but for the sake of all that we most value, let it come before it is too late. What would be our fate—how terrible would be our misery—if such a thought should come to either of us after we have linked our lots together."

There was a solemnity about her as she thus spoke which almost repressed him,—which for a time did prevent him from taking that tone of authority which on such a subject he would choose to adopt. But he recovered himself. "I hardly think that this comes well from you," he said.

"From whom else should it come? Who else can fight my battle for me; and, John, who else can fight that same battle on your behalf? I tell you this, that with your mind standing towards me as it does stand at present, you could not give me your hand at the altar with true words and a happy conscience. Am I not true? You have half repented of your bargain already. Is it not so?"

He did not answer her; but getting up from his seat walked to the front of the summer-house, and stood there with his back turned upon her. It was not that he meant to be ungracious, but in truth he did not know how to answer her. He had half repented of his bargain.

"John," she said, getting up and following him, so that she could put her hand upon his arm, "I have been very angry with you."

"Angry with me!" he said, turning sharp upon her.

"Yes, angry with you. You would have treated me like a child. But that feeling has gone now. I am not angry now. There is my hand;—the hand of a friend. Let the words that have been spoken between us be as though they had not been spoken. Let us both be free."

"Do you mean it?"

"Certainly I mean it." As she spoke these words her eyes filled with tears, in spite of all the efforts she could make; but he was not looking at her, and her efforts had sufficed to prevent any sob from being audible.

"With all my heart," he said; and it was manifest from his tone that he had no thought of her happiness as he spoke. It was true that she had been angry with him—angry, as she had herself declared; but nevertheless, in what she had said and what she had done, she had thought more of his happiness than of her own. Now she was angry once again.

"With all your heart, Captain Broughton! Well, so be it. If with all your heart, then is the necessity so much the greater. You go to-morrow. Shall we say farewell now?"

"Patience, I am not going to be lectured."

"Certainly not by me. Shall we say farewell now?"

"Yes, if you are determined."

"I am determined. Farewell, Captain Broughton. You have all my wishes for your happiness." And she held out her hand to him.

"Patience!" he said. And he looked at her with a dark frown, as though he would strive to frighten her into submission. If so, he might have saved himself any such attempt.

"Farewell, Captain Broughton. Give me your hand, for I cannot stay." He gave her his hand, hardly knowing why he did so. She lifted it to her lips and kissed it, and then, leaving him, passed from the summer-house down through the wicket-gate, and straight home to the parsonage.

During the whole of that day she said no word to anyone of what had occurred. When she was once more at home she went about her household affairs as she had done on that day of his arrival. When she sat down to dinner with her father he observed nothing to make him think that she was unhappy; nor during the evening was there any expression in her face, or any tone in her voice, which excited his attention. On the following morning Captain Broughton called at the parsonage, and the servant-girl brought word to her mistress that he was in the parlour. But she would not see him. "Laws, miss, you ain't a quarrelled with your beau?" the poor girl said. "No, not quarrelled," she said; "but give him that." It was a scrap of paper, containing a word or two in pencil. "It is better that we should not meet again. God bless you." And from that day to this, now more than ten years, they never have met.

"Papa," she said to her father that afternoon, "dear papa, do not be angry with me. It is all over between me and John Broughton. Dearest, you and I will not be separated."

It would be useless here to tell how great was the old man's surprise and how true his sorrow. As the tale was told to him no cause was given for anger with anyone. Not a word was spoken against the suitor who had on that day returned to London with a full conviction that now at least he was relieved from his engagement. "Patty, my darling child," he said, "may God grant that it be for the best!"

"It is for the best," she answered stoutly. "For this place I am fit; and I much doubt whether I am fit for any other."

On that day she did not see Miss Le Smyrger, but on the following morning, knowing that Captain Broughton had gone off, having heard the wheels of the carriage as they passed by the parsonage gate on his way to the station,—she walked up to the Combe.

"He has told you, I suppose?" said she.

"Yes," said Miss Le Smyrger. "And I will never see him again unless he asks your pardon on his knees. I have told him so. I would not even give him my hand as he went."

"But why so, thou kindest one? The fault was mine more than his."

"I understand. I have eyes in my head," said the old maid. "I have watched him for the last four or five days. If you could have kept the truth to yourself and bade him keep off from you, he would have been at your feet now, licking the dust from your shoes."

"But, dear friend, I do not want a man to lick dust from my shoes."

"Ah, you are a fool. You do not know the value of your own wealth."

"True; I have been a fool. I was a fool to think that one coming from such a life as he has led could be happy with such as I am. I know the truth now. I have bought the lesson dearly,—but perhaps not too dearly, seeing that it will never be forgotten."

There was but little more said about the matter between our three friends at Oxney Colne. What, indeed, could be said? Miss Le Smyrger for a year or two still expected that her nephew would return and claim his bride; but he has never done so, nor has there been any correspondence between them. Patience Woolsworthy had learned her lesson dearly. She had given her whole heart to the man; and, though she so bore herself that no one was aware of the violence of the struggle, nevertheless the struggle within her bosom was very violent. She never told herself that she had done wrong; she never regretted her loss; but yet—yet!—the loss was very hard to bear. He also had loved her, but he was not capable of a love which could much injure his daily peace. Her daily peace was gone for many a day to come.

Her father is still living; but there is a curate now in the parish. In conjunction with him and with Miss Le Smyrger she spends her time in the concerns of the parish. In her own eyes she is a confirmed old maid; and such is my opinion also. The romance of her life was played out in that summer. She never sits now lonely on the hill-side thinking how much she might do for one whom she really loved. But with a large heart she loves many, and, with no romance, she works hard to lighten the burdens of those she loves.

As for Captain Broughton, all the world know that he did marry that great heiress with whom his name was once before connected, and that he is now a useful member of Parliament, working on committees three or four days a week with a zeal that is indefatigable. Sometimes, not often, as he thinks of Patience Woolsworthy, a gratified smile comes across his face.

1861

THE PRUSSIAN OFFICER

D. H. Lawrence

I

THEY HAD marched more than thirty kilometres since dawn, along the white, hot road where occasional thickets of trees threw a moment of shade, then out into the glare again. On either hand, the valley, wide and shallow, glittered with heat; dark-green patches of rye, pale young corn, fallow and meadow and black pine woods spread in a dull, hot diagram under a glistening sky. But right in front the mountains ranged across, pale blue and very still, snow gleaming gently out of the deep atmosphere. And towards the mountains, on and on, the regiment marched between the rye-fields and the meadows, between the scraggy fruit trees set regularly on either side the high road. The burnished, dark-green rye threw off a suffocating heat, the mountains drew gradually nearer and more distinct. While the feet of the soldiers grew hotter, sweat ran through their hair under their helmets, and their knapsacks could burn no more in contact with their shoulders, but seemed instead to give off a cold, prickly sensation.

He walked on and on in silence, staring at the mountains ahead, that rose sheer out of the land, and stood fold behind fold, half earth, half heaven, the heaven, the barrier with slits of soft snow, in the pale, bluish peaks.

He could now walk almost without pain. At the start, he had determined not to limp. It had made him sick to take the first steps, and during the first mile or so, he had compressed his breath, and the cold drops of sweat had stood on his forehead. But he had walked it off. What were they after all but bruises! He had looked at them, as he was getting up: deep bruises on the backs of his thighs. And since he had made his first step in the morning, he had been conscious of them, till now he had a tight, hot place in his chest, with suppressing the pain, and holding himself in. There seemed no air when he breathed. But he walked almost lightly.

The Captain's hand had trembled at taking his coffee at dawn: his orderly saw it again. And he saw the fine figure of the Captain wheeling on horseback at the farmhouse ahead, a handsome figure in pale-blue uniform with facings of scarlet, and the metal gleaming on the black helmet and the sword-scabbard, and dark streaks of sweat coming on the silky bay horse. The orderly felt he was connected with that figure moving so suddenly on horseback: he followed it like a shadow, mute and inevitable and damned by it. And the officer was always aware of the tramp of the company behind, the march of his orderly among the men.

The Captain was a tall man of about forty, grey at the temples. He had a handsome, finely-knit figure, and was one of the best horsemen in the West. His orderly, having to rub him down, admired the amazing riding-muscles of his loins.

For the rest, the orderly scarcely noticed the officer any more than he noticed himself. It was rarely he saw his master's face: he did not look at it. The Captain had reddish-brown, stiff hair, that he wore short upon his skull. His moustache was also cut short and bristly over a full, brutal mouth. His face was rather rugged, the cheeks thin. Perhaps the man was the more handsome for the deep lines in his face, the irritable tension of his brow, which gave him the look of a man who fights with life. His fair eyebrows stood bushy over light-blue eyes that were always flashing with cold fire.

He was a Prussian aristocrat, haughty and overbearing. But his mother had been a Polish countess. Having made too many gambling debts when he was young, he had ruined his prospects in the Army, and remained an infantry captain. He had never married: his position did not allow of it, and no woman had ever moved him to it. His time he spent riding—occasionally he rode one of his own horses at the races—and at the officers' club. Now and then he took himself a mistress. But after such an event, he returned to duty with his brow still more tense, his eyes still more hostile and irritable. With the men, however, he was merely impersonal, though a devil when roused; so that, on the whole, they feared him, but had no great aversion from him. They accepted him as the inevitable.

To his orderly he was at first cold and just and indifferent: he did not fuss over trifles. So that his servant knew practically nothing about him, except just what orders he would give, and how he wanted them obeyed. That was quite simple. Then the change gradually came.

The orderly was a youth of about twenty-two, of medium height, and well built. He had strong, heavy limbs, was swarthy, with a soft, black, young moustache. There was something altogether warm and young about him. He had firmly marked eyebrows over dark, expressionless eyes, that seemed never to have thought, only to have received life direct through his senses, and acted straight from instinct.

Gradually the officer had become aware of his servant's young vigorous, unconscious presence about him. He could not get away from the sense of the youth's person, while he was in attendance. It was like a warm flame upon the older man's tense, rigid body, that had become almost unliving, fixed. There was something so free and self-contained about him, and something in the young fellow's movement, that made the officer aware of him. And this irritated the Prussian. He did not choose to be touched into life by his servant. He might easily have changed his man, but he did not. He now very rarely looked direct at his orderly, but kept his face averted, as if to avoid seeing him. And yet as the young soldier moved unthinking about the apartment, the elder watched him, and would notice the movement of his strong young shoulders under the blue cloth, the bend of his neck. And it irritated him. To see the soldier's young, brown, shapely peasant's hand grasp the loaf or the wine-bottle sent a flash of hate or of anger through the elder man's blood. It was not that the youth was clumsy: it was rather the blind, instinctive sureness of movement of an unhampered young animal that irritated the officer to such a degree.

Once, when a bottle of wine had gone over, and the red gushed out on to the tablecloth, the officer had started up with an oath, and his eyes, bluey like fire, had held those of the confused youth for a moment. It was a shock for the young soldier. He felt something sink deeper, deeper into his soul, where nothing had ever gone before. It left him rather blank and wondering. Some of his natural completeness in himself was gone, a little uneasiness took its place. And from that time an undiscovered feeling had held between the two men.

Henceforward the orderly was afraid of really meeting his master. His subconsciousness remembered those steely blue eyes and the harsh brows, and did not intend to meet them again. So he always stared past his master, and avoided him. Also, in a little anxiety, he waited for the three months to have gone, when his time would be up. He began to feel a constraint in the Captain's presence, and the soldier even more than the officer wanted to be left alone, in his neutrality as servant.

He had served the Captain for more than a year, and knew his duty. This he performed easily, as if it were natural to him. The officer and his commands he took for granted, as he took the sun and the rain, and he served as a matter of course. It did not implicate him personally.

But now if he were going to be forced into a personal interchange with his master he would be like a wild thing caught, he felt he must get away.

But the influence of the young soldier's being had penetrated through the officer's stiffened discipline, and perturbed the man in him. He, however, was a gentleman, with long, fine hands and cultivated movements, and was not going to allow such a thing as the stirring of his innate self. He was a man of passionate temper, who had always kept himself suppressed. Occasionally there had been a duel, an outburst before the soldiers. He knew himself to be always on the point of breaking out. But he kept himself hard to the idea of the Service. Whereas the young soldier seemed to live out his warm, full nature, to give it off in his very movements, which had a certain zest, such as wild animals have in free movement. And this irritated the officer more and more.

In spite of himself, the Captain could not regain his neutrality of feeling towards his orderly. Nor could he leave the man alone. In spite of himself, he watched him, gave him sharp orders, tried to take up as much of his time as possible. Sometimes he flew into a rage with the young soldier, and bullied him. Then the orderly shut himself off, as it were out of earshot, and waited, with sullen, flushed face, for the end of the noise. The words never pierced to his intelligence, he made himself, protectively, impervious to the feelings of his master.

He had a scar on his left thumb, a deep seam going across the knuckle. The officer had long suffered from it, and wanted to do something to it. Still it was there, ugly and brutal on the young, brown hand. At last the Captain's reserve gave way. One day, as the orderly was smoothing out the tablecloth, the officer pinned down his thumb with a pencil, asking:

"How did you come by that?"

The young man winced and drew back at attention.

"A wood axe, Herr Hauptmann," he answered.

The officer waited for further explanation. None came. The orderly went about his duties. The elder man was sullenly angry. His servant avoided him. And the next day he had to use all his will-power to avoid seeing the scarred thumb. He wanted to get hold of it and——A hot flame ran in his blood.

He knew his servant would soon be free, and would be glad. As yet, the soldier had held himself off from the elder man. The Captain grew madly irritable. He could not rest when the soldier was away, and when he was present, he glared at him with tormented eyes. He hated those fine, black brows over the unmeaning, dark eyes, he was infuriated by the free movement of the handsome limbs, which no military discipline could make stiff. And he became harsh and cruelly bullying, using contempt and satire. The young soldier only grew more mute and expressionless.

"What cattle were you bred by, that you can't keep straight eyes? Look me in the eyes when I speak to you."

And the soldier turned his dark eyes to the other's face, but there was no sight in them: he stared with the slightest possible cast, holding back his sight, perceiving the blue of his master's eyes, but receiving no look from them. And the elder man went pale, and his reddish eyebrows twitched. He gave his order, barrenly.

Once he flung a heavy military glove into the young soldier's face. Then he had the satisfaction of seeing the black eyes flare up into his own, like a blaze when straw is thrown on a fire. And he had laughed with a little tremor and a sneer.

But there were only two months more. The youth instinctively tried to keep himself intact: he tried to serve the officer as if the latter were an abstract authority and not a man. All his instinct was to avoid personal contact, even definite hate. But in spite of himself the hate grew, responsive to the officer's passion. However, he put it in the background. When he had left the Army he could dare acknowledge it. By nature he was active, and had many friends. He thought what amazing good fellows they were. But, without knowing it, he was alone. Now this solitariness was intensified. It would carry him through his term. But the officer seemed to be going irritably insane, and the youth was deeply frightened.

The soldier had a sweetheart, a girl from the mountains, independent and primitive. The two walked together, rather silently. He went with her, not to talk, but to have his arm round her, and for the physical contact. This eased him, made it easier for him to ignore the Captain; for he could rest with her held fast against his chest. And she, in some unspoken fashion, was there for him. They loved each other.

The Captain perceived it, and was mad with irritation. He kept the young man engaged all the evenings long, and took pleasure in the dark look that came on his face. Occasionally, the eyes of the two men met, those of the younger sullen and dark, doggedly unalterable, those of the elder sneering with restless contempt.

The officer tried hard not to admit the passion that had got hold of him. He would not know that his feeling for his orderly was anything but that of a man incensed by his stupid, perverse servant. So, keeping quite justified and conventional in his consciousness, he let the other thing run on. His nerves, however, were suffering. At last he slung the end of a belt in his servant's face. When he saw the youth start back, the pain-tears in his eyes and the blood on his mouth, he had felt at once a thrill of deep pleasure and of shame.

But this, he acknowledged to himself, was a thing he had never done before. The fellow was too exasperating. His own nerves must be going to pieces. He went away for some days with a woman.

'It was a mockery of pleasure. He simply did not want the woman. But he stayed on for his time. At the end of it, he came back in an agony of irritation, torment, and misery. He rode all the evening, then came straight in to supper. His orderly was out. The officer sat with his long, fine hands lying on the table, perfectly still, and all his blood seemed to be corroding.

At last his servant entered. He watched the strong, easy young figure, the fine eyebrows, the thick black hair. In a week's time the youth had got back his old well-being. The hands of the officer twitched and seemed to be full of mad flame. The young man stood at attention, unmoving, shut off.

The meal went in silence. But the orderly seemed eager. He made a clatter with the dishes.

"Are you in a hurry?" asked the officer, watching the intent, warm face of his servant. The other did not reply.

"Will you answer my question?" said the Captain.

"Yes, sir," replied the orderly, standing with his pile of deep Army plates. The Captain waited, looked at him, then asked again:

"Are you in a hurry?"

"Yes, sir," came the answer, that sent a flash through the listener.

"For what?"

"I was going out, sir."

"I want you this evening."

There was a moment's hesitation. The officer had a curious stiffness of countenance.

"Yes, sir," replied the servant, in his throat.

"I want you to-morrow evening also—in fact, you may consider your evenings occupied, unless I give you leave."

The mouth with the young moustache set close.

"Yes, sir," answered the orderly, loosening his lips for a moment.

He again turned to the door.

"And why have you a piece of pencil in your ear?"

The orderly hesitated, then continued on his way without answering. He set the plates in a pile outside the door, took the stump of pencil from his ear, and put it in his pocket. He had been copying a verse for his sweetheart's birthday card. He returned to finish clearing the table. The officer's eyes were dancing, he had a little, eager smile.

"Why have you a piece of pencil in your ear?" he asked.

The orderly took his hands full of dishes. His master was standing near the great green stove, a little smile on his face, his chin thrust forward. When the young soldier saw him his heart suddenly ran hot. He felt blind. Instead of answering, he turned dazedly to the door. As he was crouching to set down the dishes, he was pitched forward by a kick from behind. The pots went in a stream down the stairs, he clung to the pillar of the banisters. And as he was rising he was kicked heavily again and again, so that he clung sickly to the post for some moments. His master had gone swiftly into the room and closed the door. The maid-servant downstairs looked up the staircase and made a mocking face at the crockery disaster.

The officer's heart was plunging. He poured himself a glass of wine, part of which he spilled on the floor, and gulped the remainder, leaning against the cool, green stove. He heard his man collecting the dishes from the stairs. Pale, as if intoxicated, he waited. The servant entered again. The

Captain's heart gave a pang, as of pleasure, seeing the young fellow bewildered and uncertain on his feet with pain.

"Schöner!" he said.

The soldier was a little slower in coming to attention.

"Yes, sir!"

The youth stood before him, with pathetic young moustache, and fine eyebrows very distinct on his forehead of dark marble.

"I asked you a question."

"Yes, sir."

The officer's tone bit like acid.

"Why had you a pencil in your ear?"

Again the servant's heart ran hot, and he could not breathe. With dark, strained eyes, he looked at the officer, as if fascinated. And he stood there sturdily planted, unconscious. The withering smile came into the Captain's eyes, and he lifted his foot.

"I forgot it—sir," panted the soldier, his dark eyes fixed on the other man's dancing blue ones.

"What was it doing there?"

He saw the young man's breast heaving as he made an effort for words.

"I had been writing."

"Writing what?"

Again the soldier looked him up and down. The officer could hear him panting. The smile came into the blue eyes. The soldier worked his dry throat, but could not speak. Suddenly the smile lit like a flame on the officer's face, and a kick came heavily against the orderly's thigh. The youth moved a pace sideways. His face went dead, with two black, staring eyes.

"Well?" said the officer.

The orderly's mouth had gone dry, and his tongue rubbed in it as on dry brown-paper. He worked his throat. The officer raised his foot. The servant went stiff.

"Some poetry, sir," came the crackling, unrecognizable sound of his voice.

"Poetry, what poetry?" asked the Captain, with a sickly smile.

Again there was the working in the throat. The Captain's heart had suddenly gone down heavily, and he stood sick and tired.

"For my girl, sir," he heard the dry, inhuman sound.

"Oh!" he said, turning away. "Clear the table."

"Click!" went the soldier's throat; then again, "click!" and then the half-articulate:

"Yes, sir."

The young soldier was gone, looking old, and walking heavily.

The officer, left alone, held himself rigid, to prevent himself from thinking. His instinct warned him that he must not think. Deep inside him was the intense gratification of his passion, still working powerfully.

Then there was a counteraction, a horrible breaking down of something inside him, a whole agony of reaction. He stood there for an hour motionless, a chaos of sensations, but rigid with a will to keep blank his consciousness, to prevent his mind grasping. And he held himself so until the worst of the stress had passed, when he began to drink, drank himself to an intoxication, till he slept obliterated. When he woke in the morning he was shaken to the base of his nature. But he had fought off the realisation of what he had done. He had prevented his mind from taking it in, had suppressed it along with his instincts, and the conscious man had nothing to do with it. He felt only as after a bout of intoxication, weak, but the affair itself all dim and not to be recovered. Of the drunkenness of his passion he successfully refused remembrance. And when his orderly appeared with coffee, the officer assumed the same self he had had the morning before. He refused the event of the past night—denied it had ever been—and was successful in his denial. He had not done any such thing—not he himself. Whatever there might be lay at the door of a stupid, insubordinate servant.

The orderly had gone about in a stupor all the evening. He drank some beer because he was parched, but not much, the alcohol made his feeling come back, and he could not bear it. He was dulled, as if nine-tenths of the ordinary man in him were inert. He crawled about disfigured. Still, when he thought of the kicks, he went sick, and when he thought of the threat of more kicking, in the room afterwards, his heart went hot and faint, and he panted, remembering the one that had come. He had been forced to say: "For my girl." He was much too done even to want to cry. His mouth hung slightly open, like an idiot's. He felt vacant, and wasted. So, he wandered at his work, painfully, and very slowly and clumsily, fumbling blindly with the brushes, and finding it difficult, when he sat down, to summon the energy to move again. His limbs, his jaw, were slack and nerveless. But he was very tired. He got to bed at last, and slept inert, relaxed, in a sleep that was rather stupor than slumber, a dead night of stupefaction shot through with gleams of anguish.

In the morning were the manoeuvres. But he woke even before the bugle sounded. The painful ache in his chest, the dryness of his throat, the awful steady feeling of misery made his eyes come awake and dreary at once. He knew, without thinking, what had happened. And he knew that the day had come again, when he must go on with his round. The last bit of darkness was being pushed out of the room. He would have to move his inert body and go on. He was so young, and had known so little trouble, that he was bewildered. He only wished it would stay night, so that he could lie still, covered up by the darkness. And yet nothing would prevent the day from coming, nothing would save him from having to get up and saddle the Captain's horse, and make the Captain's coffee. It was there, inevitable. And then, he thought, it was impossible. Yet they would not leave him free. He must go and take the coffee to the Captain. He was too stunned to understand it. He only knew it was inevitable—inevitable, however long he lay inert.

At last, after heaving at himself, for he seemed to be a mass of inertia, he got up. But he had to force every one of his movements from behind, with his will. He felt lost, and dazed, and helpless. Then he clutched hold of the bed, the pain was so keen. And looking at his thighs he saw the darker bruises on his swarthy flesh, and he knew that if he pressed one of his fingers on one of the bruises, he should faint. But he did not want to faint—he did not want anybody to know. No one should ever know. It was between him and the Captain. There were only the two people in the world now—himself and the Captain.

Slowly, economically, he got dressed and forced himself to walk. Everything was obscure, except just what he had his hands on. But he managed to get through his work. The very pain revived his dull senses. The worst remained yet. He took the tray and went up to the Captain's room. The officer, pale and heavy, sat at the table. The orderly, as he saluted, felt himself put out of existence. He stood still for a moment submitting to his own nullification—then he gathered himself, seemed to regain himself, and then the Captain began to grow vague, unreal, and the younger soldier's heart beat up. He clung to this situation—that the Captain did not exist—so that he himself might live. But when he saw his officer's hand tremble as he took the coffee, he felt everything falling shattered. And he went away, feeling as if he himself were coming to pieces, disintegrated. And when the Captain was there on horseback, giving orders, while he himself stood, with rifle and knapsack, sick with pain, he felt as if he must shut his eyes—as if he must shut his eyes on everything. It was only the long agony of marching with a parched throat that filled him with one single, sleep-heavy intention: to save himself.

II

He was getting used even to his parched throat. That the snowy peaks were radiant among the sky, that the whity-green glacier-river twisted through its pale shoals, in the valley below, seemed almost supernatural. But he was going mad with fever and thirst. He plodded on uncomplaining. He did not want to speak, not to anybody. There were two gulls, like flakes of water and snow, over the river. The scent of green rye soaked in sunshine came like a sickness. And the march continued, monotonously, almost like a bad sleep.

At the next farmhouse, which stood low and broad near the high road, tubs of water had been put out. The soldiers clustered round to drink.

They took off their helmets, and the steam mounted from their wet hair. The Captain sat on horseback, watching. He needed to see his orderly. His helmet threw a dark shadow over his light, fierce eyes, but his moustache and mouth and chin were distinct in the sunshine. The orderly must move under the presence of the figure of the horseman. It was not that he was afraid, or cowed. It was as if he was disembowelled, made empty, like an empty shell. He felt himself as nothing, a shadow creeping under the sunshine. And, thirsty as he was, he could scarcely drink, feeling the Captain near him. He would not take off his helmet to wipe his wet hair. He wanted to stay in shadow, not to be forced into consciousness. Starting, he saw the light heel of the officer prick the belly of the horse; the Captain cantered away, and he himself could relapse into vacancy.

Nothing, however, could give him back his living place in the hot, bright morning. He felt like a gap among it all. Whereas the Captain was prouder, overriding. A hot flash went through the young servant's body. The Captain was firmer and prouder with life, he himself was empty as a shadow. Again the flash went through him, dazing him out. But his heart ran a little firmer.

The company turned up the hill, to make a loop for the return. Below, from among the trees, the farm-bell clanged. He saw the labourers, mowing bare-foot at the thick grass, leave off their work and go downhill, their scythes hanging over their shoulders, like long, bright claws curving down behind them. They seemed like dream-people, as if they had no relation to himself. He felt as in a blackish dream: as if all the other things were there and had form, but he himself was only a consciousness, a gap that could think and perceive.

The soldiers were tramping silently up the glaring hill-side. Gradually his head began to revolve, slowly, rhythmically. Sometimes it was dark before his eyes, as if he saw this world through a smoked glass, frail shadows and unreal. It gave him a pain in his head to walk.

The air was too scented, it gave no breath. All the lush green-stuff seemed to be issuing its sap, till the air was deathly, sickly with the smell of greenness. There was the perfume of clover, like pure honey and bees. Then there grew a faint acrid tang—they were near the beeches; and then a queer clattering noise, and a suffocating, hideous smell; they were passing a flock of sheep, a shepherd in a black smock, holding his crook. Why should the sheep huddle together under this fierce sun? He felt that the shepherd would not see him, though he could see the shepherd.

At last there was the halt. They stacked rifles in a conical stack, put down their kit in a scattered circle around it, and dispersed a little, sitting on a small knoll high on the hill-side. The chatter began. The soldiers were steaming with heat, but were lively. He sat still, seeing the blue mountains rising upon the land, twenty kilometres away. There was a blue fold in the ranges, then out of that, at the foot, the broad, pale bed of the river, stretches of whity-green water between pinkish-grey shoals among the dark pine woods. There it was, spread out a long way off. And it seemed to come downhill, the river. There was a raft being steered, a mile away. It was a strange country. Nearer, a red-roofed, broad farm with white base and square dots of windows crouched beside the wall of beech foliage on the wood's edge. There were long strips of rye and clover and pale green corn. And just at his feet, below the knoll, was a darkish bog, where globe flowers stood breathless still on their slim stalks. And some of the pale gold bubbles were burst, and a broken fragment hung in the air. He thought he was going to sleep.

Suddenly something moved into this coloured mirage before his eyes. The Captain, a small, light-blue and scarlet figure, was trotting evenly between the strips of corn, along the level brow of the hill. And the man making flag-signals was coming on. Proud and sure moved the horseman's figure, the quick, bright thing, in which was concentrated all the light of this morning, which for the rest lay a fragile, shining shadow. Submissive, apathetic, the young soldier sat and stared. But as the horse slowed to a walk, coming up the last steep path, the great flash flared over the body and soul of the orderly. He sat waiting. The back of his head felt as if it were weighted with a heavy piece of fire. He did not want to eat. His hands trembled slightly as he moved them. Meanwhile the officer on horseback was approaching slowly and proudly. The tension grew in the orderly's soul. Then again, seeing the Captain ease himself on the saddle, the flash blazed through him.

The Captain looked at the patch of light blue and scarlet, and dark heads, scattered closely on the hill-side. It pleased him. The command pleased him. And he was feeling proud. His orderly was among them in common subjection. The officer rose a little on his stirrups to look. The young soldier sat with averted, dumb face. The Captain relaxed on his seat. His slim-legged, beautiful horse, brown as a beech nut, walked proudly uphill. The Captain passed into the zone of the company's atmosphere: a hot smell of men, of sweat, of leather. He knew it very well. After a word with the lieutenant, he went a few paces higher, and sat there, a dominant figure, his sweat-marked horse swishing its tail, while he looked down on his men, on his orderly, a nonentity among the crowd.

The young soldier's heart was like fire in his chest, and he breathed with difficulty. The officer, looking downhill, saw three of the young soldiers, two pails of water between them, staggering across a sunny green field. A table had been set up under a tree, and there the slim lieutenant stood, importantly busy. Then the Captain summoned himself to an act of courage. He called his orderly.

The flame leapt into the young soldier's throat as he heard the command, and he rose blindly, stifled. He saluted, standing below the officer. He did not look up. But there was the flicker in the Captain's voice.

"Go to the inn and fetch me . . ." the officer gave his commands. "Quick!" he added.

At the last word, the heart of the servant leapt with a flash, and he felt the strength come over his body. But he turned in mechanical obedience, and set off at a heavy run downhill, looking almost like a bear, his trousers bagging over his military boots. And the officer watched this blind, plunging run all the way.

But it was only the outside of the orderly's body that was obeying so humbly and mechanically. Inside had gradually accumulated a core into which all the energy of that young life was compact and concentrated. He executed his commission, and plodded quickly back uphill. There was a pain in his head as he walked that made him twist his features unknowingly. But hard there in the centre of his chest was himself, himself, firm, and not to be plucked to pieces.

The Captain had gone up into the wood. The orderly plodded through the hot, powerfully smelling zone of the company's atmosphere. He had a curious mass of energy inside him now. The Captain was less real than himself. He approached the green entrance to the wood. There, in the half-shade, he saw the horse standing, the sunshine and the flickering shadow of leaves dancing over his brown body. There was a clearing where timber had lately been felled. Here, in the gold-green shade beside the brilliant cup of sunshine, stood two figures, blue and pink, the bits of pink showing out plainly. The Captain was talking to his lieutenant.

The orderly stood on the edge of the bright clearing, where great trunks of trees, stripped and glistening, lay stretched like naked, brown-skinned bodies. Chips of wood littered the trampled floor, like splashed light, and the bases of the felled trees stood here and there, with their raw, level tops. Beyond was the brilliant, sunlit green of a beech.

"Then I will ride forward," the orderly heard his Captain say. The lieutenant saluted and strode away. He himself went forward. A hot flash passed through his belly, as he tramped towards his officer.

The Captain watched the rather heavy figure of the young soldier stumble forward, and his veins, too, ran hot. This was to be man to man between them. He yielded before the solid, stumbling figure with bent head. The orderly stooped and put the food on a level-sawn tree-base. The Captain watched the glistening, sun-inflamed, naked hands. He wanted to speak to the young soldier, but could not. The servant propped a bottle against his thigh, pressed open the cork, and poured out the beer into the mug. He kept his head bent. The Captain accepted the mug.

"Hot!" he said, as if amiably.

The flame sprang out of the orderly's heart, nearly suffocating him.

"Yes, sir," he replied, between shut teeth.

And he heard the sound of the Captain's drinking, and he clenched his fists, such a strong torment came into his wrists. Then came the faint clang of the closing pot-lid. He looked up. The Captain was watching him. He glanced swiftly away. Then he saw the officer stoop and take a piece of bread from the tree-base. Again the flash of flame went through the young soldier, seeing the stiff body stoop beneath him, and his hands jerked. He looked away. He could feel the officer was nervous. The bread fell as it was being broken. The officer ate the other piece. The two men stood tense and still, the master laboriously chewing his bread, the servant staring with averted face, his fist clenched.

Then the young soldier started. The officer had pressed open the lid of the mug again. The orderly watched the lip of the mug, and the white hand that clenched the handle, as if he were fascinated. It was raised. The youth followed it with his eyes. And then he saw the thin, strong throat of the elder man moving up and down as he drank, the strong jaw working. And the instinct which had been jerking at the young man's wrists suddenly jerked free. He jumped, feeling as if it were rent in two by a strong flame.

The spur of the officer caught in a tree root, he went down backwards with a crash, the middle of his back thudding sickeningly against a sharp-edged tree-base, the pot flying away. And in a second the orderly, with serious, earnest young face, and underlip between his teeth, had got his knee in the officer's chest and was pressing the chin backward over the farther edge of the tree-stump, pressing, with all his heart behind in a passion of relief, the tension of his wrists exquisite with relief. And with the base of his palms he shoved at the chin with all his might. And it was pleasant, too, to have that chin, that hard jaw already slightly rough with beard, in his hands. He did not relax one hair's breadth, but, all the force of all his blood exulting in his thrust, he shoved back the head of the other man, till there was a little "cluck" and a crunching sensation. Then he felt as if his head went to vapour. Heavy convulsions shook the body of the officer, frightening and horrifying the young soldier. Yet it pleased him, too, to repress them. It pleased him to keep his hands pressing back the chin, to feel the chest of the other man yield in expiration to the weight of his strong, young knees, to feel the hard twitchings of the prostrate body jerking his own whole frame, which was pressed down on it.

But it went still. He could look into the nostrils of the other man, the eyes he could scarcely see. How curiously the mouth was pushed out, exaggerating the full lips, and the moustache bristling up from them. Then, with a start, he noticed the nostrils gradually filled with blood. The red brimmed, hesitated, ran over, and went in a thin trickle down the face to the eyes.

It shocked and distressed him. Slowly, he got up. The body twitched and sprawled there, inert. He stood and looked at it in silence. It was a pity *it* was broken. It represented more than the thing which had kicked and bullied him. He was afraid to look at the eyes. They were hideous now, only the whites showing, and the blood running to them. The face of the orderly was drawn with horror at the sight. Well, it was so. In his heart he was satisfied. He had hated the face of the Captain. It was extinguished now. There was a heavy relief in the orderly's soul. That was as it should be. But he could not bear to see the long, military body lying broken over the tree-base, the fine fingers crisped. He wanted to hide it away.

Quickly, busily, he gathered it up and pushed it under the felled tree trunks, which rested their beautiful, smooth length either end on the logs. The face was horrible with blood. He covered it with the helmet. Then he pushed the limbs straight and decent, and brushed the dead leaves off the fine cloth of the uniform. So, it lay quite still in the shadow under there. A little strip of sunshine ran along the breast, from a chink between the logs. The orderly sat by it for a few moments. Here his own life also ended.

Then, through his daze, he heard the lieutenant, in a loud voice, explaining to the men outside the wood, that they were to suppose the bridge on the river below was held by the enemy. Now they were to march to the attack in such and such a manner. The lieutenant had no gift of expression. The orderly, listening from habit, got muddled. And when the lieutenant began it all again he ceased to hear.

He knew he must go. He stood up. It surprised him that the leaves were glittering in the sun, and the chips of wood reflecting white from the ground. For him a change had come over the world. But for the rest it had not—all seemed the same. Only he had left it. And he could not go back. It was his duty to return with the beer-pot and the bottle. He could not. He had left all that. The lieutenant was still hoarsely explaining. He must go, or they would overtake him. And he could not bear contact with anyone now.

He drew his fingers over his eyes, trying to find out where he was. Then he turned away. He saw the horse standing in the path. He went up to it and mounted. It hurt him to sit in the saddle. The pain of keeping his seat occupied him as they cantered through the wood. He would not have minded anything, but he could not get away from the sense of being divided from the others. The path led out of the trees. On the edge of the wood he pulled up and stood watching. There in the spacious sunshine of the valley soldiers were moving in a little swarm. Every now and then, a man harrowing on a strip of fallow shouted to his oxen, at the turn. The village and the white-towered church was small in the sunshine. And he no longer belonged to it—he sat there, beyond, like a man outside in the dark. He had gone out from everyday life into the unknown and he could not, he even did not want to go back.

Turning from the sun-blazing valley, he rode deep into the wood. Tree trunks, like people standing grey and still, took no notice as he went. A doe, herself a moving bit of sunshine and shadow, went running through the flecked shade. There were bright green rents in the foliage. Then it was all pine wood, dark and cool. And he was sick with pain, and had an intolerable great pulse in his head, and he was sick. He had never been ill in his life. He felt lost, quite dazed with all this.

Trying to get down from the horse, he fell, astonished at the pain and his lack of balance. The horse shifted uneasily. He jerked its bridle and sent it cantering jerkily away. It was his last connection with the rest of things.

But he only wanted to lie down and not be disturbed. Stumbling through the trees, he came on a quiet place where beeches and pine trees grew on a slope. Immediately he had lain down and closed his eyes, his consciousness went racing on without him. A big pulse of sickness beat in him as if it throbbed through the whole earth. He was burning with dry heat. But he was too busy, too tearingly active in the incoherent race of delirium to observe.

III

He came to with a start. His mouth was dry and hard, his heart beat heavily, but he had not the energy to get up. His heart beat heavily. Where was he?—the barracks—at home? There was something knocking. And, making an effort, he looked round—trees, and litter of greenery, and reddish, bright, still pieces of sunshine on the floor. He did not believe he was himself, he did not believe what he saw. Something was knocking. He made a struggle towards consciousness, but relapsed. Then he struggled again. And gradually his surroundings fell into relationship with himself. He knew, and a great pang of fear went through his heart. Somebody was knocking. He could see the heavy, black rags of a fir tree overhead. Then everything went black. Yet he did not believe he had closed his eyes. He had not. Out of the blackness sight slowly emerged again. And someone was knocking. Quickly, he saw the blood-disfig-ured face of his Captain, which he hated. And he held himself still with horror. Yet, deep inside him, he knew that it was so, the Captain should be dead. But the physical delirium got hold of him. Someone was knocking. He lay perfectly still, as if dead, with fear. And he went unconscious.

When he opened his eyes again, he started, seeing something creeping swiftly up a tree trunk. It was a little bird. And the bird was whistling overhead. Tap-tap-tap—it was the small, quick bird rapping the tree trunk with its beak, as if its head were a little round hammer. He watched it curiously. It shifted sharply, in its creeping fashion. Then, like a mouse, it slid down the bare trunk. Its swift creeping sent a flash of revulsion through him. He raised his head. It felt a great weight. Then, the little bird ran out of the shadow across a still patch of sunshine, its little head bobbing swiftly, its white legs twinkling brightly for a moment. How neat it was in its build, so compact, with pieces of white on its wings. There were several of them. They were so pretty—but they crept like swift, erratic mice, running here and there among the beech-mast.

He lay down again exhausted, and his consciousness lapsed. He had a horror of the little creeping birds. All his blood seemed to be darting and creeping in his head. And yet he could not move.

He came to with a further ache of exhaustion. There was the pain in his head, and the horrible sickness, and his inability to move. He had never been ill in his life. He did not know where he was or what he was. Probably he had got sunstroke. Or what else?—he had silenced the Captain for ever—some time ago—oh, a long time ago. There had been blood on his face, and his eyes had turned upwards. It was all right, somehow. It was peace. But now he had got beyond himself. He had never been here before. Was it life, or not life? He was by himself. They were in a big, bright place, those others, and he was outside. The town, all the country, a big bright place of light: and he was outside, here, in the darkened open beyond, where each thing existed alone. But they would all have to come out there sometime, those others. Little, and left behind him, they all were. There had been father and mother and sweetheart. What did they all matter? This was the open land.

He sat up. Something scuffled. It was a little brown squirrel running in lovely undulating bounds over the floor, its red tail completing the undulation of its body—and then, as it sat up, furling and unfurling. He watched it, pleased. It ran on again, friskily, enjoying itself. It flew wildly at another squirrel, and they were chasing each other, and making little scolding, chattering noises. The soldier wanted to speak to them. But only a hoarse sound came out of his throat. The squirrels burst away—they flew up the trees. And then he saw the one peeping round at him, half-way up a tree trunk. A start of fear went through him, though in so far as he was conscious, he was amused. It still stayed, its little keen face staring at him half-way up the tree trunk, its little ears pricked up, its clawey little hands clinging to the bark, its white breast reared. He started from it in panic.

Struggling to his feet, he lurched away. He went on walking, walking, looking for something—for a drink. His brain felt hot and inflamed for want of water. He stumbled on: Then he did not know anything. He went unconscious as he walked. Yet he stumbled on, his mouth open.

When, to his dumb wonder, he opened his eyes on the world again, he no longer tried to remember what it was. There was thick, golden light behind golden-green glitterings, and tall, grey-purple shafts, and darknesses farther off, surrounding him, growing deeper. He was conscious of a sense of arrival. He was amid the reality, on the real, dark bottom. But there was the thirst burning in his brain. He felt lighter, not so heavy. He supposed it was newness. The air was muttering with thunder. He thought he was walking wonderfully swiftly and was coming straight to relief—or was it to water?

Suddenly he stood still with fear. There was a tremendous flare of gold, immense—just a few dark trunks like bars between him and it. All the young level wheat was burnished gold glaring on its silky green. A woman, full-skirted, a black cloth on her head for head-dress, was passing like a block of shadow through the glistening, green corn, into the full glare. There was a farm, too, pale blue in shadow, and the timber black. And there was a church spire, nearly fused away in the gold. The woman moved on, away from him. He had no language with which to speak to her. She was the bright, solid unreality. She would make a noise of words that would confuse him, and her eyes would look at him without seeing him. She was crossing there to the other side. He stood against a tree.

When at last he turned, looking down the long, bare grove whose flat bed was already filling dark, he saw the mountains in a wonder-light, not far away, and radiant. Behind the soft, grey ridge of the nearest range the farther mountains stood golden and pale grey, the snow all radiant like pure, soft gold. So still, gleaming in the sky, fashioned pure out of the ore of the sky, they shone in their silence. He stood and looked at them, his face illuminated. And like the golden, lustrous gleaming of the snow he felt his own thirst bright in him. He stood and gazed, leaning against a tree. And then everything slid away into space.

During the night the lightning fluttered perpetually, making the whole sky white. He must have walked again. The world hung livid round him for moments, fields a level sheen of grey-green light, trees in dark bulk, and the range of clouds black across a white sky. Then the darkness fell like a shutter, and the night was whole. A faint flutter of a half-revealed world, that could not quite leap out of the darkness!— Then there again stood a sweep of pallor for the land, dark shapes looming, a range of clouds hanging overhead. The world was a ghostly shadow, thrown for a moment upon the pure darkness, which returned ever whole and complete.

And the mere delirium of sickness and fever went on inside him—his brain opening and shutting like the night—then sometimes convulsions of terror from something with great eyes that stared round a tree—then the long agony of the march, and the sun decomposing his blood—then the pang of hate for the Captain, followed by a pang of tenderness and ease. But everything was distorted, born of an ache and resolving into an ache.

In the morning he came definitely awake. Then his brain flamed with the sole horror of thirstiness! The sun was on his face, the dew was steaming from his wet clothes. Like one possessed, he got up. There, straight in front of him, blue and cool and tender, the mountains ranged across the pale edge of the morning sky. He wanted them—he wanted them alone—he wanted to leave himself and be identified with them. They did not move, they were still and soft, with white, gentle markings of snow. He stood still, mad with suffering, his hands crisping and clutching. Then he was twisting in a paroxysm on the grass.

He lay still, in a kind of dream of anguish. His thirst seemed to have separated itself from him, and to stand apart, a single demand. Then the pain he felt was another single self. Then there was the clog of his body, another separate thing. He was divided among all kinds of separate things. There was some strange, agonised connection between them, but they were drawing farther apart. Then they would all split. The sun, drilling down on him, was drilling through the bond. Then they would all fall, fall through the everlasting lapse of space. Then again, his consciousness reasserted itself. He roused on to his elbow and stared at the gleaming mountains. There they ranked, all still and wonderful between earth and heaven. He stared till his eyes went black, and the mountains, as they stood in their beauty, so clean and cool, seemed to have it, that which was lost in him.

IV

When the soldiers found him, three hours later, he was lying with his face over his arm, his black hair giving off heat under the sun. But he was still alive. Seeing the open, black mouth the young soldiers dropped him in horror.

He died in the hospital at night, without having seen again.

The doctors saw the bruises on his legs, behind, and were silent.

The bodies of the two men lay together, side by side, in the mortuary, the one white and slender, but laid rigidly at rest, the other looking as if every moment it must rouse into life again, so young and unused, from a slumber.

1914

THE PHANTOM 'RICKSHAW

Rudyard Kipling

> May no ill dreams disturb my rest,
> Nor Powers of Darkness me molest.
>
> "Evening Hymn."

ONE OF the few advantages that India has over England is a great Knowability. After five years' service a man is directly or indirectly acquainted with the two or three hundred Civilians in his Province, all the Messes of ten or twelve Regiments and Batteries, and some fifteen hundred other people of non-official caste. In ten years his knowledge should be doubled and at the end of twenty he knows, or knows something about, every Englishman in the Empire, and may travel anywhere and everywhere without paying hotel-bills.

Globe-trotters who expect entertainment as a right have, even within my memory, blunted this open-heartedness, but none the less to-day, if you belong to the Inner Circle and are neither a Bear nor a Black Sheep, all houses are open to you, and our small world is very, very kind and helpful.

Rickett of Kamartha stayed with Polder of Kumaon some fifteen years ago. He meant to stay two nights, but was knocked down by rheumatic fever, and for six weeks disorganised Polder's establishment, stopped Polder's work, and nearly died in Polder's bedroom. Polder behaves as though he had been placed under eternal obligation by Rickett, and yearly sends the little Ricketts a box of presents and toys. It is the same everywhere. The men who do not take the trouble to conceal from you their opinion that you are an incompetent ass, and the women who blacken your character and misunderstand your wife's amusements, will work themselves to the bone in your behalf if you fall sick or into serious trouble.

Heatherlegh, the Doctor, kept, in addition to his regular practice, a hospital on his private account—an arrangement of loose boxes for Incurables, his friends called it—but it was really a sort of fitting-up shed for craft that had been damaged by stress of weather. The weather in India is often sultry, and since the tale of bricks is always a fixed quantity, and the only liberty allowed is permission to work overtime and get no thanks, men occasionally break down and become as mixed as the metaphors in this sentence.

Heatherlegh is the dearest doctor that ever was, and his invariable prescription to all his patients is, "Lie low, go slow, and keep cool." He says that more men are killed by overwork than the importance of this world justifies. He maintains that overwork slew Pansay, who died under his hands about three years ago. He has, of course, the right to speak authoritatively, and he laughs at my theory that there was a crack in Pansay's head and a little bit of the Dark World came through and pressed him to death. "Pansay went off the handle," says Heatherlegh, "after the stimulus of long leave at Home. He may or he may not have behaved like a blackguard to Mrs. Keith-Wessington. My notion is that the work of the Katabundi Settlement ran him off his legs, and that he took to brooding and making much of an ordinary P. & O. flirtation. He certainly was engaged to Miss Mannering, and she certainly broke off the engagement. Then he took a feverish chill and all that nonsense about ghosts developed. Overwork started his illness, kept it alight, and killed him, poor devil. Write him off to the System that uses one man to do the work of two and a half men."

I do not believe this. I used to sit up with Pansay sometimes when Heatherlegh was called out to patients and I happened to be within claim. The man would make me most unhappy by describing, in a low, even voice, the procession that was always passing at the bottom of his bed. He had a sick man's command of language. When he recovered I suggested that he should write of the whole affair from beginning to end, knowing that ink might assist him to ease his mind.

He was in a high fever while he was writing, and the blood-and-thunder Magazine diction he adopted did not calm him. Two months afterwards he was reported fit for duty, but, in spite of the fact that he was urgently needed to help an undermanned Commission stagger through a deficit, he preferred to die; vowing at the last that he was hag-ridden. I got his manuscript before he died, and this is his version of the affair, dated 1885, exactly as he wrote it:—

My doctor tells me that I need rest and change of air. It is not improbable that I shall get both ere long—rest that neither the red-coated messenger nor the mid-day gun can break, and change of air far beyond that which any homeward-bound steamer can give me. In the meantime I am resolved to stay where I am; and, in flat defiance of my doctor's orders, to take all the world into my confidence. You shall learn for your-selves the precise nature of my malady, and shall, too, judge for yourselves whether any man born of woman on this weary earth was ever so tor-mented as I.

Speaking now as a condemned criminal might speak ere the drop-bolts are drawn, my story, wild and hideously improbable as it may appear, demands at least attention. That it will ever receive credence I utterly disbelieve. Two months ago I should have scouted as mad or drunk the man who had dared tell me the like. Two months ago I was the happiest man in India. To-day, from Peshawar to the sea, there is no one more wretched. My doctor and I are the only two who know this. His explanation is that my brain, digestion, and eyesight are all slightly affected; giving rise to my frequent and persistent "delusions." Delusions, indeed! I call him a fool; but he attends me still with the same unwea-ried smile, the same bland professional manner, the same neatly-trimmed red whiskers, till I begin to suspect that I am an ungrateful, evil-tempered invalid. But you shall judge for yourselves.

Three years ago it was my fortune—my great misfortune—to sail from Gravesend to Bombay, on return from long leave, with one Agnes Keith-Wessington, wife of an officer on the Bombay side. It does not in the least concern you to know what manner of woman she was. Be content with the knowledge that, ere the voyage had ended, both she and I were desperately and unreasoningly in love with one another. Heaven knows that I can make the admission now without one particle of vanity. In matters of this sort there is always one who gives and another who accepts. From the first day of our ill-omened attachment, I was conscious that Agnes's passion was a stronger, a more dominant, and—if I may use the expression—a purer sentiment than mine. Whether she recognised the fact then, I do not know. Afterwards it was bitterly plain to both of us.

Arrived at Bombay in the spring of the year, we went our respective ways, to meet no more for the next three or four months, when my leave and her love took us both to Simla. There we spent the season together; and there my fire of straw burnt itself out to a pitiful end with the closing year. I attempt no excuse. I make no apology. Mrs. Wessington had given up much for my sake, and was prepared to give up all. From my own lips, in August 1882, she learnt that I was sick of her presence, tired of her com-pany, and weary of the sound of her voice. Ninety-nine women out of a hundred would have wearied of me as I wearied of them; seventy-five of that number would have promptly avenged themselves by active and obtrusive flirtation with other men. Mrs. Wessington was the hundredth. On her neither my openly-expressed aversion nor the cutting brutalities with which I garnished our interviews had the least effect.

"Jack, darling!" was her one eternal cuckoo cry: "I'm sure it's all a mistake—a hideous mistake; and we'll be good friends again some day. Please forgive me, Jack, dear."

I was the offender, and I knew it. That knowledge transformed my pity into passive endurance, and, eventually, into blind hate—the same instinct, I suppose, which prompts a man to savagely stamp on the spider he has but half killed. And with this hate in my bosom the season of 1882 came to an end.

Next year we met again in Simla—she with her monotonous face and timid attempts at reconciliation, and I with loathing of her in every fibre of my frame. Several times I could not avoid meeting her alone; and on each occasion her words were identically the same. Still the unreasoning wail that it was all a "mistake"; and still the hope of eventually "making friends." I might have seen, had I cared to look, that that hope only was keeping her alive. She grew more wan and thin month by month. You will agree with me, at least, that such conduct would have driven any one to despair. It was uncalled for; childish, unwomanly. I maintain that she was much to blame. And again, sometimes, in the black, fever-stricken night-watches, I have begun to think that I might have been a little kinder to her. But that really is a "delusion." I could not have continued pretending to love her when I didn't; could I? It would have been unfair to us both.

Last year we met again—on the same terms as before. The same weary appeals, and the same curt answers from my lips. At least I would make her see how wholly wrong and hopeless were her attempts at resuming the old relationship. As the season wore on, we fell apart—that is to say, she found it difficult to meet me, for I had other and more absorbing interests to attend to. When I think it over quietly in my sickroom, the season of 1884 seems a confused nightmare wherein light and shade were fantastically intermingled: my courtship of little Kitty Mannering; my hopes, doubts, and fears; our long rides together; my trembling avowal of attachment; her reply; and now and again a vision of a white face flitting by in the 'rickshaw with the black and white liveries I once watched for so earnestly; the wave of Mrs. Wessington's gloved hand; and, when she met me alone, which was but seldom, the irksome monotony of her appeal. I loved Kitty Mannering; honestly, heartily loved her, and with my love for her grew my hatred for Agnes. In August Kitty and I were engaged. The next day I met those accursed "magpie" jhampanies at the back of Jakko, and, moved by some passing sentiment of pity, stopped to tell Mrs. Wessington everything. She knew it already.

"So I hear you're engaged, Jack, dear." Then, without a moment's pause: "I'm sure it's all a mistake—a hideous mistake. We shall be as good friends some day, Jack, as we ever were."

My answer might have made even a man wince. It cut the dying woman before me like the blow of a whip. "Please forgive me, Jack; I didn't mean to make you angry; but it's true, it's true!"

And Mrs. Wessington broke down completely. I turned away and left her to finish her journey in peace, feeling, but only for a moment or two, that I had been an unutterably mean hound. I looked back, and saw that she had turned her 'rickshaw with the idea, I suppose, of overtaking me.

The scene and its surroundings were photographed on my memory. The rain-swept sky (we were at the end of the wet weather), the sodden, dingy pines, the muddy road, and the black powder-riven cliffs formed a gloomy background against which the black and white liveries of the jhampanies, the yellow-panelled 'rickshaw, and Mrs. Wessington's down-bowed golden head stood out clearly. She was holding her handkerchief in her left hand and was leaning back exhausted against the 'rickshaw cushions. I turned my horse up a bypath near the Sanjowlie Reservoir and literally ran away. Once I fancied I heard a faint call of "Jack!" This may have been imagination. I never stopped to verify it. Ten minutes later I came across Kitty on horseback; and, in the delight of a long ride with her, forgot all about the interview.

A week later Mrs. Wessington died, and the inexpressible burden of her existence was removed from my life. I went Plainsward perfectly happy. Before three months were over I had forgotten all about her, except that at times the discovery of some of her old letters reminded me unpleasantly of our bygone relationship. By January I had disinterred what was left of our correspondence from among my scattered belongings and had burnt it. At the beginning of April of this year, 1885, I was at Simla—semi-deserted Simla—once more, and was deep in lover's talks and walks with Kitty. It was decided that we should be married at the end of June. You will understand, therefore, that, loving Kitty as I did, I am not saying too much when I pronounce myself to have been at that time the happiest man in India.

Fourteen delightful days passed almost before I noticed their flight. Then, aroused to the sense of what was proper among mortals circumstanced as we were, I pointed out to Kitty that an engagement ring was the outward and visible sign of her dignity as an engaged girl, and that she must forthwith come to Hamilton's to be measured for one. Up to that moment, I give you my word, we had completely forgotten so trivial a matter. To Hamilton's we accordingly went on the 15th of April, 1885. Remember that—whatever my doctor may say to the contrary—I was then in perfect health, enjoying a well-balanced mind and an absolutely tranquil spirit. Kitty and I entered Hamilton's shop together, and there, regardless of the order of affairs, I measured Kitty for the ring in the presence of the amused assistant. The ring was a sapphire with

two diamonds. We then rode out down the slope that leads to the
Combermere Bridge and Peliti's shop.

While my Waler was cautiously feeling his way over the loose shale,
and Kitty was laughing and chattering at my side,—while all Simla, that
is to say, as much of it as had then come from the Plains, was grouped
round the Reading-room and Peliti's verandah,—I was aware that some
one, apparently at a vast distance, was calling me by my Christian name.
It struck me that I had heard the voice before, but when and where I
could not at once determine. In the short space it took to cover the road
between the path from Hamilton's shop and the first plank of the
Combermere Bridge I had thought over half-a-dozen people who might
have committed such a solecism, and had eventually decided that it must
have been some singing in my ears. Immediately opposite Peliti's shop
my eye was arrested by the sight of four jhampanies in "magpie" livery
pulling a yellow-panelled, cheap, bazar 'rickshaw. In a moment my mind
flew back to the previous season and Mrs. Wessington with a sense of
irritation and disgust. Was it not enough that the woman was dead and
done with, without her black and white servitors reappearing to spoil the
day's happiness? Whoever employed them now I thought I would call
upon, and ask as a personal favour to change her jhampanies' livery. I
would hire the men myself, and, if necessary, buy their coats from off
their backs. It is impossible to say here what a flood of undesirable memories their presence evoked.

"Kitty," I cried, "there are poor Mrs. Wessington's jhampanies turned
up again! I wonder who has them now?"

Kitty had known Mrs. Wessington slightly last season, and had always
been interested in the sickly woman.

"What? Where?" she asked. "I can't see them anywhere."

Even as she spoke, her horse, swerving from a laden mule, threw himself directly in front of the advancing 'rickshaw. I had scarcely time to
utter a word of warning when, to my unutterable horror, horse and rider
passed through men and carriage as if they had been thin air.

"What's the matter?" cried Kitty; "what made you call out so foolishly,
Jack? If I am engaged I don't want all creation to know about it. There
was lots of space between the mule and the verandah; and, if you think I
can't ride—There!"

Whereupon wilful Kitty set off, her dainty little head in the air, at a
hand-gallop in the direction of the Band-stand, fully expecting, as she
herself afterwards told me, that I should follow her. What was the matter? Nothing indeed. Either that I was mad or drunk, or that Simla was
haunted with devils. I reined in my impatient cob, and turned round.
The 'rickshaw had turned too, and now stood immediately facing me,
near the left railing of the Combermere Bridge.

"Jack! Jack, darling!" (There was no mistake about the words this time: they rang through my brain as if they had been shouted in my ear.) "It's some hideous mistake, I'm sure. Please forgive me, Jack, and let's be friends again."

The 'rickshaw-hood had fallen back, and inside, as I hope and pray daily for the death I dread by night, sat Mrs. Keith-Wessington, handkerchief in hand, and golden head bowed on her breast.

How long I stared motionless I do not know. Finally, I was aroused by my syce taking the Waler's bridle and asking whether I was ill. From the horrible to the commonplace is but a step. I tumbled off my horse and dashed, half fainting, into Peliti's for a glass of cherry-brandy. There two or three couples were gathered round the coffee-tables discussing the gossip of the day. Their trivialities were more comforting to me just then than the consolations of religion could have been. I plunged into the midst of the conversation at once; chatted, laughed, and jested with a face (when I caught a glimpse of it in a mirror) as white and drawn as that of a corpse. Three or four men noticed my condition, and, evidently setting it down to the results of over-many pegs, charitably endeavoured to draw me apart from the rest of the loungers. But I refused to be led away. I wanted the company of my kind—as a child rushes into the midst of the dinner-party after a fright in the dark. I must have talked for about ten minutes or so, though it seemed an eternity to me, when I heard Kitty's clear voice outside inquiring for me. In another minute she had entered the shop, prepared to upbraid me for failing so signally in my duties. Something in my face stopped her.

"Why, Jack," she cried, "what have you been doing? What has happened? Are you ill?" Thus driven into a direct lie, I said that the sun had been a little too much for me. It was close upon five o'clock of a cloudy April afternoon, and the sun had been hidden all day. I saw my mistake as soon as the words were out of my mouth; attempted to recover it; blundered hopelessly, and followed Kitty in a regal rage out of doors, amid the smiles of my acquaintances. I made some excuse (I have forgotten what) on the score of my feeling faint, and cantered away to my hotel, leaving Kitty to finish the ride by herself.

In my room I sat down and tried calmly to reason out the matter. Here I was, Theobald Jack Pansay, a well-educated Bengal Civilian in the year of grace 1885, presumably sane, certainly healthy, driven in terror from my sweetheart's side by the apparition of a woman who had been dead and buried eight months ago. These were facts that I could not blink. Nothing was farther from my thought than any memory of Mrs. Wessington when Kitty and I left Hamilton's shop. Nothing was more utterly commonplace than the stretch of wall opposite Peliti's. It was broad daylight. The road was full of people; and yet here, look you, in defiance of every law of probability, in direct outrage of Nature's ordinance, there had appeared to me a face from the grave.

Kitty's Arab had gone through the 'rickshaw: so that my first hope that some woman marvellously like Mrs. Wessington had hired the carriage and the coolies with their old livery was lost. Again and again I went round this treadmill of thought; and again and again gave up baffled and in despair. The voice was as inexplicable as the apparition. I had originally some wild notion of confiding it all to Kitty; of begging her to marry me at once, and in her arms defying the ghostly occupant of the 'rickshaw. "After all," I argued, "the presence of the 'rickshaw is in itself enough to prove the existence of a spectral illusion. One may see ghosts of men and women, but surely never coolies and carriages. The whole thing is absurd. Fancy the ghost of a hillman!"

Next morning I sent a penitent note to Kitty, imploring her to overlook my strange conduct of the previous afternoon. My Divinity was still very wroth, and a personal apology was necessary. I explained, with a fluency born of night-long pondering over a falsehood, that I had been attacked with a sudden palpitation of the heart—the result of indigestion. This eminently practical solution had its effect; and Kitty and I rode out that afternoon with the shadow of my first lie dividing us.

Nothing would please her save a canter round Jakko. With my nerves still unstrung from the previous night, I feebly protested against the notion, suggesting Observatory Hill, Jutogh, the Boileaugunge road—anything rather than the Jakko round. Kitty was angry and a little hurt; so I yielded from fear of provoking further misunderstanding, and we set out together toward Chota Simla. We walked a greater part of the way, and, according to our custom, cantered from a mile or so below the Convent to the stretch of level road by the Sanjowlie Reservoir. The wretched horses appeared to fly, and my heart beat quicker and quicker as we neared the crest of the ascent. My mind had been full of Mrs. Wessington all the afternoon; and every inch of the Jakko road bore witness to our old-time walks and talks. The boulders were full of it; the pines sang it aloud overhead; the rain-fed torrents giggled and chuckled unseen over the shameful story; and the wind in my ears chanted the iniquity aloud.

As a fitting climax, in the middle of the level men call the Ladies' Mile, the Horror was awaiting me. No other 'rickshaw was in sight—only the four black and white jhampanies, the yellow-panelled carriage, and the golden head of the woman within—all apparently just as I had left them eight months and one fortnight ago! For an instant I fancied that Kitty must see what I saw—we were so marvellously sympathetic in all things. Her next words undeceived me—"Not a soul in sight! Come along, Jack, and I'll race you to the Reservoir buildings!" Her wiry little Arab was off like a bird, my Waler following close behind, and in this order we dashed under the cliffs. Half a minute brought us within fifty yards of the 'rickshaw. I pulled my Waler and fell back a little. The 'rickshaw was directly in the middle of the road; and once more the Arab passed through it, my horse following. "Jack! Jack dear! Please forgive me," rang with a wail in my ears, and, after an interval: "It's all a mistake, a hideous mistake!"

I spurred my horse like a man possessed. When I turned my head at the Reservoir works, the black and white liveries were still waiting—patiently waiting—under the gray hillside, and the wind brought me a mocking echo of the words I had just heard. Kitty bantered me a good deal on my silence throughout the remainder of the ride. I had been talking up till then wildly and at random. To save my life I could not speak afterwards naturally, and from Sanjowlie to the Church wisely held my tongue.

I was to dine with the Mannerings that night, and had barely time to canter home to dress. On the road to Elysium Hill I overheard two men talking together in the dusk.—"It's a curious thing," said one, "how completely all trace of it disappeared. You know my wife was insanely fond of the woman (never could see anything in her myself), and wanted me to pick up her old 'rickshaw and coolies if they were to be got for love or money. Morbid sort of fancy I call it; but I've got to do what the Memsahib tells me. Would you believe that the man she hired it from tells me that all four of the men—they were brothers—died of cholera on the way to Hardwar, poor devils; and the 'rickshaw has been broken up by the man himself. Told me he never used a dead Memsahib's 'rickshaw. Spoilt his luck. Queer notion, wasn't it? Fancy poor little Mrs. Wessington spoiling any one's luck except her own!" I laughed aloud at this point, and my laugh jarred on me as I uttered it. So there were ghosts of 'rickshaws after all, and ghostly employments in the other world! How much did Mrs. Wessington give her men? What were their hours? Where did they go?

And for visible answer to my last question I saw the infernal Thing blocking my path in the twilight. The dead travel fast, and by short cuts unknown to ordinary coolies. I laughed aloud a second time and checked my laughter suddenly, for I was afraid I was going mad. Mad to a certain extent I must have been, for I recollect that I reined in my horse at the head of the 'rickshaw, and politely wished Mrs. Wessington "Good-evening." Her answer was one I knew only too well. I listened to the end; and replied that I had heard it all before, but should be delighted if she had anything further to say. Some malignant devil stronger than I must have entered into me that evening, for I have a dim recollection of talking the commonplaces of the day for five minutes to the Thing in front of me.

"Mad as a hatter, poor devil—or drunk. Max, try and get him to come home."

Surely that was not Mrs. Wessington's voice! The two men had overheard me speaking to the empty air, and had returned to look after me. They were very kind and considerate, and from their words evidently gathered that I was extremely drunk. I thanked them confusedly and cantered away to my hotel, there changed and arrived at the Mannerings' ten minutes late. I pleaded the darkness of the night as an excuse; was rebuked by Kitty for my unloverlike tardiness; and sat down.

The conversation had already become general; and, under cover of it, I was addressing some tender small talk to my sweetheart when I was aware that at the farther end of the table a short red-whiskered man was describing, with much broidery, his encounter with a mad unknown that evening.

A few sentences convinced me that he was repeating the incident of half an hour ago. In the middle of the story he looked round for applause, as professional story-tellers do, caught my eye, and straightway collapsed. There was a moment's awkward silence, and the red-whiskered man muttered something to the effect that he had "forgotten the rest," thereby sacrificing a reputation as a good story-teller which he had built up for six seasons past. I blessed him from the bottom of my heart, and—went on with my fish.

In the fulness of time that dinner came to an end; and with genuine regret I tore myself away from Kitty—as certain as I was of my own existence that It would be waiting for me outside the door. The red-whiskered man, who had been introduced to me as Doctor Heatherlegh of Simla, volunteered to bear me company as far as our roads lay together. I accepted his offer with gratitude.

My instinct had not deceived me. It lay in readiness in the Mall, and, in what seemed devilish mockery of our ways, with a lighted head-lamp. The red-whiskered man went to the point at once, in a manner that showed he had been thinking over it all dinner-time.

"I say, Pansay, what the deuce was the matter with you this evening on the Elysium road?" The suddenness of the question wrenched an answer from me before I was aware.

"That!" said I, pointing to It.

"That may be either D. T. or Eyes for aught I know. Now you don't liquor. I saw as much at dinner, so it can't be D. T. There's nothing whatever where you're pointing, though you're sweating and trembling with fright like a scared pony. Therefore, I conclude that it's Eyes. And I ought to understand all about them. Come along home with me. I'm on the Blessington lower road."

To my intense delight the 'rickshaw, instead of waiting for us, kept about twenty yards ahead—and this, too, whether we walked, trotted, or cantered. In the course of that long night ride I had told my companion almost as much as I have told you here.

"Well, you've spoilt one of the best tales I've ever laid tongue to," said he, "but I'll forgive you for the sake of what you've gone through. Now come home and do what I tell you; and when I've cured you, young man, let this be a lesson to you to steer clear of women and indigestible food till the day of your death."

The 'rickshaw kept steady in front; and my red-whiskered friend seemed to derive great pleasure from my account of its exact whereabouts.

"Eyes, Pansay—all Eyes, Brain, and Stomach. And the greatest of these three is Stomach. You've too much conceited Brain, too little Stomach, and thoroughly unhealthy Eyes. Get your Stomach straight and the rest follows. And all that's French for a liver pill. I'll take sole medical charge of you from this hour, for you're too interesting a phenomenon to be passed over."

By this time we were deep in the shadow of the Blessington lower road, and the 'rickshaw came to a dead stop under a pine-clad, over-hanging shale cliff. Instinctively I halted too, giving my reason. Heatherlegh rapped out an oath.

"Now, if you think I'm going to spend a cold night on the hillside for the sake of a Stomach-cum-Brain-cum-Eye illusion—Lord, ha' mercy! What's that?"

There was a muffled report, a blinding smother of dust just in front of us, a crack, the noise of rent boughs, and about ten yards of the cliff-side—pines, undergrowth, and all—slid down into the road below, completely blocking it up. The uprooted trees swayed and tottered for a moment like drunken giants in the gloom, and then fell prone among their fellows with a thunderous crash. Our two horses stood motionless and sweating with fear. As soon as the rattle of falling earth and stone had subsided, my companion muttered: "Man, if we'd gone forward we should have been ten feet deep in our graves by now. 'There are more things in heaven and earth.' . . . Come home, Pansay, and thank God. I want a peg badly."

We retraced our way over the Church Ridge, and I arrived at Dr. Heatherlegh's house shortly after midnight.

His attempts toward my cure commenced almost immediately, and for a week I never left his sight. Many a time in the course of that week did I bless the good-fortune which had thrown me in contact with Simla's best and kindest doctor. Day by day my spirits grew lighter and more equable. Day by day, too, I became more and more inclined to fall in with Heatherlegh's "spectral illusion" theory, implicating eyes, brain, and stomach. I wrote to Kitty, telling her that a slight sprain caused by a fall from my horse kept me indoors for a few days; and that I should be recovered before she had time to regret my absence.

Heatherlegh's treatment was simple to a degree. It consisted of liver pills, cold-water baths, and strong exercise, taken in the dusk or at early dawn—for, as he sagely observed: "A man with a sprained ankle doesn't walk a dozen miles a day, and your young woman might be wondering if she saw you."

At the end of the week, after much examination of pupil and pulse, and strict injunctions as to diet and pedestrianism, Heatherlegh dismissed me as brusquely as he had taken charge of me. Here is his parting bene-diction: "Man, I can certify to your mental cure, and that's as much as to say I've cured most of your bodily ailments. Now, get your traps out of this as soon as you can; and be off to make love to Miss Kitty."

I was endeavouring to express my thanks for his kindness. He cut me short.

"Don't think I did this because I like you. I gather that you've behaved like a blackguard all through. But, all the same, you're a phenomenon, and as queer a phenomenon as you are a blackguard. No!"—checking me a second time—"not a rupee, please. Go out and see if you can find the eyes-brain-and-stomach business again. I'll give you a lakh for each time you see it."

Half an hour later I was in the Mannerings' drawing-room with Kitty—drunk with the intoxication of present happiness and the fore-knowledge that I should never more be troubled with Its hideous pres-ence. Strong in the sense of my new-found security, I proposed a ride at once, and, by preference, a canter round Jakko.

Never had I felt so well, so overladen with vitality and mere animal spir-its, as I did on the afternoon of the 30th of April. Kitty was delighted at the change in my appearance, and complimented me on it in her delightfully frank and outspoken manner. We left the Mannerings' house together, laughing and talking, and cantered along the Chota Simla road as of old.

I was in haste to reach the Sanjowlie Reservoir and there make my assur-ance doubly sure. The horses did their best, but seemed all too slow to my impatient mind. Kitty was astonished at my boisterousness. "Why, Jack!" she cried at last, "you are behaving like a child. What are you doing?"

We were just below the Convent, and from sheer wantonness I was making my Waler plunge and curvet across the road as I tickled it with the loop of my riding-whip.

"Doing?" I answered; "nothing, dear. That's just it. If you'd been doing nothing for a week except lie up, you'd be as riotous as I."

> "'Singing and murmuring in your feastful mirth,
>   Joying to feel yourself alive;
> Lord over Nature, Lord of the visible Earth,
>   Lord of the senses five.'"

My quotation was hardly out of my lips before we had rounded the corner above the Convent, and a few yards farther on could see across to Sanjowlie. In the centre of the level road stood the black and white liveries, the yellow-panelled 'rickshaw, and Mrs. Keith-Wessington. I pulled up, looked, rubbed my eyes, and, I believe, must have said something. The next thing I knew was that I was lying face downward on the road, with Kitty kneeling above me in tears.

"Has it gone, child!" I gasped. Kitty only wept more bitterly.

"Has what gone, Jack dear? what does it all mean? There must be a mistake somewhere, Jack. A hideous mistake." Her last words brought me to my feet—mad—raving for the time being.

"Yes, there is a mistake somewhere," I repeated, "a hideous mistake. Come and look at It."

I have an indistinct idea that I dragged Kitty by the wrist along the road up to where It stood, and implored her for pity's sake to speak to It; to tell It that we were betrothed; that neither Death nor Hell could break the tie between us; and Kitty only knows how much more to the same effect. Now and again I appealed passionately to the Terror in the 'rickshaw to bear witness to all I had said, and to release me from a torture that was killing me. As I talked I suppose I must have told Kitty of my old relations with Mrs. Wessington, for I saw her listen intently with white face and blazing eyes.

"Thank you, Mr. Pansay," she said, "that's quite enough."

The syces, impassive as Orientals always are, had come up with the recaptured horses; and as Kitty sprang into her saddle I caught hold of her bridle, entreating her to hear me out and forgive. My answer was the cut of her riding-whip across my face from mouth to eye, and a word or two of farewell that even now I cannot write down. So I judged, and judged rightly, that Kitty knew all; and I staggered back to the side of the 'rickshaw. My face was cut and bleeding, and the blow of the riding-whip had raised a livid blue wheal on it. I had no self-respect. Just then, Heatherlegh, who must have been following Kitty and me at a distance, cantered up.

"Doctor," I said, pointing to my face, "here's Miss Mannering's signature to my order of dismissal and—I'll thank you for that lakh as soon as convenient."

Heatherlegh's face, even in my abject misery, moved me to laughter.

"I'll stake my professional reputation—" he began.

"Don't be a fool," I whispered. "I've lost my life's happiness and you'd better take me home."

As I spoke the 'rickshaw was gone. Then I lost all knowledge of what was passing. The crest of Jakko seemed to heave and roll like the crest of a cloud and fall in upon me.

Seven days later (on the 7th of May, that is to say) I was aware that I goes back to the doctor again

was lying in Heatherlegh's room as weak as a little child. Heatherlegh was watching me intently from behind the papers on his writing-table. His first words were not encouraging; but I was too far spent to be much moved by them.

(2) Kitty returns her engagement ring
11

"Here's Miss Kitty has sent back your letters. You corresponded a good deal, you young people. Here's a packet that looks like a ring, and a cheerful sort of a note from Mannering Papa, which I've taken the liberty of reading and burning. The old gentleman's not pleased with you."

"And Kitty?" I asked dully.

"Rather more drawn than her father from what she says. By the same token you must have been letting out any number of queer reminiscences just before I met you. Says that a man who would have behaved to a woman as you did to Mrs. Wessington ought to kill himself out of sheer pity for his kind. She's a hot-headed little virago, your girl. Will have it too that you were suffering from D. T. when that row on the Jakko road turned up. Says she'll die before she ever speaks to you again."

I groaned and turned over on the other side.

"Now you've got your choice, my friend. This engagement has to be broken off; and the Mannerings don't want to be too hard on you. Was it broken through D. T. or epileptic fits? Sorry I can't offer you a better exchange unless you'd prefer hereditary insanity. Say the word and I'll tell 'em it's fits. All Simla knows about that scene on the Ladies' Mile. Come! I'll give you five minutes to think over it."

During those five minutes I believe that I explored thoroughly the lowest circles of the Inferno which it is permitted man to tread on earth. And at the same time I myself was watching myself faltering through the dark labyrinths of doubt, misery, and utter despair. I wondered, as Heatherlegh in his chair might have wondered, which dreadful alternative I should adopt. Presently I heard myself answering in a voice that I hardly recognised—

"They're confoundedly particular about morality in these parts. Give 'em fits, Heatherlegh, and my love. Now let me sleep a bit longer."

Then my two selves joined, and it was only I (half-crazed, devil-driven I) that tossed in my bed tracing step by step the history of the past month.

"But I am in Simla," I kept repeating to myself. "I, Jack Pansay, am in Simla, and there are no ghosts here. It's unreasonable of that woman to pretend there are. Why couldn't Agnes have left me alone? I never did her any harm. It might just as well have been me as Agnes. Only I'd never have come hack on purpose to kill her. Why can't I be left alone—left alone and happy?"

It was high noon when I first awoke; and the sun was low in the sky before I slept—slept as the tortured criminal sleeps on his rack, too worn to feel further pain.

→ talk of the town

[margin: whole town knows that he's dealing w/ Smthn mental]

Next day I could not leave my bed. Heatherlegh told me in the morning that he had received an answer from Mr. Mannering, and that, thanks to his (Heatherlegh's) friendly offices, the story of my affliction had travelled through the length and breadth of Simla, where I was on all sides much pitied.

[margin: Dr. many times to cure him]

"And that's rather more than you deserve," he concluded pleasantly, "though the Lord knows you've been going through a pretty severe mill. Never mind; we'll cure you yet, you perverse phenomenon."

I declined firmly to be cured. "You've been much too good to me already, old man," said I; "but I don't think I need trouble you further."

In my heart I knew nothing Heatherlegh could do would lighten the burden that had been laid upon me. → hopeless!

[margin: why me!!]

With that knowledge came also a sense of hopeless, impotent rebellion against the unreasonableness of it all. There were scores of men no better than I whose punishments had at least been reserved for another world; and I felt that it was bitterly, cruelly unfair that I alone should have been singled out for so hideous a fate. This mood would in time give place to another where it seemed that the 'rickshaw and I were the only realities in a world of shadows; that Kitty was a ghost; that Mannering, Heatherlegh, and all the other men and women I knew were all ghosts; and the great, grey hills themselves but vain shadows devised to torture me. From mood to mood I tossed backwards and forwards for seven weary days; my body growing daily stronger and stronger, until the bedroom looking-glass told me that I had returned to everyday life, and was as other men once more. Curiously enough my face showed no signs of the struggle I had gone through. It was pale indeed, but as expressionless and commonplace as ever. I had expected some permanent alteration—visible evidence of the disease that was eating me away. I found nothing.

[margin: time? healed?]

On the 15th of May, I left Heatherlegh's house at eleven o'clock in the morning; and the instinct of the bachelor drove me to the Club. There I found that every man knew my story as told by Heatherlegh, and was, in clumsy fashion, abnormally kind and attentive. Nevertheless I recognised that for the rest of my natural life I should be among but not of my fellows; and I envied very bitterly indeed the laughing coolies on the Mall below. I lunched at the Club, and at four o'clock wandered aimlessly down the Mall in the vague hope of meeting Kitty. Close to the Bandstand the black and white liveries joined me, and I heard Mrs. Wessington's old appeal at my side. I had been expecting this ever since I came out, and was only surprised at her delay. The phantom 'rickshaw and I went side by side along the Chota Simla road in silence. Close to the bazar, Kitty and a man on horseback overtook and passed us. For any sign she gave I might have been a dog in the road. She did not even pay

me the compliment of quickening her pace, though the rainy afternoon
had served for an excuse.

So Kitty and her companion, and I and my ghostly Light-o'-Love,
crept round Jakko in couples. The road was streaming with water; the
pines dripped like roof-pipes on the rocks below, and the air was full of
fine driving rain. Two or three times I found myself saying to myself
almost aloud: "I'm Jack Pansay on leave at Simla—at Simla! Everyday,
ordinary Simla. I mustn't forget that—I mustn't forget that." Then I
would try to recollect some of the gossip I had heard at the Club: the
prices of So-and-So's horses—anything, in fact, that related to the worka-
day Anglo-Indian world I knew so well. I even repeated the multiplica-
tion-table rapidly to myself, to make quite sure that I was not taking leave
of my senses. It gave me much comfort, and must have prevented my
hearing Mrs. Wessington for a time.

Once more I wearily climbed the Convent slope and entered the level
road. Here Kitty and the man started off at a canter, and I was left alone
with Mrs. Wessington. "Agnes," said I, "will you put back your hood and
tell me what it all means?" The hood dropped noiselessly, and I was face
to face with my dead and buried mistress. She was wearing the dress in
which I had last seen her alive; carried the same tiny handkerchief in her
right hand, and the same card-case in her left. (A woman eight months
dead with a card-case!) I had to pin myself down to the multiplication-
table, and to set both hands on the stone parapet of the road, to assure
myself that that at least was real.

"Agnes," I repeated, "for pity's sake tell me what it all means." Mrs.
Wessington leaned forward, with that odd, quick turn of the head I used
to know so well, and spoke.

If my story had not already so madly overleaped the bounds of all
human belief I should apologise to you now. As I know that no one—
no, not even Kitty, for whom it is written as some sort of justification of
my conduct—will believe me, I will go on. Mrs. Wessington spoke, and
I walked with her from the Sanjowlie road to the turning below the
Commander-in-Chief's house as I might walk by the side of any living
woman's 'rickshaw, deep in conversation. The second and most torment-
ing of my moods of sickness had suddenly laid hold upon me, and, like
the Prince in Tennyson's poem, "I seemed to move amid a world of
ghosts." There had been a garden-party at the Commander-in-Chief's,
and we two joined the crowd of homeward-bound folk. As I saw them
it seemed that they were the shadows—impalpable, fantastic shadows—
that divided for Mrs. Wessington's 'rickshaw to pass through. What we
said during the course of that weird interview, I cannot—indeed, I dare
not—tell. Heatherlegh's comment would have been a short laugh and a
remark that I had been "mashing a brain-eye-and-stomach chimera." It

goes on a date w/ Mrs. W's ghest?

Rudyard Kipling

was a ghastly and yet in some indefinable way a marvellously dear experience. Could it be possible, I wondered, that I was in this life to woo a second time the woman I had killed by my own neglect and cruelty?

I met Kitty on the homeward road—a shadow among shadows.

If I were to describe all the incidents of the next fortnight in their order, my story would never come to an end, and your patience would be exhausted. Morning after morning and evening after evening the ghostly 'rickshaw and I used to wander through Simla together. Wherever I went there the four black and white liveries followed me and bore me company to and from my hotel. At the Theatre I found them amid the crowd of yelling jhampanies; outside the Club verandah, after a long evening of whist; at the Birthday Ball, waiting patiently for my reappearance; and in broad daylight when I went calling. Save that it cast no shadow, the 'rickshaw was in every respect as real to look upon as one of wood and iron. More than once, indeed, I have had to check myself from warning some hard-riding friend against cantering over it. More than once I have walked down the Mall deep in conversation with Mrs. Wessington, to the unspeakable amazement of the passers-by. ← everyone thinks he is talking to himself

Before I had been out and about a week I learned that the "fit" theory had been discarded in favour of insanity. However, I made no change in my mode of life. I called, rode, and dined out as freely as ever. I had a passion for the society of my kind which I had never felt before; I hungered to be among the realities of life; and at the same time I felt vaguely unhappy when I had been separated too long from my ghostly companion. It would be almost impossible to describe my varying moods from the 15th of May up to to-day.

The presence of the 'rickshaw filled me by turns with horror, blind fear, a dim sort of pleasure, and utter despair. I dared not leave Simla; and I knew that my stay there was killing me. I knew, moreover, that it was my destiny to die slowly and a little every day. My only anxiety was to get the penance over as quietly as might be. Alternately I hungered for a sight of Kitty, and watched her outrageous flirtations with my successor—to speak more accurately, my successors—with amused interest. She was as much out of my life as I was out of hers. By day I wandered with Mrs. Wessington almost content. By night I implored Heaven to let me return to the world as I used to know it. Above all these varying moods lay the sensation of dull, numbing wonder that the Seen and the Unseen should mingle so strangely on this earth to hound one poor soul to its grave.

August 27.—Heatherlegh has been indefatigable in his attendance on me; and only yesterday told me that I ought to send in an application for sick leave. An application to escape the company of a phantom! A request that the Government would graciously permit me to get rid of five ghosts and an airy 'rickshaw by going to England! Heatherlegh's proposition moved me to almost hysterical laughter. I told him that I should await the end quietly at Simla; and I am sure that the end is not far off. Believe me that I dread its advent more than any word can say; and I torture myself nightly with a thousand speculations as to the manner of my death.

Shall I die in my bed decently and as an English gentleman should die; or, in one last walk on the Mall, will my soul be wrenched from me to take its place for ever and ever by the side of that ghastly Phantasm? Shall I return to my old lost allegiance in the next world, or shall I meet Agnes loathing her and bound to her side through all eternity? Shall we two hover over the scene of our lives till the end of Time? As the day of my death draws nearer, the intense horror that all living flesh feels toward escaped spirits from beyond the grave grows more and more powerful. It is an awful thing to go down quick among the dead with scarcely one-half of your life completed. It is a thousand times more awful to wait as I do in your midst for I know not what unimaginable terror. Pity me, at least on the score of my "delusion," for I know you will never believe what I have written here. Yet as surely as ever a man was done to death by the Powers of Darkness I am that man.

In justice, too, pity her. For as surely as ever woman was killed by man, I killed Mrs. Wessington. And the last portion of my punishment is even now upon me.

1885

UNDER THE KNIFE

H. G. Wells

"WHAT IF I die under it?" The thought recurred again and again as I
walked home from Haddon's. It was a purely personal question. I was
spared the deep anxieties of a married man, and I knew there were few
of my intimate friends but would find my death troublesome chiefly on
account of their duty of regret. I was surprised indeed and perhaps a little
humiliated, as I turned the matter over, to think how few could possibly
exceed the conventional requirement. Things came before me stripped
of glamour, in a clear dry light, during that walk from Haddon's house
over Primrose Hill. There were the friends of my youth; I perceived now
that our affection was a tradition which we foregathered rather laboriously to maintain. There were the rivals and helpers of my later career: I
suppose I had been cold-blooded or undemonstrative—one perhaps
implies the other. It may be that even the capacity for friendship is a
question of physique. There had been a time in my own life when I had
grieved bitterly enough at the loss of a friend; but as I walked home that
afternoon the emotional side of my imagination was dormant. I could
not pity myself, nor feel sorry for my friends, nor conceive of them as
grieving for me.

I was interested in this deadness of my emotional nature—no doubt a
concomitant of my stagnating physiology; and my thoughts wandered off
along the line it suggested. Once before, in my hot youth, I had suffered
a sudden loss of blood and had been within an ace of death. I remembered now that my affections as well as my passions had drained out of
me, leaving scarcely anything but a tranquil resignation, a dreg of self-
pity. It had been weeks before the old ambitions, and tendernesses, and
all the complex moral interplay of a man, had reasserted themselves.
Now again I was bloodless; I had been feeding down for a week or more.
I was not even hungry. It occurred to me that the real meaning of this
numbness might be a gradual slipping away from the pleasure–pain guid-
ance of the animal man. It has been proven, I take it, as thoroughly as

98

anything can be proven in this world, that the higher emotions, the moral feelings, even the subtle tendernesses of love, are evolved from the elemental desires and fears of the simple animal: they are the harness in which man's mental freedom goes. And it may be that, as death overshadows us, as our possibility of acting diminishes, this complex growth of balanced impulse, propensity, and aversion whose interplay inspires our acts, goes with it. Leaving what?

I was suddenly brought back to reality by an imminent collision with a butcher-boy's tray. I found that I was crossing the bridge over the Regent's Park Canal which runs parallel with that in the Zoological Gardens. The boy in blue had been looking over his shoulder at a black barge advancing slowly, towed by a gaunt white horse. In the Gardens a nurse was leading three happy little children over the bridge. The trees were bright green; the spring hopefulness was still unstained by the dusts of summer; the sky in the water was bright and clear, but broken by long waves, by quivering bands of black, as the barge drove through. The breeze was stirring; but it did not stir me as the spring breeze used to do.

Was this dullness of feeling in itself an anticipation? It was curious that I could reason and follow out a network of suggestion as clearly as ever: so, at least, it seemed to me. It was calmness rather than dullness that was coming upon me. Was there any ground for the belief in the presentiment of death? Did a man near to death begin instinctively to withdraw himself from the meshes of matter and sense, even before the cold hand was laid upon his? I felt strangely isolated—isolated without regret—from the life and existence about me. The children playing in the sun and gathering strength and experience for the business of life, the park-keeper gossiping with a nursemaid, the nursing mother, the young couple intent upon each other as they passed me, the trees by the wayside spreading new pleading leaves to the sunlight, the stir in their branches—I had been part of it all, but I had nearly done with it now.

Some way down the Broad Walk I perceived that I was tired, and that my feet were heavy. It was hot that afternoon, and I turned aside and sat down on one of the green chairs that line the way. In a minute I had dozed into a dream, and the tide of my thoughts washed up a vision of the resurrection. I was still sitting in the chair, but I thought myself actually dead, withered, tattered, dried, one eye (I saw) pecked out by birds. "Awake!" cried a voice; and incontinently the dust of the path and the mould under the grass became insurgent. I had never before thought of Regent's Park as a cemetery, but now through the trees, stretching as far as eye could see, I beheld a flat plain of writhing graves and heeling tombstones. There seemed to be some trouble: the rising dead appeared to stifle as they struggled upward, they bled in their struggles, the red flesh was tattered away from the white bones. "Awake!" cried a voice: but

I determined I would not rise to such horrors. "Awake!" They would not let me alone. "Wike up!" said an angry voice. A cockney angel! The man who sells the tickets was shaking me, demanding my penny.

I paid my penny, pocketed my ticket, yawned, stretched my legs, and, feeling now rather less torpid, got up and walked on towards Langham Place. I speedily lost myself again in a shifting maze of thoughts about death. Going across Marylebone Road into that crescent at the end of Langham Place, I had the narrowest escape from the shaft of a cab, and went on my way with a palpitating heart and a bruised shoulder. It struck me that it would have been curious if my meditations on my death on the morrow had led to my death that day.

But I will not weary you with more of my experiences that day and the next. I knew more and more certainly that I should die under the operation; at, times I think I was inclined to pose to myself. At home I found everything prepared; my room cleared of needless objects and hung with white sheets; a nurse installed and already at loggerheads with my housekeeper. They wanted me to go to bed early, and after a little resistance I obeyed.

In the morning I was very indolent, and though I read my newspapers and the letters that came by the first post, I did not find them very interesting. There was a friendly note from Addison, my old school friend, calling my attention to two discrepancies and a printer's error in my new book, with one from Langridge venting some vexation over Minton. The rest were business communications. I had a cup of tea but nothing to eat. The glow of pain at my side seemed more massive. I knew it was pain, and yet, if you can understand, I did not find it very painful. I had been awake and hot and thirsty in the night, but in the morning bed felt comfortable. In the night-time I had lain thinking of things that were past; in the morning I dozed over the question of immortality. Haddon came, punctual to the minute, with a neat black bag; and Mowbray soon followed. Their arrival stirred me up a little. I began to take a more personal interest in the proceedings. Haddon moved the little octagonal table close to the bedside, and, with his broad black back to me, began taking things out of his bag. I heard the light click of steel upon steel. My imagination, I found, was not altogether stagnant. "Will you hurt me much?" I said in an off-hand tone.

"Not a bit," Haddon answered over his shoulder. "We shall chloroform you. Your heart's as sound as a bell." And as he spoke, I had a whiff of the pungent sweetness of the anaesthetic.

They stretched me out, with a convenient exposure of my side, and, almost before I realized what was happening, the chloroform was being administered. It stings the nostrils, and there is a suffocating sensation, at first. I knew I should die—that this was the end of consciousness for me.

And suddenly I felt that I was not prepared for death: I had a vague sense of a duty overlooked—I knew not what. What was it I had not done? I could think of nothing more to do, nothing desirable left in life; and yet I had the strangest disinclination for death. And the physical sensation was painfully oppressive. Of course the doctors did not know they were going to kill me. Possibly I struggled. Then I fell motionless, and a great silence, a monstrous silence, and an impenetrable blackness came upon me.

There must have been an interval of absolute unconsciousness, seconds or minutes. Then, with a chilly, unemotional clearness, I perceived that I was not yet dead. I was still in my body; but all the multitudinous sensations that come sweeping from it to make up the background of consciousness had gone, leaving me free of it all. No, not free of it all; for as yet something still held me to the poor stark flesh upon the bed—held me, yet not so closely that I did not feel myself external to it, independent of it, straining away from it. I do not think I saw, I do not think I heard; but I perceived all that was going on, and it was as if I both heard and saw. Haddon was bending over me. Mowbray behind me; the scalpel—it was a large scalpel—was cutting my flesh at the side under the flying ribs. It was interesting to see myself cut like cheese, without a pang, without even a qualm. The interest was much of a quality with that one might feel in a game of chess between strangers. Haddon's face was firm and his hand steady; but I was surprised to perceive (*how* I know not) that he was feeling the gravest doubt as to his own wisdom in the conduct of the operation.

Mowbray's thoughts, too, I could see. He was thinking that Haddon's manner showed too much of the specialist. New suggestions came up like bubbles through a stream of frothing meditation, and burst one after another in the little bright spot of his consciousness. He could not help noticing and admiring Haddon's swift dexterity, in spite of his envious quality and his disposition to detract. I saw my liver exposed. I was puzzled at my own condition. I did not feel that I was dead, but I was different in some way from my living self. The grey depression that had weighed on me for a year or more and coloured all my thoughts, was gone. I perceived and thought without any emotional tint at all. I wondered if everyone perceived things in this way under chloroform, and forgot it again when he came out of it. It would be inconvenient to look into some heads, and not forget.

Although I did not think that I was dead, I still perceived quite clearly that I was soon to die. This brought me back to the consideration of Haddon's proceedings. I looked into his mind, and saw that he was afraid of cutting a branch of the portal vein. My attention was distracted from details by the curious changes going on in his mind. His consciousness was like the quivering little spot of light which is thrown by the mirror of a galvanometer. His thoughts ran under it like a stream, some through the focus bright and distinct, some shadowy in the half-light of the edge. Just now the little glow was steady; but the least movement on Mowbray's part, the slightest sound from outside, even a faint difference in the slow movement of the living flesh he was cutting, set the light-spot shivering and spinning. A new sense-impression came rushing up through the flow of thoughts, and lo! the light-spot jerked away towards it, swifter than a frightened fish. It was wonderful to think that upon that unstable, fitful thing depended all the complex motions of the man; that for the next five minutes, therefore, my life hung upon its movements. And he was growing more and more nervous in his work. It was as if a little picture of a cut vein grew brighter, and struggled to oust from his brain another picture of a cut falling short of the mark. He was afraid: his dread of cutting too little was battling with his dread of cutting too far.

Then, suddenly, like an escape of water from under a lock-gate, a great uprush of horrible realization set all his thoughts swirling, and simultaneously I perceived that the vein was cut. He started back with a hoarse exclamation, and I saw the brown-purple blood gather in a swift bead, and run trickling. He was horrified. He pitched the red-stained scalpel on to the octagonal table; and instantly both doctors flung themselves upon me, making hasty and ill-conceived efforts to remedy the disaster. "Ice!" said Mowbray, gasping. But I knew that I was killed, though my body still clung to me.

I will not describe their belated endeavours to save me, though I perceived every detail. My perceptions were sharper and swifter than they had ever been in my life; my thoughts rushed through my mind with incredible swiftness, but with perfect definition. I can only compare their crowded clarity to the effects of a reasonable dose of opium. In a moment it would all be over, and I should be free. I knew I was immortal, but what would happen I did not know. Should I drift off presently, like a puff of smoke from a gun, in some kind of half-material body, an attenuated version of my material self? Should I find myself suddenly among the innumerable hosts of the dead, and know the world about me for the phantasmagoria it had always seemed? Should I drift to some spiritualistic *séance,* and there make foolish, incomprehensible attempts to affect a purblind medium? It was a state of unemotional curiosity, of colourless expectation. And then I realized a growing stress upon me, a feeling as though some huge human magnet was drawing me upward out of my body. The stress grew and grew. I seemed an atom for which monstrous forces were fighting. For one brief, terrible moment sensation came back to me. That feeling of falling headlong which comes in nightmares, that feeling a thousand times intensified, that and a black horror swept across my thoughts in a torrent. Then the two doctors, the naked body with its cut side, the little room, swept away from under me and vanished as a speck of foam vanishes down an eddy.

I was in mid-air. Far below was the West End of London, receding rapidly,—for I seemed to be flying swiftly upward,—and, as it receded, passing westward, like a panorama. I could see, through the faint haze of smoke the innumerable roofs chimney-set, the narrow roadways stippled with people and conveyances, the little specks of squares, and the church steeples like thorns sticking out of the fabric. But it spun away as the earth rotated on its axis, and in a few seconds (as it seemed) I was over the scattered clumps of town about Ealing, the little Thames a thread of blue to the south, and the Chiltern Hills and the North Downs coming up like the rim of a basin, far away and faint with haze. Up I rushed. And at first I had not the faintest conception what this headlong rush upward could mean.

Every moment the circle of scenery beneath me grew wider and wider, and the details of town and field, of hill and valley, got more and more hazy and pale and indistinct, a luminous grey was mingled more and more with the blue of the hills and the green of the open meadows; and a little patch of cloud, low and far to the west, shone ever more dazzlingly white. Above, as the veil of atmosphere between myself and outer space grew thinner, the sky, which had been a fair springtime blue at first, grew deeper and richer in colour, passing steadily through the intervening shades until presently it was as dark as the blue sky of midnight, and presently as black as the blackness of a frosty starlight, and at last as black as no blackness I had ever beheld. And first one star and then many, and at last an innumerable host broke out upon the sky: more stars than anyone has ever seen from the face of the earth. For the blueness of the sky is the light of the sun and stars sifted and spread abroad blindingly: there is diffused light even in the darkest skies of winter, and we do not see the stars by day only because of the dazzling irradiation of the sun. But now I saw things—I know not how; assuredly with no mortal eyes—and that defect of bedazzlement blinded me no longer. The sun was incredibly strange and wonderful. The body of it was a disc of blinding white light: not yellowish as it seems to those who live upon the earth, but livid white, all streaked with scarlet streaks and rimmed about with a fringe of writhing tongues of red fire. And, shooting half way across the heavens from either side of it, and brighter than the Milky Way, were two pinions of silver-white, making it look more like those winged globes I have seen in Egyptian sculpture, than anything else I can remember upon earth. These I knew for the solar corona, though I had never seen anything of it but a picture during the days of my earthly life.

When my attention came back to the earth again, I saw that it had fallen very far away from me. Field and town were long since indistinguishable, and all the varied hues of the country were merging into a uniform bright grey, broken only by the brilliant white of the clouds that lay scattered in flocculent masses over Ireland and the west of England. For now I could see the outlines of the north of France and Ireland, and all this island of Britain save where Scotland passed over the horizon to the north, or where the coast was blurred or obliterated by cloud. The sea was a dull grey, and darker than the land; and the whole panorama was rotating slowly towards the east.

All this had happened so swiftly that, until I was some thousand miles or so from the earth, I had no thought for myself. But now I perceived I had neither hands nor feet, neither parts nor organs, and that I felt neither alarm nor pain. All about me I perceived that the vacancy (for I had already left the air behind) was cold beyond the imagination of man; but it troubled me not. The sun's rays shot through the void, powerless to light or heat until they should strike on matter in their course. I saw things with a serene self-forgetfulness, even as if I were God. And down below there, rushing away from me,—countless miles in a second,—where a little dark spot on the grey marked the position of London, two doctors were struggling to restore life to the poor hacked and outworn shell I had abandoned. I felt then such release, such serenity as I can compare to no mortal delight I have ever known.

It was only after I had perceived all these things that the meaning of that headlong rush of the earth grew into comprehension. Yet it was so simple, so obvious, that I was amazed at my never anticipating the thing that was happening to me. I had suddenly been cut adrift from matter: all that was material of me was there upon earth, whirling away through space, held to the earth by gravitation, partaking of the earth's inertia, moving in its wreath of epicycles round the sun, and with the sun and the planets on their vast march through space. But the immaterial has no inertia, feels nothing of the pull of matter for matter: where it parts from its garment of flesh, there it remains (so far as space concerns it any longer) immovable in space. I was not leaving the earth: the earth was leaving *me,* and not only the earth, but the whole solar system was streaming past. And about me in space, invisible to me, scattered in the wake of the earth upon its journey, there must be an innumerable multitude of souls, stripped like myself of the material, stripped like myself of passions of the individual and the generous emotions of the gregarious brute, naked intelligences, things of newborn wonder and thought, marvelling at the strange release that had suddenly come on them!

As I receded faster and faster from the strange white sun in the black heavens, and from the broad and shining earth upon which my being had begun, I seemed to grow, in some incredible manner, vast: vast as regards this world I had left, vast as regards the moments and periods of a human life. Very soon I saw the full circle of the earth, slightly gibbous, like the moon when she nears her full, but very large; and the silvery shape of America was now in the noonday blaze wherein (as it seemed) little England had been basking but a few minutes ago. At first the earth was large and shone in the heavens, filling a great part of them; but every moment she grew smaller and more distant. As she shrunk, the broad moon in its third quarter crept into view over the rim of her disc. I looked for the constellations. Only that part of Aries directly behind the sun, and the Lion, which the earth covered, were hidden. I recognized the tortuous, tattered band of the Milky Way, with Vega very bright between sun and earth; and Sirius and Orion shone splendid against the unfathomable blackness in the opposite quarter of the heavens. The Pole Star was overhead, and the Great Bear hung over the circle of the earth. And away beneath and beyond the shining corona of the sun were strange groupings of stars I had never seen in my life—notably, a dagger-shaped group that I knew for the Southern Cross. All these were no larger than when they had shone on earth; but the little stars that one scarcely sees shone now against the setting of black vacancy as brightly as the first-magnitudes had done, while the larger worlds were points of indescribable glory and colour. Aldebaran was a spot of blood-red fire, and Sirius condensed to one point the light of a world of sapphires. And they shone steadily: they did not scintillate, they were calmly glorious. My impressions had an adamantine hardness and brightness: there was no blurring softness, no atmosphere, nothing but infinite darkness set with the myriads of these acute and brilliant points and specks of light. Presently, when I looked again, the little earth seemed no bigger than the sun, and it dwindled and turned as I looked until, in a second's space (as it seemed to me), it was halved; and so it went on swiftly dwindling. Far away in the opposite direction, a little pinkish pin's head of light, shining steadily, was the planet Mars. I swam motionless in vacancy, and, without a trace of terror or astonishment, watched the speck of cosmic dust we call the world fall away from me.

Presently it dawned upon me that my sense of duration had changed: that my mind was moving not faster but infinitely slower, that between each separate impression there was a period of many days. The moon spun once round the earth as I noted this; and I perceived clearly the motion of Mars in his orbit. Moreover, it appeared as if the time between thought and thought grew steadily greater, until at last a thousand years was but a moment in my perception.

At first the constellations had shone motionless against the black background of infinite space; but presently it seemed as though the group of

stars about Hercules and the Scorpion was contracting, while Orion and
Aldebaran and their neighbours were scattering apart. Flashing suddenly
out of the darkness there came a flying multitude of particles of rock,
glittering like dust-specks in a sunbeam, and encompassed in a faintly
luminous haze. They swirled all about me, and vanished again in a twinkling far behind. And then I saw that a bright spot of light, that shone a
little to one side of my path, was growing very rapidly larger, and perceived that it was the planet Saturn rushing towards me. Larger and larger
it grew, swallowing up the heavens behind it, and hiding every moment
a fresh multitude of stars. I perceived its flattened, whirling body, its disc-
like belt, and seven of its little satellites. It grew and grew, till it towered
enormous; and then I plunged amid a streaming multitude of clashing
stones and dancing dust-particles and gas-eddies, and saw for a moment
the mighty triple belt like three concentric arches of moonlight above
me, its shadow black on the boiling tumult below. These things happened
in one-tenth of the time it takes to tell them. The planet went by like a
flash of lightning; for a few seconds it blotted out the sun, and there and
then became a mere black, dwindling, winged patch against the light.
The earth, the mother mote of my being, I could no longer see.

So with a stately swiftness, in the profoundest silence, the solar system
fell from me, as it had been a garment, until the sun was a mere star amid
the multitude of stars, with its eddy of planet-specks, lost in the confused
glittering of the remoter light. I was no longer a denizen of the solar
system: I had come to the Outer Universe, I seemed to grasp and com-
prehend the whole world of matter. Ever more swiftly the stars closed in
about the spot where Antares and Vega had vanished in a luminous haze,
until that part of the sky had the semblance of a whirling mass of nebu-
lae, and ever before me yawned vaster gaps of vacant blackness and the
stars shone fewer and fewer. It seemed as if I moved towards a point
between Orion's belt and sword; and the void about that region opened
vaster and vaster every second, an incredible gulf of nothingness, into
which I was falling. Faster and ever faster the universe rushed by, a hurry
of whirling motes at last, speeding silently into the void. Stars glowing
brighter and brighter, with their circling planets catching the light in a
ghostly fashion as I neared them, shone out and vanished again into inex-
istence; faint comets, clusters of meteorites, winking specks of matter,
eddying light-points, whizzed past, some perhaps a hundred millions of
miles or so from me at most, few nearer, travelling with unimaginable
rapidity, shooting constellations, momentary darts of fire, through that
black, enormous night. More than anything else it was like a dusty
draught, sunbeam-lit. Broader, and wider, and deeper grew the starless
space, the vacant Beyond, into which I was being drawn. At last a quarter of the heavens was black and blank, and the whole headlong rush of

stellar universe closed in behind me like a veil of light that is gathered together. It drove away from me like a monstrous jack-o'-lantern driven by the wind. I had come out into the wilderness of space. Ever the vacant blackness grew broader, until the hosts of the stars seemed only like a swarm of fiery specks hurrying away from me, inconceivably remote, and the darkness, the nothingness and emptiness, was about me on every side. Soon the little universe of matter, the cage of points in which I had begun to be, was dwindling, now to a whirling disc of luminous glittering, and now to one minute disc of hazy light. In a little while it would shrink to a point, and at last would vanish altogether.

Suddenly feeling came back to me—feeling in the shape of overwhelming terror: such a dread of those dark vastitudes as no words can describe, a passionate resurgence of sympathy and social desire. Were there other souls, invisible to me as I to them, about me in the blackness? Or was I indeed, even as I felt, alone? Had I passed out of being into something that was neither being nor not-being? The covering of the body, the covering of matter, had been torn from me, and the hallucinations of companionship and security. Everything was black and silent. I had ceased to be. I was nothing. There was nothing, save only that infinitesimal dot of light that dwindled in the gulf. I strained myself to hear and see, and for a while there was naught but infinite silence, intolerable darkness, horror, and despair.

Then I saw that about the spot of light into which the whole world of matter had shrunk there was a faint glow. And in a band on either side of that the darkness was not absolute. I watched it for ages, as it seemed to me, and through the long waiting the haze grew imperceptibly more distinct. And then about the band appeared an irregular cloud of the faintest, palest brown. I felt a passionate impatience; but the things grew brighter so slowly that they scarcely seemed to change. What was unfolding itself? What was this strange reddish dawn in the interminable night of space?

The cloud's shape was grotesque. It seemed to be looped along its lower side into four projecting masses, and, above, it ended in a straight line. What phantom was it? I felt assured I had seen that figure before; but I could not think what, nor where, nor when it was. Then the realization rushed upon me. *It was a clenched Hand.* I was alone in space, alone with his huge, shadowy Hand, upon which the whole Universe of Matter lay like an unconsidered speck of dust. It seemed as though I watched it through vast periods of time. On the forefinger glittered a ring; and the universe from which I had come was but a spot of light upon the ring's curvature. And the thing that the hand gripped had the likeness of a black rod. Through a long eternity I watched this Hand, with the ring and the rod, marvelling and fearing and waiting helplessly on what might follow. It seemed as though nothing could follow: that I should watch for ever, seeing only the Hand and the thing it held, and understanding nothing of its import. Was the whole universe but a refracting speck upon some greater Being? Were our worlds but the atoms of another universe, and those again of another, and so on through an endless progression? And what was I? Was I indeed immaterial? A vague persuasion of a body gathering about me came into my suspense. The abysmal darkness about the Hand filled with impalpable suggestion, with uncertain, fluctuating shapes.

Came a sound, like the sound of a tolling bell; faint, as if infinitely far, muffled as though heard through thick swathings of darkness: a deep, vibrating resonance, with vast gulfs of silence between each stroke. And the Hand appeared to tighten on the rod. And I saw far above the Hand, towards the apex of the darkness, a circle of dim phosphorescence, a ghostly sphere whence these sounds came throbbing; and at the last stroke the Hand vanished, for the hour had come, and I heard a noise of many waters. But the black rod remained as a great band across the sky. And then a voice, which seemed to run to the uttermost parts of space, spoke, saying, "There will be no more pain."

At that an almost intolerable gladness and radiance rushed upon me, and I saw the circle shining white and bright, and the rod black and shining, and many things else distinct and clear. And the circle was the face of the clock, and the rod the rail of my bed. Haddon was standing at the foot, against the rail, with a small pair of scissors on his fingers; and the hands of my clock on the mantel over his shoulder were clasped together over the hour of twelve. Mowbray was washing something in a basin at the octagonal table, and at my side I felt a subdued feeling that could scarce be spoken of as pain.

The operation had not killed me. And I perceived, suddenly, that the dull melancholy of half a year was lifted from my mind.

1896

THE DEAD HAND

Wilkie Collins

WHEN THIS present nineteenth century was younger by a good many years than it is now, a certain friend of mine, named Arthur Holliday, happened to arrive in the town of Doncaster exactly in the middle of the race-week, or, in other words, in the middle of the month of September.

He was one of those reckless, rattle-pated, open-hearted, and open-mouthed young gentlemen who possess the gift of familiarity in its highest perfection, and who scramble carelessly along the journey of life, making friends, as the phrase is, wherever they go. His father was a rich manufacturer, and had bought landed property enough in one of the midland counties to make all the born squires in his neighborhood thoroughly envious of him. Arthur was his only son, possessor in prospect of the great business after his father's death; well supplied with money, and not too rigidly looked after during his father's lifetime. Report, or scandal, whichever you please, said that the old gentleman had been rather wild in his youthful days, and that, unlike most parents, he was not disposed to be violently indignant when he found that his son took after him. This may be true or not. I myself only knew the elder Mr. Holliday when he was getting on in years, and then he was as quiet and as respectable a gentleman as ever I met with.

Well, one September, as I told you, young Arthur comes to Doncaster, having decided all of a sudden, in his hare-brained way, that he would go to the races. He did not reach the town till towards the close of evening, and he went at once to see about his dinner and bed at the principal hotel. Dinner they were ready enough to give him, but as for a bed, they laughed when he mentioned it. In the race-week at Doncaster it is no uncommon thing for visitors who have not bespoken apartments to pass the night in their carriages at the inn doors. As for the lower sort of strangers, I myself have often seen them, at that full time, sleeping out on the door-steps for want of a covered place to creep under. Rich as he was, Arthur's chance of getting a night's lodging (seeing that he had not

109

written beforehand to secure one) was more than doubtful. He tried the second hotel, and the third hotel, and two of the inferior inns after that, and was met everywhere with the same form of answer. No accommodation for the night of any sort was left. All the bright golden sovereigns in his pocket would not buy him a bed at Doncaster in the race-week.

To a young fellow of Arthur's temperament, the novelty of being turned away into the street like a penniless vagabond, at every house where he asked for a lodging, presented itself in the light of a new and highly amusing piece of experience. He went on with his carpet-bag in his hand, applying for a bed at every place of entertainment for travellers that he could find in Doncaster, until he wandered into the outskirts of the town.

By this time the last glimmer of twilight had faded out, the moon was rising dimly in a mist, the wind was getting cold, the clouds were gathering heavily, and there was every prospect that it was soon going to rain!

The look of the night had rather a lowering effect on young Holliday's good spirits. He began to contemplate the houseless situation in which he was placed from the serious rather than the humorous point of view, and he looked about him for another public house to inquire at with something very like downright anxiety in his mind on the subject of a lodging for the night.

The suburban part of the town towards which he had now strayed was hardly lighted at all, and he could see nothing of the houses as he passed them, except that they got progressively smaller and dirtier the farther he went. Down the winding road before him shone the dull gleam of an oil lamp, the one faint lonely light that struggled ineffectually with the foggy darkness all round him. He resolved to go on as far as this lamp, and then, if it showed him nothing in the shape of an inn, to return to the central part of the town, and to try if he could not at least secure a chair to sit down on through the night at one of the principal hotels.

As he got near the lamp he heard voices, and, walking close under it, found that it lighted the entrance to a narrow court, on the wall of which was painted a long hand in faded flesh color, pointing with a lean forefinger to this inscription: THE TWO ROBINS.

Arthur turned into the court without hesitation to see what The Two Robins could do for him. Four or five men were standing together round the door of the house, which was at the bottom of the court, facing the entrance from the street. The men were all listening to one other man, better dressed than the rest, who was telling his audience something, in a low voice, in which they were apparently very much interested.

On entering the passage, Arthur was passed by a stranger with a knapsack in his hand, who was evidently leaving the house.

"No," said the traveller with the knapsack, turning round and addressing himself cheerfully to a fat, sly-looking, bald-headed man, with a dirty white apron, who had followed him down the passage, "no, Mr. Landlord, I am not easily scared by trifles; but I don't mind confessing that I can't stand that."

It occurred to young Holliday, the moment he heard these words, that the stranger had been asked an exorbitant price for a bed at The Two Robins, and that he was unable or unwilling to pay it. The moment his back was turned, Arthur, comfortably conscious of his own well-filled pockets, addressed himself in a great hurry, for fear any other benighted traveller should slip in and forestall him, to the sly-looking landlord with the dirty apron and the bald head.

"If you have got a bed to let," he said, "and if that gentleman who has just gone out won't pay your price for it, I will."

The sly landlord looked hard at Arthur.

"Will you, sir?" he asked, in a meditative, doubtful way.

"Name your price," said young Holliday, thinking that the landlord's hesitation sprang from some boorish distrust of him. "Name your price, and I'll give you the money at once, if you like."

"Are you game for five shillings?" inquired the landlord, rubbing his stubby double chin, and looking up thoughtfully at the ceiling above him.

Arthur nearly laughed in the man's face; but, thinking it prudent to control himself, offered the five shillings as seriously as he could. The sly landlord held out his hand, then suddenly drew it back again.

"You're acting all fair and aboveboard by me," he said, "and, before I take your money, I'll do the same by you. Look here, this is how it stands. You can have a bed all to yourself for five shillings, but you can't have more than a half share of the room it stands in. Do you see what I mean, young gentleman?"

"Of course I do," returned Arthur, a little irritably. "You mean that it is a double-bedded room, and that one of the beds is occupied?"

The landlord nodded his head, and rubbed his double chin harder than ever. Arthur hesitated, and mechanically moved back a step or two toward the door. The idea of sleeping in the same room with a total stranger did not present an attractive prospect to him. He felt more than inclined to drop his five shillings into his pocket, and go out into the street once more.

"Is it yes or no?" asked the landlord. "Settle it as quick as you can, because there's lots of people wanting a bed at Doncaster tonight, besides you."

Arthur looked towards the court, and heard the rain falling heavily in the street outside. He thought he would ask a question or two before he rashly decided on leaving the shelter of The Two Robins.

"What sort of a man is it who has got the other bed?" he inquired. "Is he a gentleman? I mean, is he a quiet, well-behaved person?"

"The quietest man I ever came across," said the landlord, rubbing his fat hands stealthily one over the other. "As sober as a judge, and as regular as clock-work in his habits. It hasn't struck nine not ten minutes ago, and he's in his bed already. I don't know whether that comes up to your notion of a quiet man: it does a long way ahead of mine, I can tell you."

"Is he asleep, do you think?" asked Arthur.

"I know he's asleep," returned the landlord; "and what's more, he's gone off so fast that I'll warrant you don't wake him. This way, sir," said the landlord, speaking over young Holliday's shoulder, as if he was addressing some new guest who was approaching the house.

"Here you are," said Arthur, determined to be beforehand with the stranger, whoever he might be. "I'll take the bed." And he handed the five shillings to the landlord, who nodded, dropped the money carelessly into his waistcoat pocket, and lighted a candle.

"Come up and see the room," said the host of The Two Robins, leading the way to the staircase quite briskly, considering how fat he was.

They mounted to the second floor of the house. The landlord half opened a door fronting the landing, then stopped, and turned round to Arthur.

"It's a fair bargain, mind, on my side as well as on yours," he said. "You give me five shillings, and I give you in return a clean, comfortable bed; and I warrant, beforehand, that you won't be interfered with, or annoyed in any way, by the man who sleeps in the same room with you." Saying those words, he looked hard, for a moment, in young Holliday's face, and then led the way into the room.

It was larger and cleaner than Arthur had expected it would be. The two beds stood parallel with each other, a space of about six feet intervening between them. They were both of the same medium size, and both had the same plain white curtains, made to draw, if necessary, all round them.

The occupied bed was the bed nearest the window. The curtains were all drawn round it except the half curtain at the bottom, on the side of the bed farthest from the window.

Arthur saw the feet of the sleeping man raising the scanty clothes into a sharp little eminence, as if he was lying flat on his back. He took the candle, and advanced softly to draw the curtain; he stopped half way, and listened for a moment; then he turned to the landlord.

"He is a very quiet sleeper," said Arthur.

"Yes," said the landlord, "very quiet."

Young Holliday advanced with the candle, and looked in at the man cautiously.

"How pale he is," said Arthur.

"Yes," returned the landlord, "pale enough, isn't he?"

Arthur looked closer at the man. The bed-clothes were drawn up to his chin, and they lay perfectly still over the region of his chest. Surprised and vaguely startled as he noticed this, Arthur stooped down closer over the stranger, looked at his ashy, parted lips, listened breathlessly for an instant; looked again at the strangely still face, and the motionless lips and chest, and turned round suddenly on the landlord with his own cheeks as pale for the moment as the hollow cheeks of the man on the bed.

"Come here," he whispered, under his breath. "Come, for God's sake! The man's not asleep. He is dead."

"You have found that out sooner than I thought you would," said the landlord, composedly. "Yes, he's dead, sure enough. He died at five o'clock to-day."

"How did he die? Who is he?" asked Arthur, staggered for the moment by the audacious coolness of the answer.

"As to who is he?" rejoined the landlord, "I know no more about him than you do. There are his books, and letters, and things all sealed up in that brown paper parcel for the coroner's inquest to open to-morrow or next day. He's been here a week, paying his way fairly enough, and stopping indoors, for the most part, as he was ailing. My girl brought him up his tea at five to-day, and as he was pouring of it out, he fell down in a faint, or a fit, or a compound of both, for anything I know. We couldn't bring him to, and I said he was dead. And the doctor couldn't bring him to, and the doctor said he was dead. And there he is. And the coroner's inquest's coming as soon as it can. And that's as much as I know about it."

Arthur held the candle close to the man's lips. The flame still burned straight up as steadily as ever. There was a moment of silence, and the rain pattered drearily through it against the panes of the window.

"If you haven't got nothing more to say to me," continued the landlord, "I suppose I may go. You don't expect your five shillings back, do you? There's the bed I promised you, clean and comfortable. There's the man I warranted not to disturb you, quiet in this world forever. If you're frightened to stop alone with him, that's not my lookout. I've kept my part of the bargain and I mean to keep the money. I'm not Yorkshire myself, young gentleman, but I've lived long enough in these parts to have my wits sharpened, and I shouldn't wonder if you found out the way to brighten up yours next time you come among us."

With these words the landlord turned towards the door, and laughed to himself softly, in high satisfaction at his own sharpness.

Startled and shocked as he was, Arthur had by this time sufficiently recovered himself to feel indignant at the trick that had been played on him, and at the insolent manner in which the landlord exulted in it.

"Don't laugh," he said sharply, "till you are sure you have got the laugh against me. You shan't have the five shillings for nothing, my man. I'll keep the bed."

"Will you?" said the landlord. "Then I wish you a good night's rest." With that brief farewell he went out and shut the door after him.

A good night's rest! The words had hardly been spoken, the door had hardly been closed, before Arthur half repented the hasty words that had just escaped him. Though not naturally over-sensitive, and not wanting in courage of the moral as well as the physical sort, the presence of the dead man had an instantaneously chilling effect on his mind when he found himself alone in the room; alone, and bound by his own rash words to stay there till the next morning, an older man would have thought nothing of those words, and would have acted, without reference to them, as his calmer sense suggested. But Arthur was too young to treat the ridicule even of his inferiors with contempt; too young not to fear the momentary humiliation of falsifying his own foolish boast more than he feared the trial of watching out the long night in the same chamber with the dead.

"It's but a few hours," he thought to himself, "and I can get away the first thing in the morning."

He was looking towards the occupied bed as that idea passed through his mind, and the sharp angular eminence made in the clothes by the dead man's upturned feet again caught his eye. He advanced and drew the curtains, purposely abstaining, as he did so, from looking at the face of the corpse, lest he might unnerve himself at the outset by fastening some ghastly impression of it on his mind. He drew the curtain very gently, and sighed involuntarily as he closed it.

"Poor fellow," he said, almost as sadly as if he had known the man. "Ah! poor fellow!"

He went next to the window. The night was black, and he could see nothing from it. The rain still pattered heavily against the glass. He inferred, from hearing it, that the window was at the back of the house, remembering that the front was sheltered from the weather by the court and the buildings over it.

While he was still standing at the window; for even the dreary rain was a relief, because of the sound it made; a relief, also, because it moved, and had some faint suggestion, in consequence, of life and companionship in it; while he was standing at the window, and looking vacantly into the black darkness outside, he heard a distant church clock strike ten. Only ten! How was he to pass the time till the house was astir the next morning?

Under any other circumstances he would have gone down to the public-house parlour, would have called for his grog, and would have laughed and talked with the company, assembled as familiarly as if he had known them all his life. But the very thought of whiling away the time in this manner was now distasteful to him. The new situation in which he was placed seemed to have altered him to himself already. Thus far his life had been the common, trifling, prosaic, surface-life of a prosperous young man, with no troubles to conquer and no trials to face. He had lost no relation whom he loved, no friend whom he treasured. Till this night, what share he had of the immortal inheritance that is divided among us all had lain dormant within him. Till this night, Death and he had not once met, even in thought.

He took a few turns up and down the room, then stopped. The noise made by his boots on the poorly carpeted floor jarred on his ear. He hesitated a little, and ended by taking his boots off, and walking backwards and forwards noiselessly.

All desire to sleep or to rest had left him. The bare thought of lying down on the unoccupied bed instantly drew the picture on his mind of a dreadful mimicry of the position of the dead man. Who was he? What was the story of his past life? Poor he must have been, or he would not have stopped at such a place as The Two Robins Inn; and weakened, probably, by long illness, or he could hardly have died in the manner which the landlord had described. Poor, ill, lonely, dead in a strange place, dead, with nobody but a stranger to pity him. A sad story; truly, on the mere face of it, a very sad story.

While these thoughts were passing through his mind, he had stopped insensibly at the window, close to which stood the foot of the bed with the closed curtains. At first he looked at it absently, then he became conscious that his eyes were fixed on it; and then a perverse desire took possession of him to do the very thing which he had resolved not to do up to this time: to look at the dead man.

He stretched out his hand towards the curtains, but checked himself in the very act of undrawing them, turned his back sharply on the bed, and walked towards the chimney-piece, to see what things were placed on it, and to try if he could keep the dead man out of his mind in that way.

There was a pewter inkstand on the chimney-piece, with some mildewed remains of ink in the bottle. There were two coarse china ornaments of the commonest kind; and there was a square of embossed card, dirty and fly-blown, with a collection of wretched riddles printed on it, in all sorts of zigzag directions, and in variously colored inks. He took the card and went away to read it at the table on which the candle was placed, sitting down with his back turned to the curtained bed.

He read the first riddle, the second, the third, all in one corner of the card, then turned it round impatiently to look at another. Before he could begin reading the riddles printed here the sound of the church clock stopped him.

Eleven.

He had got through an hour of the time in the room with the dead man.

Once more he looked at the card. It was not easy to make out the letters printed on it in consequence of the dimness of the light which the landlord had left him: a common tallow candle, furnished with a pair of heavy old-fashioned steel snuffers. Up to this time his mind had been too much occupied to think of the light. He had left the wick of the candle unsnuffed till it had risen higher than the flame, and had burned into an odd pent-house shape at the top, from which morsels of the charred cotton fell off from time to time in little flakes. He took up the snuffers now and trimmed the wick. The light brightened directly, and the room became less dismal.

Again he turned to the riddles, reading them doggedly and resolutely, now in one corner of the card, now in another. All his efforts, however, could not fix his attention on them. He pursued his occupation mechanically, deriving no sort of impression from what he was reading. It was as if a shadow from the curtained bed had got between his mind and the gaily-printed letters: a shadow that nothing could dispel. At last, he gave up the struggle, threw the card from him impatiently, and took to walking softly up and down the room again.

The dead man, the dead man, the hidden dead man on the bed!

There was the one persistent idea still haunting him. Hidden! Was it only the body being there, or was it the body being there, concealed, that was preying on his mind? He stopped at the window with that doubt in him, once more listening to the pattering rain, once more looking out into the black darkness.

Still the dead man!

The darkness forced his mind back upon itself, and set his memory at work, reviving with a painfully-vivid distinctness the momentary impression it had received from his first sight of the corpse. Before long the face seemed to be hovering out in the middle of the darkness, confronting him through the window, with the paleness whiter, with the dreadful dull line of light between the imperfectly closed eyelids broader than he had seen it, with the parted lips slowly dropping farther and farther away from each other, with the features growing larger and moving closer, till they seemed to fill the window, and to silence the rain, and to shut out the night.

The sound of a voice shouting below stairs woke him suddenly from the dream of his own distempered fancy. He recognized it as the voice of the landlord.

"Shut up at twelve, Ben," he heard it say. "I'm off to bed."

He wiped away the damp that had gathered on his forehead, reasoned with himself for a little while, and resolved to shake his mind free of the ghastly counterfeit which still clung to it by forcing himself to confront, if it was only for a moment, the solemn reality. Without allowing himself an instant to hesitate, he parted the curtains at the foot of the bed, and looked through.

There was the sad, peaceful, white face, with the awful mystery of stillness on it, laid back upon the pillow. No stir, no change there! He only looked at it for a moment before he closed the curtains again, but that moment steadied him, calmed him, restored him, mind and body, to himself. He returned to his old occupation of walking up and down the room, persevering in it this time till the clock struck again.

Twelve.

As the sound of the clock-bell died away, it was succeeded by the confused noise downstairs of the drinkers in the taproom leaving the house. The next sound, after an interval of silence, was caused by the barring of the door and the closing of the shutters at the back of the inn. Then the silence followed again, and was disturbed no more.

He was alone now: absolutely, hopelessly alone with the dead man till the next morning.

The wick of the candle wanted trimming again. He took up the snuffers, but paused suddenly on the very point of using them, and looked attentively at the candle, then back, over his shoulder, at the curtained bed, then again at the candle. It had been lighted for the first time to show him the way up stairs, and three parts of it, at least, were already consumed. In another hour it would be burned out. In another hour, unless he called at once to the man who had shut up the inn for a fresh candle, he would be left in the dark.

Strongly as his mind had been affected since he had entered the room, his unreasonable dread of encountering ridicule and of exposing his courage to suspicion had not altogether lost its influence over him even yet.

He lingered irresolutely by the table, waiting till he could prevail on himself to open the door, and call from the landing to the man who had shut up the inn. In his present hesitating frame of mind, it was a kind of relief to gain a few moments only by engaging in the trifling occupation of snuffing the candle. His hand trembled a little, and the snuffers were heavy and awkward to use. When he closed them on the wick, he closed them a hair's breadth too low. In an instant the candle was out, and the room was plunged in pitch darkness.

The one impression which the absence of light immediately produced on his mind was distrust of the curtained bed, distrust which shaped itself into no distinct idea, but which was powerful enough, in its very vagueness, to bind him down to his chair, to make his heart beat fast, and to set him listening intently. No sound stirred in the room, but the familiar sound of the rain against the window, louder and sharper now than he had heard it yet.

Still the vague distrust, the inexpressible dread possessed him, and kept him in his chair. He had put his carpet-bag on the table when he first entered the room, and he now took the key from his pocket, reached out his hand softly, opened the bag, and groped in it for his travelling writing-case, in which he knew that there was a small store of matches. When he had got one of the matches, he waited before he struck it on the coarse wooden table, and listened intently again without knowing why. Still there was no sound in the room but the steady, ceaseless rattling sound of the rain.

He lighted the candle again without another moment of delay, and, on the instant of its burning up, the first object in the room that his eyes sought for was the curtained bed.

Just before the light had been put out he had looked in that direction, and had seen no change, no disarrangement of any sort in the folds of the closely-drawn curtains.

When he looked at the bed now, he saw hanging over the side of it a long white hand.

It lay perfectly motionless midway on the side of the bed, where the curtain at the head and the curtain at the foot met. Nothing more was visible. The clinging curtains hid everything but the long white hand.

He stood looking at it, unable to stir, unable to call out, feeling nothing, knowing nothing, every faculty he possessed gathered up and lost in the one seeing faculty. How long that first panic held him he never could tell afterwards. It might have been only for a moment; it might have been for many minutes together. How he got to the bed; whether he ran to it headlong, or whether he approached it slowly: how he wrought himself up to unclose the curtains and look in, he never has remembered, and never will remember to his dying day. It is enough that he did go to the bed, and that he did look inside the curtains.

The man had moved. One of his arms was outside the clothes; his face was turned a little on the pillow; his eyelids were wide open. Changed as to position and as to one of the features, the face was otherwise fearfully and wonderfully unaltered. The dead paleness and the dead quiet were on it still.

One glance showed Arthur this; one glance before he flew breathlessly to the door and alarmed the house.

The man whom the landlord called "Ben" was the first to appear on the stairs. In three words Arthur told him what had happened, and sent him for the nearest doctor.

I, who tell you this story, was then staying with a medical friend of mine, in practice at Doncaster, taking care of his patients for him during his absence in London; and I, for the time being, was the nearest doctor. They had sent for me from the inn when the stranger was taken ill in the afternoon but I was not at home, and medical assistance was sought for elsewhere. When the man from The Two Robins rang the night-bell, I was just thinking of going to bed. Naturally enough, I did not believe a word of his story about a dead man who had come to life again. However, I put on my hat, armed myself with one or two bottles of restorative medicine, and ran to the inn, expecting to find nothing more remarkable, when I got there, than a patient in a fit.

My surprise at finding that the man had spoken the literal truth was almost, if not quite, equaled by my astonishment at finding myself face to face with Arthur Holliday as soon as I entered the bedroom. It was no time then for giving or seeking explanations. We just shook hands amazedly, and then I ordered everybody but Arthur out of the room, and hurried to the man on the bed.

The kitchen fire had not been long out. There was plenty of hot water in the boiler, and plenty of flannel to be had. With these, with my medicines, and with such help as Arthur could render under my direction, I dragged the man literally out of the jaws of death. In less than an hour from the time when I had been called in, he was alive and talking in the bed on which he had been laid out to wait for the coroner's inquest.

You will naturally ask me what had been the matter with him, and I might treat you, in reply, to a long theory, plentifully sprinkled with what the children call hard words. I prefer telling you that, in this case, cause and effect could not be satisfactorily joined together by any theory whatever. There are mysteries in life and the conditions of it which human science has not fathomed yet; and I candidly confess to you that, in bringing that man back to existence, I was, morally speaking, groping haphazard in the dark. I know (from the testimony of the doctor who attended him in the afternoon) that the vital machinery, so far as its action is appreciable by our senses, had, in this case, unquestionably stopped, and I am equally certain (seeing that I recovered him) that the vital principle was not extinct. When I add that he had suffered from a long and complicated illness, and that his whole nervous system was utterly deranged, I have told you all I really know of the physical condition of my dead-alive patient at The Two Robins Inn.

When he "came to," as the phrase goes, he was a startling object to look at, with his colorless face, his sunken cheeks, his wild black eyes, and his long black hair. The first question he asked me about himself when he could speak made me suspect that I had been called in to a man in my own profession. I mentioned to him my surmise, and he told me that I was right.

He said he had come last from Paris, where he had been attached to a hospital; that he had lately returned to England, on his way to Edinburgh, to continue his studies; that he had been taken ill on the journey; and that he had stopped to rest and recover himself at Doncaster. He did not add a word about his name, or who he was, and of course I did not question him on the subject. All I inquired when he ceased speaking was what branch of the profession he intended to follow.

"Any branch," he said, bitterly, "which will put bread into the mouth of a poor man."

At this, Arthur, who had been hitherto watching him in silent curiosity, burst out impetuously in his usual good-humored way:

"My dear fellow" (everybody was "my dear fellow" with Arthur), "now you have come to life again, don't begin by being downhearted about your prospects. I'll answer for it I can help you to some capital thing in the medical line, or, if I can't, I know my father can."

The medical student looked at him steadily.

"Thank you," he said, coldly; then added, "May I ask who your father is?"

"He's well enough known all about this part of the country; he is a great manufacturer, and his name is Holliday," replied Arthur.

My hand was on the man's wrist during this brief conversation. The instant the name of Holliday was pronounced I felt the pulse under my fingers flutter, stop, go on suddenly with a bound, and beat afterwards for a minute or two at the fever rate.

"How did you come here?" asked the stranger, quickly, excitably, passionately almost.

Arthur related briefly what had happened from the time of his first taking the bed at the inn.

"I am indebted to Mr. Holliday's son, then, for the help that has saved my life," said the medical student, speaking to himself, with a singular sarcasm in his voice. "Come here!"

He held out, as he spoke, his long, white, bony right hand.

"With all my heart," said Arthur, taking his hand cordially. "I may confess it now," he continued, laughing, "upon my honor, you almost frightened me out of my wits."

The stranger did not seem to listen. His wild black eyes were fixed with a look of eager interest on Arthur's face, and his long bony fingers kept tight hold of Arthur's hand. Young Holliday, on his side, returned the gaze, amazed and puzzled by the medical student's odd language and manners. The two faces were close together; I looked at them, and, to my amazement, I was suddenly impressed by the sense of a likeness between them: not in features or complexion, but solely in expression. It must have been a strong likeness, or I should certainly not have found it out, for I am naturally slow at detecting resemblances between faces.

"You have saved my life," said the strange man, still looking hard in Arthur's face, still holding tightly by his hand. "If you had been my own brother, you could not have done more for me than that."

He laid a singularly strong emphasis on those three words "my own brother," and a change passed over his face as he pronounced them; a change that no language of mine is competent to describe.

"I hope I have not done being of service to you yet," said Arthur. "I'll speak to my father as soon as I get home."

"You seem to be fond and proud of your father," said the medical student. "I suppose, in return, he is fond and proud of you?"

"Of course, he is," answered Arthur, laughing, "is there anything wonderful in that? Isn't your father fond . . ."

The stranger suddenly dropped young Holliday's hand and turned his face away.

"I beg your pardon," said Arthur. "I hope I have not unintentionally pained you. I hope you have not lost your father?"

"I can't well lose what I have never had," retorted the medical student, with a harsh mocking laugh.

"What you have never had!"

The strange man suddenly caught Arthur's hand again, suddenly looked once more hard in his face.

"Yes," he said, with a repetition of the bitter laugh. "You have brought a poor devil back into the world who has no business there. Do I astonish you? Well, I have a fancy of my own for telling you what men in my situation generally keep a secret. I have no name and no father. The merciful law of society tells me I am nobody's son! Ask your father if he will be my father too, and help me on in life with the family name."

Arthur looked at me more puzzled than ever.

I signed to him to say nothing, and laid my fingers again on the man's wrist. No. In spite of the extraordinary speech that he had just made, he was not, as I have been disposed to suspect, beginning to get light-headed. His pulse, by this time, had fallen back to a quiet, slow beat, and his skin was moist and cool. Not a symptom of fever or agitation about him.

Finding that neither of us answered him, he turned to me, and began talking of the extraordinary nature of his case, and asking my advice about the future course of medical treatment to which he ought to subject himself. I said the matter required careful thinking over, and suggested that I should send him a prescription a little later. He told me to write it at once, as he would most likely be leaving Doncaster in the morning before I was up. It was quite useless to represent to him the folly and danger of such a proceeding as this. He heard me politely and patiently, but held to his resolution, without offering any reasons or explanations, and repeated to me that, if I wished to give him a chance of seeing my prescription, I must write it at once.

Hearing this, Arthur volunteered the loan of a travelling writing-case which he said he had with him, and, bringing it to the bed, shook the note-paper out of the pocket of the case forthwith in his usual careless way. With the paper there fell out on the counterpane of the bed a small packet of sticking-plaster, and a little water-color drawing of a landscape.

The medical student took up the drawing and looked at it. His eye fell on some initials neatly written in cipher in one corner. He started and trembled; his pale face grew whiter than ever; his wild black eyes turned on Arthur, and looked through and through him.

"A pretty drawing," he said, in a remarkably quiet voice.

"Ah! and done by such a pretty girl," said Arthur. "Oh, such a pretty girl! I wish it was not a landscape; I wish it was a portrait of her!"

"You admire her very much?"

Arthur, half in jest, half in earnest, kissed his hand for answer.

"Love at first sight," said young Holliday, putting the drawing away again. "But the course of it doesn't run smooth. It's the old story. She's monopolized, as usual; trammelled by a rash engagement to some poor man who is never likely to get money enough to marry her. It was lucky I heard of it in time, or I should certainly have risked a declaration when she gave me that drawing. Here, doctor, here is pen, ink, and paper all ready for you."

"When she gave you that drawing? Gave it? gave it?"

He repeated the words slowly to himself, and suddenly closed his eyes. A momentary distortion passed across his face, and I saw one of his hands clutch up the bedclothes and squeeze them hard. I thought he was going to be ill again, and begged that there might be no more talking. He opened his eyes when I spoke, fixed them once more searchingly on Arthur, and said, slowly and distinctly,

"You like her, and she likes you. The poor man may die out of your way. Who can tell that she may not give you herself as well as her drawing, after all?"

Before young Holliday could answer, he turned to me, and said in a whisper, "Now for the prescription." From that time, though he spoke to Arthur again, he never looked at him more.

When I had written the prescription, he examined it, approved of it, and then astonished us both by abruptly wishing us good night. I offered to sit up with him, and he shook his head. Arthur offered to sit up with him, and he said, shortly, with his face turned away, "No." I insisted on having somebody left to watch him. He gave way when he found I was determined, and said he would accept the services of the waiter at the inn.

"Thank you both," he said, as we rose to go. "I have one last favor to ask: not of you, doctor, for I leave you to exercise your professional discretion, but of Mr. Holliday." His eyes, while he spoke, still rested steadily on me, and never once turned towards Arthur. "I beg that Mr. Holliday will not mention to anyone, least of all his father, the events that have occurred and the words that have passed in this room. I entreat him to bury me in his memory as, but for him, I might have been buried in my grave. I cannot give my reason for making this strange request. I can only implore him to grant it."

His voice faltered for the first time, and he hid his face on the pillow. Arthur, completely bewildered, gave the required pledge. I took young Holliday away with me immediately afterwards to the house of my friend, determined to go back to the inn and to see the medical student again before he had left in the morning.

I returned to the inn at eight o'clock, purposely abstaining from waking Arthur, who was sleeping off the past night's excitement on one of my friend's sofas. A suspicion had occurred to me, as soon as I was alone in my bedroom, which made me resolve that Holliday and the stranger whose life he had saved should not meet again, if I could prevent it.

I have already alluded to certain reports or scandals which I knew of relating to the early life of Arthur's father. While I was thinking, in my bed, of what had passed at the inn; of the change in the student's pulse when he heard the name of Holliday; of the resemblance of expression that I had discovered between his face and Arthur's; of the emphasis he had laid on those three words, "my own brother"; and of his incomprehensible acknowledgement of his own illegitimacy; while I was thinking of these things, the reports I have mentioned suddenly flew into my mind, and linked themselves fast to the chain of my previous reflections. Something within me whispered, "It is best that those two young men should not meet again." I felt it before I slept; I felt it when I woke; and I went, as I told you, alone to the inn the next morning.

I had missed my only opportunity of seeing my nameless patient again. He had been gone nearly an hour when I inquired for him.

I have now told you everything that I know for certain in relation to the man whom I brought back to life in the double-bedded room of the inn at Doncaster. What I have next to add is matter of inference and surmise, and is not, strictly speaking, matter of fact.

I have to tell you, first, that the medical student turned out to be strangely and unaccountably right in assuming it as more than probable that Arthur Holliday would marry the young lady who had given him the water-color drawing of the landscape. That marriage took place a little more than a year after the events occurred which I have just been relating.

The young couple came to live in the neighborhood in which I was then established in practice. I was present at the wedding and was rather surprised to find that Arthur was singularly reserved with me, both before and after his marriage, on the subject of the young lady's prior engagement. He only referred to it once when we were alone, merely telling me, on that occasion, that his wife had done all that honor and duty required of her in the matter, and that the engagement had been broken off with the full approval of her parents. I never heard more from him than this. For three years he and his wife lived together happily. At the expiration of that time the symptoms of a serious illness first declared themselves in Mrs. Arthur Holliday. It turned out to be a long, lingering, hopeless malady. I attended her throughout. We had been great friends when she was well, and we became more attached to each other than ever when she was ill. I had many long and interesting conversations with her in the intervals when she suffered least. The result of one of those conversations I may briefly relate, leaving you to draw any inferences from it that you please.

The interview to which I refer occurred shortly before her death.

I called one evening, as usual, and found her alone, with a look in her eyes which told me she had been crying. She only informed me at first that she had been depressed in spirits, but by little and little she became more communicative, and confessed to me that she had been looking over some old letter which had been addressed to her, before she had seen Arthur, by a man to whom she had been engaged to be married. I asked her how the engagement came to be broken off. She replied that it had not been broken off, but that it had died out in a very mysterious way. The person to whom she was engaged, her first love, she called him, was very poor and there was no immediate prospect of their being married. He followed my profession, and went abroad to study. They had corresponded regularly until the time when, as she believed, he had returned to England. From that period she heard no more of him. He was of a fretful, sensitive temperament, and she feared that she might have inadvertently done or said something to offend him. However that might be, he had never written to her again, and after waiting a year she had married Arthur. I asked when the first estrangement had begun, and found that the time at which she ceased to hear anything of her first lover exactly corresponded with the time at which I had been called in to my mysterious patient at The Two Robins Inn.

A fortnight after that conversation she died. In course of time Arthur married again. Of late years he has lived principally in London, and I have seen little or nothing of him.

I have some years to pass before I can approach to anything like a conclusion of this fragmentary narrative. And even when that later period is reached, the little that I have to say will not occupy your attention for more than a few minutes.

One rainy evening, while I was still practising as a country doctor, I was sitting alone, thinking over a case then under my charge, which sorely perplexed me, when I heard a low knock at the door of my room.

"Come in," I cried, looking up curiously to see who wanted me.

After a momentary delay, the lock moved, and a long, white, bony hand stole round the door as it opened, gently pushing it over a fold in the carpet which hindered it from working freely on the hinges. The hand was followed by a man whose face instantly struck me with a very strange sensation. There was something familiar to me in the look of him, and yet it was also something that suggested the idea of change.

He quietly introduced himself as "Mr. Lorn," presented to me some excellent professional recommendations, and proposed to fill the place, then vacant, of my assistant. While he was speaking, I noticed it as singular that we did not appear to be meeting each other like strangers, and that, while I was certainly startled at seeing him, he did not appear to be at all startled at seeing me.

It was on the tip of my tongue to say that I thought I had met with him before. But there was something in his face, and something in my own recollections, I can hardly say what, which unaccountably restrained me from speaking, and which as unaccountably attracted me to him at once, and made me feel ready and glad to accept his proposal.

He took his assistant's place on that very day. We got on together as if we had been old friends from the first; but, throughout the whole time of his residence in my house, he never volunteered any confidences on the subject of his past life, and I never approached the forbidden topic except by hints, which he resolutely refused to understand.

I had long had a notion that my patient at the inn might have been a natural son of the elder Mr. Holliday's, and that he might also have been the man who was engaged to Arthur's first wife. And now another idea occurred to me, that Mr. Lorn was the only person in existence who could, if he chose, enlighten me on both those doubtful points. But he never did choose, and I was never enlightened. He remained with me till I removed to London to try my fortune there as a physician for the second time, and then he went his way and I went mine, and we have never seen each other since.

I can add no more. I may have been right in my suspicion, or I may have been wrong. All I know is that, in those days of my country practice, when I came home late, and found my assistant asleep, and woke him, he used to look, in coming to, wonderfully like the stranger at Doncaster as he raised himself in the bed on that memorable night.

1857

· satirical → mocking

TOBERMORY

Saki (H. H. Munro)

IT WAS a chill, rain-washed afternoon of a late August day, that indefinite season when partridges are still in security or cold storage, and there is nothing to hunt—unless one is bounded on the north by the Bristol Channel, in which case one may lawfully gallop after fat red stags. Lady Blemley's house-party was not bounded on the north by the Bristol Channel, hence there was a full gathering of her guests round the tea-table on this particular afternoon. And, in spite of the blankness of the season and the triteness of the occasion, there was no trace in the company of that fatigued restlessness which means a dread of the pianola and a subdued hankering for auction bridge. The undisguised open-mouthed attention of the entire party was fixed on the homely negative personality of Mr. Cornelius Appin. Of all her guests, he was the one who had come to Lady Blemley with the vaguest reputation. Some one had said he was "clever," and he had got his invitation in the moderate expectation, on the part of his hostess, that some portion at least of his cleverness would be contributed to the general entertainment. Until tea-time that day she had been unable to discover in what direction, if any, his cleverness lay. He was neither a wit nor a croquet champion, a hypnotic force nor a begetter of amateur theatricals. Neither did his exterior suggest the sort of man in whom women are willing to pardon a generous measure of mental deficiency. He had subsided into mere Mr. Appin, and the Cornelius seemed a piece of transparent baptismal bluff. And now he was claiming to have launched on the world a discovery beside which the invention of gunpowder, of the printing-press, and of steam locomotion were inconsiderable trifles. Science had made bewildering strides in many directions during recent decades, but this thing seemed to belong to the domain of miracle rather than to scientific achievement.

"And do you really ask us to believe," Sir Wilfrid was saying, "that you

Supernatural ?

126

have discovered a means for instructing animals in the art of human speech, and that dear old Tobermory has proved your first successful pupil?"

"It is a problem at which I have worked for the last seventeen years," said Mr. Appin, "but only during the last eight or nine months have I been rewarded with glimmerings of success. Of course I have experimented with thousands of animals, but latterly only with cats, those wonderful creatures which have assimilated themselves so marvellously with our civilization while retaining all their highly developed feral instincts. Here and there among cats one comes across an outstanding superior intellect, just as one does among the ruck of human beings, and when I made the acquaintance of Tobermory a week ago I saw at once that I was in contact with a 'Beyond-cat' of extraordinary intelligence. I had gone far along the road to success in recent experiments; with Tobermory, as you call him, I have reached the goal."

Mr. Appin concluded his remarkable statement in a voice which he strove to divest of a triumphant inflection. No one said "Rats," though Clovis's lips moved in a monosyllabic contortion which probably invoked those rodents of disbelief.

"And do you mean to say," asked Miss Resker, after a slight pause, "that you have taught Tobermory to say and understand easy sentences of one syllable?"

"My dear Miss Resker," said the wonder-worker patiently, "one teaches little children and savages and backward adults in that piecemeal fashion; when one has once solved the problem of making a beginning with an animal of highly developed intelligence one has no need for those halting methods. Tobermory can speak our language with perfect correctness."

This time Clovis very distinctly said, "Beyond-rats!" Sir Wilfrid was more polite, but equally sceptical.

"Hadn't we better have the cat in and judge for ourselves?" suggested Lady Blemley.

Sir Wilfrid went in search of the animal, and the company settled themselves down to the languid expectation of witnessing some more or less adroit drawing-room ventriloquism.

In a minute Sir Wilfrid was back in the room, his face white beneath its tan and his eyes dilated with excitement.

"By Gad, it's true!"

His agitation was unmistakably genuine, and his hearers started forward in a thrill of awakened interest.

Collapsing into an armchair he continued breathlessly: "I found him dozing in the smoking-room and called out to him to come for his tea. He blinked at me in his usual way, and I said, 'Come on, Toby; don't keep us waiting'; and, by Gad! he drawled out in a most horribly natural voice that he'd come when he dashed well pleased! I nearly jumped out of my skin!"

Appin had preached to absolutely incredulous hearers; Sir Wilfred's statement carried instant conviction. A Babel-like chorus of startled exclamation arose, amid which the scientist sat mutely enjoying the first fruit of his stupendous discovery.

In the midst of the clamour Tobermory entered the room and made his way with velvet tread and studied unconcern across to the group seated round the tea-table.

A sudden hush of awkwardness and constraint fell on the company. Somehow there seemed an element of embarrassment in addressing on equal terms a domestic cat of acknowledged mental ability.

"Will you have some milk, Tobermory?" asked Lady Blemley in a rather strained voice.

"I don't mind if I do," was the response, couched in a tone of even indifference. A shiver of suppressed excitement went through the listeners, and Lady Blemley might be excused for pouring out the saucerful of milk rather unsteadily.

"I'm afraid I've spilt a good deal of it," she said apologetically.

"After all, it's not my Axminster," was Tobermory's rejoinder.

Another silence fell on the group, and then Miss Resker, in her best district-visitor manner, asked if the human language had been difficult to learn. Tobermory looked squarely at her for a moment and then fixed his gaze serenely on the middle distance. It was obvious that boring questions lay outside his scheme of life.

"What do you think of human intelligence?" asked Mavis Pellington lamely.

"Of whose intelligence in particular?" asked Tobermory coldly.

"Oh, well, mine for instance," said Mavis, with a feeble laugh.

"You put me in an embarrassing position," said Tobermory, whose tone and attitude certainly did not suggest a shred of embarrassment. "When your inclusion in this house-party was suggested Sir Wilfrid protested that you were the most brainless woman of his acquaintance, and that there was a wide distinction between hospitality and the care of the feeble-minded. Lady Blemley replied that your lack of brain-power was the precise quality which had earned you your invitation, as you were the only person she could think of who might be idiotic enough to buy their old car. You know, the one they call 'The Envy of Sisyphus,' because it goes quite nicely up-hill if you push it."

Lady Blemley's protestations would have had greater effect if she had not casually suggested to Mavis only that morning that the car in question would be just the thing for her down at her Devonshire home.

Major Barfield plunged in heavily to effect a diversion.

"How about your carryings-on with the tortoise-shell puss up at the stables, eh?"

The moment he had said it every one realized the blunder.

"One does not usually discuss these matters in public," said Tobermory frigidly. "From a slight observation of your ways since you've been in this house I should imagine you'd find it inconvenient if I were to shift the conversation on to your own little affairs."

The panic which ensued was not confined to the Major.

"Would you like to go and see if cook has got your dinner ready?" suggested Lady Blemley hurriedly, affecting to ignore the fact that it wanted at least two hours to Tobermory's dinner-time.

"Thanks," said Tobermory, "not quite so soon after my tea. I don't want to die of indigestion."

"Cats have nine lives, you know," said Sir Wilfrid heartily.

"Possibly," answered Tobermory; "but only one liver."

"Adelaide!" said Mrs. Cornett, "do you mean to encourage that cat to go out and gossip about us in the servants' hall?"

The panic had indeed become general. A narrow ornamental balustrade ran in front of most of the bedroom windows at the Towers, and it was recalled with dismay that this had formed a favourite promenade for Tobermory at all hours, whence he could watch the pigeons—and heaven knew what else besides. If he intended to become reminiscent in his present outspoken strain the effect would be something more than disconcerting. Mrs. Cornett, who spent much time at her toilet table, and whose complexion was reputed to be of a nomadic though punctual disposition, looked as ill at ease as the Major. Miss Scrawen, who wrote fiercely sensuous poetry and led a blameless life, merely displayed irritation; if you are methodical and virtuous in private you don't necessarily want every one to know it. Bertie van Tahn, who was so depraved at seventeen that he had long ago given up trying to be any worse, turned a dull shade of gardenia white, but he did not commit the error of dashing out of the room like Odo Finsberry, a young gentleman who was understood to be reading for the Church and who was possibly disturbed at the thought of scandals he might hear concerning other people. Clovis had the presence of mind to maintain a composed exterior; privately he was calculating how long it would take to procure a box of fancy mice through the agency of the *Exchange and Mart* as a species of hush-money.

Even in a delicate situation like the present, Agnes Resker could not endure to remain too long in the background.

"Why did I ever come down here?" she asked dramatically.

Tobermory immediately accepted the opening.

"Judging by what you said to Mrs. Cornett on the croquet-lawn yesterday, you were out for food. You described the Blemleys as the dullest people to stay with that you knew, but said they were clever enough to employ a first-rate cook; otherwise they'd find it difficult to get any one to come down a second time."

"There's not a word of truth in it! I appeal to Mrs. Cornett—" exclaimed the discomfited Agnes.

"Mrs. Cornett repeated your remark afterwards to Bertie van Tahn," continued Tobermory, "and said, 'That woman is a regular Hunger Marcher; she'd go anywhere for four square meals a day,' and Bertie van Tahn said—"

At this point the chronicle mercifully ceased. Tobermory had caught a glimpse of the big yellow Tom from the Rectory working his way through the shrubbery towards the stable wing. In a flash he had vanished through the open French window.

With the disappearance of his too brilliant pupil Cornelius Appin found himself beset by a hurricane of bitter upbraiding, anxious inquiry, and frightened entreaty. The responsibility for the situation lay with him, and he must prevent matters from becoming worse. Could Tobermory impart his dangerous gift to other cats? was the first question he had to answer. It was possible, he replied, that he might have initiated his intimate friend the stable puss into his new accomplishment, but it was unlikely that his teaching could have taken a wider range as yet.

"Then," said Mrs. Cornett, "Tobermory may be a valuable cat and a great pet; but I'm sure you'll agree, Adelaide, that both he and the stable cat must be done away with without delay."

"You don't suppose I've enjoyed the last quarter of an hour, do you?" said Lady Blemley bitterly. "My husband and I are very fond of Tobermory—at least, we were before this horrible accomplishment was infused into him; but now, of course, the only thing is to have him destroyed as soon as possible."

"We can put some strychnine in the scraps he always gets at dinner-time," said Sir Wilfrid, "and I will go and drown the stable cat myself. The coachman will be very sore at losing his pet, but I'll say a very catching form of mange has broken out in both cats and we're afraid of its spreading to the kennels."

"But my great discovery!" expostulated Mr. Appin; "after all my years of research and experiment—"

"You can go and experiment on the short-horns at the farm, who are under proper control," said Mrs. Cornett, "or the elephants at the Zoological Gardens. They're said to be highly intelligent, and they have this recommendation, that they don't come creeping about our bedrooms and under chairs, and so forth."

An archangel ecstatically proclaiming the Millennium, and then finding that it clashed unpardonably with Henley and would have to be indefinitely postponed, could hardly have felt more crestfallen than Cornelius Appin at the reception of his wonderful achievement. Public opinion, however, was against him—in fact, had the general voice been consulted on the subject it is probable that a strong minority vote would have been in favour of including him in the strychnine diet.

Defective train arrangements and a nervous desire to see matters brought to a finish prevented an immediate dispersal of the party, but dinner that evening was not a social success. Sir Wilfrid had had rather a trying time with the stable cat and subsequently with the coachman. Agnes Resker ostentatiously limited her repast to a morsel of dry toast, which she bit as though it were a personal enemy; while Mavis Pellington maintained a vindictive silence throughout the meal. Lady Blemley kept up a flow of what she hoped was conversation, but her attention was fixed on the doorway. A plateful of carefully dosed fish scraps was in readiness on the sideboard, but sweets and savoury and dessert went their way, and no Tobermory appeared either in the dining-room or kitchen.

The sepulchral dinner was cheerful compared with the subsequent vigil in the smoking-room. Eating and drinking had at least supplied a distraction and cloak to the prevailing embarrassment. Bridge was out of the question in the general tension of nerves and tempers, and after Odo Finsberry had given a lugubrious rendering of "Mélisande in the Wood" to a frigid audience, music was tacitly avoided. At eleven the servants went to bed, announcing that the small window in the pantry had been left open as usual for Tobermory's private use. The guests read steadily through the current batch of magazines, and fell back gradually on the "Badminton Library" and bound volumes of *Punch*. Lady Blemley made periodic visits to the pantry, returning each time with an expression of listless depression which forestalled questioning.

At two o'clock Clovis broke the dominating silence.

"He won't turn up tonight. He's probably in the local newspaper office at the present moment, dictating the first instalment of his reminiscences. Lady What's-her-name's book won't be in it. It will be the event of the day."

Having made this contribution to the general cheerfulness, Clovis went to bed. At long intervals the various members of the house-party followed his example.

The servants taking round the early tea made a uniform announcement in reply to a uniform question. Tobermory had not returned.

Breakfast was, if anything, a more unpleasant function than dinner had been, but before its conclusion the situation was relieved. Tobermory's

→ RIP TOBERMORY ✗ ✗
                                       b/c got into
                                          a fight

Saki

corpse was brought in <u>from the shrubbery</u>, where a gardener had just discovered it. From the <u>bites on his throat</u> and the yellow fur which coated
his claws it was evident that he had fallen in unequal combat with the
big Tom from the Rectory.   → *true arson*

By midday most of the guests had quitted the Towers, and after lunch
<u>Lady Blemley</u> had sufficiently recovered her spirits to write an extremely
nasty letter to the Rectory about the loss of her valuable pet.

Tobermory had been Appin's one successful pupil, and he was destined
to have no successor. A few weeks later an elephant in the Dresden
Zoological Garden, which had shown no previous signs of irritability,
broke loose and <u>killed an Englishman who had apparently been teasing
it.</u> The victim's name was variously reported in the papers as Oppin and
Eppelin, but his front name was faithfully rendered Cornelius.

"If he was trying German irregular verbs on the poor beast," said
Clovis, "he deserved all he got."

1911

A LODGING FOR THE NIGHT

Robert Louis Stevenson

IT WAS late in November 1456. The snow fell over Paris with rigorous, relentless persistence; sometimes the wind made a sally and scattered it in flying vortices; sometimes there was a lull, and flake after flake descended out of the black night air, silent, circuitous, interminable. To poor people, looking up under moist eyebrows, it seemed a wonder where it all came from. Master Francis Villon had propounded an alternative that afternoon, at a tavern window: was it only Pagan Jupiter plucking geese upon Olympus, or were the holy angels moulting? He was only a poor Master of Arts, he went on; and as the question somewhat touched upon divinity, he durst not venture to conclude. A silly old priest from Montargis, who was among the company, treated the young rascal to a bottle of wine in honour of the jest and the grimaces with which it was accompanied, and swore on his own white beard that he had been just such another irreverent dog when he was Villon's age.

The air was raw and pointed, but not far below freezing; and the flakes were large, damp, and adhesive. The whole city was sheeted up. An army might have marched from end to end and not a footfall given the alarm. If there were any belated birds in heaven, they saw the island like a large white patch, and the bridges like slim white spars, on the black ground of the river. High up overhead the snow settled among the tracery of the cathedral towers. Many a niche was drifted full; many a statue wore a long white bonnet on its grotesque or sainted head. The gargoyles had been transformed into great false noses, drooping towards the point. The crockets were like upright pillows swollen on one side. In the intervals of the wind there was a dull sound of dripping about the precincts of the church.

The cemetery of St. John had taken its own share of the snow. All the graves were decently covered; tall, white housetops stood around in grave array; worthy burghers were long ago in bed, benightcapped like their domiciles; there was no light in all the neighbourhood but a little peep from a lamp that hung swinging in the church choir, and tossed the shadows to and fro in time to its oscillations. The clock was hard on ten when the patrol went by with halberds and a lantern, beating their hands; and they saw nothing suspicious about the cemetery of St. John.

Yet there was a small house, backed up against the cemetery wall, which was still awake, and awake to evil purpose, in that snoring district. There was not much to betray it from without; only a stream of warm vapour from the chimney-top, a patch where the snow melted on the roof, and a few half-obliterated footprints at the door. But within, behind the shuttered windows, Master Francis Villon, the poet, and some of the thievish crew with whom he consorted, were keeping the night alive and passing round the bottle.

A great pile of living embers diffused a strong and ruddy glow from the arched chimney. Before this straddled Dom Nicolas, the Picardy monk, with his skirts picked up and his fat legs bared to the comfortable warmth. His dilated shadow cut the room in half; and the firelight only escaped on either side of his broad person, and in a little pool between his outspread feet. His face had the beery, bruised appearance of the continual drinker's; it was covered with a network of congested veins, purple in ordinary circumstances, but now pale violet, for even with his back to the fire the cold pinched him on the other side. His cowl had half fallen back, and made a strange excrescence on either side of his bull neck. So he straddled, grumbling, and cut the room in half with the shadow of his portly frame.

On the right, Villon and Guy Tabary were huddled together over a scrap of parchment; Villon making a ballade which he was to call the *Ballade of Roast Fish,* and Tabary spluttering admiration at his shoulder. The poet was a rag of a man, dark, little, and lean, with hollow cheeks and thin black locks. He carried his four-and-twenty years with feverish animation. Greed had made folds about his eyes, evil smiles had puckered his mouth. The wolf and pig struggled together in his face. It was an eloquent, sharp, ugly, earthly countenance. His hands were small and prehensile, with fingers knotted like a cord; and they were continually flickering in front of him in violent and expressive pantomime. As for Tabary, a broad, complacent, admiring imbecility breathed from his squash nose and slobbering lips: he had become a thief, just as he might have become the most decent of burgesses, by the imperious chance that rules the lives of human geese and human donkeys.

At the monk's other hand, Montigny and Thevenin Pensete played a game of chance. About the first there clung some flavour of good birth and training, as about a fallen angel; something long, lithe, and courtly in the person; something aquiline and darkling in the face. Thevenin, poor soul, was in great feather: he had done a good stroke of knavery that afternoon in the Faubourg St. Jacques, and all night he had been gaining from Montigny. A flat smile illuminated his face; his bald head shone rosily in a garland of red curls; his little protuberant stomach shook with silent chucklings as he swept in his gains.

"Doubles or quits?" said Thevenin.

Montigny nodded grimly.

"Some may prefer to dine in state," wrote Villon, *"On bread and cheese on silver plate.* Or—or—help me out, Guido!"

Tabary giggled.

"Or parsley on a golden dish," scribbled the poet.

The wind was freshening without; it drove the snow before it, and sometimes raised its voice in a victorious whoop, and made sepulchral grumblings in the chimney. The cold was growing sharper as the night went on. Villon, protruding his lips, imitated the gust with something between a whistle and a groan. It was an eerie, uncomfortable talent of the poet's, much detested by the Picardy monk.

"Can't you hear it rattle in the gibbet?" said Villon. "They are all dancing the devil's jig on nothing, up there. You may dance, my gallants, you'll be none the warmer! Whew, what a gust! Down went somebody just now! A medlar the fewer on the three-legged medlar-tree!—I say, Dom Nicolas, it'll be cold to-night on the St. Denis Road?" he asked.

Dom Nicolas winked both his big eyes, and seemed to choke upon his Adam's apple. Montfaucon, the great grisly Paris gibbet, stood hard by the St. Denis Road, and the pleasantry touched him on the raw. As for Tabary, he laughed immoderately over the medlars; he had never heard anything more light-hearted; and he held his sides and crowed. Villon fetched him a fillip on the nose, which turned his mirth into an attack of coughing.

"Oh, stop that row," said Villon, "and think of rhymes to 'fish.'"

"Doubles or quits," said Montigny doggedly.

"With all my heart," quoth Thevenin.

"Is there any more in that bottle?" asked the monk.

"Open another," said Villon. "How do you ever hope to fill that big hogshead, your body, with little things like bottles? And how do you expect to get to heaven? How many angels, do you fancy, can be spared to carry up a single monk from Picardy? Or do you think yourself another Elias—and they'll send the coach for you?"

"Hominibus impossibile," replied the monk, as he filled his glass.

Tabary was in ecstasies.

Villon filliped his nose again.

"Laugh at my jokes, if you like," he said.

"It was very good," objected Tabary.

Villon made a face at him. "Think of rhymes to 'fish,'" he said. "What have you to do with Latin? You'll wish you knew none of it at the great assizes, when the devil calls for Guido Tabary, clericus—the devil with the humpback and red-hot finger-nails. Talking of the devil," he added in a whisper, "look at Montigny!"

All three peered covertly at the gamester. He did not seem to be enjoying his luck. His mouth was a little to a side; one nostril nearly shut, and the other much inflated. The black dog was on his back, as people say, in terrifying nursery metaphor; and he breathed hard under the gruesome burden.

"He looks as if he could knife him," whispered Tabary, with round eyes.

The monk shuddered, and turned his face and spread his open hands to the red embers. It was the cold that thus affected Dom Nicolas, and not any excess of moral sensibility.

"Come now," said Villon—"about this ballade. How does it run so far?" And beating time with his hand, he read it aloud to Tabary.

They were interrupted at the fourth rhyme by a brief and fatal movement among the gamesters. The round was completed, and Thevenin was just opening his mouth to claim another victory, when Montigny leaped up, swift as an adder, and stabbed him to the heart. The blow took effect before he had time to utter a cry, before he had time to move. A tremor or two convulsed his frame; his hands opened and shut, his heels rattled on the floor; then his head rolled backward over one shoulder with the eyes wide open, and Thevenin Pensete's spirit had returned to Him who made it.

Everyone sprang to his feet; but the business was over in two twos. The four living fellows looked at each other in rather a ghastly fashion; the dead man contemplating a corner of the roof with a singular and ugly leer.

"My God!" said Tabary, and he began to pray in Latin.

Villon broke out into hysterical laughter. He came a step forward and ducked a ridiculous bow at Thevenin, and laughed still louder. Then he sat down suddenly, all of a heap, upon a stool, and continued laughing bitterly as though he would shake himself to pieces.

Montigny recovered his composure first.

"Let's see what he has about him," he remarked; and he picked the dead man's pockets with a practised hand, and divided the money into four equal portions on the table. "There's for you," he said.

The monk received his share with a deep sigh, and a single stealthy glance at the dead Thevenin, who was beginning to sink into himself and topple sideways off the chair.

"We're all in for it," cried Villon, swallowing his mirth. "It's a hanging job for every man jack of us that's here—not to speak of those who aren't." He made a shocking gesture in the air with his raised right hand, and put out his tongue and threw his head on one side, so as to counterfeit the appearance of one who has been hanged. Then he pocketed his share of the spoil, and executed a shuffle with his feet as if to restore the circulation.

Tabary was the last to help himself; he made a dash at the money, and retired to the other end of the apartment.

Montigny stuck Thevenin upright in the chair, and drew out the dagger, which was followed by a jet of blood.

"You fellows had better be moving," he said, as he wiped the blade on his victim's doublet.

"I think we had," returned Villon with a gulp. "Damn his fat head!" he broke out. "It sticks in my throat like phlegm. What right has a man to have red hair when he is dead?" And he fell all of a heap again upon the stool, and fairly covered his face with his hands.

Montigny and Dom Nicolas laughed aloud, even Tabary feebly chiming in.

"Cry baby," said the monk.

"I always said he was a woman," added Montigny with a sneer. "Sit up, can't you?" he went on, giving another shake to the murdered body. "Tread out that fire, Nick!"

But Nick was better employed; he was quietly taking Villon's purse, as the poet sat, limp and trembling, on the stool where he had been making a ballade not three minutes before. Montigny and Tabary dumbly demanded a share of the booty, which the monk silently promised as he passed the little bag into the bosom of his gown. In many ways an artistic nature unfits a man for practical existence.

No sooner had the theft been accomplished than Villon shook himself, jumped to his feet, and began helping to scatter and extinguish the embers. Meanwhile Montigny opened the door and cautiously peered into the street. The coast was clear; there was no meddlesome patrol in sight. Still it was judged wiser to slip out severally; and as Villon was himself in a hurry to escape from the neighbourhood of the dead Thevenin, and the rest were in a still greater hurry to get rid of him before he should discover the loss of his money, he was the first by general consent to issue forth into the street.

The wind had triumphed and swept all the clouds from heaven. Only a few vapours, as thin as moonlight, fleeted rapidly across the stars. It was bitter cold; and by a common optical effect, things seemed almost more definite than in the broadest daylight. The sleeping city was absolutely still: a company of white hoods, a field full of little Alps, below the twinkling stars. Villon cursed his fortune. Would it were still snowing! Now, wherever he went he left an indelible trail behind him on the glittering

streets; wherever he went he was still tethered to the house by the cemetery of St. John; wherever he went he must weave, with his own plod-
ding feet, the rope that bound him to the crime and would bind him to
the gallows. The leer of the dead man came back to him with a new significance. He snapped his fingers as if to pluck up his own spirits, and
choosing a street at random, stepped boldly forward in the snow.

Two things preoccupied him as he went: the aspect of the gallows at
Montfaucon in this bright windy phase of the night's existence, for one;
and for another, the look of the dead man with his bald head and garland
of red curls. Both struck cold upon his heart, and he kept quickening his
pace as if he could escape from unpleasant thoughts by mere fleetness of
foot. Sometimes he looked back over his shoulder with a sudden nervous
jerk; but he was the only moving thing in the white streets, except when
the wind swooped round a corner and threw up the snow, which was
beginning to freeze, in spouts of glittering dust.

Suddenly he saw, a long way before him, a black clump and a couple
of lanterns. The clump was in motion, and the lanterns swung as though
carried by men walking. It was a patrol. And though it was merely crossing his line of march, he judged it wiser to get out of eyeshot as speedily as he could. He was not in the humour to be challenged, and he was
conscious of making a very conspicuous mark upon the snow. Just on his
left hand there stood a great hotel, with some turrets and a large porch
before the door; it was half-ruinous, he remembered, and had long stood
empty; and so he made three steps of it and jumped into the shelter of
the porch. It was pretty dark inside, after the glimmer of the snowy
streets, and he was groping forward with outspread hands, when he stumbled over some substance which offered an indescribable mixture of
resistances, hard and soft, firm and loose. His heart gave a leap, and he
sprang two steps back and stared dreadfully at the obstacle. Then he gave
a little laugh of relief. It was only a woman, and she dead. He knelt
beside her to make sure upon this latter point. She was freezing cold, and
rigid like a stick. A little ragged finery fluttered in the wind about her
hair, and her cheeks had been heavily rouged that same afternoon. Her
pockets were quite empty; but in her stocking, underneath the garter,
Villon found two of the small coins that went by the name of whites. It
was little enough; but it was always something; and the poet was moved
with a deep sense of pathos that she should have died before she had
spent her money. That seemed to him a dark and pitiable mystery; and
he looked from the coins in his hand to the dead woman, and back again
to the coins, shaking his head over the riddle of man's life. Henry V. of
England, dying at Vincennes just after he had conquered France, and this
poor jade cut off by a cold draught in a great man's doorway, before she
had time to spend her couple of whites—it seemed a cruel way to carry

on the world. Two whites would have taken such a little while to squander; and yet it would have been one more good taste in the mouth, one more smack of the lips, before the devil got the soul, and the body was left to birds and vermin. He would like to use all his tallow before the light was blown out and the lantern broken.

While these thoughts were passing through his mind, he was feeling, half-mechanically, for his purse. Suddenly his heart stopped beating; a feeling of cold scales passed up the back of his legs, and a cold blow seemed to fall upon his scalp. He stood petrified for a moment; then he felt again with one feverish movement; and then his loss burst upon him, and he was covered with perspiration. To spendthrifts money is so living and actual—it is such a thin veil between them and their pleasures! There is only one limit to their fortune—that of time; and a spendthrift with only a few crowns is the Emperor of Rome until they are spent. For such a person to lose his money is to suffer the most shocking reverse, and fall from heaven to hell, from all to nothing, in a breath. And all the more if he has put his head in the halter for it; if he may be hanged to-morrow for that same purse, so dearly earned, so foolishly departed. Villon stood and cursed; he threw the two whites into the street; he shook his fist at heaven; he stamped, and was not horrified to find himself trampling the poor corpse. Then he began rapidly to retrace his steps towards the house beside the cemetery. He had forgotten all fear of the patrol, which was long gone by at any rate, and had no idea but that of his lost purse. It was in vain that he looked right and left upon the snow; nothing was to be seen. He had not dropped it in the streets. Had it fallen in the house? He would have liked dearly to go in and see; but the idea of the grisly occupant unmanned him. And he saw besides, as he drew near, that their efforts to put out the fire had been unsuccessful; on the contrary, it had broken into a blaze, and a changeful light played in the chinks of door and window, and revived his terror for the authorities and Paris gibbet.

He returned to the hotel with the porch, and groped about upon the snow for the money he had thrown away in his childish passion. But he could only find one white; the other had probably struck sideways and sunk deeply in. With a single white in his pocket, all his projects for a rousing night in some wild tavern vanished utterly away. And it was not only pleasure that fled laughing from his grasp; positive discomfort, positive pain, attacked him as he stood ruefully before the porch. His perspiration had dried upon him; and though the wind had now fallen, a binding frost was setting in stronger with every hour, and he felt benumbed and sick at heart. What was to be done? Late as was the hour, improbable as was success, he would try the house of his adopted father, the chaplain of St. Benoît.

He ran there all the way, and knocked timidly. There was no answer.

He knocked again and again, taking heart with every stroke; and at last steps were heard approaching from within. A barred wicket fell open in the iron-studded door, and emitted a gush of yellow light.

"Hold up your face to the wicket," said the chaplain from within.

"It's only me," whimpered Villon.

"Oh, it's only you, is it?" returned the chaplain; and he cursed him with foul unpriestly oaths for disturbing him at such an hour, and bade him be off to hell, where he came from.

"My hands are blue to the wrists," pleaded Villon; "my feet are dead and full of twinges; my nose aches with the sharp air; the cold lies at my heart. I may be dead before morning. Only this once, father, and before God I will never ask again."

"You should have come earlier," said the ecclesiastic, coolly. "Young men require a lesson now and then." He shut the wicket and retired deliberately into the interior of the house.

Villon was beside himself; he beat upon the door with his hands and feet, and shouted hoarsely after the chaplain.

"Wormy old fox!" he cried. "If I had my hand under your twist, I would send you flying headlong into the bottomless pit."

A door shut in the interior, faintly audible to the poet down long passages. He passed his hand over his mouth with an oath. And then the humour of the situation struck him, and he laughed and looked lightly up to heaven, where the stars seemed to be winking over his discomfiture.

What was to be done? It looked very like a night in the frosty streets. The idea of the dead woman popped into his imagination, and gave him a hearty fright; what had happened to her in the early night might very well happen to him before morning. And he so young! and with such immense possibilities of disorderly amusement before him! He felt quite pathetic over the notion of his own fate, as if it had been some one else's, and made a little imaginative vignette of the scene in the morning when they should find his body.

He passed all his chances under review, turning the white between his thumb and forefinger. Unfortunately he was on bad terms with some old friends who would once have taken pity on him in such a plight. He had lampooned them in verses, he had beaten and cheated them; and yet now, when he was in so close a pinch, he thought there was at least one who might perhaps relent. It was a chance. It was worth trying at least, and he would go and see.

On the way, two little accidents happened to him which coloured his musings in a very different manner. For, first, he fell in with the track of a patrol, and walked in it for some yards, although it lay out of his direction. And this spirited him up; at least he had confused his trail; for he was still possessed with the idea of people tracking him all about Paris over the snow, and collaring him next morning before he was awake. The other matter affected him very differently. He passed a street corner, where, not so long before, a woman and her child had been devoured by wolves. This was just the kind of weather, he reflected, when wolves might take it into their heads to enter Paris again; and a lone man in these deserted streets would run the chance of something worse than a mere scare. He stopped and looked upon the place with an unpleasant inter-est—it was a centre where several lanes intersected each other; and he looked down them all one after another, and held his breath to listen, lest he should detect some galloping black things on the snow or hear the sound of howling between him and the river. He remembered his mother telling him the story and pointing out the spot, while he was yet a child. His mother! If he only knew where she lived, he might make sure at least of shelter. He determined he would inquire upon the mor-row: nay, he would go and see her too, poor old girl! So thinking, he arrived at his destination—his last hope for the night.

The house was quite dark, like its neighbours, and yet after a few taps, he heard a movement overhead, a door opening, and a cautious voice asking who was there. The poet named himself in a loud whisper, and waited, not without some trepidation, the result. Nor had he to wait long. A window was suddenly opened, and a pailful of slops splashed down upon the doorstep. Villon had not been unprepared for something of the sort, and had put himself as much in shelter as the nature of the porch admitted; but for all that, he was deplorably drenched below the waist. His hose began to freeze almost at once. Death from cold and exposure stared him in the face; he remembered he was of phthisical ten-dency, and began coughing tentatively. But the gravity of the danger steadied his nerves. He stopped a few hundred yards from the door where he had been so rudely used, and reflected with his finger to his nose. He could only see one way of getting a lodging, and that was to take it. He had noticed a house not far away which looked as if it might be easily broken into, and thither he betook himself promptly, entertain-ing himself on the way with the idea of a room still hot, with a table still loaded with the remains of supper, where he might pass the rest of the black hours, and whence he should issue, on the morrow, with an arm-ful of valuable plate. He even considered on what viands and what wines he should prefer; and as he was calling the roll of his favourite dainties, roast fish presented itself to his mind with an odd mixture of amusement and horror.

"I shall never finish that ballade," he thought to himself; and then, with another shudder at the recollection, "Oh, damn his fat head!" he repeated fervently, and spat upon the snow.

The house in question looked dark at first sight; but as Villon made a preliminary inspection in search of the handiest point of attack, a little twinkle of light caught his eye from behind a curtained window.

"The devil!" he thought. "People awake! Some student or some saint, confound the crew! Can't they get drunk and lie in bed snoring like their neighbours! What's the good of curfew, and poor devils of bell-ringers jumping at a rope's end in bell-towers? What's the use of day, if people sit up all night? The gripes to them!" He grinned as he saw where his logic was leading him. "Every man to his business, after all," added he, "and if they're awake, by the Lord, I may come by a supper honestly for this once, and cheat the devil."

He went boldly to the door, and knocked with an assured hand. On both previous occasions he had knocked timidly and with some dread of attracting notice; but now, when he had just discarded the thought of a burglarious entry, knocking at a door seemed a mighty simple and innocent proceeding. The sound of his blows echoed through the house with thin, phantasmal reverberations, as though it were quite empty; but these had scarcely died away before a measured tread drew near, a couple of bolts were withdrawn, and one wing was opened broadly, as though no guile or fear of guile were known to those within. A tall figure of a man, muscular and spare, but a little bent, confronted Villon. The head was massive in bulk, but finely sculptured; the nose blunt at the bottom but refining upward to where it joined a pair of strong and honest eyebrows; the mouth and eyes surrounded with delicate markings, and the whole face based upon a thick white beard, boldly and squarely trimmed. Seen as it was by the light of a flickering hand-lamp, it looked perhaps nobler than it had a right to do; but it was a fine face, honourable rather than intelligent, strong, simple, and righteous.

"You knock late, sir," said the old man in resonant, courteous tones.

Villon cringed, and brought up many servile words of apology; at a crisis of this sort, the beggar was uppermost in him, and the man of genius hid his head with confusion.

"You are cold," repeated the old man, "and hungry? Well, step in." And he ordered him into the house with a noble enough gesture.

"Some great seigneur," thought Villon, as his host, setting down the lamp on the flagged pavement of the entry, shot the bolts once more into their places.

"You will pardon me if I go in front," he said, when this was done; and he preceded the poet up-stairs into a large apartment, warmed with a pan of charcoal and lit by a great lamp hanging from the roof. It was very bare of furniture; only some gold plate on a sideboard; some folios; and a stand of armour between the windows. Some smart tapestry hung upon the walls, representing the crucifixion of our Lord in one piece, and in another a scene of shepherds and shepherdesses by a running stream. Over the chimney was a shield of arms.

"Will you seat yourself," said the old man, "and forgive me if I leave you? I am alone in my house to-night, and if you are to eat I must forage for you myself."

No sooner was his host gone than Villon leaped from the chair on which he had just seated himself, and began examining the room, with the stealth and passion of a cat. He weighed the gold flagons in his hand, opened all the folios, and investigated the arms upon the shield, and the stuff with which the seats were lined. He raised the window-curtains, and saw that the windows were set with rich stained glass in figures, so far as he could see, of martial import. Then he stood in the middle of the room, drew a long breath, and retaining it with puffed cheeks, looked round and round him, turning on his heels, as if to impress every feature of the apartment on his memory.

"Seven pieces of plate," he said. "If there had been ten I would have risked it. A fine house, and a fine old master, so help me all the saints."

And just then, hearing the old man's tread returning along the corridor, he stole back to his chair, and began toasting his wet legs before the charcoal pan.

His entertainer had a plate of meat in one hand and a jug of wine in the other. He set down the plate upon the table, motioning Villon to draw in his chair, and going to the sideboard, brought back two goblets, which he filled.

"I drink to your better fortune," he said, gravely touching Villon's cup with his own.

"To our better acquaintance," said the poet, growing bold. A mere man of the people would have been awed by the courtesy of the old seigneur, but Villon was hardened in that matter; he had made mirth for great lords before now, and found them as black rascals as himself. And so he devoted himself to the viands with a ravenous gusto, while the old man, leaning backward, watched him with steady, curious eyes.

"You have blood on your shoulder, my man," he said.

Montigny must have laid his wet right hand upon him as he left the house. He cursed Montigny in his heart.

"It was none of my shedding," he stammered.

"I had not supposed so," returned his host quietly. "A brawl?"

"Well, something of that sort," Villon admitted with a quaver.

"Perhaps a fellow murdered?"

"Oh, no, not murdered," said the poet, more and more confused. "It was all fair play—murdered by accident. I had no hand in it, God strike me dead!" he added fervently.

"One rogue the fewer, I dare say," observed the master of the house.

"You may dare to say that," agreed Villon, infinitely relieved. "As big a rogue as there is between here and Jerusalem. He turned up his toes like a lamb. But it was a nasty thing to look at. I dare say you've seen dead men in your time, my lord?" he added, glancing at the armour.

"Many," said the old man. "I have followed the wars, as you imagine." Villon laid down his knife and fork, which he had just taken up again. "Were any of them bald?" he asked.

"Oh, yes, and with hair as white as mine."

"I don't think I would mind the white so much," said Villon. "His was red." And he had a return of his shuddering and tendency to laughter, which he drowned with a great draught of wine. "I'm a little put out when I think of it," he went on. "I knew him—damn him! And then the cold gives a man fancies—or the fancies give a man cold, I don't know which."

"Have you any money?" asked the old man.

"I have one white," returned the poet, laughing. "I got it out of a dead jade's stocking in a porch. She was as dead as Caesar, poor wench, and as cold as a church, with bits of ribbon sticking in her hair. This is a hard world in winter for wolves and wenches and poor rogues like me."

"I," said the old man, "am Enguerrand de la Feuillée, seigneur de Brisetout, bailly du Patatrac. Who and what may you be?"

Villon rose and made a suitable reverence. "I am called Francis Villon," he said, "a poor Master of Arts of this university. I know some Latin, and a deal of vice. I can make chansons, ballades, lais, virelais, and roundels, and I am very fond of wine. I was born in a garret, and I shall not improbably die upon the gallows. I may add, my lord, that from this night forward I am your lordship's very obsequious servant to command."

"No servant of mine," said the knight; "my guest for this evening, and no more."

"A very grateful guest," said Villon politely; and he drank in dumb show to his entertainer.

"You are shrewd," began the old man, tapping his forehead, "very shrewd; you have learning; you are a clerk; and yet you take a small piece of money off a dead woman in the street. Is it not a kind of theft?"

"It is a kind of theft much practised in the wars, my lord."

"The wars are the field of honour," returned the old man proudly. "There a man plays his life upon the cast; he fights in the name of his lord the king, his Lord God, and all their lordships the holy saints and angels."

"Put it," said Villon, "that I were really a thief, should I not play my life also, and against heavier odds?"

"For gain, and not for honour."

"Gain?" repeated Villon with a shrug. "Gain! The poor fellow wants supper, and takes it. So does the soldier in a campaign. Why, what are all these requisitions we hear so much about? If they are not gain to those who take them, they are loss enough to the others. The men-at-arms drink by a good fire, while the burgher bites his nails to buy them wine and wood. I have seen a good many ploughmen swinging on trees about the country; ay, I have seen thirty on one elm, and a very poor figure they made; and when I asked some one how all these came to be hanged, I was told it was because they could not scrape together enough crowns to satisfy the men-at-arms."

"These things are a necessity of war, which the low-born must endure with constancy. It is true that some captains drive over hard; there are spirits in every rank not easily moved by pity; and, indeed, many follow arms who are no better than brigands."

"You see," said the poet, "you cannot separate the soldier from the brigand; and what is a thief but an isolated brigand with circumspect manners? I steal a couple of mutton chops, without so much as disturbing the farmer's sheep; the farmer grumbles a bit, but sups none the less wholesomely on what remains. You come up blowing gloriously on a trumpet, take away the whole sheep, and beat the farmer pitifully into the bargain. I have no trumpet; I am only Tom, Dick, or Harry; I am a rogue and a dog, and hanging's too good for me—with all my heart—but just you ask the farmer which of us he prefers, just find out which of us he lies awake to curse on cold nights."

"Look at us two," said his lordship. "I am old, strong, and honoured. If I were turned from my house to-morrow, hundreds would be proud to shelter me. Poor people would go out and pass the night in the streets with their children, if I merely hinted that I wished to be alone. And I find you up, wandering homeless, and picking farthings off dead women by the wayside! I fear no man and nothing; I have seen you tremble and lose countenance at a word. I wait God's summons contentedly in my own house, or, if it please the king to call me out again, upon the field of battle. You look for the gallows; a rough, swift death, without hope or honour. Is there no difference between these two?"

"As far as to the moon," Villon acquiesced. "But if I had been born lord of Brisetout, and you had been the poor scholar Francis, would the difference have been any the less? Should not I have been warming my knees at this charcoal pan, and would not you have been groping for farthings in the snow? Should not I have been the soldier, and you the thief?"

"A thief!" cried the old man. "I a thief! If you understood your words, you would repent them."

Villon turned out his hands with a gesture of inimitable impudence. "If your lordship had done me the honour to follow my argument!" he said.

"I do you too much honour in submitting to your presence," said the knight. "Learn to curb your tongue when you speak with old and honourable men, or some one hastier than I may reprove you in a sharper fashion." And he rose and paced the lower end of the apartment, struggling with anger and antipathy. Villon surreptitiously refilled his cup, and settled himself more comfortably in the chair, crossing his knees and leaning his head upon one hand and the elbow against the back of the chair. He was now replete and warm; and he was in nowise frightened for his host, having gauged him as justly as was possible between two such different characters. The night was far spent, and in a very comfortable fashion after all; and he felt morally certain of a safe departure on the morrow.

"Tell me one thing," said the old man, pausing in his walk. "Are you really a thief?"

"I claim the sacred rights of hospitality," returned the poet. "My lord, I am."

"You are very young," the knight continued.

"I should never have been so old," replied Villon, showing his fingers, "if I had not helped myself with these ten talents. They have been my nursing mothers and my nursing fathers."

"You may still repent and change."

"I repent daily," said the poet. "There are few people more given to repentance than poor Francis. As for change, let somebody change my circumstances. A man must continue to eat, if it were only that he may continue to repent."

"The change must begin in the heart," returned the old man solemnly.

"My dear lord," answered Villon, "do you really fancy that I steal for pleasure? I hate stealing, like any other piece of work or danger. My teeth chatter when I see a gallows. But I must eat, I must drink, I must mix in society of some sort. What the devil! Man is not a solitary animal—*Cui Deus foeminam tradit.* Make me king's pantler—make me abbot of St. Denis; make me bailly of the Patatrac; and then I shall be changed indeed. But as long as you leave me the poor scholar Francis Villon, without a farthing, why, of course, I remain the same."

"The grace of God is all-powerful."

"I should be a heretic to question it," said Francis. "It has made you lord of Brisetout, and bailly of the Patatrac; it has given me nothing but the quick wits under my hat and these ten toes upon my hands. May I help myself to wine? I thank you respectfully. By God's grace, you have a very superior vintage."

The lord of Brisetout walked to and fro with his hands behind his back. Perhaps he was not yet quite settled in his mind about the parallel between thieves and soldiers; perhaps Villon had interested him by some cross-thread of sympathy; perhaps his wits were simply muddled by so much unfamiliar reasoning; but whatever the cause, he somehow yearned to convert the young man to a better way of thinking, and could not make up his mind to drive him forth again into the street.

"There is something more than I can understand in this," he said at length. "Your mouth is full of subtleties, and the devil has led you very far astray; but the devil is only a very weak spirit before God's truth, and all his subtleties vanish at a word of true honour, like darkness at morning. Listen to me once more. I learned long ago that a gentleman should live chivalrously and lovingly to God, and the king, and his lady; and though I have seen many strange things done, I have still striven to command my ways upon that rule. It is not only written in all noble histories, but in every man's heart, if he will take care to read. You speak of food and wine, and I know very well that hunger is a difficult trial to endure; but you do not speak of other wants; you say nothing of honour, of faith to God and other men, of courtesy, of love without reproach. It may be that I am not very wise—and yet I think I am—but you seem to me like one who has lost his way and made a great error in life. You are attending to the little wants, and you have totally forgotten the great and only real ones, like a man who should be doctoring a toothache on the Judgment Day. For such things as honour and love and faith are not only nobler than food and drink, but, indeed, I think that we desire them more, and suffer more sharply for their absence. I speak to you as I think you will most easily understand me. Are you not, while careful to fill your belly, disregarding another appetite in your heart, which spoils the pleasure of your life and keeps you continually wretched?"

Villon was sensibly nettled under all this sermonising. "You think I have no sense of honour!" he cried. "I'm poor enough, God knows! It's hard to see rich people with their gloves, and you blowing your hands. An empty belly is a bitter thing, although you speak so lightly of it. If you had had as many as I, perhaps you would change your tune. Anyway, I'm a thief—make the most of that—but I'm not a devil from hell, God strike me dead. I would have you to know I've an honour of my own, as good as yours, though I don't prate about it all day long, as if it were a God's miracle to have any. It seems quite natural to me; I keep it in its box till it's wanted. Why now, look you here, how long have I been in this room with you? Did you not tell me you were alone in the house? Look at your gold plate! You're strong, if you like, but you're old and unarmed, and I have my knife. What did I want but a jerk of the elbow, and here would have been you with the cold steel in your bowels, and there would have been me, linking in the streets, with an armful of gold cups! Did you suppose I hadn't wit enough to see that? And I scorned the action. There are your damned goblets, as safe as in a church; there are you, with your heart ticking as good as new; and here am I, ready to go out again as poor as I came in, with my one white that you threw in my teeth! And you think I have no sense of honour—God strike me dead!"

The old man stretched out his right arm. "I will tell you what you are," he said. "You are a rogue, my man, an impudent and a black-hearted rogue and vagabond. I have passed an hour with you. Oh! believe me, I feel myself disgraced! And you have eaten and drank at my table. But now I am sick at your presence; the day has come, and the night-bird should be off to his roost. Will you go before, or after?"

"Which you please," returned the poet, rising. "I believe you to be strictly honourable." He thoughtfully emptied his cup. "I wish I could add you were intelligent," he went on, knocking on his head with his knuckles. "Age, age! the brains stiff and rheumatic."

The old man preceded him from a point of self-respect; Villon followed, whistling, with his thumbs in his girdle.

"God pity you," said the lord of Brisetout at the door.

"Good-bye, papa," returned Villon, with a yawn. "Many thanks for the cold mutton."

The door closed behind him. The dawn was breaking over the white roofs. A chill, uncomfortable morning ushered in the day. Villon stood and heartily stretched himself in the middle of the road.

"A very dull old gentleman," he thought. "I wonder what his goblets may be worth."

1877

"OH, WHISTLE, AND I'LL COME TO YOU, MY LAD"

M. R. James

"I SUPPOSE you will be getting away pretty soon, now Full term is over, Professor," said a person not in the story to the Professor of Ontography, soon after they had sat down next to each other at a feast in the hospitable hall of St. James's College.

The Professor was young, neat, and precise in speech.

"Yes," he said; "my friends have been making me take up golf this term, and I mean to go to the East Coast—in point of fact to Burnstow—(I dare say you know it) for a week or ten days, to improve my game. I hope to get off to-morrow."

"Oh, Parkins," said his neighbour on the other side, "if you are going to Burnstow, I wish you would look at the site of the Templars' preceptory, and let me know if you think it would be any good to have a dig there in the summer."

It was, as you might suppose, a person of antiquarian pursuits who said this, but, since he merely appears in this prologue, there is no need to give his entitlements.

"Certainly," said Parkins, the Professor: "if you will describe to me whereabouts the site is, I will do my best to give you an idea of the lie of the land when I get back; or I could write to you about it, if you would tell me where you are likely to be."

"Don't trouble to do that, thanks. It's only that I'm thinking of taking my family in that direction in the Long, and it occurred to me that, as very few of the English preceptories have ever been properly planned, I might have an opportunity of doing something useful on off-days."

The Professor rather sniffed at the idea that planning out a preceptory could be described as useful. His neighbour continued:

"The site—I doubt if there is anything showing above ground—must be down quite close to the beach now. The sea has encroached tremendously, as you know, all along that bit of coast. I should think, from the map, that it must be about three-quarters of a mile from the Globe Inn, at the north end of the town. Where are you going to stay?"

"Well, *at* the Globe Inn, as a matter of fact," said Parkins; "I have engaged a room there. I couldn't get in anywhere else; most of the lodging-houses are shut up in winter, it seems; and, as it is, they tell me that the only room of any size I can have is really a double-bedded one, and that they haven't a corner in which to store the other bed, and so on. But I must have a fairly large room, for I am taking some books down, and mean to do a bit of work; and though I don't quite fancy having an empty bed—not to speak of two—in what I may call for the time being my study, I suppose I can manage to rough it for the short time I shall be there."

"Do you call having an extra bed in your room roughing it, Parkins?" said a bluff person opposite. "Look here, I shall come down and occupy it for a bit; it'll be company for you."

The Professor quivered, but managed to laugh in a courteous manner.

"By all means, Rogers; there's nothing I should like better. But I'm afraid you would find it rather dull; you don't play golf, do you?"

"No, thank Heaven!" said rude Mr. Rogers.

"Well, you see, when I'm not writing I shall most likely be out on the links, and that, as I say, would be rather dull for you, I'm afraid."

"Oh, I don't know! There's certain to be somebody I know in the place; but, of course, if you don't want me, speak the word, Parkins; I shan't be offended. Truth, as you always tell us, is never offensive."

Parkins was, indeed, scrupulously polite and strictly truthful. It is to be feared that Mr. Rogers sometimes practised upon his knowledge of these characteristics. In Parkins's breast there was a conflict now raging, which for a moment or two did not allow him to answer. That interval being over, he said:

"Well, if you want the exact truth, Rogers, I was considering whether the room I speak of would really be large enough to accommodate us both comfortably; and also whether (mind, I shouldn't have said this if you hadn't pressed me) you would not constitute something in the nature of a hindrance to my work."

Rogers laughed loudly.

"Well done, Parkins!" he said. "It's all right. I promise not to interrupt your work; don't you disturb yourself about that. No, I won't come if you don't want me; but I thought I should do so nicely to keep the ghosts off." Here he might have been seen to wink and to nudge his next neighbour. Parkins might also have been seen to become pink. "I beg pardon, Parkins," Rogers continued; "I oughtn't to have said that. I forgot you didn't like levity on these topics."

"Well," Parkins said, "as you have mentioned the matter, I freely own that I do *not* like careless talk about what you call ghosts. A man in my position," he went on, raising his voice a little, "cannot, I find, be too careful about appearing to sanction the current beliefs on such subjects. As you know, Rogers, or as you ought to know; for I think I have never concealed my views——"

"No, you certainly have not, old man," put in Rogers *sotto voce*.

"——I hold that any semblance, any appearance of concession to the view that such things might exist is equivalent to a renunciation of all that I hold most sacred. But I'm afraid I have not succeeded in securing your attention."

"Your *undivided* attention, was what Dr. Blimber actually *said*," Rogers interrupted, with every appearance of an earnest desire for accuracy. "But I beg your pardon, Parkins: I'm stopping you."

"No, not at all," said Parkins. "I don't remember Blimber; perhaps he was before my time. But I needn't go on. I'm sure you know what I mean."

"Yes, yes," said Rogers, rather hastily—"just so. We'll go into it fully at Burnstow, or somewhere."

In repeating the above dialogue I have tried to give the impression which it made on me, that Parkins was something of an old woman—rather henlike, perhaps, in his little ways; totally destitute, alas! of the sense of humour, but at the same time dauntless and sincere in his convictions, and a man deserving of the greatest respect. Whether or not the reader has gathered so much, that was the character which Parkins had.

On the following day Parkins did, as he had hoped, succeed in getting away from his college, and in arriving at Burnstow. He was made welcome at the Globe Inn, was safely installed in the large double-bedded room of which we have heard, and was able before retiring to rest to arrange his materials for work in apple-pie order upon a commodious table which occupied the outer end of the room, and was surrounded on three sides by windows looking out seaward; that is to say, the central window looked straight out to sea, and those on the left and right commanded prospects along the shore to the north and south respectively. On the south you saw the village of Burnstow. On the north no houses were to be seen, but only the beach and the low cliff backing it. Immediately in front was a strip—not considerable—of rough grass, dotted with old anchors, capstans, and so forth; then a broad path; then the beach. Whatever may have been the original distance between the Globe Inn and the sea, not more than sixty yards now separated them.

The rest of the population of the inn was, of course, a golfing one, and included few elements that call for a special description. The most conspicuous figure was, perhaps, that of an *ancien militaire*, secretary of a

London club, and possessed of a voice of incredible strength, and of views of a pronouncedly Protestant type. These were apt to find utterance after his attendance upon the ministrations of the Vicar, an estimable man with inclinations towards a picturesque ritual, which he gallantly kept down as far as he could out of deference to East Anglian tradition.

Professor Parkins, one of whose principal characteristics was pluck, spent the greater part of the day following his arrival at Burnstow in what he had called improving his game, in company with this Colonel Wilson: and during the afternoon—whether the process of improvement were to blame or not, I am not sure—the Colonel's demeanour assumed a colouring so lurid that even Parkins jibbed at the thought of walking home with him from the links. He determined, after a short and furtive look at that bristling moustache and those incarnadined features, that it would be wiser to allow the influences of tea and tobacco to do what they could with the Colonel before the dinner-hour should render a meeting inevitable.

"I might walk home to-night along the beach," he reflected—"yes, and take a look—there will be light enough for that—at the ruins of which Disney was talking. I don't exactly know where they are, by the way; but I expect I can hardly help stumbling on them."

This he accomplished, I may say, in the most literal sense, for in picking his way from the links to the shingle beach his foot caught, partly in a gorse-root and partly in a biggish stone, and over he went. When he got up and surveyed his surroundings, he found himself in a patch of somewhat broken ground covered with small depressions and mounds. These latter, when he came to examine them, proved to be simply masses of flints embedded in mortar and grown over with turf. He must, he quite rightly concluded, be on the site of the preceptory he had promised to look at. It seemed not unlikely to reward the spade of the explorer; enough of the foundations was probably left at no great depth to throw a good deal of light on the general plan. He remembered vaguely that the Templars, to whom this site had belonged, were in the habit of building round churches, and he thought a particular series of the humps or mounds near him did appear to be arranged in something of a circular form. Few people can resist the temptation to try a little amateur research in a department quite outside their own, if only for the satisfaction of showing how successful they would have been had they only taken it up seriously. Our Professor, however, if he felt something of this mean desire, was also truly anxious to oblige Mr. Disney. So he paced with care the circular area he had noticed, and wrote down its rough dimensions in his pocket-book. Then he proceeded to examine an oblong eminence which lay east of the centre of the circle, and seemed to his thinking likely to be the base of a platform or altar. At one end of it, the northern, a patch of the turf was gone—removed by some boy or other creature *ferae naturae*. It might, he thought, be as well to probe the soil here for evidences of masonry, and he took out his knife and began scraping away the earth. And now followed another little discovery: a portion of soil fell inward as he scraped, and disclosed a small cavity. He lighted one match after another to help him to see of what nature the hole was, but the wind was too strong for them all. By tapping and scratching the sides with his knife, however, he was able to make out that it must be an artificial hole in masonry. It was rectangular, and the sides, top, and bottom, if not actually plastered, were smooth and regular. Of course it was empty. No! As he withdrew the knife he heard a metallic clink, and when he introduced his hand it met with a cylindrical object lying on the floor of the hole. Naturally enough, he picked it up, and when he brought it into the light, now fast fading, he could see that it, too, was of man's making—a metal tube about four inches long, and evidently of some considerable age.

By the time Parkins had made sure that there was nothing else in this odd receptacle, it was too late and too dark for him to think of undertaking any further search. What he had done had proved so unexpectedly interesting that he determined to sacrifice a little more of the daylight on the morrow to archaeology. The object which he now had safe in his pocket was bound to be of some slight value at least, he felt sure.

Bleak and solemn was the view on which he took a last look before starting homeward. A faint yellow light in the west showed the links, on which a few figures moving towards the club-house were still visible, the squat martello tower, the lights of Aldsey village, the pale ribbon of sands intersected at intervals by black wooden groynes, the dim and murmuring sea. The wind was bitter from the north, but was at his back when he set out for the Globe. He quickly rattled and clashed through the shingle and gained the sand, upon which, but for the groynes which had to be got over every few yards, the going was both good and quiet. One last look behind, to measure the distance he had made since leaving the ruined Templars' church, showed him a prospect of company on his walk, in the shape of a rather indistinct personage, who seemed to be making great efforts to catch up with him, but made little, if any, progress. I mean that there was an appearance of running about his movements, but that the distance between him and Parkins did not seem materially to lessen. So, at least, Parkins thought, and decided that he almost certainly did not know him, and that it would be absurd to wait until he came up. For all that, company, he began to think, would really be very welcome on that lonely shore, if only you could choose your companion. In his unenlightened days he had read of meetings in such places which even now would hardly bear thinking of. He went on thinking of them, however, until he reached home, and particularly of one which catches most people's fancy at some time of their childhood. "Now I saw in my dream that Christian had gone but a very little way when he saw a foul fiend coming over the field to meet him." "What should I do now," he thought, "if I looked back and caught sight of a black figure sharply defined against the yellow sky, and saw that it had horns and wings? I wonder whether I should stand or run for it. Luckily, the gentleman behind is not of that kind, and he seems to be about as far off now as when I saw him first. Well, at this rate he won't get his dinner as soon as I shall; and, dear me! it's within a quarter of an hour of the time now. I must run!"

Parkins had, in fact, very little time for dressing. When he met the Colonel at dinner, Peace—or as much of her as that gentleman could manage—reigned once more in the military bosom; nor was she put to flight in the hours of bridge that followed dinner, for Parkins only was a more than respectable player. When, therefore, he retired towards twelve o'clock, he felt that he had spent his evening in quite a satisfactory way, and that, even for so long as a fortnight or three weeks, life at the Globe would be supportable under similar conditions—"especially," thought he, "if I go on improving my game."

As he went along the passages he met the boots of the Globe, who stopped and said:

"Beg your pardon, sir, but as I was a-brushing your coat just now there was somethink fell out of the pocket. I put it on your chest of drawers, sir, in your room, sir—a piece of a pipe or somethink of that, sir. Thank you, sir. You'll find it on your chest of drawers, sir—yes, sir. Good night, sir."

The speech served to remind Parkins of his little discovery of that afternoon. It was with some considerable curiosity that he turned it over by the light of his candles. It was of bronze, he now saw, and was shaped very much after the manner of the modern dog-whistle; in fact it was—yes, certainly it was—actually no more nor less than a whistle. He put it to his lips, but it was quite full of a fine, caked-up sand or earth, which would not yield to knocking, but must be loosened with a knife. Tidy as ever in his habits, Parkins cleared out the earth on to a piece of paper, and took the latter to the window to empty it out. The night was clear and bright, as he saw when he had opened the casement, and he stopped for an instant to look at the sea and note a belated wanderer stationed on the shore in front of the inn. Then he shut the window, a little surprised at the late hours people kept at Burnstow, and took his whistle to the light again. Why, surely there were marks on it, not merely marks, but letters! A very little rubbing rendered the deeply-cut inscription quite legible, but the Professor had to confess, after some earnest thought, that the meaning of it was as obscure to him as the writing on the wall to Belshazzar. There were legends both on the front and on the back of the whistle. The one read thus:

$$\text{FUR} \begin{array}{c} \text{FLA} \\ \text{FLE} \end{array} \text{BIS}$$

The other:

⚜ QUIS EST ISTE QUI UENIT ⚜

"I ought to be able to make it out," he thought; "but I suppose I am a little rusty in my Latin. When I come to think of it, I don't believe I even know the word for a whistle. The long one does seem simple enough. It ought to mean, 'Who is this who is coming?' Well, the best way to find out is evidently to whistle for him."

He blew tentatively and stopped suddenly, startled and yet pleased at the note he had elicited. It had a quality of infinite distance in it, and, soft as it was, he somehow felt it must be audible for miles round. It was a sound, too, that seemed to have the power (which many scents possess) of forming pictures in the brain. He saw quite clearly for a moment a vision of a wide, dark expanse at night, with a fresh wind blowing, and in the midst a lonely figure—how employed, he could not tell. Perhaps he would have seen more had not the picture been broken by the sudden surge of a gust of wind against his casement, so sudden that it made him look up, just in time to see the white glint of a sea-bird's wing somewhere outside the dark panes.

The sound of the whistle had so fascinated him that he could not help trying it once more, this time more boldly. The note was little, if at all, louder than before, and repetition broke the illusion—no picture followed, as he had half hoped it might. "But what is this? Goodness! what force the wind can get up in a few minutes! What a tremendous gust! There! I knew that window-fastening was no use! Ah! I thought so—both candles out. It's enough to tear the room to pieces."

The first thing was to get the window shut. While you might count twenty Parkins was struggling with the small casement, and felt almost as if he were pushing back a sturdy burglar, so strong was the pressure. It slackened all at once, and the window banged to and latched itself. Now to relight the candles and see what damage, if any, had been done. No, nothing seemed amiss; no glass even was broken in the casement. But the noise had evidently roused at least one member of the household: the Colonel was to be heard stumping in his stockinged feet on the floor above, and growling.

Quickly as it had risen, the wind did not fall at once. On it went, moaning and rushing past the house, at times rising to a cry so desolate that, as Parkins disinterestedly said, it might have made fanciful people feel quite uncomfortable; even the unimaginative, he thought after a quarter of an hour, might be happier without it.

Whether it was the wind, or the excitement of golf, or of the researches in the preceptory that kept Parkins awake, he was not sure. Awake he remained, in any case, long enough to fancy (as I am afraid I often do myself under such conditions) that he was the victim of all manner of fatal disorders: he would lie counting the beats of his heart, convinced that it was going to stop work every moment, and would entertain grave suspicions of his lungs, brain, liver, etc.—suspicions which he was sure would be dispelled by the return of daylight, but which until then refused to be put aside. He found a little vicarious comfort in the idea that someone else was in the same boat. A near neighbour (in the darkness it was not easy to tell his direction) was tossing and rustling in his bed, too.

The next stage was that Parkins shut his eyes and determined to give sleep every chance. Here again over-excitement asserted itself in another form—that of making pictures. *Experto crede,* pictures do come to the closed eyes of one trying to sleep, and are often so little to his taste that he must open his eyes and disperse them.

Parkins's experience on this occasion was a very distressing one. He found that the picture which presented itself to him was continuous. When he opened his eyes, of course, it went; but when he shut them once more it framed itself afresh, and acted itself out again, neither quicker nor slower than before. What he saw was this:

A long stretch of shore—shingle edged by sand, and intersected at short intervals with black groynes running down to the water—a scene, in fact, so like that of his afternoon's walk that, in the absence of any landmark, it could not be distinguished therefrom. The light was obscure, conveying an impression of gathering storm, late winter evening, and slight cold rain. On this bleak stage at first no actor was visible. Then, in the distance, a bobbing black object appeared; a moment more, and it was a man running, jumping, clambering over the groynes, and every few seconds looking eagerly back. The nearer he came the more obvious it was that he was not only anxious, but even terribly frightened, though his face was not to be distinguished. He was, moreover, almost at the end of his strength. On he came; each successive obstacle seemed to cause him more difficulty than the last. "Will he get over this next one?" thought Parkins; "it seems a little higher than the others." Yes; half climbing, half throwing himself, he did get over, and fell all in a heap on the other side (the side nearest to the spectator). There, as if really unable to get up again, he remained crouching under the groyne, looking up in an attitude of painful anxiety.

So far no cause whatever for the fear of the runner had been shown; but now there began to be seen, far up the shore, a little flicker of something light-coloured moving to and fro with great swiftness and irregularity. Rapidly growing larger, it, too, declared itself as a figure in pale, fluttering draperies, ill-defined. There was something about its motion which made Parkins very unwilling to see it at close quarters. It would stop, raise arms, bow itself toward the sand, then run stooping across the beach to the water-edge and back again; and then, rising upright, once more continue its course forward at a speed that was startling and terrifying. The moment came when the pursuer was hovering about from left to right only a few yards beyond the groyne where the runner lay in hiding. After two or three ineffectual castings hither and thither it came to a stop, stood upright, with arms raised high, and then darted straight forward towards the groyne.

It was at this point that Parkins always failed in his resolution to keep his eyes shut. With many misgivings as to incipient failure of eyesight, overworked brain, excessive smoking, and so on, he finally resigned himself to light his candle, get out a book, and pass the night waking, rather than be tormented by this persistent panorama, which he saw clearly enough could only be a morbid reflection of his walk and his thoughts on that very day.

The scraping of match on box and the glare of light must have startled some creatures of the night—rats or what not—which he heard scurry across the floor from the side of his bed with much rustling. Dear, dear! the match is out! Fool that it is! But the second one burnt better, and a candle and book were duly procured, over which Parkins pored till sleep of a wholesome kind came upon him, and that in no long space. For about the first time in his orderly and prudent life he forgot to blow out the candle, and when he was called next morning at eight there was still a flicker in the socket and a sad mess of guttered grease on the top of the little table.

After breakfast he was in his room, putting the finishing touches to his golfing costume—fortune had again allotted the Colonel to him for a partner—when one of the maids came in.

"Oh, if you please," she said, "would you like any extra blankets on your bed, sir?"

"Ah! thank you," said Parkins. "Yes, I think I should like one. It seems likely to turn rather colder."

In a very short time the maid was back with the blanket.

"Which bed should I put it on, sir?" she asked.

"What? Why, that one—the one I slept in last night," he said, pointing to it.

"Oh yes! I beg your pardon, sir, but you seemed to have tried both of 'em; leastways, we had to make 'em both up this morning."

"Really? How very absurd!" said Parkins. "I certainly never touched the other, except to lay some things on it. Did it actually seem to have been slept in?"

"Oh yes, sir!" said the maid. "Why, all the things was crumpled and throwed about all ways, if you'll excuse me, sir—quite as if anyone 'adn't passed but a very poor night, sir."

"Dear me," said Parkins. "Well, I may have disordered it more than I thought when I unpacked my things. I'm very sorry to have given you the trouble, I'm sure. I expect a friend of mine soon, by the way—a gentleman from Cambridge—to come and occupy it for a night or two. That will be all right, I suppose, won't it?"

"Oh yes, to be sure, sir. Thank you, sir. It's no trouble, I'm sure," said the maid, and departed to giggle with her colleagues.

Parkins set forth, with a stern determination to improve his game.

I am glad to be able to report that he succeeded so far in this enterprise that the Colonel, who had been rather repining at the prospect of a second day's play in his company, became quite chatty as the morning advanced; and his voice boomed out over the flats, as certain also of our own minor poets have said, "like some great bourdon in a minster tower."

"Extraordinary wind, that, we had last night," he said. "In my old home we should have said someone had been whistling for it."

"Should you, indeed!" said Parkins. "Is there a superstition of that kind still current in your part of the country?"

"I don't know about superstition," said the Colonel. "They believe in it all over Denmark and Norway, as well as on the Yorkshire coast; and my experience is, mind you, that there's generally something at the bottom of what these country-folk hold to, and have held to for generations. But it's your drive" (or whatever it might have been: the golfing reader will have to imagine appropriate digressions at the proper intervals).

When conversation was resumed, Parkins said, with a slight hesitancy:

"Apropos of what you were saying just now, Colonel, I think I ought to tell you that my own views on such subjects are very strong. I am, in fact, a convinced disbeliever in what is called the 'supernatural.'"

"What!" said the Colonel, "do you mean to tell me you don't believe in second-sight, or ghosts, or anything of that kind?"

"In nothing whatever of that kind," returned Parkins firmly.

"Well," said the Colonel, "but it appears to me at that rate, sir, that you must be little better than a Sadducee."

Parkins was on the point of answering that, in his opinion, the Sadducees were the most sensible persons he had ever read of in the Old Testament; but, feeling some doubt as to whether much mention of them was to be found in that work, he preferred to laugh the accusation off.

"Perhaps I am," he said; "but——Here, give me my cleek, boy!—Excuse me one moment, Colonel." A short interval. "Now, as to whistling for the wind, let me give you my theory about it. The laws which govern winds are really not at all perfectly known—to fisher-folk and such, of course, not known at all. A man or woman of eccentric habits, perhaps, or a stranger, is seen repeatedly on the beach at some unusual hour, and is heard whistling. Soon afterwards a violent wind rises; a man who could read the sky perfectly or who possessed a barometer could have foretold that it would. The simple people of a fishing-village have no barometers, and only a few rough rules for prophesying weather. What more natural than that the eccentric personage I postulated should be regarded as having raised the wind, or that he or she should clutch eagerly at the reputation of being able to do so? Now, take last night's wind: as it happens, I myself was whistling. I blew a whistle twice, and the wind seemed to come absolutely in answer to my call. If anyone had seen me——"

The audience had been a little restive under this harangue, and Parkins had, I fear, fallen somewhat into the tone of a lecturer; but at the last sentence the Colonel stopped.

"Whistling, were you?" he said. "And what sort of whistle did you use? Play this stroke first." Interval.

"About that whistle you were asking, Colonel. It's rather a curious one. I have it in my——No; I see I've left it in my room. As a matter of fact, I found it yesterday."

And then Parkins narrated the manner of his discovery of the whistle, upon hearing which the Colonel grunted, and opined that, in Parkins's place, he should himself be careful about using a thing that had belonged to a set of Papists, of whom, speaking generally, it might be affirmed that you never knew what they might not have been up to. From this topic he diverged to the enormities of the Vicar, who had given notice on the previous Sunday that Friday would be the Feast of St. Thomas the Apostle, and that there would be service at eleven o'clock in the church. This and other similar proceedings constituted in the Colonel's view a strong presumption that the Vicar was a concealed Papist, if not a Jesuit; and Parkins, who could not very readily follow the Colonel in this region, did not disagree with him. In fact, they got on so well together in the morning that there was no talk on either side of their separating after lunch.

Both continued to play well during the afternoon, or, at least, well enough to make them forget everything else until the light began to fail them. Not until then did Parkins remember that he had meant to do some more investigating at the preceptory; but it was of no great importance, he reflected. One day was as good as another; he might as well go home with the Colonel.

As they turned the corner of the house, the Colonel was almost knocked down by a boy who rushed into him at the very top of his speed, and then, instead of running away, remained hanging on to him and panting. The first words of the warrior were naturally those of reproof and objurgation, but he quickly discerned that the boy was almost speechless with fright. Inquiries were useless at first. When the boy got his breath he began to howl, and still clung to the Colonel's legs. He was at last detached, but continued to howl.

"What in the world *is* the matter with you? What have you been up to? What have you seen?" said the two men.

"Ow, I seen it wive at me out of the winder," wailed the boy, "and I don't like it."

"What window?" said the irritated Colonel. "Come, pull yourself together, my boy."

"The front winder it was, at the 'otel," said the boy.

At this point Parkins was in favour of sending the boy home, but the Colonel refused; he wanted to get to the bottom of it, he said; it was most dangerous to give a boy such a fright as this one had had, and if it turned out that people had been playing jokes, they should suffer for it in some way. And by a series of questions he made out this story: The boy had been playing about on the grass in front of the Globe with some others; then they had gone home to their teas, and he was just going, when he happened to look up at the front winder and see it a-wiving at him. *It* seemed to be a figure of some sort, in white as far as he knew—couldn't see its face; but it wived at him, and it warn't a right thing—not to say not a right person. Was there a light in the room? No, he didn't think to look if there was a light. Which was the window? Was it the top one or the second one? The seckind one it was—the big winder what got two little uns at the sides.

"Very well, my boy," said the Colonel, after a few more questions. "You run away home now. I expect it was some person trying to give you a start. Another time, like a brave English boy, you just throw a stone—well, no, not that exactly, but you go and speak to the waiter, or to Mr. Simpson, the landlord, and—yes—and say that I advised you to do so."

The boy's face expressed some of the doubt he felt as to the likelihood of Mr. Simpson's lending a favourable ear to his complaint, but the Colonel did not appear to perceive this, and went on:

"And here's a sixpence—no, I see it's a shilling—and you be off home, and don't think any more about it."

The youth hurried off with agitated thanks, and the Colonel and Parkins went round to the front of the Globe and reconnoitred. There was only one window answering to the description they had been hearing.

"Well, that's curious," said Parkins; "it's evidently my window the lad was talking about. Will you come up for a moment, Colonel Wilson? We ought to be able to see if anyone has been taking liberties in my room."

They were soon in the passage, and Parkins made as if to open the door. Then he stopped and felt in his pockets.

"This is more serious than I thought," was his next remark. "I remember now that before I started this morning I locked the door. It is locked now, and, what is more, here is the key." And he held it up. "Now," he went on, "if the servants are in the habit of going into one's room during the day when one is away, I can only say that—well, that I don't approve of it at all." Conscious of a somewhat weak climax, he busied himself in opening the door (which was indeed locked) and in lighting candles. "No," he said, "nothing seems disturbed."

"Except your bed," put in the Colonel.

"Excuse me, that isn't my bed," said Parkins. "I don't use that one. But it does look as if someone had been playing tricks with it."

It certainly did: the clothes were bundled up and twisted together in a most tortuous confusion. Parkins pondered.

"That must be it," he said at last: "I disordered the clothes last night in unpacking, and they haven't made it since. Perhaps they came in to make it, and that boy saw them through the window; and then they were called away and locked the door after them. Yes, I think that must be it."

"Well, ring and ask," said the Colonel, and this appealed to Parkins as practical.

The maid appeared, and, to make a long story short, deposed that she had made the bed in the morning when the gentleman was in the room, and hadn't been there since. No, she hadn't no other key. Mr. Simpson he kep' the keys; he'd be able to tell the gentleman if anyone had been up.

This was a puzzle. Investigation showed that nothing of value had been taken, and Parkins remembered the disposition of the small objects on tables and so forth well enough to be pretty sure that no pranks had been played with them. Mr. and Mrs. Simpson furthermore agreed that neither of them had given the duplicate key of the room to any person whatever during the day. Nor could Parkins, fair-minded man as he was, detect anything in the demeanour of master, mistress, or maid that indicated guilt. He was much more inclined to think that the boy had been imposing on the Colonel.

The latter was unwontedly silent and pensive at dinner and throughout the evening. When he bade good night to Parkins, he murmured in a gruff undertone:

"You know where I am if you want me during the night."

"Why, yes, thank you, Colonel Wilson, I think I do; but there isn't much prospect of my disturbing you, I hope. By the way," he added, "did I show you that old whistle I spoke of? I think not. Well, here it is."

The Colonel turned it over gingerly in the light of the candle.

"Can you make anything of the inscription?" asked Parkins, as he took it back.

"No, not in this light. What do you mean to do with it?"

"Oh, well, when I get back to Cambridge I shall submit it to some of the archaeologists there, and see what they think of it; and very likely, if they consider it worth having, I may present it to one of the museums."

"'M!" said the Colonel. "Well, you may be right. All I know is that, if it were mine, I should chuck it straight into the sea. It's no use talking, I'm well aware, but I expect that with you it's a case of live and learn. I hope so, I'm sure, and I wish you a good night."

He turned away, leaving Parkins in act to speak at the bottom of the stair, and soon each was in his own bedroom.

By some unfortunate accident, there were neither blinds nor curtains in the windows of the Professor's room. The previous night he had thought little of this, but to-night there seemed every prospect of a bright moon rising to shine directly on his bed, and probably wake him later on. When he noticed this he was a good deal annoyed, but, with an ingenuity which I can only envy, he succeeded in rigging up, with the help of a railway-rug, some safety-pins, and a stick and umbrella, a screen which, if it only held together, would completely keep the moonlight off his bed. And shortly afterwards he was comfortably in that bed. When he had read a somewhat solid work long enough to produce a decided wish for sleep, he cast a drowsy glance round the room, blew out the candle, and fell back upon the pillow.

He must have slept soundly for an hour or more, when a sudden clatter shook him up in a most unwelcome manner. In a moment he realized what had happened: his carefully-constructed screen had given way, and a very bright frosty moon was shining directly on his face. This was highly annoying. Could he possibly get up and reconstruct the screen? or could he manage to sleep if he did not?

For some minutes he lay and pondered over the possibilities; then he turned over sharply, and with all his eyes open lay breathlessly listening. There had been a movement, he was sure, in the empty bed on the opposite side of the room. To-morrow he would have it moved, for there must be rats or something playing about in it. It was quiet now. No! the commotion began again. There was a rustling and shaking: surely more than any rat could cause.

I can figure to myself something of the Professor's bewilderment and horror, for I have in a dream thirty years back seen the same thing happen; but the reader will hardly, perhaps, imagine how dreadful it was to him to see a figure suddenly sit up in what he had known was an empty bed. He was out of his own bed in one bound, and made a dash towards the window, where lay his only weapon, the stick with which he had propped his screen. This was, as it turned out, the worst thing he could have done, because the personage in the empty bed, with a sudden motion, slipped from the bed and took up a position, with outspread arms, between the two beds, and in front of the door. Parkins watched it in a horrid perplexity. Somehow, the idea of getting past it and escaping through the door was intolerable to him; he could not have borne—he didn't know why—to touch it; and as for its touching him, he would sooner dash himself through the window than have that happen. It stood for the moment in a band of dark shadow, and he had not seen what its face was like. Now it began to move, in a stooping posture, and all at once the spectator realized, with some horror and some relief, that it must be blind, for it seemed to feel about it with its muffled arms in a groping and random fashion. Turning half away from him, it became suddenly conscious of the bed he had just left, and darted towards it, and bent over and felt the pillows in a way which made Parkins shudder as he had never in his life thought it possible. In a very few moments it seemed to know that the bed was empty, and then, moving forward into the area of light and facing the window, it showed for the first time what manner of thing it was.

Parkins, who very much dislikes being questioned about it, did once describe something of it in my hearing, and I gathered that what he chiefly remembers about it is a horrible, an intensely horrible, face *of crumpled linen*. What expression he read upon it he could not or would not tell, but that the fear of it went nigh to maddening him is certain.

But he was not at leisure to watch it for long. With formidable quickness it moved into the middle of the room, and, as it groped and waved, one corner of its draperies swept across Parkins's face. He could not—though he knew how perilous a sound was—he could not keep back a cry of disgust, and this gave the searcher an instant clue. It leapt towards him upon the instant, and the next moment he was half-way through the window backwards, uttering cry upon cry at the utmost pitch of his voice, and the linen face was thrust close into his own. At this, almost the last possible second, deliverance came, as you will have guessed: the Colonel burst the door open, and was just in time to see the dreadful group at the window. When he reached the figures only one was left. Parkins sank forward into the room in a faint, and before him on the floor lay a tumbled heap of bedclothes.

Colonel Wilson asked no questions, but busied himself in keeping everyone else out of the room and in getting Parkins back to his bed; and himself wrapped in a rug, occupied the other bed for the rest of the night. Early on the next day Rogers arrived, more welcome than he would have been a day before, and the three of them held a very long consultation in the Professor's room. At the end of it the Colonel left the hotel door carrying a small object between his finger and thumb, which he cast as far into the sea as a very brawny arm could send it. Later on the smoke of a burning ascended from the back premises of the Globe.

Exactly what explanation was patched up for the staff and visitors at the hotel I must confess I do not recollect. The Professor was somehow cleared of the ready suspicion of delirium tremens, and the hotel of the reputation of a troubled house.

There is not much question as to what would have happened to Parkins if the Colonel had not intervened when he did. He would either have fallen out of the window or else lost his wits. But it is not so evident what more the creature that came in answer to the whistle could have done than frighten. There seemed to be absolutely nothing material about it save the bedclothes of which it had made itself a body. The Colonel, who remembered a not very dissimilar occurrence in India, was of opinion that if Parkins had closed with it it could really have done very little, and that its one power was that of frightening. The whole thing, he said, served to confirm his opinion of the Church of Rome.

There is really nothing more to tell, but, as you may imagine, the Professor's views on certain points are less clear cut than they used to be. His nerves, too, have suffered: he cannot even now see a surplice hanging on a door quite unmoved, and the spectacle of a scarecrow in a field late on a winter afternoon has cost him more than one sleepless night.

1904

THE BROKEN BOOT

John Galsworthy

THE ACTOR, Gilbert Caister, who had been "out" for six months, emerged from his East Coast seaside lodging about noon in the day, after the opening of "Shooting the Rapids," on tour, in which he was playing Dr. Dominick in the last act. A salary of four pounds a week would not, he was conscious, remake his fortunes, but a certain jauntiness had returned to the gait and manner of one employed again at last.

Fixing his monocle, he stopped before a fishmonger's and, with a faint smile on his face, regarded a lobster. Ages since he had eaten a lobster! One could long for a lobster without paying, but the pleasure was not solid enough to detain him. He moved upstreet and stopped again, before a tailor's window. Together with the actual tweeds, in which he could so easily fancy himself refitted, he could see a reflection of himself, in the faded brown suit wangled out of the production of "Marmaduke Mandeville" the year before the war. The sunlight in this damned town was very strong, very hard on seams and buttonholes, on knees and elbows! Yet he received the ghost of aesthetic pleasure from the reflected elegance of a man long fed only twice a day, of an eyeglass well rimmed out from a soft brown eye, of a velour hat salved from the production of "Educating Simon" in 1912; and, in front of the window he removed that hat, for under it was his new phenomenon, not yet quite evaluated, his *mêche blanche*. Was it an asset, or the beginning of the end? It reclined backwards on the right side, conspicuous in his dark hair, above that shadowy face always interesting to Gilbert Caister. They said it came from atrophy of the—er—something nerve, an effect of the war, or of under-nourished tissue. Rather distinguished, perhaps, but——!

He walked on, and became conscious that he had passed a face he knew. Turning, he saw it also turned on a short and dapper figure—a face rosy, bright, round, with an air of cherubic knowledge, as of a getter-up of amateur theatricals.

Bryce-Green, by George!

165

"Caister? It is! Haven't seen you since you left the old camp. Remember what sport we had over 'Gotta Grampus'? By Jove! I am glad to see you. Doing anything with yourself? Come and have lunch with me."

Bryce-Green, the wealthy patron, the moving spirit of entertainment in that South Coast convalescent camp. And, drawling slightly, Caister answered:

"Shall be delighted." But within him something did not drawl: "By God, you're going to have a feed, my boy!"

And—elegantly threadbare, roundabout and dapper—the two walked side by side.

"Know this place? Let's go in here! Phyllis, cocktails for my friend Mr. Caister and myself, and caviare on biscuits. Mr. Caister is playing here! you must go and see him."

The girl who served the cocktails and the caviare looked up at Caister with interested blue eyes. Precious! He had been "out" for six months!

"Nothing of a part," he drawled; "took it to fill a gap." And below his waistcoat the gap echoed: "Yes, and it'll take some filling."

"Bring your cocktail along, Caister; we'll go into the little further room, there'll be nobody there. What shall we have—a lobstah?"

And Caister murmured: "I love lobstahs."

"Very fine and large here. And how are you, Caister? So awfully glad to see you—only real actor we had."

"Thanks," said Caister, "I'm all right." And he thought: "He's a damned amateur, but a nice little man."

"Sit here. Waiter, bring us a good big lobstah and a salad; and then—er—a small fillet of beef with potatoes fried crisp, and a bottle of my special hock. Ah! and a rum omelette—plenty of rum and sugah. Twig?"

And Caister thought: "Thank God, I do."

They had sat down opposite each other at one of the two small tables in the little recessed room.

"Luck!" said Bryce-Green.

"Luck!" replied Caister; and the cocktail trickling down him echoed: "Luck!"

"And what do you think of the state of the drama?" Oh! ho! A question after his own heart. Balancing his monocle by a sweetish smile on the opposite side of his mouth, Caister drawled his answer: "Quite too bally awful!"

"H'm! Yes," said Bryce-Green; "nobody with any genius, is there?"

And Caister thought: "Nobody with any money."

"Have you been playing anything great? You were so awfully good in 'Gotta Grampus'!"

"Nothing particular. I've been—er—rather slack." And with their feel around his waist his trousers seemed to echo: "Slack!"

"Ah!" said Bryce-Green. "Here we are! Do you like claws?"

"Tha-a-nks, Anything!" To eat—until warned by the pressure of his waist against his trousers! Huh! What a feast! And what a flow of his own tongue suddenly released—on drama, music, art; mellow and critical, stimulated by the round eyes and interjections of his little provincial host.

"By Jove, Caister! You've got a *mèche blanche*. Never noticed. I'm awfully interested in *mèches blanches*. Don't think me too frightfully rude—but did it come suddenly?"

"No, gradually."

"And how do you account for it?"

"Try starvation," trembled on Caister's lips.

"I don't."

"I think it's ripping. Have some more omelette? I often wish I'd gone on the regular stage myself. Must be a topping life, if one has talent, like you."

Topping?

"Have a cigar. Waiter! Coffee and cigars. I shall come and see you to-night. Suppose you'll be here a week?"

Topping! The laughter and applause—"Mr. Caister's rendering left nothing to be desired; its ——and its —— are in the true spirit of ——!"

Silence recalled him from his rings of smoke. Bryce-Green was sitting, with cigar held out and mouth a little open, and bright eyes round as pebbles, fixed—fixed on some object near the floor, past the corner of the tablecloth. Had he burnt his mouth? The eyelids fluttered; he looked at Caister, licked his lips like a dog, nervously, and said:

"I say, old chap, don't think me a beast, but are you at all—er—er—rocky? I mean—if I can be of any service, don't hesitate! Old acquaintance, don't you know, and all that——"

His eyes rolled out again towards the object, and Caister followed them. Out there above the carpet he saw it—his own boot. It dangled, because his knees were crossed, six inches off the ground—split—right across, twice, between lace and toecap. Quite! He knew it. A boot left him from the rôle of Bertie Carstairs, in "The Dupe," just before the war. Good boots. His only pair, except the boots of Dr. Dominick, which he was nursing. And from the boot he looked back at Bryce-Green, sleek and concerned. A drop, black when it left his heart, suffused his eye behind the monocle; his smile curled bitterly; he said:

"Not at all, thanks! Why?"

"Oh! n-n-nothing. It just occurred to me." His eyes—but Caister had withdrawn the boot. Bryce-Green paid the bill and rose.

"Old chap, if you'll excuse me; engagement at half-past two. So awf'ly glad to have seen you. Good-bye!"

"Good-bye!" said Caister. "And thanks!"

He was alone. And, chin on hand, he stared through his monocle into an empty coffee cup. Alone with his heart, his boot, his life to come. . . . "And what have you been in lately, Mr. Caister?" "Nothing very much lately. Of course I've played almost everything." "Quite so. Perhaps you'll leave your address; can't say anything definite, I'm afraid." "I—I should—er—be willing to rehearse on approval; or—if I could read the part?" "Thank you, afraid we haven't got as far as that." "No? Quite! Well, I shall hear from you, perhaps." And Caister could see his own eyes looking at the manager. God! What a look. . . . A topping life! A dog's life! Cadging—cadging—cadging for work! A life of draughty waiting, of concealed beggary, of terrible depressions, of want of food!

The waiter came skating round as if he desired to clear. Must go! Two young women had come in and were sitting at the other table between him and the door. He saw them look at him, and his sharpened senses caught the whisper:

"Sure—in the last act. Don't you see his *mêche blanche?*"

"Oh! yes—of course! Isn't it—wasn't he——!"

Caister straightened his back; his smile crept out, he fixed his monocle. They had spotted his Dr. Dominick!

"If you've quite finished, sir, may I clear?"

"Certainly. I'm going." He gathered himself and rose. The young women were gazing up. Elegant, with faint smile, he passed them close, managing—so that they could not see—his broken boot.

1923

THE HOUSE OF COBWEBS

George Gissing

IT WAS five o'clock on a June morning. The dirty-buff blind of the lodging-house bedroom shone like cloth of gold as the sun's unclouded rays poured through it, transforming all they illumined, so that things poor and mean seemed to share in the triumphant glory of new-born day. In the bed lay a young man who had already been awake for an hour. He kept stirring uneasily, but with no intention of trying to sleep again. His eyes followed the slow movement of the sunshine on the wall-paper, and noted, as they never had done before, the details of the flower pattern, which represented no flower wherewith botanists are acquainted, yet, in this summer light, turned the thoughts to garden and field and hedgerow. The young man had a troubled mind, and his thoughts ran thus:—

"I must have three months at least, and how am I to live? . . . Fifteen shillings a week—not quite that, if I spread my money out. Can one live on fifteen shillings a week—rent, food, washing? . . . I shall have to leave these lodgings at once. They're not luxurious, but I can't live here under twenty-five, that's clear. . . . Three months to finish my book. It's good; I'm hanged if it isn't! This time I shall find a publisher. All I have to do is to stick at my work and keep my mind easy. . . . Lucky that it's summer; I don't need fires. Any corner would do for me where I can be quiet and see the sun. . . . Wonder whether some cottager in Surrey would house and feed me for fifteen shillings a week? . . . No use lying here. Better get up and see how things look after an hour's walk."

So the young man arose and clad himself, and went out into the shining street. His name was Goldthorpe. His years were not yet three-and-twenty. Since the age of legal independence he had been living alone in London, solitary and poor, very proud of a wholehearted devotion to the career of authorship. As soon as he slipped out of the stuffy house, the live air, perfumed with freshness from meadows and hills afar, made his blood pulse joyously. He was at the age of hope, and something within him, which did not represent mere youthful illusion,

169

supported his courage in the face of calculations such as would have damped sober experience. With boyish step, so light and springy that it seemed anxious to run and leap, he took his way through a suburb south of Thames, and pushed on towards the first rising of the Surrey hills. And as he walked resolve strengthened itself in his heart. Somehow or other he would live independently through the next three months. If the worst came to the worst, he could earn bread as clerk or labourer, but as long as his money lasted he would pursue his purpose, and that alone. He sang to himself in this gallant determination, happy as if some one had left him a fortune.

In an ascending road, quiet and tree-shadowed, where the dwellings on either side were for the most part old and small, though here and there a brand-new edifice on a larger scale showed that the neighbourhood was undergoing change such as in our time destroys the picturesque in all London suburbs, the cheery dreamer chanced to turn his eyes upon a spot of desolation which aroused his curiosity and set his fancy at work. Before him stood three deserted houses, a little row once tenanted by middle-class folk, but now for some time unoccupied and unrepaired. They were of brick, but the fronts had a stucco facing cut into imitation of ashlar, and weathered to the sombrest grey. The windows of the ground floor and of that above, and the fanlights above the doors, were boarded up, a guard against unlicensed intrusion; the top story had not been thought to stand in need of this protection, and a few panes were broken. On these dead frontages could be traced the marks of climbing plants, which once hung their leaves about each doorway; dry fragments of the old stem still adhered to the stucco. What had been the narrow strip of fore-garden, railed from the pavement, was now a little wilderness of coarse grass, docks, nettles, and degenerate shrubs. The paint on the doors had lost all colour, and much of it was blistered off; the three knockers had disappeared, leaving indications of rough removal, as if— which was probably the case—they had fallen a prey to marauders. Standing full in the brilliant sunshine, this spectacle of abandonment seemed sadder, yet less ugly, than it would have looked under a gloomy sky. Goldthorpe began to weave stories about its musty squalor. He crossed the road to make a nearer inspection; and as he stood gazing at the dishonoured thresholds, at the stained and cracked boarding of the blind windows, at the rusty paling and the broken gates, there sounded from somewhere near a thin, shaky strain of music, the notes of a con-certina played with uncertain hand. The sound seemed to come from within the houses, yet how could that be? Assuredly no one lived under these crazy roofs. The musician was playing "Home, Sweet Home," and as Goldthorpe listened it seemed to him that the sound was not station-ary. Indeed, it moved; it became more distant, then again the notes sounded more distinctly, and now as if the player were in the open air. Perhaps he was at the back of the houses?

On either side ran a narrow passage, which parted the spot of desolation from inhabited dwellings. Exploring one of these, Goldthorpe found that there lay in the rear a tract of gardens. Each of the three lifeless houses had its garden of about twenty yards long. The bordering wall along the passage allowed a man of average height to peer over it, and Goldthorpe searched with curious eye the piece of ground which was nearest to him. Many a year must have gone by since any gardening was done here. Once upon a time the useful and ornamental had both been represented in this modest space; now, flowers and vegetables, such of them as survived in the struggle for existence, mingled together, and all alike were threatened by a wild, rank growth of grasses and weeds, which had obliterated the beds, hidden the paths, and made of the whole garden plot a green jungle. But Goldthorpe gave only a glance at this still life; his interest was engrossed by a human figure, seated on a campstool near the back wall of the house, and holding a concertina, whence, at this moment, in slow, melancholy strain, "Home, Sweet Home" began to wheeze forth. The player was a middle-aged man, dressed like a decent clerk or shopkeeper, his head shaded with an old straw hat rather too large for him, and on his feet—one of which swung as he sat with legs crossed—a pair of still more ancient slippers, also too large. With head aside, and eyes looking upward, he seemed to listen in a mild ecstasy to the notes of his instrument. He had a round face of much simplicity and good-nature, semicircular eyebrows, pursed little mouth with abortive moustache, and short thin beard fringing the chinless lower jaw. Having observed this unimposing person for a minute or two, himself unseen, Goldthorpe surveyed the rear of the building, anxious to discover any sign of its still serving as human habitation; but nothing spoke of tenancy. The windows on this side were not boarded, and only a few panes were broken; but the chief point of contrast with the desolate front was made by a Virginia creeper, which grew luxuriantly up to the eaves, hiding every sign of decay save those dim, dusty apertures which seemed to deny all possibility of life within. And yet, on looking steadily, did he not discern something at one of the windows on the top story—something like a curtain or a blind? And had not that same window the appearance of having been more recently cleaned than the others? He could not be sure; perhaps he only fancied these things. With neck aching from the strained position in which he had made his survey over the wall, the young man turned away. In the same moment "Home, Sweet Home" came to an end, and, but for the cry of a milkman, the early-morning silence was undisturbed.

Goldthorpe pursued his walk, thinking of what he had seen, and won-

dering what it all meant. On his way back he made a point of again passing the deserted houses, and again he peered over the wall of the passage.
The man was still there, but no longer seated with the concertina; wearing a round felt hat instead of the straw, he stood almost knee-deep in
vegetation, and appeared to be examining the various growths about
him. Presently he moved forward, and, with head still bent, approached
the lower end of the garden, where, in a wall higher than that over which
Goldthorpe made his espial, there was a wooden door. This the man
opened with a key, and, having passed out, could be heard to turn a lock
behind him. A minute more, and this short, respectable figure came into
sight at the end of the passage. Goldthorpe could not resist the opportunity thus offered. Affecting to turn a look of interest towards the nearest
roof, he waited until the stranger was about to pass him, then, with civil
greeting, ventured upon a question.

"Can you tell me how these houses come to be in this neglected
state?"

The stranger smiled; a soft, modest, deferential smile such as became
his countenance, and spoke in a corresponding voice, which had a
vaguely provincial accent.

"No wonder it surprises you, sir. I should be surprised myself. It
comes of quarrels and lawsuits."

"So I supposed. Do you know who the property belongs to?"

"Well, yes, sir. The fact is—it belongs to me."

The avowal was made apologetically, and yet with a certain timid
pride. Goldthorpe exhibited all the interest he felt. An idea had suddenly
sprung up in his mind; he met the stranger's look, and spoke with the
easy good-humour natural to him.

"It seems a great pity that houses should be standing empty like that.
Are they quite uninhabitable? Couldn't one camp here during this fine
summer weather? To tell you the truth, I'm looking for a room—as cheap
a room as I can get. Could you let me one for the next three months?"

The stranger was astonished. He regarded the young man with an
uneasy smile.

"You are joking, sir."

"Not a bit of it. Is the thing quite impossible? Are all the rooms in too
bad a state?"

"I won't say *that*," replied the other cautiously, still eyeing his inter-
locutor with surprised glances. "The upper rooms are really not so bad—
that is to say, from a humble point of view. I—I have been looking at
them just now. You really mean, sir——?"

"I'm quite in earnest, I assure you," cried Goldthorpe cheerily. "You
see I'm tolerably well dressed still, but I've precious little money, and I
want to eke out the little I've got for about three months. I'm writing a

book. I think I shall manage to sell it when it's done, but it'll take me about three months yet. I don't care what sort of place I live in, so long as it's quiet. Couldn't we come to terms?"

The listener's visage seemed to grow rounder in progressive astonishment; his eyes declared an emotion akin to awe; his little mouth shaped itself as if about to whistle.

"A book, sir? You are writing a book? You are a literary man?"

"Well, a beginner. I have poverty on my side, you see."

"Why, it's like Dr. Johnson!" cried the other, his face glowing with interest. "It's like Chatterton!—though I'm sure I hope you won't end like him, sir. It's like Goldsmith!—indeed it is!"

"I've got half Oliver's name, at all events," laughed the young man. "Mine is Goldthorpe."

"You don't say so, sir! What a strange coincidence! Mine, sir, is Spicer. I—I don't know whether you'd care to come into my garden? We might talk there——"

In a minute or two they were standing amid the green jungle, which Goldthorpe viewed with delight. He declared it the most picturesque garden he had ever seen.

"Why, there are potatoes growing there. And what are those things? Jerusalem artichokes? And look at that magnificent thistle; I never saw a finer thistle in my life! And poppies—and marigolds—and broad-beans—and isn't that lettuce?"

Mr. Spicer was red with gratification.

"I feel that something might be done with the garden, sir," he said. "The fact is, sir, I've only lately come into this property, and I'm sorry to say it'll only be mine for a little more than a year—a year from next midsummer day, sir. There's the explanation of what you see. It's leasehold property, and the lease is just coming to its end. Five years ago, sir, an uncle of mine inherited the property from his brother. The houses were then in a very bad state, and only one of them let, and there had been lawsuits going on for a long time between the leaseholder and the ground-landlord—I can't quite understand these matters, they're not at all in my line, sir; but at all events there were quarrels and lawsuits, and I'm told one of the tenants was somehow mixed up in it. The fact is, my uncle wasn't a very well-to-do man, and perhaps he didn't feel able to repair the houses, especially as the lease was drawing to its end. Would you like to go in and have a look round?"

They entered by the back door, which admitted them to a little wash-house. The window was over-spun with cobwebs, thick, hoary; each corner of the ceiling was cobweb-packed; long, dusty filaments depended along the walls. Notwithstanding, Goldthorpe noticed that the house had a water-supply; the sink was wet, the tap above it looked new. This confirmed a suspicion in his mind, but he made no remark. They passed into the kitchen. Here again the work of the spider showed thick on every hand. The window, however, though uncleaned for years, had recently been opened; one knew that by the torn and ragged condition of the webs where the sashes joined. And lo! on the window-sill stood a plate, a cup and saucer, a knife, a fork, a spoon—all of them manifestly new-washed. Goldthorpe affected not to see these objects; he averted his face to hide an involuntary smile.

"I must light a candle," said Mr. Spicer. "The staircase is quite dark."

A candle stood ready, with a box of matches, on the rusty cooking-stove. No fire had burned in the grate for many a long day; of that the visitor assured himself. Save the objects on the window-sill, no evidence of human occupation was discoverable. Having struck a light, Mr. Spicer advanced. In the front passage, on the stairs, on the landing, every angle and every projection had its drapery of cobwebs. The stuffy, musty air smelt of cobwebs; so, at all events, did Goldthorpe explain to himself a peculiar odour which he seemed never to have smelt. It was the same in the two rooms on the first floor. Through the boarded windows of that in front penetrated a few thin rays from the golden sky; they gleamed upon dust and web, on faded, torn wall-paper and a fireplace in ruins.

"I shouldn't recommend you to take either of *these* rooms," said Mr. Spicer, looking nervously at his companion. "They really can't be called attractive."

"Those on the top are healthier, no doubt," was the young man's reply. "I noticed that some of the window-glass is broken. That must have been good for airing."

Mr. Spicer grew more and more nervous. He opened his little round mouth, very much like a fish gasping, but seemed unable to speak. Silently he led the way to the top story, still amid cobwebs; the atmosphere was certainly purer up here, and when they entered the first room they found themselves all at once in such a flood of glorious sunshine that Goldthorpe shouted with delight.

"Ah, I could live here! Would it cost much to have panes put in? An old woman with a broom would do the rest." He added in a moment, "But the back windows are not broken, I think?"

"No—I think not—I—no——"

Mr. Spicer gasped and stammered. He stood holding the candle (its light invisible) so that the grease dripped steadily on his trousers.

"Let's have a look at the other," cried Goldthorpe. "It gets the afternoon sun, no doubt. And one would have a view of the garden."

"Stop, sir!" broke from his companion, who was red and perspiring. "There's something I should like to tell you before you go into that room. I—it—the fact is, sir, that—temporarily—I am occupying it myself."

"Oh, I beg your pardon, Mr. Spicer!"

"Not at all, sir! Don't mention it, sir. I have a reason—it seemed to me—I've merely put in a bed and a table, sir, that's all—a temporary arrangement."

"Yes, yes; I quite understand. What could be more sensible? If the house were mine, I should do the same. What's the good of owning a house, and making no use of it?"

Great was Mr. Spicer's satisfaction.

"See what it is, sir," he exclaimed, "to have to do with a literary man! You are large-minded, sir; you see things from an intellectual point of view. I can't tell you how it gratifies me, sir, to have made your acquaintance. Let us go into the back room."

With nervous boldness he threw the door open. Goldthorpe, advancing respectfully, saw that Mr. Spicer had not exaggerated the simplicity of his arrangements. In a certain measure the room had been cleaned, but along the angle of walls and ceiling there still clung a good many cobwebs, and the state of the paper was deplorable. A blind hung at the window, but the floor had no carpet. In one corner stood a little camp bed, neatly made for the day; a table and a chair, of the cheapest species, occupied the middle of the floor, and on the hearth was an oil cooking-stove.

"It's wonderful how little one really wants," remarked Mr. Spicer, "at all events in weather such as this. I find that I get along here very well indeed. The only expense I had was for the water-supply. And really, sir, when one comes to think of it, the situation is pleasant. If one doesn't mind loneliness—and it happens that I don't. I have my books, sir——"

He opened the door of a cupboard containing several shelves. The first thing Goldthorpe's eye fell upon was the concertina; he saw also sundry articles of clothing, neatly disposed, a little crockery, and, ranged on the two top shelves, some thirty volumes, all of venerable aspect.

"Literature, sir," pursued Mr. Spicer modestly, "has always been my comfort. I haven't had very much time for reading, but my motto, sir, has been *nulla dies sine linea*."

It appeared from his pronunciation that Mr. Spicer was no classical scholar, but he uttered the Latin words with infinite gusto, and timidly watched their effect upon the listener.

"This is delightful," cried Mr. Goldthorpe. "Will you let me have the front room? I could work here splendidly—splendidly! What rent do you ask, Mr. Spicer?"

"Why really, sir, to tell you the truth I don't know what to say. Of course the windows must be seen to. The fact is, sir, if you felt disposed to do that at your own expense, and—and to have the room cleaned, and—and, let us say, to bear half the water-rate whilst you are here, why, really, I hardly feel justified in asking anything more."

It was Goldthorpe's turn to be embarrassed, for, little as he was prepared to pay, he did not like to accept a stranger's generosity. They discussed the matter in detail, with the result that for the arrangement which Mr. Spicer had proposed there was substituted a weekly rent of two shillings, the lease extending over a period of three months. Goldthorpe was to live quite independently, asking nothing in the way of domestic service; moreover, he was requested to introduce no other person to the house, even as casual visitor. These conditions Mr. Spicer set forth, in a commercial hand, on a sheet of notepaper, and the agreement was solemnly signed by both contracting parties.

On the way home to breakfast Goldthorpe reviewed his position now that he had taken this decisive step. It was plain that he must furnish his room with the articles which Mr. Spicer found indispensable, and this outlay, be as economical as he might, would tell upon the little capital which was to support him for three months. Indeed, when all had been done, and he found himself, four days later, dwelling on the top story of the house of cobwebs, a simple computation informed him that his total expenditure, after payment of rent, must not exceed fifteenpence a day. What matter? He was in the highest spirits, full of energy and hope. His landlord had been kind and helpful in all sorts of ways, helping him to clean the room, to remove his property from the old lodgings, to make purchases at the lowest possible rate, to establish himself as comfortably as circumstances permitted. And when, on the first morning of his tenancy, he was awakened by a brilliant sun, the young man had a sensation of comfort and satisfaction quite new in his experience; for he was really at home; the bed he slept on, the table he ate at and wrote upon, were his own possessions; he thought with pity of his lodging-house life, and felt a joyous assurance that here he would do better work than ever before.

In less than a week Mr. Spicer and he were so friendly that they began to eat together, taking it in turns to prepare the meal. Now and then they walked in company, and every evening they sat smoking (very cheap tobacco) in the wild garden. Little by little Mr. Spicer revealed the facts of his history. He had begun life, in a midland town, as a chemist's errand-boy, and by steady perseverance, with a little pecuniary help from relatives, had at length risen to the position of chemist's assistant. For five-and-twenty years he practised such rigid economy that, having no one but himself to provide for, he began to foresee a possibility of passing his old age elsewhere than in the workhouse. Then befell the death of his uncle, which was to have important consequences for him. Mr. Spicer told the story of this exciting moment late one evening, when, kept indoors by rain, the companions sat together upstairs, one on each side of the rusty and empty fireplace.

"All my life, Mr. Goldthorpe, I've thought what a delightful thing it must be to have a house of one's own. I mean, really of one's own; not only a rented house, but one in which you could live and die, feeling that no one had a right to turn you out. Often and often I've dreamt of it, and tried to imagine what the feeling would be like. Not a large, fine house—oh dear, no! I didn't care how small it might be; indeed, the smaller the better for a man of my sort. Well, then, you can imagine how it came upon me when I heard——But let me tell you first that I hadn't seen my uncle for fifteen years or more. I had always thought him a well-to-do man, and I knew he wasn't married, but the truth is, it never came into my head that he might leave me something. Picture me, Mr. Goldthorpe—you have imagination, sir—standing behind the counter and thinking about nothing but business, when in comes a young gentleman—I see him now—and asks for Mr. Spicer. 'Spicer is my name, sir,' I said. 'And you are the nephew,' were his next words, 'of the late Mr. Isaac Spicer, of Clapham, London?' That shook me, sir, I assure you it did, but I hope I behaved decently. The young gentleman went on to tell me that my uncle had left no will, and that I was believed to be his next-of-kin, and that if so, I inherited all his property, the principal part of which was three houses in London. Now try and think, Mr. Goldthorpe, what sort of state I was in after hearing that. You're an intellectual man, and you can enter into another's mind. Three houses! Well, sir, you know what houses those were. I came up to London at once (it was last autumn), and I saw my uncle's lawyer, and he told me all about the property, and I saw it for myself. Ah, Mr. Goldthorpe! If ever a man suffered a bitter disappointment, sir!"

He ended on a little laugh, as if excusing himself for making so much of his story, and sat for a moment with head bowed.

"Fate played you a nasty trick there," said Goldthorpe. "A knavish trick."

"One felt almost justified in using strong language, sir—though I always avoid it on principle. However, I must tell you that the houses weren't all. Luckily there was a little money as well, and, putting it with my own savings, sir, I found it would yield me an income. When I say an income, I mean, of course, for a man in my position. Even when I have to go into lodgings, when my houses become the property of the ground-landlord—to my mind, Mr. Goldthorpe, a very great injustice, but I don't set myself up against the law of the land—I shall just be able to live. And that's no small blessing, sir, as I think you'll agree."

"Rather! It's the height of human felicity, Mr. Spicer. I envy you vastly."

"Well, sir, I'm rather disposed to look at it in that light myself. My nature is not discontented, Mr. Goldthorpe. But, sir, if you could have seen me when the lawyer began to explain about the houses! I was absolutely ignorant of the leasehold system; and at first I really couldn't understand. The lawyer thought me a fool, I fear, sir. And when I came down here and saw the houses themselves! I'm afraid, Mr. Goldthorpe, I'm really afraid, sir, I was weak enough to shed a tear."

They were sitting by the light of a very small lamp, which did not tend to cheerfulness.

"Come," cried Goldthorpe, "after all, the houses are yours for a twelvemonth. Why shouldn't we both live on here all the time? It'll be a little breezy in winter, but we could have the fireplaces knocked into shape, and keep up good fires. When I've sold my book I'll pay a higher rent, Mr. Spicer. I like the old house, upon my word I do! Come, let us have a tune before we go to bed."

Smiling and happy, Mr. Spicer fetched from the cupboard his concertina, and after the usual apology for what he called his "imperfect mastery of the instrument," sat down to play "Home, Sweet Home." He had played it for years, and evidently would never improve in his execution. After "Home, Sweet Home" came "The Bluebells of Scotland," after that "Annie Laurie"; and Mr. Spicer's repertory was at an end. He talked of learning new pieces, but there was not the slightest hope of this achievement.

Mr. Spicer's mental development had ceased more than twenty years ago, when, after extreme efforts, he had attained the qualification of chemist's assistant. Since then the world had stood still with him. Though a true lover of books, he knew nothing of any that had been published during his own lifetime. His father, though very poor, had possessed a little collection of volumes, the very same which now stood in Mr. Spicer's cupboard. The authors represented in this library were either English classics or obscure writers of the early part of the nineteenth century. Knowing these books very thoroughly, Mr. Spicer sometimes indulged in a quotation which would have puzzled even the erudite. His favourite poet was Cowper, whose moral sentiments greatly soothed him. He spoke of Byron like some contemporary who, whilst admitting his lordship's genius, felt an abhorrence of his life. He judged literature solely from the moral point of view, and was incapable of understanding any other. Of fiction he had read very little indeed, for it was not regarded with favour by his parents. Scott was hardly more than a name to him. And though he avowed acquaintance with one or two works of Dickens, he spoke of them with an uneasy smile, as if in some doubt as to their tendency. With these intellectual characteristics, Mr. Spicer naturally found it difficult to appreciate the attitude of his literary friend, a young man whose brain thrilled in response to modern ideas, and who regarded himself as the destined leader of a new school of fiction. Not indiscreet,

Goldthorpe soon became aware that he had better talk as little as possible of the work which absorbed his energies. He had enough liberality
and sense of humour to understand and enjoy his landlord's conversation, and the simple goodness of the man inspired him with no little
respect. Thus they got along together remarkably well. Mr. Spicer never
ceased to feel himself honoured by the presence under his roof of one
who—as he was wont to say—wielded the pen. The tradition of Grub
Street was for him a living fact. He thought of all authors as struggling
with poverty, and continued to cite eighteenth-century examples by
way of encouraging Goldthorpe and animating his zeal. Whilst the
young man was at work Mr. Spicer moved about the house with sound-
less footsteps. When invited into his tenant's room he had a reverential
demeanour, and the sight of manuscript on the bare deal table caused
him to subdue his voice.

The weeks went by, and Goldthorpe's novel steadily progressed. In
London he had only two or three acquaintances, and from them he held
aloof, lest necessity or temptation should lead to his spending money
which he could not spare. The few letters which he received were
addressed to a post-office—impossible to shock the nerves of a postman
by requesting him to deliver correspondence at this dead house, of which
the front door had not been opened for years. The weather was perfect;
a great deal of sunshine, but as yet no oppressive heat, even in the chambers under the roof. Towards the end of June Mr. Spicer began to amuse
himself with a little gardening. He had discovered in the coal-hole an
ancient fork, with one prong broken and the others rusting away. This
implement served him in his slow, meditative attack on that part of the
jungle which seemed to offer least resistance. He would work for a quarter of an hour, then, resting on his fork, contemplate the tangled mass of
vegetation which he had succeeded in tearing up.

"Our aim should be," he said gravely, when Goldthorpe came to
observe his progress, "to clear the soil round about those vegetables and
flowers which seem worth preserving. These broad-beans, for instance—
they seem to be a very fine sort. And the Jerusalem artichokes. I've been
making inquiry about the artichokes, and I'm told they are not ready to
eat till the autumn. The first frost is said to improve them. They're fine
plants—very fine plants."

Already the garden had supplied them with occasional food, but they
had to confess that, for the most part, these wild vegetables lacked savour.
The artichokes, now shooting up into a leafy grove, were the great hope
of the future. It would be deplorable to quit the house before this tuber
came to maturity.

"The worst of it is," remarked Mr. Spicer one day, when he was perspiring freely, "that I can't help thinking of how different it would be if

this garden was really my own. The fact is, Mr. Goldthorpe, I can't put much heart into the work; no, I can't. The more I reflect, the more indignant I become. Really now, Mr. Goldthorpe, speaking as an intellectual man, as a man of imagination, could anything be more cruelly unjust than this leasehold system? I assure you, it keeps me awake at night; it really does."

The tenor of his conversation proved that Mr. Spicer had no intention of leaving the house until he was legally obliged to do so. More than once he had an interview with his late uncle's solicitor, and each time he came back with melancholy brow. All the details of the story were now familiar to him; he knew all about the lawsuits which had ruined the property. Whenever he spoke of the ground-landlord, known to him only by name, it was with a severity such as he never permitted himself on any other subject. The ground-landlord was, to his mind, an embodiment of social injustice.

"Never in my life, Mr. Goldthorpe, did I grudge any payment of money as I grudge the ground-rent of these houses. I feel it as robbery, sir, as sheer robbery, though the sum is so small. When, in my ignorance, the matter was first explained to me, I wondered why my uncle had continued to pay this rent, the houses being of no profit to him. But now I understand, Mr. Goldthorpe; the sense of possession is very sweet. Property's property, even when it's leasehold and in ruins. I grudge the ground-rent bitterly, but I feel, sir, that I couldn't bear to lose my houses until the fatal moment, when lose them I must."

In August the thermometer began to mark high degrees. Goldthorpe found it necessary to dispense with coat and waistcoat when he was working, and at times a treacherous languor whispered to him of the delights of idleness. After one particularly hot day, he and his landlord smoked together in the dusking garden, both unusually silent. Mr. Spicer's eye dwelt upon the great heap of weeds which was resulting from his labour; an odour somewhat too poignant arose from it upon the close air. Goldthorpe, who had been rather headachy all day, was trying to think into perfect clearness the last chapters of his book, and found it difficult.

"You know," he said all at once, with an impatient movement, "we ought to be at the seaside."

"The seaside?" echoed his companion, in surprise. "Ah, it's a long time since I saw the sea, Mr. Goldthorpe. Why, it must be—yes, it is at least twenty years."

"Really? I've been there every year of my life till this. One gets into the way of thinking of luxuries as necessities. I tell you what it is. If I sell my book as soon as it's done, we'll have a few days somewhere on the south coast together."

Mr. Spicer betrayed uneasiness.

"I should like it much," he murmured, "but I fear, Mr. Goldthorpe, I greatly fear I can't afford it."

"Oh, but I mean that you shall go with me as my guest! But for you, Mr. Spicer, I might never have got my book written at all."

"I feel it an honour, sir, I assure you, to have a literary man in my house," was the genial reply. "And you think the *work* will soon be finished, sir?"

Mr. Spicer always spoke of his tenant's novel as "the work"—which on his lips had a very large and respectful sound.

"About a fortnight more," answered Goldthorpe with grave intensity.

The heat continued. As he lay awake before getting up, eager to finish his book, yet dreading the torrid temperature of his room, which made the brain sluggish and the hand slow, Goldthorpe saw how two or three energetic spiders had begun to spin webs once more at the corners of the ceiling; now and then he heard the long buzzing of a fly entangled in one of these webs. The same thing was happening in Mr. Spicer's chamber. It did not seem worth while to brush the new webs away.

"When you come to think of it, sir," said the landlord, "it's the spiders who are the real owners of these houses. When I go away, they'll be pulled down; they're not fit for human habitation. Only the spiders are really at home here, and the fact is, sir, I don't feel I have the right to disturb them. As a man of imagination, Mr. Goldthorpe, you'll understand my thoughts!"

Only with a great effort was the novel finished. Goldthorpe had lost his appetite (not, perhaps, altogether a disadvantage), and he could not sleep; a slight fever seemed to be constantly upon him. But this work was a question of life and death to him, and he brought it to an end only a few days after the term he had set himself. The complete manuscript was exhibited to Mr. Spicer, who expressed his profound sense of the privilege. Then, without delay, Goldthorpe took it to the publishing house in which he had most hope.

The young author could now do nothing but wait, and, under the circumstances, waiting meant torture. His money was all but exhausted; if he could not speedily sell the book, his position would be that of a mere pauper. Supported thus long by the artist's enthusiasm, he fell into despondency, saw the dark side of things. To be sure, his mother (a widow in narrow circumstances) had written pressing him to take a holiday "at home," but he dreaded the thought of going penniless to his mother's house, and there, perchance, receiving bad news about his book. An ugly feature of the situation was that he continued to feel anything but well; indeed, he felt sure that he was getting worse. At night he suffered severely; sleep had almost forsaken him. Hour after hour he lay listening

to mysterious noises, strange crackings and creakings through the desolate house; sometimes he imagined the sound of footsteps in the bare
rooms below; even hushed voices, from he knew not where, chilled his
blood at midnight. Since crumbs had begun to lie about, mice were
common; they scampered as if in revelry above the ceiling, and under the
floor, and within the walls. Goldthorpe began to dislike this strange
abode. He felt that under any circumstances it would be impossible for
him to dwell here much longer.

When his last coin was spent, and he had no choice but to pawn or
sell something for a few days' subsistence, the manuscript came back
upon his hands. It had been judged—declined.

That morning he felt seriously unwell. After making known the catas-
trophe to Mr. Spicer—who was stricken voiceless—he stood silent for a
minute or two, then said with quiet resolve:

"It's all up. I've no money, and I feel as if I were going to have an illness. I must say good-bye to you, old friend."

"Mr. Goldthorpe!" exclaimed the other solemnly; "I entreat you, sir,
to do nothing rash! Take heart, sir! Think of Samuel Johnson, think of
Goldsmith——"

"The extent of my rashness, Mr. Spicer, will be to raise enough money
on my watch to get down into Derbyshire. I must go home. If I don't,
you'll have the pleasant job of taking me to a hospital."

Mr. Spicer insisted on lending him the small sum he needed. An hour
or two later they were at St. Pancras Station, and before sunset
Goldthorpe had found harbourage under his mother's roof. There he lay
ill for more than a month, and convalescent for as long again. His doctor
declared that he must have been living in some very unhealthy place, but
the young man preferred to explain his illness by overwork. It seemed to
him sheer ingratitude to throw blame on Mr. Spicer's house, where he
had been so contented and worked so well until the hot days of latter
August. Mr. Spicer himself wrote kind and odd little letters, giving an
account of the garden, and earnestly hoping that his literary friend would
be back in London to taste the Jerusalem artichokes. But Christmas came
and went, and Goldthorpe was still at his mother's house.

Meanwhile the manuscript had gone from publisher to publisher, and
at length, on a day in January—date ever memorable in Goldthorpe's
life—there arrived a short letter in which a certain firm dryly intimated
their approval of the story offered them, and their willingness to purchase
the copyright for a sum of fifty pounds. The next morning the triumphant author travelled to London. For two or three days a violent gale
had been blowing, with much damage throughout the country; on his
journey Goldthorpe saw many great trees lying prostrate, beaten, as
though scornfully, by the cold rain which now descended in torrents.

Arrived in town, he went to the house where he had lodged in the time
of comparative prosperity, and there was lucky enough to find his old
rooms vacant. On the morrow he called upon the gracious publishers,
and after that, under a sky now become more gentle, he took his way
towards the abode of Mr. Spicer.

Eager to communicate the joyous news, glad in the prospect of seeing
his simple-hearted friend, he went at a great pace up the ascending road.
There were the three houses, looking drearier than ever in a faint gleam
of winter sunshine. There were his old windows. But—what had happened to the roof? He stood in astonishment and apprehension, for, just
above the room where he had dwelt, the roof was an utter wreck, showing a great hole, as if something had fallen upon it with crushing weight.
As indeed was the case; evidently the chimney-stack had come down,
and doubtless in the recent gale. Seized with anxiety on Mr. Spicer's
account, he ran round to the back of the garden and tried the door; but
it was locked as usual. He strained to peer over the garden wall, but could
discover nothing that threw light on his friend's fate; he noticed, however, a great grove of dead, brown artichoke stems, seven or eight feet
high. Looking up at the back windows, he shouted Mr. Spicer's name; it
was useless. Then, in serious alarm, he betook himself to the house on
the other side of the passage, knocked at the door, and asked of the
woman who presented herself whether anything was known of a gentleman who dwelt where the chimney-stack had just fallen. News was at
once forthcoming; the event had obviously caused no small local excitement. It was two days since the falling of the chimney, which happened
towards evening, when the gale blew its hardest. Mr. Spicer was at that
moment sitting before the fire, and only by a miracle had he escaped
destruction, for an immense weight of material came down through the
rotten roof, and even broke a good deal of the flooring. Had the occupant been anywhere but close by the fireplace, he must have been
crushed to a mummy; as it was, only a few bricks struck him, inflicting
severe bruises on back and arms. But the shock had been serious. When
his shouts from the window at length attracted attention and brought
help, the poor man had to be carried downstairs, and in a thoroughly
helpless state was removed to the nearest hospital.

"Which room was he in?" inquired Goldthorpe. "Back or front?"

"In the front room. The back wasn't touched."

Musing on Mr. Spicer's bad luck—for it seemed as if he had changed
from the back to the front room just in order that the chimney might fall
on him—Goldthorpe hastened away to the hospital. He could not be
admitted to-day, but heard that his friend was doing very well; on the
morrow he would be allowed to see him.

So at the visitors' hour Goldthorpe returned. Entering the long accident ward, he searched anxiously for the familiar face, and caught sight of it just as it began to beam recognition. Mr. Spicer was sitting up in bed; he looked pale and meagre, but not seriously ill; his voice quivered with delight as he greeted the young man.

"I heard of your inquiring for me yesterday, Mr. Goldthorpe, and I've hardly been able to live for impatience to see you. How are you, sir? How are you? And what news about the *work,* sir?"

"We'll talk about that presently, Mr. Spicer. Tell me all about your accident. How came you to be in the front room?"

"Ah, sir," replied the patient, with a little shake of the head, "that indeed was singular. Only a few days before, I had made a removal from my room into yours. I call it yours, sir, for I always thought of it as yours; but thank heaven you were not there. Only a few days before. I took that step, Mr. Goldthorpe, for two reasons: first, because water was coming through the roof at the back in rather unpleasant quantities, and secondly, because I hoped to get a little morning sun in the front. The fact is, sir, my room had been just a little depressing. Ah, Mr. Goldthorpe, if you knew how I have missed you, sir! But the *work*—what news of the *work?*"

Smiling as though carelessly, the author made known his good fortune. For a quarter of an hour Mr. Spicer could talk of nothing else.

"This has completed my cure!" he kept repeating. "The work was composed under my roof, my own roof, sir! Did I not tell you to take heart?"

"And where are you going to live?" asked Goldthorpe presently. "You can't go back to the old house."

"Alas! no, sir. All my life I have dreamt of the joy of owning a house. You know how the dream was realised, Mr. Goldthorpe, and you see what has come of it at last. Probably it is a chastisement for overweening desires, sir. I should have remembered my position, and kept my wishes within bounds. But, Mr. Goldthorpe, I shall continue to cultivate the garden, sir. I shall put in spring lettuces, and radishes, and mustard and cress. The property is mine till midsummer day. You shall eat a lettuce of my growing, Mr. Goldthorpe; I am bent on that. And how I grieve that you were not with me at the time of the artichokes—just at the moment when they were touched by the first frost!"

"Ah! They were really good, Mr. Spicer?"

"Sir, they seemed good to *me,* very good. Just at the moment of the first frost!"

1906

THE LIFTED VEIL

George Eliot

Give me no light, great Heaven, but such as turns
To energy of human fellowship;
No powers beyond the growing heritage
That makes completer manhood.

[handwritten: chest pain due to ♡ disease]

Chapter 1

[handwritten: dismal prognosis]

THE TIME of my end approaches. I have lately been subject to attacks of *angina pectoris*; and in the ordinary course of things, my physician tells me, I may fairly hope that my life will not be protracted many months. Unless, then, I am cursed with an exceptional physical constitution, as I am cursed with an exceptional mental character, I shall not much longer groan under the wearisome burden of this earthly existence. If it were to be otherwise,—if I were to live on to the age most men desire and provide for,—I should for once have known whether the miseries of delusive expectation can outweigh the miseries of true provision. For I foresee when I shall die, and everything that will happen in my last moments.

Just a month from this day, on September 20, 1850, I shall be sitting in this chair, in this study, at ten o'clock at night, longing to die, weary of incessant insight and foresight, without delusions and without hope. Just as I am watching a tongue of blue flame rising in the fire, and my lamp is burning low, the horrible contraction will begin at my chest. I shall only have time to reach the bell, and pull it violently, before the sense of suffocation will come. No one will answer my bell. I know why. My two servants are lovers, and will have quarrelled. My housekeeper will have rushed out of the house in a fury, two hours before, hoping that Perry will believe she has gone to drown herself. Perry is alarmed at last, and is gone out after her. The little scullery-maid is asleep on a bench: she never answers the bell; it does not wake her. The sense of suffocation increases: my lamp goes out with a horrible stench: I make a great effort, and snatch at the bell again. I long for life, and there is no help. I thirsted

[handwritten right margin: no one is taking care of Latimer?]

[handwritten bottom: attend to each other, not Latimer]

for the unknown: the thirst is gone. O God, let me stay with the known, and be weary of it: I am content. Agony of pain and suffocation—and all the while the earth, the fields, the pebbly brook at the bottom of the rookery, the fresh scent after the rain, the light of the morning through my chamber-window, the warmth of the hearth after the frosty air,—will darkness close over them forever?

Darkness,—darkness,—no pain,—nothing but darkness: but I am passing on and on through the darkness: my thought stays in the darkness, but always with a sense of moving onward. . . .

Before that time comes, I wish to use my last hours of ease and strength in telling the strange story of my experience. I have never fully unbosomed myself to any human being; I have never been encouraged to trust much in the sympathy of my fellow-men. But we have all a chance of meeting with some pity, some tenderness, some charity, when we are dead: it is the living only who cannot be forgiven,—the living only from whom men's indulgence and reverence are held off, like the rain by the hard east wind. While the heart beats, bruise it,—it is your only opportunity; while the eye can still turn towards you with moist, timid entreaty, freeze it with an icy unanswering gaze; while the ear, that delicate messenger to the inmost sanctuary of the soul, can still take in the tones of kindness, put it off with hard civility, or sneering compliment, or envious affectation of indifference; while the creative brain can still throb with the sense of injustice, with the yearning for brotherly recognition,—make haste,—oppress it with your ill-considered judgments, your trivial comparisons, your careless misrepresentations. The heart will by and by be still—*ubi saeva indignatio ulterius cor lacerare nequit;* the eye will cease to entreat; the ear will be deaf; the brain will have ceased from all wants as well as from all work. Then your charitable speeches may find vent; then you may remember and pity the toil and the struggle and the failure; then you may give due honour to the work achieved; then you may find extenuation for errors, and may consent to bury them.

That is a trivial schoolboy text; why do I dwell on it? It has little reference to me, for I shall leave no works behind me for men to honour. I have no near relatives who will make up, by weeping over my grave, for the wounds they inflicted on me when I was among them. It is only the story of my life that will perhaps win a little more sympathy from strangers when I am dead, than I ever believed it would obtain from my friends while I was living.

My childhood perhaps seems happier to me than it really was, by contrast with all the after-years. For then the curtain of the future was as impenetrable to me as to other children: I had all their delight in the present hour, their sweet indefinite hopes for the morrow; and I had a tender mother: even now, after the dreary lapse of long years, a slight trace of sensation accompanies the remembrance of her caress as she held me on her knee,—her arms round my little body, her cheek pressed on mine. I had a complaint of the eyes that made me blind for a little while, and she kept me on her knee from morning till night. That unequalled love soon vanished out of my life, and even to my childish consciousness it was as if that life had become more chill. I rode my little white pony, with the groom by my side as before, but there were no loving eyes looking at me as I mounted, no glad arms opened to me when I came back. Perhaps I missed my mother's love more than most children of seven or eight would have done, to whom the other pleasures of life remained as before; for I was certainly a very sensitive child. I remember still the mingled trepidation and delicious excitement with which I was affected by the tramping of the horses on the pavement in the echoing stables, by the loud resonance of the grooms' voices, by the booming bark of the dogs as my father's carriage thundered under the archway of the courtyard, by the din of the gong as it gave notice of luncheon and dinner. The measured tramp of soldiery which I sometimes heard—for my father's house lay near a country town where there were large barracks—made me sob and tremble; and yet when they were gone past, I longed for them to come back again.

I fancy my father thought me an odd child, and had little fondness for me; though he was very careful in fulfilling what he regarded as a parent's duties. But he was already past the middle of life, and I was not his only son. My mother had been his second wife, and he was five-and-forty when he married her. He was a firm, unbending, intensely orderly man, in root and stem a banker, but with a flourishing graft of the active landholder, aspiring to county influence: one of those people who are always like themselves from day to day, who are uninfluenced by the weather, and neither know melancholy nor high spirits. I held him in great awe, and appeared more timid and sensitive in his presence than at other times; a circumstance which, perhaps, helped to confirm him in the intention to educate me on a different plan from the prescriptive one with which he had complied in the case of my elder brother, already a tall youth at Eton. My brother was to be his representative and successor; he must go to Eton and Oxford, for the sake of making connections, of course: my father was not a man to underrate the bearing of Latin satirists or Greek dramatists on the attainment of an aristocratic position. But, intrinsically, he had slight esteem for "those dead but sceptred spirits"; having qualified himself for forming an independent opinion by reading Potter's "Æschylus," and dipping into Francis's "Horace." To this negative view he added a positive one, derived from a recent connection with mining speculations; namely, that a scientific education was the really useful training for a younger son. Moreover, it was clear that a shy, sensitive boy like me was not fit to encounter the rough experience of a public school. Mr. Letherall had said so very decidedly. Mr. Letherall was a large man in spectacles, who one day took my small head between his large hands, and pressed it here and there in an exploratory, auspicious manner—then placed each of his great thumbs on my temples, and pushed me a little way from him, and stared at me with glittering spectacles. The contemplation appeared to displease him, for he frowned sternly, and said to my father, drawing his thumbs across my eyebrows,—

"The deficiency is there, sir,—there; and here," he added, touching the upper sides of my head,—"here is the excess. That must be brought out, sir, and this must be laid to sleep."

I was in a state of tremor, partly at the vague idea that I was the object of reprobation, partly in the agitation of my first hatred—hatred of this big, spectacled man, who pulled my head about as if he wanted to buy and cheapen it.

I am not aware how much Mr. Letherall had to do with the system afterwards adopted towards me, but it was presently clear that private tutors, natural history, science, and the modern languages were the appliances by which the defects of my organization were to be remedied. I was very stupid about machines, so I was to be greatly occupied with them; I had no memory for classification, so it was particularly necessary that I should study systematic zoology and botany; I was hungry for human deeds and human emotions, so I was to be plentifully crammed with the mechanical powers, the elementary bodies, and the phenomena of electricity and magnetism. A better-constituted boy would certainly have profited under my intelligent tutors, with their scientific apparatus; and would, doubtless, have found the phenomena of electricity and magnetism as fascinating as I was, every Thursday, assured they were. As it was, I could have paired off, for ignorance of whatever was taught me, with the worst Latin scholar that was ever turned out of a classical academy. I read Plutarch, and Shakespeare, and Don Quixote by the sly, and supplied myself in that way with wandering thoughts, while my tutor was assuring me that "an improved man, as distinguished from an ignorant one, was a man who knew the reason why water ran down-hill." I had no desire to be this improved man; I was glad of the running water; I could watch it and listen to it gurgling among the pebbles, and bathing the bright green water-plants, by the hour together. I did not want to know *why* it ran; I had perfect confidence that there were good reasons for what was so very beautiful.

There is no need to dwell on this part of my life. I have said enough to indicate that my nature was of the sensitive, unpractical order, and that it grew up in an uncongenial medium, which could never foster it into happy, healthy development. When I was sixteen I was sent to Geneva to complete my course of education; and the change was a very happy one to me, for the first sight of the Alps, with the setting sun on them, as we descended the Jura, seemed to me like an entrance into heaven; and the three years of my life there were spent in a perpetual sense of exaltation, as if from a draught of delicious wine, at the presence of Nature in all her

awful loveliness. You will think, perhaps, that I must have been a poet,
from this early sensibility to Nature. But my lot was not so happy as that.
A poet pours forth his song and *believes* in the listening ear and answering soul, to which his song will be floated sooner or later. But the poet's
sensibility without his voice,—the poet's sensibility that finds no vent but
in silent tears on the sunny bank, when the noonday light sparkles on the
water or in an inward shudder at the sound of harsh human tones, the
sight of a cold human eye,—this dumb passion brings with it a fatal solitude of soul in the society of one's fellow-men. My least solitary
moments were those in which I pushed off in my boat, at evening,
towards the centre of the lake; it seemed to me that the sky, and the glowing mountain-tops, and the wide blue water surrounded me with a cher-
ishing love such as no human face had shed on me since my mother's
love had vanished out of my life. I used to do as Jean Jacques did,—lie
down in my boat and let it glide where it would, while I looked up at
the departing glow leaving one mountain-top after the other, as if the
prophet's chariot of fire were passing over them on its way to the home
of light. Then, when the white summits were all sad and corpse-like, I
had to push homeward, for I was under careful surveillance, and was
allowed no late wanderings. This disposition of mine was not favourable
to the formation of intimate friendships among the numerous youths of
my own age who are always to be found studying at Geneva. Yet I made
one such friendship; and, singularly enough, it was with a youth whose
intellectual tendencies were the very reverse of my own. I shall call him
Charles Meunier; his real surname—an English one, for he was of
English extraction—having since become celebrated. He was an orphan,
who lived on a miserable pittance while he pursued the medical studies
for which he had a special genius. Strange! that with my vague mind, susceptible and unobservant, hating inquiry and given up to contemplation,
I should have been drawn towards a youth whose strongest passion was
science. But the bond was not an intellectual one; it came from a source
that can happily blend the stupid with the brilliant, the dreamy with the
practical: it came from community of feeling. Charles was poor and ugly,
derided by Genevese *gamins,* and not acceptable in drawing-rooms. I saw
that he was isolated, as I was, though from a different cause, and, stimulated by a sympathetic resentment, I made timid advances towards him.
It is enough to say that there sprang up as much comradeship between
us as our different habits would allow; and in Charles's rare holidays we
went up the Salève together, or took the boat to Vevey, while I listened
dreamily to the monologues in which he unfolded his bold conceptions
of future experiment and discovery. I mingled them confusedly in my
thought with glimpses of blue water and delicate floating cloud, with the
notes of birds and the distant glitter of the glacier. He knew quite well
that my mind was half absent, yet he liked to talk to me in this way; for
don't we talk of our hopes and our projects even to dogs and birds, when

they love us? I have mentioned this one friendship because of its connection with a strange and terrible scene which I shall have to narrate in
my subsequent life.

This happier life at Geneva was put an end to by a severe illness, which
is partly a blank to me, partly a time of dimly-remembered suffering,
with the presence of my father by my bed from time to time. Then came
the languid monotony of convalescence, the days gradually breaking into
variety and distinctness as my strength enabled me to take longer and
longer drives. On one of these more vividly remembered days, my father
said to me, as he sat beside my sofa,—

"When you are quite well enough to travel, Latimer, I shall take you
home with me. The journey will amuse you and do you good, for I shall
go through the Tyrol and Austria, and you will see many new places. Our
neighbours, the Filmores, are come; Alfred will join us at Basle, and we
shall all go together to Vienna, and back by Prague—"

My father was called away before he had finished his sentence, and he
left my mind resting on the word *Prague,* with a strange sense that a new
and wondrous scene was breaking upon me: a city under the broad sunshine, that seemed to me as if it were the summer sunshine of a long-past
century arrested in its course,—unrefreshed for ages by the dews of night
or the rushing rain-cloud; scorching the dusty, weary, time-eaten grandeur
of a people doomed to live on in the stale repetition of memories, like
deposed and superannuated kings in their regal gold-inwoven tatters. The
city looked so thirsty that the broad river seemed to me a sheet of metal;
and the blackened statues, as I passed under their blank gaze, along the
unending bridge, with their ancient garments and their saintly crowns,
seemed to me the real inhabitants and owners of this place, while the
busy, trivial men and women, hurrying to and fro, were a swarm of
ephemeral visitants infesting it for a day. It is such grim, stony beings as
these, I thought, who are the fathers of ancient faded children, in those
tanned time-fretted dwellings that crowd the steep before me; who pay
their court in the worn and crumbling pomp of the palace which
stretches its monotonous length on the height; who worship wearily in
the stifling air of the churches, urged by no fear or hope, but compelled
by their doom to be ever old and undying, to live on in the rigidity of
habit, as they live on in perpetual midday, without the repose of night or
the new birth of morning.

A stunning clang of metal suddenly thrilled through me, and I became
conscious of the objects in my room again: one of the fire-irons had
fallen as Pierre opened the door to bring me my draught. My heart was
palpitating violently, and I begged Pierre to leave my draught beside me;
I would take it presently.

As soon as I was alone again, I began to ask myself whether I had been
sleeping. Was this a dream,—this wonderfully distinct vision,—minute in
its distinctness down to a patch of rainbow light on the pavement, trans-

mitted through a coloured lamp in the shape of a star—of a strange city, quite unfamiliar to my imagination? I had seen no picture of Prague: it lay in my mind as a mere name, with vaguely-remembered historical associations,—ill-defined memories of imperial grandeur and religious wars.

Nothing of this sort had ever occurred in my dreaming experience before, for I had often been humiliated because my dreams were only saved from being utterly disjointed and commonplace by the frequent terrors of nightmare. But I could not believe that I had been asleep, for I remembered distinctly the gradual breaking-in of the vision upon me, like the new images in a dissolving view, or the growing distinctness of the landscape as the sun lifts up the veil of the morning mist. And while I was conscious of this incipient vision, I was also conscious that Pierre came to tell my father Mr. Filmore was waiting for him, and that my father hurried out of the room. No, it was not a dream; was it—the thought was full of tremulous exultation—was it the poet's nature in me, hitherto only a troubled yearning sensibility, now manifesting itself suddenly as spontaneous creation? Surely it was in this way that Homer saw the plain of Troy, that Dante saw the abodes of the departed, that Milton saw the earthward flight of the Tempter. Was it that my illness had wrought some happy change in my organization—given a firmer tension to my nerves—carried off some dull obstruction? I had often read of such effects—in works of fiction at least. Nay; in genuine biographies I had read of the subtilizing or exalting influence of some diseases on the mental powers. Did not Novalis feel his inspiration intensified under the progress of consumption?

When my mind had dwelt for some time on this blissful idea, it seemed to me that I might perhaps test it by an exertion of my will. The vision had begun when my father was speaking of our going to Prague. I did not for a moment believe it was really a representation of that city; I believed—I hoped it was a picture that my newly-liberated genius had painted in fiery haste, with the colours snatched from lazy memory. Suppose I were to fix my mind on some other place,—Venice, for example, which was far more familiar to my imagination than Prague: perhaps the same sort of result would follow. I concentrated my thoughts on Venice; I stimulated my imagination with poetic memories, and strove to feel myself present in Venice, as I had felt myself present in Prague. But in vain. I was only colouring the Canaletto engravings that hung in my old bedroom at home; the picture was a shifting one, my mind wandering uncertainly in search of more vivid images; I could see no accident of form or shadow without conscious labour after the necessary conditions. It was all prosaic effort, not rapt passivity, such as I had experienced half an hour before. I was discouraged; but I remembered that inspiration was fitful.

For several days I was in a state of excited expectation, watching for a recurrence of my new gift. I sent my thoughts ranging over my world of knowledge, in the hope that they would find some object which would send a reawakening vibration through my slumbering genius. But no; my world remained as dim as ever, and that flash of strange light refused to come again, though I watched for it with palpitating eagerness.

My father accompanied me every day in a drive, and a gradually lengthening walk as my powers of walking increased; and one evening he had agreed to come and fetch me at twelve the next day, that we might go together to select a musical box, and other purchases rigorously demanded of a rich Englishman visiting Geneva. He was one of the most punctual of men and bankers, and I was always nervously anxious to be quite ready for him at the appointed time. But, to my surprise, at a quarter past twelve he had not appeared. I felt all the impatience of a convalescent who has nothing particular to do, and who has just taken a tonic in the prospect of immediate exercise that would carry off the stimulus.

Unable to sit still and reserve my strength, I walked up and down the room, looking out on the current of the Rhone, just where it leaves the dark-blue lake; but thinking all the while of the possible causes that could detain my father.

Suddenly I was conscious that my father was in the room, but not alone: there were two persons with him. Strange! I had heard no footstep, I had not seen the door open; but I saw my father, and at his right hand our neighbour Mrs. Filmore, whom I remembered very well, though I had not seen her for five years. She was a commonplace middle-aged woman, in silk and cashmere; but the lady on the left of my father was not more than twenty, a tall, slim, willowy figure, with luxuriant blond hair, arranged in cunning braids and folds that looked almost too massive for the slight figure and the small-featured, thin-lipped face they crowned. But the face had not a girlish expression: the features were sharp, the pale grey eyes at once acute, restless, and sarcastic. They were fixed on me in half-smiling curiosity, and I felt a painful sensation as if a sharp wind were cutting me. The pale-green dress, and the green leaves that seemed to form a border about her pale blond hair, made me think of a Water-Nixie—for my mind was full of German lyrics, and this pale, fatal-eyed woman, with the green weeds, looked like a birth from some cold sedgy stream, the daughter of an aged river.

"Well, Latimer, you thought me long," my father said. . . .

But while the last word was in my ears, the whole group vanished, and there was nothing between me and the Chinese printed folding-screen that stood before the door. I was cold and trembling; I could only totter forward and throw myself on the sofa. This strange new power had manifested itself again. . . . But *was* it a power? Might it not rather be a disease—a sort of intermittent delirium, concentrating my energy of brain into moments of unhealthy activity, and leaving my saner hours all the more barren? I felt a dizzy sense of unreality in what my eye rested on;

I grasped the bell convulsively, like one trying to free himself from night-mare, and rang it twice. Pierre came with a look of alarm in his face.

"Monsieur ne se trouve pas bien?" he said anxiously.

"I'm tired of waiting, Pierre," I said, as distinctly and emphatically as I could, like a man determined to be sober in spite of wine; "I'm afraid something has happened to my father,—he's usually so punctual. Run to the Hôtel des Bergues and see if he is there."

Pierre left the room at once, with a soothing "Bien, Monsieur"; and I felt the better for this scene of simple, waking prose. Seeking to calm myself still further, I went into my bedroom, adjoining the *salon,* and opened a case of eau-de-Cologne; took out a bottle; went through the process of taking out the cork very neatly, and then rubbed the reviving spirit over my hands and forehead, and under my nostrils, drawing a new delight from the scent because I had procured it by slow details of labour, and by no strange sudden madness. Already I had begun to taste some-thing of the horror that belongs to the lot of a human being whose nature is not adjusted to simple human conditions.

Still enjoying the scent, I returned to the *salon,* but it was not unoc-cupied, as it had been before I left it. In front of the Chinese folding-screen there was my father, with Mrs. Filmore on his right hand, and on his left,—the slim blond-haired girl, with the keen face and the keen eyes fixed on me in half-smiling curiosity.

"Well, Latimer, you thought me long," my father said.

I heard no more, felt no more, till I became conscious that I was lying with my head low on the sofa, Pierre and my father by my side. As soon as I was thoroughly revived, my father left the room, and presently returned, saying,—

"I've been to tell the ladies how you are, Latimer. They were waiting in the next room. We shall put off our shopping expedition to-day."

Presently he said, "That young lady is Bertha Grant, Mrs. Filmore's orphan niece. Filmore has adopted her, and she lives with them, so you will have her for a neighbour when we go home,—perhaps for a near relation; for there is a tenderness between her and Alfred, I suspect, and I should be gratified by the match, since Filmore means to provide for her in every way as if she were his daughter. It had not occurred to me that you knew nothing about her living with the Filmores."

He made no further allusion to the fact of my having fainted at the moment of seeing her, and I would not for the world have told him the reason: I shrank from the idea of disclosing to any one what might be regarded as a pitiable peculiarity, most of all from betraying it to my father, who would have suspected my sanity ever after.

I do not mean to dwell with particularity on the details of my expe-rience. I have described these two cases at length, because they had definite, clearly traceable results in my after-lot.

Shortly after this last occurrence—I think the very next day—I began to be aware of a phase in my abnormal sensibility, to which, from the languid and slight nature of my intercourse with others since my illness, I had not been alive before. This was the obtrusion on my mind of the mental process going forward in first one person, and then another, with whom I happened to be in contact: the vagrant, frivolous ideas and emotions of some uninteresting acquaintance—Mrs. Filmore, for example—would force themselves on my consciousness like an importunate, ill-played musical instrument, or the loud activity of an imprisoned insect. But this unpleasant sensibility was fitful, and left me moments of rest, when the souls of my companions were once more shut out from me, and I felt a relief such as silence brings to wearied nerves. I might have believed this importunate insight to be merely a diseased activity of the imagination, but that my prevision of incalculable words and actions proved it to have a fixed relation to the mental process in other minds. But this superadded consciousness, wearying and annoying enough when it urged on me the trivial experience of indifferent people, became an intense pain and grief when it seemed to be opening to me the souls of those who were in a close relation to me,—when the rational talk, the graceful attentions, the wittily-turned phrases, and the kindly deeds, which used to make the web of their characters, were seen as if thrust asunder by a microscopic vision, that showed all the intermediate frivolities, all the suppressed egoism, all the struggling chaos of puerilities, meanness, vague capricious memories, and indolent make-shift thoughts, from which human words and deeds emerge like leaflets covering a fermenting heap.

At Basle we were joined by my brother Alfred, now a handsome self-confident man of six-and-twenty,—a thorough contrast to my fragile, nervous, ineffectual self. I believe I was held to have a sort of half-womanish, half-ghostly beauty; for the portrait-painters, who are thick as weeds at Geneva, had often asked me to sit to them, and I had been the model of a dying minstrel in a fancy picture. But I thoroughly disliked my own *physique,* and nothing but the belief that it was a condition of poetic genius would have reconciled me to it. That brief hope was quite fled, and I saw in my face now nothing but the stamp of a morbid organization, framed for passive suffering,—too feeble for the sublime resistance of poetic production. Alfred, from whom I had been almost constantly separated, and who, in his present stage of character and appearance, came before me as a perfect stranger, was bent on being extremely friendly and brother-like to me. He had the superficial kindness of a good-humoured, self-satisfied nature, that fears no rivalry, and has encountered no contrarieties. I am not sure that my disposition was good enough for me to have been quite free from envy towards him, even if our desires had not clashed, and if I had been in the healthy human condition which admits of generous confidence and charitable construction. There must always have been an antipathy between our natures. As it was, he became in a few weeks an object of intense hatred to me; and when he entered the room, still more when he spoke, it was as if a sensation of grating metal had set my teeth on edge. My diseased consciousness was more intensely and continually occupied with his thoughts and emotions than with those of any other person who came in my way. I was perpetually exasperated with the petty promptings of his conceit and his love of patronage, with his self-complacent belief in Bertha Grant's passion for him, with his half-pitying contempt for me—seen not in the ordinary indications of into-nation and phrase and slight action, which an acute and suspicious mind is on the watch for, but in all their naked skinless complication.

For we were rivals, and our desires clashed, though he was not aware of it. I have said nothing yet of the effect Bertha Grant produced in me on a nearer acquaintance. That effect was chiefly determined by the fact that she made the only exception, among all the human beings about me, to my unhappy gift of insight. About Bertha I was always in a state of uncertainty: I could watch the expression of her face, and speculate on its meaning; I could ask for her opinion with the real interest of igno-rance; I could listen for her words and watch for her smile with hope and fear: she had for me the fascination of an unravelled destiny. I say it was this fact that chiefly determined the strong effect she produced on me: for, in the abstract, no womanly character could seem to have less affin-ity for that of a shrinking, romantic, passionate youth than Bertha's. She was keen, sarcastic, unimaginative, prematurely cynical, remaining critical and unmoved in the most impressive scenes, inclined to dissect all my favourite poems, and especially contemptuous towards the German lyrics which were my pet literature at that time. To this moment I am unable to define my feeling towards her: it was not ordinary boyish admiration, for she was the very opposite, even to the colour of her hair, of the ideal woman who still remained to me the type of loveliness; and she was without that enthusiasm for the great and good, which, even at the moment of her strongest dominion over me, I should have declared to be the highest element of character. But there is no tyranny more complete than that which a self-centred negative nature exercises over a morbidly sensitive nature perpetually craving sympathy and support. The most independent people feel the effect of a man's silence in heightening their value for his opinion,—feel an additional triumph in conquering the reverence of a critic habitually captious and satirical: no wonder, then, that an enthusiastic self-distrusting youth should watch and wait before the closed secret of a sarcastic woman's face, as if it were the shrine of the doubtfully benignant deity who ruled his destiny. For a young enthusi-ast is unable to imagine the total negation in another mind of the emo-tions which are stirring his own: they may be feeble, latent, inactive, he thinks, but they are there,—they may be called forth; sometimes, in moments of happy hallucination, he believes they may be there in all the greater strength because he sees no outward sign of them. And this effect, as I have intimated, was heightened to its utmost intensity in me, because Bertha was the only being who remained for me in the mysterious seclusion of soul that renders such youthful delusion possible. Doubtless there was another sort of fascination at work,—that subtle physical attraction which delights in cheating our psychological predictions, and in compelling the men who paint sylphs to fall in love with some *bonne et brave femme,* heavy-heeled and freckled.

Bertha's behaviour towards me was such as to encourage all my illusions, to heighten my boyish passion, and make me more and more dependent on her smiles. Looking back with my present wretched knowledge, I conclude that her vanity and love of power were intensely gratified by the belief that I had fainted on first seeing her purely from the strong impression her person had produced on me. The most prosaic woman likes to believe herself the object of a violent, a poetic passion; and without a grain of romance in her, Bertha had that spirit of intrigue which gave piquancy to the idea that the brother of the man she meant to marry was dying with love and jealousy for her sake. That she meant to marry my brother was what at that time I did not believe; for though he was assiduous in his attentions to her, and I knew well enough that both he and my father had made up their minds to this result, there was not yet an understood engagement,—there had been no explicit declaration; and Bertha habitually, while she flirted with my brother, and accepted his homage in a way that implied to him a thorough recognition of its intention, made me believe, by the subtlest looks and phrases,—feminine nothings which could never be quoted against her,— that he was really the object of her secret ridicule; that she thought him, as I did, a coxcomb, whom she would have pleasure in disappointing. Me she openly petted in my brother's presence, as if I were too young and sickly ever to be thought of as a lover; and that was the view he took of me. But I believe she must inwardly have delighted in the tremors into which she threw me by the coaxing way in which she patted my curls, while she laughed at my quotations. Such caresses were always given in the presence of our friends; for when we were alone together, she affected a much greater distance towards me, and now and then took the opportunity, by words or slight actions, to stimulate my foolish timid hope that she really preferred me. And why should she not follow her inclination? I was not in so advantageous a position as my brother, but I had fortune, I was not a year younger than she was, and she was an heiress, who would soon be of age to decide for herself.

The fluctuations of hope and fear, confined to this one channel, made each day in her presence a delicious torment. There was one deliberate act of hers which especially helped to intoxicate me. When we were at Vienna her twentieth birthday occurred, and as she was very fond of ornaments, we all took the opportunity of the splendid jewellers' shops in that Teutonic Paris to purchase her a birthday present of jewelry. Mine, naturally, was the least expensive; it was an opal ring,—the opal was my favourite stone, because it seems to blush and turn pale as if it had a soul. I told Bertha so when I gave it her, and said that it was an emblem of the poetic nature, changing with the changing light of heaven and of woman's eyes. In the evening she appeared elegantly dressed, and wearing conspicuously all the birthday presents except mine. I looked eagerly at her fingers, but saw no opal. I had no opportunity of noticing this to her during the evening; but the next day, when I found her seated near the window alone, after breakfast, I said, "You scorn to wear my poor opal. I should have remembered that you despised poetic natures, and should have given you coral, or turquoise, or some other opaque unresponsive stone." "Do I despise it?" she answered, taking hold of a delicate gold chain which she always wore round her neck and drawing out the end from her bosom with my ring hanging to it; "it hurts me a little, I can tell you," she said, with her usual dubious smile, "to wear it in that secret place; and since your poetical nature is so stupid as to prefer a more public position, I shall not endure the pain any longer."

She took off the ring from the chain and put it on her finger, smiling still, while the blood rushed to my cheeks, and I could not trust myself to say a word of entreaty that she would keep the ring where it was before.

I was completely fooled by this, and for two days shut myself up in my own room whenever Bertha was absent, that I might intoxicate myself afresh with the thought of this scene and all it implied.

I should mention that during these two months,—which seemed a long life to me from the novelty and intensity of the pleasures and pains I underwent,—my diseased participation in other people's consciousness continued to torment me; now it was my father, and now my brother, now Mrs. Filmore or her husband, and now our German courier, whose stream of thought rushed upon me like a ringing in the ears not to be got rid of, though it allowed my own impulses and ideas to continue their uninterrupted course. It was like a preternaturally heightened sense of hearing, making audible to one a roar of sound where others find perfect stillness. The weariness and disgust of this involuntary intrusion into other souls was counteracted only by my ignorance of Bertha, and my growing passion for her—a passion enormously stimulated, if not produced, by that ignorance. She was my oasis of mystery in the dreary desert of knowledge. I had never allowed my diseased condition to betray itself, or to drive me into any unusual speech or action, except once, when, in a moment of peculiar bitterness against my brother, I had forestalled some words which I knew he was going to utter—a clever observation, which he had prepared beforehand. He had occasionally a slightly affected hesitation in his speech, and when he paused an instant after the second word, my impatience and jealousy impelled me to continue the speech for him, as if it were something we had both learned by rote. He coloured and looked astonished, as well as annoyed; and the words had no sooner escaped my lips than I felt a shock of alarm lest such an anticipation of words—very far from being words of course, easy to divine—should have betrayed me as an exceptional being, a sort of quiet energumen, whom every one, Bertha above all, would shudder at and avoid. But I magnified, as usual, the impression any word or deed of mine could produce on others; for no one gave any sign of having noticed my interruption as more than a rudeness, to be forgiven me on the score of my feeble nervous condition.

While this superadded consciousness of the actual was almost constant with me, I had never had a recurrence of that distinct prevision which I have described in relation to my first interview with Bertha; and I was waiting with eager curiosity to know whether or not my vision of Prague would prove to have been an instance of the same kind. A few days after the incident of the opal ring, we were paying one of our frequent visits to the Lichtenberg Palace. I could never look at many pictures in succession; for pictures, when they are at all powerful, affect me so strongly that one or two exhaust all my capability of contemplation. This morning I had been looking at Giorgione's picture of the cruel-eyed woman, said to be a likeness of Lucrezia Borgia. I had stood long alone before it, fascinated by the terrible reality of that cunning, relentless face, till I felt a strange poisoned sensation, as if I had long been inhaling a fatal odour, and was just beginning to be conscious of its effects. Perhaps even then I should not have moved away, if the rest of the party had not returned to this room, and announced that they were going to the Belvedere Gallery to settle a bet which had arisen between my brother and Mr. Filmore about a portrait. I followed them dreamily, and was hardly alive to what occurred till they had all gone up to the gallery, leaving me below; for I refused to come within sight of another picture that day. I made my way to the Grand Terrace, since it was agreed that we should saunter in the gardens when the dispute had been decided. I had been sitting here a short space, vaguely conscious of trim gardens, with a city and green hills in the distance, when, wishing to avoid the proximity of the sentinel, I rose and walked down the broad stone steps, intending to seat myself farther on in the gardens. Just as I reached the gravel-walk, I felt an arm slipped within mine, and a light hand gently pressing my wrist. In the same instant a strange intoxicating numbness passed over me, like the continuance or climax of the sensation I was still feeling from the gaze of Lucrezia Borgia. The gardens, the summer sky, the consciousness of Bertha's arm being within mine, all vanished, and I seemed to be suddenly in darkness, out of which there gradually broke a dim firelight, and I felt myself sitting in my father's leather chair in the library at home. I knew the fireplace,—the dogs for the wood-fire,—the black marble chimney-piece with the white marble medallion of the dying Cleopatra in the centre. Intense and hopeless misery was pressing on my soul; the light became stronger, for Bertha was entering with a candle in her hand—Bertha, my wife—with cruel eyes, with green jewels and green leaves on her white ball-dress; every hateful thought within her present to me. . . . "Madman, idiot! why don't you kill yourself, then?" It was a moment of hell. I saw into her pitiless soul,—saw its barren worldliness, its scorching hate,—and felt it clothe me round like an air I was obliged to breathe. She came with her candle and stood over me with a bitter smile of contempt; I saw the great emerald brooch on her bosom, a studded serpent with diamond eyes. I shuddered,—I despised this woman with the barren soul and mean thoughts; but I felt helpless before her, as if she clutched my bleeding heart, and would clutch it till the last drop of life-blood ebbed away. She was my wife, and we hated each other. Gradually the hearth, the dim library, the candle-light disappeared,—seemed to melt away into a background of light, the green serpent with the diamond eyes remaining a dark image on the retina. Then I had a sense of my eyelids quivering, and the living daylight broke in upon me; I saw gardens, and heard voices; I was seated on the steps of the Belvedere Terrace, and my friends were round me.

The tumult of mind into which I was thrown by this hideous vision made me ill for several days, and prolonged our stay at Vienna. I shuddered with horror as the scene recurred to me; and it recurred constantly, with all its minutiæ, as if they had been burnt into my memory; and yet, such is the madness of the human heart under the influence of its immediate desires, I felt a wild hell-braving joy that Bertha was to be mine; for the fulfilment of my former prevision concerning her first appearance before me, left me little hope that this last hideous glimpse of the future was the mere diseased play of my own mind, and had no relation to external realities. One thing alone I looked towards as a possible means of casting doubt on my terrible conviction,—the discovery that my vision of Prague had been false,—and Prague was the next city on our route.

Meanwhile, I was no sooner in Bertha's society again, than I was as completely under her sway as before. What if I saw into the heart of Bertha, the matured woman—Bertha, my wife? Bertha, the *girl*, was a fascinating secret to me still: I trembled under her touch; I felt the witchery of her presence; I yearned to be assured of her love. The fear of poison is feeble against the sense of thirst. Nay, I was just as jealous of my brother as before—just as much irritated by his small patronizing ways; for my pride, my diseased sensibility, were there as they had always been, and winced as inevitably under every offence as my eye winced from an intruding mote. The future, even when brought within the compass of feeling by a vision that made me shudder, had still no more than the force of an idea, compared with the force of present emotion,—of my love for Bertha, of my dislike and jealousy towards my brother.

It is an old story, that men sell themselves to the tempter, and sign a bond with their blood, because it is only to take effect at a distant day; then rush on to snatch the cup their souls thirst after with an impulse not the less savage because there is a dark shadow beside them forevermore. There is no short cut, no patent tram-road, to wisdom: after all the centuries of invention, the soul's path lies through the thorny wilderness which must be still trodden in solitude, with bleeding feet, with sobs for help, as it was trodden by them of old time.

My mind speculated eagerly on the means by which I should become my brother's successful rival, for I was still too timid, in my ignorance of Bertha's actual feeling, to venture on any step that would urge from her an avowal of it. I thought I should gain confidence even for this, if my vision of Prague proved to have been veracious; and yet, the horror of that certitude! Behind the slim girl Bertha, whose words and looks I watched for, whose touch was bliss, there stood continually that Bertha with the fuller form, the harder eyes, the more rigid mouth,—with the barren selfish soul laid bare; no longer a fascinating secret, but a measured fact, urging itself perpetually on my unwilling sight. Are you unable to give me your sympathy—you who read this? Are you unable to imagine this double consciousness at work within me, flowing on like two parallel streams which never mingle their waters and blend into a common hue? Yet you must have known something of the presentiments that spring from an insight at war with passion; and my visions were only like presentiments intensified to horror. You have known the powerlessness of ideas before the might of impulse; and my visions, when once they had passed into memory, were mere ideas—pale shadows that beckoned in vain, while my hand was grasped by the living and the loved.

In after days I thought with bitter regret that if I had foreseen something more or something different—if instead of that hideous vision which poisoned the passion it could not destroy, or if even along with it I could have had a foreshadowing of that moment when I looked on my brother's face for the last time, some softening influence would have been shed over my feeling towards him: pride and hatred would surely have been subdued into pity, and the record of those hidden sins would have been shortened. But this is one of the vain thoughts with which we men flatter ourselves. We try to believe that the egoism within us would have easily been melted, and that it was only the narrowness of our knowledge which hemmed in our generosity, our awe, our human piety, and hindered them from submerging our hard indifference to the sensations and emotions of our fellow. Our tenderness and self-renunciation seem strong when our egoism has had its day,—when, after our mean striving for a triumph that is to be another's loss, the triumph comes suddenly, and we shudder at it, because it is held out by the chill hand of death.

Our arrival in Prague happened at night, and I was glad of this, for it seemed like a deferring of a terribly decisive moment, to be in the city for hours without seeing it. As we were not to remain long in Prague, but to go on speedily to Dresden, it was proposed that we should drive out the next morning and take a general view of the place, as well as visit some of its specially interesting spots, before the heat became oppressive—for we were in August, and the season was hot and dry. But it happened that the ladies were rather late at their morning toilet, and to my father's politely-repressed but perceptible annoyance, we were not in the carriage till the morning was far advanced. I thought with a sense of relief, as we entered the Jews' quarter, where we were to visit the old synagogue, that we should be kept in this flat, shut-up part of the city, until we should all be too tired and too warm to go farther, and so we should return without seeing more than the streets through which we had already passed. That would give me another day's suspense,—suspense, the only form in which a fearful spirit knows the solace of hope. But as I stood under the blackened, groined arches of that old synagogue, made dimly visible by the seven thin candles in the sacred lamp, while our Jewish cicerone reached down the Book of the Law, and read to us in its ancient tongue,—I felt a shuddering impression that this strange building, with its shrunken lights, this surviving withered remnant of medieval Judaism, was of a piece with my vision. Those darkened dusty Christian saints, with their loftier arches and their larger candles, needed the consolatory scorn with which they might point to a more shrivelled death-in-life than their own.

As I expected, when we left the Jews' quarter the elders of our party wished to return to the hotel. But now, instead of rejoicing in this, as I had done beforehand, I felt a sudden overpowering impulse to go on at once to the bridge, and put an end to the suspense I had been wishing to protract. I declared, with unusual decision, that I would get out of the carriage and walk on alone; they might return without me. My father, thinking this merely a sample of my usual "poetic nonsense," objected that I should only do myself harm by walking in the heat; but when I persisted, he said angrily that I might follow my own absurd devices, but that Schmidt (our courier) must go with me. I assented to this, and set off with Schmidt towards the bridge. I had no sooner passed from under the archway of the grand old gate leading on to the bridge, than a trembling seized me, and I turned cold under the mid-day sun; yet I went on; I was in search of something,—a small detail which I remembered with special intensity as part of my vision. There it was,—the patch of rainbow light on the pavement transmitted through a lamp in the shape of a star.

Chapter 2

Before the autumn was at an end, and while the brown leaves still stood thick on the beeches in our park, my brother and Bertha were engaged to each other, and it was understood that their marriage was to take place early in the next spring. In spite of the certainty I had felt from that moment on the bridge at Prague, that Bertha would one day be my wife, my constitutional timidity and distrust had continued to benumb me, and the words in which I had sometimes premeditated a confession of my love had died away unuttered. The same conflict had gone on within me as before,—the longing for an assurance of love from Bertha's lips, the dread lest a word of contempt and denial should fall upon me like a corrosive acid. What was the conviction of a distant necessity to me? I trembled under a present glance, I hungered after a present joy, I was clogged and chilled by a present fear. And so the days passed on: I witnessed Bertha's engagement and heard her marriage discussed as if I were under a conscious nightmare,—knowing it was a dream that would vanish, but feeling stifled under the grasp of hard-clutching fingers.

When I was not in Bertha's presence,—and I was with her very often, for she continued to treat me with a playful patronage that wakened no jealousy in my brother—I spent my time chiefly in wandering, in strolling, or taking long rides while the daylight lasted, and then shutting myself up with my unread books; for books had lost the power of chaining my attention. My self-consciousness was heightened to that pitch of intensity in which our own emotions take the form of a drama which urges itself imperatively on our contemplation, and we begin to weep, less under the sense of our suffering than at the thought of it. I felt a sort of pitying anguish over the pathos of my own lot: the lot of a being finely organized for pain, but with hardly any fibres that responded to pleasure,—to whom the idea of future evil robbed the present of its joy, and for whom the idea of future good did not still the uneasiness of a present yearning or a present dread. I went dumbly through that stage of the poet's suffering, in which he feels the delicious pang of utterance, and makes an image of his sorrows.

I was left entirely without remonstrance concerning this dreamy way-ward life: I knew my father's thought about me: "That lad will never be good for anything in life: he may waste his years in an insignificant way on the income that falls to him: I shall not trouble myself about a career for him."

One mild morning in the beginning of November, it happened that I was standing outside the portico patting lazy old Cæsar, a Newfoundland almost blind with age, the only dog that ever took any notice of me,—for the very dogs shunned me, and fawned on the happier people about me,—when the groom brought up my brother's horse which was to carry him to the hunt, and my brother himself appeared at the door, florid, broad-chested, and self-complacent, feeling what a good-natured fellow he was not to behave insolently to us all on the strength of his great advantages.

"Latimer, old boy," he said to me in a tone of compassionate cordiality, "what a pity it is you don't have a run with the hounds now and then! The finest thing in the world for low spirits!"

"Low spirits!" I thought bitterly, as he rode away; "that is the sort of phrase with which coarse, narrow natures like yours think to describe experience of which you can know no more than your horse knows. It is to such as you that the good of this world falls: ready dulness, healthy selfishness, good-tempered conceit,—these are the keys to happiness."

The quick thought came, that my selfishness was even stronger than his,—it was only a suffering selfishness instead of an enjoying one. But then, again, my exasperating insight into Alfred's self-complacent soul, his freedom from all the doubts and fears, the unsatisfied yearnings, the exquisite tortures of sensitiveness, that had made the web of my life, seemed to absolve me from all bonds towards him. This man needed no pity, no love; those fine influences would have been as little felt by him as the delicate white mist is felt by the rock it caresses. There was no evil in store for *him*: if he was not to marry Bertha, it would be because he had found a lot pleasanter to himself.

Mr. Filmore's house lay not more than half a mile beyond our own gates, and whenever I knew my brother was gone in another direction, I went there for the chance of finding Bertha at home. Later on in the day I walked thither. By a rare accident she was alone, and we walked out in the grounds together, for she seldom went on foot beyond the trimly swept gravel-walks. I remember what a beautiful sylph she looked to me as the low November sun shone on her blond hair, and she tripped along teasing me with her usual light banter, to which I listened half fondly, half moodily; it was all the sign Bertha's mysterious inner self ever made to me. To-day perhaps the moodiness predominated, for I had not yet shaken off the access of jealous hate which my brother had raised in me by his parting patronage. Suddenly I interrupted and startled her by saying, almost fiercely, "Bertha, how can you love Alfred?"

She looked at me with surprise for a moment, but soon her light smile came again, and she answered sarcastically, "Why do you suppose I love him?"

"How can you ask that, Bertha?"

"What! your wisdom thinks I must love the man I'm going to marry? The most unpleasant thing in the world. I should quarrel with him; I should be jealous of him; our *ménage* would be conducted in a very ill-bred manner. A little quiet contempt contributes greatly to the elegance of life."

"Bertha, that is not your real feeling. Why do you delight in trying to deceive me by inventing such cynical speeches?"

"I need never take the trouble of invention in order to deceive you, my small Tasso" (that was the mocking name she usually gave me). "The easiest way to deceive a poet is to tell him the truth."

She was testing the validity of her epigram in a daring way, and for a moment the shadow of my vision—the Bertha whose soul was no secret to me—passed between me and the radiant girl, the playful sylph whose feelings were a fascinating mystery. I suppose I must have shuddered, or betrayed in some other way my momentary chill of horror.

"Tasso!" she said, seizing my wrist and peeping round into my face, "are you really beginning to discern what a heartless girl I am? Why, you are not half the poet I thought you were; you are actually capable of believing the truth about me."

The shadow passed from between us, and was no longer the object nearest to me. The girl whose light fingers grasped me, whose elfish charming face looked into mine—who, I thought, was betraying an interest in my feelings that she would not have directly avowed,—this warm-breathing presence again possessed my senses and imagination like a returning siren melody which had been overpowered for an instant by the roar of threatening waves. It was a moment as delicious to me as the waking up to a consciousness of youth after a dream of middle age. I forgot everything but my passion, and said with swimming eyes,—

"Bertha, shall you love me when we are first married? I wouldn't mind if you really loved me only for a little while."

Her look of astonishment, as she loosed my hand and started away from me, recalled me to a sense of my strange, my criminal indiscretion.

"Forgive me," I said hurriedly, as soon as I could speak again; "I did not know what I was saying."

"Ah, Tasso's mad fit has come on, I see," she answered quietly, for she had recovered herself sooner than I had. "Let him go home and keep his head cool. I must go in, for the sun is setting."

I left her—full of indignation against myself. I had let slip words which, if she reflected on them, might rouse in her a suspicion of my abnormal mental condition—a suspicion which of all things I dreaded. And besides that, I was ashamed of the apparent baseness I had committed in uttering them to my brother's betrothed wife. I wandered home slowly, entering our park through a private gate instead of by the lodges. As I approached the house, I saw a man dashing off at full speed from the stable-yard across the park. Had any accident happened at home? No; perhaps it was only one of my father's peremptory business errands that required this headlong haste. Nevertheless I quickened my pace without any distinct motive, and was soon at the house. I will not dwell on the scene I found there. My brother was dead,—had been pitched from his horse, and killed on the spot by a concussion of the brain.

I went up to the room where he lay, and where my father was seated beside him with a look of rigid despair. I had shunned my father more than any one since our return home, for the radical antipathy between our natures made my insight into his inner self a constant affliction to me. But now, as I went up to him, and stood beside him in sad silence, I felt the presence of a new element that blended us as we had never been blent before. My father had been one of the most successful men in the money-getting world: he had had no sentimental sufferings, no illness. The heaviest trouble that had befallen him was the death of his first wife. But he married my mother soon after; and I remember he seemed exactly the same, to my keen childish observation, the week after her death as before. But now, at last, a sorrow had come,—the sorrow of old age, which suffers the more from the crushing of its pride and its hopes, in proportion as the pride and hope are narrow and prosaic. His son was to have been married soon,—would probably have stood for the borough at the next election. That son's existence was the best motive that could be alleged for making new purchases of land every year to round off the estate. It is a dreary thing to live on doing the same things year after year, without knowing why we do them. Perhaps the tragedy of disappointed youth and passion is less piteous than the tragedy of disappointed age and worldliness.

As I saw into the desolation of my father's heart, I felt a movement of deep pity towards him, which was the beginning of a new affection,—an affection that grew and strengthened in spite of the strange bitterness with which he regarded me in the first month or two after my brother's death. If it had not been for the softening influence of my compassion for him—the first deep compassion I had ever felt,—I should have been stung by the perception that my father transferred the inheritance of an eldest son to me with a mortified sense that fate had compelled him to the unwelcome course of caring for me as an important being. It was only in spite of himself that he began to think of me with anxious regard. There is hardly any neglected child for whom death has made vacant a more favoured place, who will not understand what I mean.

Gradually, however, my new deference to his wishes, the effect of that patience which was born of my pity for him, won upon his affection, and he began to please himself with the endeavour to make me fill my brother's place as fully as my feebler personality would admit. I saw that the prospect which by and by presented itself of my becoming Bertha's husband was welcome to him, and he even contemplated in my case what he had not intended in my brother's,—that his son and daughter-in-law should make one household with him. My softened feeling towards my father made this the happiest time I had known since childhood;—these last months in which I retained the delicious illusion of loving Bertha, of longing and doubting and hoping that she might love me. She behaved with a certain new consciousness and distance towards me after my brother's death; and I too was under a double constraint,—that of delicacy towards my brother's memory, and of anxiety as to the impression my abrupt words had left on her mind. But the additional screen this mutual reserve erected between us only brought me more completely under her power: no matter how empty the adytum, so that the veil be thick enough. So absolute is our soul's need of something hidden and uncertain for the maintenance of that doubt and hope and effort which are the breath of its life, that if the whole future were laid bare to us beyond to-day, the interest of all mankind would be bent on the hours that lie between; we should pant after the uncertainties of our one morning and our one afternoon; we should rush fiercely to the

Exchange for our last possibility of speculation, of success, of disappointment: we should have a glut of political prophets foretelling a crisis or a no-crisis within the only twenty-four hours left open to prophecy. Conceive the condition of the human mind if all propositions whatsoever were self-evident except one, which was to become self-evident at the close of a summer's day, but in the mean time might be the subject of question, of hypothesis, of debate. Art and philosophy, literature and science, would fasten like bees on that one proposition which had the honey of probability in it, and be the more eager because their enjoyment would end with sunset. Our impulses, our spiritual activities, no more adjust themselves to the idea of their future nullity, than the beating of our heart, or the irritability of our muscles.

Bertha, the slim, fair-haired girl, whose present thoughts and emotions were an enigma to me amidst the fatiguing obviousness of the other minds around me, was as absorbing to me as a single unknown to-day— as a single hypothetic proposition to remain problematic till sunset; and all the cramped, hemmed-in belief and disbelief, trust and distrust, of my nature welled out in this one narrow channel.

And she made me believe that she loved me. Without ever quitting her tone of *badinage* and playful superiority, she intoxicated me with the sense that I was necessary to her, that she was never at ease unless I was near her, submitting to her playful tyranny. It costs a woman so little effort to besot us in this way! A half-repressed word, a moment's unexpected silence, even an easy fit of petulance on our account, will serve us as *hashish* for a long while. Out of the subtlest web of scarcely perceptible signs, she set me weaving the fancy that she had always unconsciously loved me better than Alfred, but that, with the ignorant fluttered sensibility of a young girl, she had been imposed on by the charm that lay for her in the distinction of being admired and chosen by a man who made so brilliant a figure in the world as my brother. She satirized herself in a very graceful way for her vanity and ambition. What was it to me that I had the light of my wretched prevision on the fact that now it was I who possessed at least all but the personal part of my brother's advantages? Our sweet illusions are half of them conscious illusions, like effects of colour that we know to be made up of tinsel, broken glass, and rags.

We were married eighteen months after Alfred's death, one cold, clear morning in April, when there came hail and sunshine both together; and Bertha, in her white silk and pale-green leaves, and the pale hues of her hair and face, looked like the spirit of the morning. My father was happier than he had thought of being again: my marriage, he felt sure, would complete the desirable modification of my character, and make me practical and worldly enough to take my place in society among sane men. For he delighted in Bertha's tact and acuteness, and felt sure she would be mistress of me, and make me what she chose: I was only twenty-one, and madly in love with her. Poor father! He kept that hope a little while after our first year of marriage, and it was not quite extinct when paralysis came and saved him from utter disappointment.

I shall hurry through the rest of my story, not dwelling so much as I have hitherto done on my inward experience. When people are well known to each other, they talk rather of what befalls them externally, leaving their feelings and sentiments to be inferred.

We lived in a round of visits for some time after our return home, giving splendid dinner-parties, and making a sensation in our neighbourhood by the new lustre of our equipage, for my father had reserved this display of his increased wealth for the period of his son's marriage; and we gave our acquaintances liberal opportunity for remarking that it was a pity I made so poor a figure as an heir and a bridegroom. The nervous fatigue of this existence, the insincerities and platitudes which I had to live through twice over,—through my inner and outward sense,—would have been maddening to me, if I had not had that sort of intoxicated callousness which came from the delights of a first passion. A bride and bride-groom, surrounded by all the appliances of wealth, hurried through the day by the whirl of society, filling their solitary moments with hastily snatched caresses, are prepared for their future life together as the *novice* is prepared for the cloister—by experiencing its utmost contrast.

Through all these crowded excited months, Bertha's inward self remained shrouded from me, and I still read her thoughts only through the language of her lips and demeanour: I had still the human interest of wondering whether what I did and said pleased her, of longing to hear a word of affection, of giving a delicious exaggeration of meaning to her smile. But I was conscious of a growing difference in her manner towards me; sometimes strong enough to be called haughty coldness, cutting and chilling me as the hail had done that came across the sunshine on our marriage morning; sometimes only perceptible in the dexterous avoidance of a *tête-à-tête* walk or dinner to which I had been looking forward. I had been deeply pained by this,—had even felt a sort of crushing of the heart, from the sense that my brief day of happiness was near its setting; but still I remained dependent on Bertha, eager for the last rays of a bliss that would soon be gone forever, hoping and watching for some afterglow more beautiful from the impending night.

I remember—how should I not remember?—the time when that dependence and hope utterly left me, when the sadness I had felt in Bertha's growing estrangement became a joy that I looked back upon with longing as a man might look back on the last pains in a paralysed limb. It was just after the close of my father's last illness, which had necessarily withdrawn us from society and thrown us more on each other. It was the evening of my father's death. On that evening the veil which had shrouded Bertha's soul from me—had made me find in her alone among my fellow-beings the blessed possibility of mystery and doubt and expectation—was first withdrawn. Perhaps it was the first day since the beginning of my passion for her, in which that passion was completely neutralized by the presence of an absorbing feeling of another kind. I had been watching by my father's death-bed: I had been witnessing the last fitful yearning glance his soul had cast back on the spent inheritance of life,—the last faint consciousness of love he had gathered from the pressure of my hand. What are all our personal loves when we have been sharing in that supreme agony? In the first moments when we come away from the presence of death, every other relation to the living is merged, to our feeling, in the great relation of a common nature and a common destiny.

In that state of mind I joined Bertha in her private sitting-room. She was seated in a leaning posture on a settee, with her back towards the door; the great rich coils of her pale blond hair surmounting her small neck, visible above the back of the settee. I remember, as I closed the door behind me, a cold tremulousness seizing me, and a vague sense of being hated and lonely,—vague and strong, like a presentiment. I know how I looked at that moment, for I saw myself in Bertha's thought as she lifted her cutting grey eyes, and looked at me: a miserable ghost-seer, surrounded by phantoms in the noonday, trembling under a breeze when the leaves were still, without appetite for the common objects of human desire, but pining after the moonbeams. We were front to front with each other, and judged each other. The terrible moment of complete illumination had come to me, and I saw that the darkness had hidden no landscape from me, but only a blank prosaic wall: from that evening forth, through the sickening years which followed, I saw all round the narrow room of this woman's soul,—saw petty artifice and mere negation where I had delighted to believe in coy sensibilities and in wit at war with latent feeling,—saw the light floating vanities of the girl defining themselves into the systematic coquetry, the scheming selfishness, of the woman—saw repulsion and antipathy harden into cruel hatred, giving pain only for the sake of wreaking itself.

For Bertha too; after her kind, felt the bitterness of disillusion. She had believed that my wild poet's passion for her would make me her slave; and that, being her slave, I should execute her will in all things. With the essential shallowness of a negative, unimaginative nature, she was unable to conceive the fact that sensibilities were anything else than weaknesses. She had thought my weaknesses would put me in her power, and she found them unmanageable forces. Our positions were reversed. Before marriage she had completely mastered my imagination, for she was a secret to me; and I created the unknown thought before which I trembled as if it were hers. But now that her soul was laid open to me, now that I was compelled to share the privacy of her motives, to follow all the petty devices that preceded her words and acts, she found herself powerless with me, except to produce in me the chill shudder of repulsion,—powerless, because I could be acted on by no lever within her reach. I was dead to worldly ambitions, to social vanities, to all the incentives within the compass of her narrow imagination, and I lived under influences utterly invisible to her.

She was really pitiable to have such a husband, and so all the world thought. A graceful, brilliant woman, like Bertha, who smiled on morning callers, made a figure in ball-rooms, and was capable of that light repartee which, from such a woman, is accepted as wit, was secure of carrying off all sympathy from a husband who was sickly, abstracted, and, as some suspected, crack-brained. Even the servants in our house gave her the balance of their regard and pity. For there were no audible quarrels between us; our alienation, our repulsion from each other, lay within the silence of our own hearts; and if the mistress went out a great deal, and seemed to dislike the master's society, was it not natural, poor thing? The master was odd. I was kind and just to my dependants, but I excited in them a shrinking, half-contemptuous pity; for this class of men and women are but slightly determined in their estimate of others by general considerations, or even experience, of character. They judge of persons as they judge of coins, and value those who pass current at a high rate.

After a time I interfered so little with Bertha's habits, that it might seem wonderful how her hatred towards me could grow so intense and active as it did. But she had begun to suspect, by some involuntary betrayal of mine, that there was an abnormal power of penetration in me—that fitfully, at least, I was strangely cognizant of her thoughts and intentions, and she began to be haunted by a terror of me, which alternated every now and then with defiance. She meditated continually how the incubus could be shaken off her life,—how she could be freed from this hateful bond to a being whom she at once despised as an imbecile, and dreaded as an inquisitor. For a long while she lived in the hope that my evident wretchedness would drive me to the commission of suicide; but suicide was not in my nature. I was too completely swayed by the sense that I was in the grasp of unknown forces, to believe in my power of self-release. Towards my own destiny I had become entirely passive; for my one ardent desire had spent itself, and impulse no longer predominated over knowledge. For this reason I never thought of taking any steps towards a complete separation, which would have made our alienation evident to the world. Why should I rush for help to a new course, when I was only suffering from the consequences of a deed which had been the act of my intensest will? That would have been the logic of one who had desires to gratify, and I had no desires. But Bertha and I lived more and more aloof from each other. The rich find it easy to live married and apart.

That course of our life which I have indicated in a few sentences filled the space of years. So much misery, so slow and hideous a growth of hatred and sin, may be compressed into a sentence! And men judge of each other's lives through this summary medium. They epitomize the experience of their fellow-mortal, and pronounce judgment on him in neat syntax, and feel themselves wise and virtuous,—conquerors over the temptations they define in well-selected predicates. Seven years of wretchedness glide glibly over the lips of the man who has never counted them out in moments of chill disappointment, of head and heart throbbings, of dread and vain wrestling, of remorse and despair. We learn *words* by rote, but not their meaning; *that* must be paid for with our life-blood, and printed in the subtle fibres of our nerves.

But I will hasten to finish my story. Brevity is justified at once to those who readily understand, and to those who will never understand.

Some years after my father's death, I was sitting by the dim firelight in my library one January evening,—sitting in the leather chair that used to be my father's,—when Bertha appeared at the door, with a candle in her hand, and advanced towards me. I knew the ball-dress she had on,—the white ball-dress with the green jewels, shone upon by the light of the wax candle which lit up the medallion of the dying Cleopatra on the mantelpiece. Why did she come to me before going out? I had not seen her in the library, which was my habitual place, for months. Why did she stand before me with the candle in her hand, with her cruel contemptuous eyes fixed on me, and the glittering serpent, like a familiar demon, on her breast? For a moment I thought this fulfilment of my vision at Vienna marked some dreadful crisis in my fate, but I saw nothing in Bertha's mind, as she stood before me, except scorn for the look of overwhelming misery with which I sat before her. . . . "Fool, idiot, why don't you kill yourself, then?"—that was her thought. But at length her thoughts reverted to her errand, and she spoke aloud. The apparently indifferent nature of the errand seemed to make a ridiculous anticlimax to my prevision and my agitation.

"I have had to hire a new maid. Fletcher is going to be married, and she wants me to ask you to let her husband have the public-house and farm at Molton. I wish him to have it. You must give the promise now, because Fletcher is going to-morrow morning—and quickly, because I'm in a hurry."

"Very well; you may promise her," I said indifferently, and Bertha swept out of the library again.

I always shrank from the sight of a new person, and all the more when it was a person whose mental life was likely to weary my reluctant insight with worldly ignorant trivialities. But I shrank especially from the sight of this new maid, because her advent had been announced to me at a moment to which I could not cease to attach some fatality: I had a vague dread that I should find her mixed up with the dreary drama of my life,—that some new sickening vision would reveal her to me as an evil genius. When at last I did unavoidably meet her, the vague dread was

changed into definite disgust. She was a tall, wiry, dark-eyed woman, this
Mrs. Archer, with a face handsome enough to give her coarse hard nature
the odious finish of bold, self-confident coquetry. That was enough to
make me avoid her, quite apart from the contemptuous feeling with
which she contemplated me. I seldom saw her; but I perceived that she
rapidly became a favourite with her mistress, and, after the lapse of eight
or nine months, I began to be aware that there had arisen in Bertha's
mind towards this woman a mingled feeling of fear and dependence, and
that this feeling was associated with ill-defined images of candle-light
scenes in her dressing-room, and the locking-up of something in Bertha's
cabinet. My interviews with my wife had become so brief and so rarely
solitary that I had no opportunity of perceiving these images in her mind
with more definiteness. The recollections of the past become contracted
in the rapidity of thought till they sometimes bear hardly a more distinct
resemblance to the external reality than the forms of an oriental alpha-
bet to the objects that suggested them.

Besides, for the last year or more a modification had been going forward in my mental condition, and was growing more and more marked.
My insight into the minds of those around me was becoming dimmer
and more fitful, and the ideas that crowded my double consciousness
became less and less dependent on any personal contact. All that was personal in me seemed to be suffering a gradual death, so that I was losing
the organ through which the personal agitations and projects of others
could affect me. But along with this relief from wearisome insight, there
was a new development of what I concluded—as I have since found
rightly,—to be a prevision of external scenes. It was as if the relation
between me and my fellow-men was more and more deadened, and my
relation to what we call the inanimate was quickened into new life. The
more I lived apart from society, and in proportion as my wretchedness
subsided from the violent throb of agonized passion into the dulness of
habitual pain, the more frequent and vivid became such visions as that I
had had of Prague,—of strange cities, of sandy plains, of gigantic ruins,
of midnight skies with strange bright constellations, of mountain-passes,
of grassy nooks flecked with the afternoon sunshine through the boughs:
I was in the midst of such scenes, and in all of them one presence seemed
to weigh on me in all these mighty shapes,—the presence of something
unknown and pitiless. For continual suffering had annihilated religious
faith within me: to the utterly miserable—the unloving and the
unloved—there is no religion possible, no worship but a worship of devils. And beyond all these, and continually recurring, was the vision of my
death,—the pangs, the suffocation, the last struggle, when life would be
grasped at in vain.

Things were in this state near the end of the seventh year. I had
become entirely free from insight, from my abnormal cognizance of any
other consciousness than my own, and instead of intruding involuntarily

into the world of other minds, was living continually in my own solitary future. Bertha was aware that I was greatly changed. To my surprise she had of late seemed to seek opportunities of remaining in my society, and had cultivated that kind of distant yet familiar talk which is customary between a husband and wife who live in polite and irrevocable alienation. I bore this with languid submission, and without feeling enough interest in her motives to be roused into keen observation; yet I could not help perceiving something triumphant and excited in her carriage and the expression of her face,—something too subtle to express itself in words or tones, but giving one the idea that she lived in a state of expectation or hopeful suspense. My chief feeling was satisfaction that her inner self was once more shut out from me; and I almost revelled for the moment in the absent melancholy that made me answer her at cross purposes, and betray utter ignorance of what she had been saying. I remember well the look and the smile with which she one day said, after a mistake of this kind on my part: "I used to think you were a clairvoyant, and that was the reason why you were so bitter against other clairvoyants, wanting to keep your monopoly; but I see now you have become rather duller than the rest of the world."

I said nothing in reply. It occurred to me that her recent obtrusion of herself upon me might have been prompted by the wish to test my power of detecting some of her secrets; but I let the thought drop again at once: her motives and her deeds had no interest for me, and whatever pleasures she might be seeking, I had no wish to balk her. There was still pity in my soul for every living thing, and Bertha was living,—was surrounded with possibilities of misery.

Just at this time there occurred an event which roused me somewhat from my inertia, and gave me an interest in the passing moment that I had thought impossible for me. It was a visit from Charles Meunier, who had written me word that he was coming to England for relaxation from too strenuous labour, and would like to see me. Meunier had now a European reputation; but his letter to me expressed that keen remembrance of an early regard, an early debt of sympathy, which is inseparable from nobility of character: and I too felt as if his presence would be to me like a transient resurrection into a happier pre-existence.

He came, and as far as possible, I renewed our old pleasure of making *tête-à-tête* excursions, though, instead of mountains and glaciers and the wide blue lake, we had to content ourselves with mere slopes and ponds and artificial plantations. The years had changed us both, but with what different result! Meunier was now a brilliant figure in society, to whom elegant women pretended to listen, and whose acquaintance was boasted of by noblemen ambitious of brains. He repressed with the utmost delicacy all betrayal of the shock which I am sure he must have received from our meeting, or of a desire to penetrate into my condition and circumstances, and sought by the utmost exertion of his charming social powers to make our reunion agreeable. Bertha was much struck by the unexpected fascinations of a visitor whom she had expected to find presentable only on the score of his celebrity, and put forth all her coquetries and accomplishments. Apparently she succeeded in attracting his admiration, for his manner towards her was attentive and flattering. The effect of his presence on me was so benignant, especially in those renewals of our old *tête-à-tête* wanderings, when he poured forth to me wonderful narratives of his professional experience, that more than once, when his talk turned on the psychological relations of disease, the thought crossed my mind that, if his stay with me were long enough, I might possibly bring myself to tell this man the secrets of my lot. Might there not lie some remedy for *me, too, in his science*? Might there not at least lie some comprehension and sympathy ready for me in his large and susceptible mind? But the thought only flickered feebly now and then, and died out before it could become a wish. The horror I had of again breaking in on the privacy of another soul made me, by an irrational instinct, draw the shroud of concealment more closely around my own, as we automatically perform the gesture we feel to be wanting in another.

When Meunier's visit was approaching its conclusion, there happened an event which caused some excitement in our household, owing to the surprisingly strong effect it appeared to produce on Bertha,—on Bertha, the self-possessed, who usually seemed inaccessible to feminine agitations, and did even her hate in a self-restrained hygienic manner. This event was the sudden severe illness of her maid, Mrs. Archer. I have reserved to this moment the mention of a circumstance which had forced itself on my notice shortly before Meunier's arrival, namely, that there had been some quarrel between Bertha and this maid, apparently during a visit to a distant family, in which she had accompanied her mistress. I had overheard Archer speaking in a tone of bitter insolence, which I should have thought an adequate reason for immediate dismissal. No dismissal followed; on the contrary, Bertha seemed to be silently putting up with personal inconveniences from the exhibitions of this woman's temper. I was the more astonished to observe that her illness seemed a cause of strong solicitude to Bertha; that she was at the bedside night and day, and would allow no one else to officiate as head-nurse. It happened that our family doctor was out on a holiday, an accident which made Meunier's presence in the house doubly welcome, and he apparently entered into the case with an interest which seemed so much stronger than the ordinary professional feeling, that one day when he had fallen into a long fit of silence after visiting her, I said to him,—

"Is this a very peculiar case of disease, Meunier?"

"No," he answered, "it is an attack of peritonitis which will be fatal, but which does not differ physically from many other cases that have come under my observation. But I'll tell you what I have on my mind. I want to make an experiment on this woman, if you will give me permission. It can do her no harm,—will give her no pain,—for I shall not make it until life is extinct to all purposes of sensation. I want to try the effect of transfusing blood into her arteries after the heart has ceased to beat for some minutes. I have tried the experiment again and again with animals that have died of this disease, with astounding results, and I want to try it on a human subject. I have the small tubes necessary, in a case I have with me, and the rest of the apparatus could be prepared readily. I should use my own blood,—take it from my own arm. This woman won't live through the night, I'm convinced, and I want you to promise me your assistance in making the experiment. I can't do without another hand, but it would perhaps not be well to call in a medical assistant from among your provincial doctors. A disagreeable foolish version of the thing might get abroad."

"Have you spoken to my wife on the subject?" I said, "because she appears to be peculiarly sensitive about this woman: she has been a favourite maid."

"To tell you the truth," said Meunier, "I don't want her to know about it. There are always insuperable difficulties with women in these matters, and the effect on the supposed dead body may be startling. You and I will sit up together, and be in readiness. When certain symptoms appear I shall take you in, and at the right moment we must manage to get every one else out of the room."

I need not give our farther conversation on the subject. He entered very fully into the details, and overcame my repulsion from them, by exciting in me a mingled awe and curiosity concerning the possible results of his experiment.

We prepared everything, and he instructed me in my part as assistant. He had not told Bertha of his absolute conviction that Archer would not survive through the night, and endeavoured to persuade her to leave the patient and take a night's rest. But she was obstinate, suspecting the fact that death was at hand, and supposing that he wished merely to save her nerves. She refused to leave the sick-room. Meunier and I sat up together in the library, he making frequent visits to the sick-room, and returning with the information that the case was taking precisely the course he expected. Once he said to me, "Can you imagine any cause of ill feeling this woman has against her mistress, who is so devoted to her?"

"I think there was some misunderstanding between them before her illness. Why do you ask?"

"Because I have observed for the last five or six hours,—since, I fancy, she has lost all hope of recovery,—there seems a strange prompting in her to say something which pain and failing strength forbid her to utter; and there is a look of hideous meaning in her eyes, which she turns continually towards her mistress. In this disease the mind often remains singularly clear to the last."

"I am not surprised at an indication of malevolent feeling in her," I said. "She is a woman who has always inspired me with distrust and dislike, but she managed to insinuate herself into her mistress's favour." He was silent after this, looking at the fire with an air of absorption, till he went upstairs again. He stayed away longer than usual, and on returning, said to me quietly, "Come now."

I followed him to the chamber where death was hovering. The dark hangings of the large bed made a background that gave a strong relief to Bertha's pale face as I entered. She started forward as she saw me enter, and then looked at Meunier with an expression of angry inquiry; but he lifted up his hand as if to impose silence, while he fixed his glance on the dying woman and felt her pulse. The face was pinched and ghastly, a cold perspiration was on the forehead, and the eyelids were lowered so as to conceal the large dark eyes. After a minute or two, Meunier walked round to the other side of the bed where Bertha stood, and with his usual air of gentle politeness towards her begged her to leave the patient under our care,—everything should be done for her,—she was no longer in a state to be conscious of an affectionate presence. Bertha was hesitating, apparently almost willing to believe his assurance and to comply. She looked round at the ghastly dying face, as if to read the confirmation of that assurance, when for a moment the lowered eyelids were raised again, and it seemed as if the eyes were looking towards Bertha, but blankly. A shudder passed through Bertha's frame, and she returned to her station near the pillow, tacitly implying that she would not leave the room.

The eyelids were lifted no more. Once I looked at Bertha as she watched the face of the dying one. She wore a rich *peignoir*, and her blond hair was half covered by a lace cap: in her attire she was, as always, an elegant woman, fit to figure in a picture of modern aristocratic life: but I asked myself how that face of hers could ever have seemed to me the face of a woman born of woman, with memories of childhood, capable of pain, needing to be fondled? The features at that moment seemed so preternaturally sharp, the eyes were so hard and eager,—she looked like a cruel immortal, finding her spiritual feast in the agonies of a dying race. For across those hard features there came something like a flash when the last hour had been breathed out, and we all felt that the dark veil had completely fallen. What secret was there between Bertha and this woman? I turned my eyes from her with a horrible dread lest my insight should return, and I should be obliged to see what had been breeding about two unloving women's hearts. I felt that Bertha had been watching for the moment of death as the sealing of her secret: I thanked Heaven it could remain sealed for me.

Meunier said quietly, "She is gone." He then gave his arm to Bertha, and she submitted to be led out of the room.

I suppose it was at her order that two female attendants came into the room, and dismissed the younger one who had been present before. When they entered, Meunier had already opened the artery in the long thin neck that lay rigid on the pillow, and I dismissed them, ordering them to remain at a distance till we rang: the doctor, I said, had an operation to perform,—he was not sure about the death. For the next twenty minutes I forgot everything but Meunier and the experiment in which he was so absorbed that I think his senses would have been closed against all sounds or sights which had no relation to it. It was my task at first to keep up the artificial respiration in the body after the transfusion had been effected, but presently Meunier relieved me, and I could see the wondrous slow return of life; the breast began to heave, the inspirations became stronger, the eyelids quivered, and the soul seemed to have returned beneath them. The artificial respiration was withdrawn: still the breathing continued, and there was a movement of the lips.

Just then I heard the handle of the door moving: I suppose Bertha had heard from the women that they had been dismissed: probably a vague fear had arisen in her mind, for she entered with a look of alarm. She came to the foot of the bed and gave a stifled cry.

The dead woman's eyes were wide open, and met hers in full recognition,—the recognition of hate. With a sudden strong effort, the hand that Bertha had thought forever still was pointed towards her, and the haggard face moved. The gasping eager voice said,—

"You mean to poison your husband . . . the poison is in the black cabinet . . . I got it for you . . . you laughed at me, and told lies about me behind my back, to make me disgusting . . . because you were jealous . . . are you sorry . . . now?"

The lips continued to murmur, but the sounds were no longer distinct. Soon there was no sound,—only a slight movement: the flame had leaped out, and was being extinguished the faster. The wretched woman's heart-strings had been set to hatred and vengeance; the spirit of life had swept the chords for an instant, and was gone again forever. Great God! Is this what it is to live again . . . to wake up with our unstilled thirst upon us, with our unuttered curses rising to our lips, with our muscles ready to act out their half-committed sins?

Bertha stood pale at the foot of the bed, quivering and helpless, despairing of devices, like a cunning animal whose hiding-places are surrounded by swift-advancing flame. Even Meunier looked paralysed; life for that moment ceased to be a scientific problem to him. As for me, this scene seemed of one texture with the rest of my existence: horror was my familiar, and this new revelation was only like an old pain recurring with new circumstances.

Since then Bertha and I have lived apart,—she in her own neighbourhood, the mistress of half our wealth; I as a wanderer in foreign countries, until I came to this Devonshire nest to die. Bertha lives pitied and admired; for what had I against that charming woman, whom every one but myself could have been happy with? There had been no witness of the scene in the dying room except Meunier, and while Meunier lived his lips were sealed by a promise to me.

Once or twice, weary of wandering, I rested in a favourite spot, and my heart went out towards the men and women and children whose faces were becoming familiar to me; but I was driven away again in terror at the approach of my old insight,—driven away to live continually with the one Unknown Presence revealed and yet hidden by the moving curtain of the earth and sky. Till at last disease took hold of me and forced me to rest here,—forced me to live in dependence on my servants. And then the curse of insight, of my double consciousness, came again, and has never left me. I know all their narrow thoughts, their feeble regard, their half-wearied pity.

It is the 20th of September, 1850. I know these figures I have just written, as if they were a long familiar inscription. I have seen them on this page in my desk unnumbered times, when the scene of my dying struggle has opened upon me. . . .

1859

FICTION

FLATLAND: A ROMANCE OF MANY DIMENSIONS, Edwin A. Abbott. (0-486-27263-X)

PRIDE AND PREJUDICE, Jane Austen. (0-486-28473-5)

CIVIL WAR SHORT STORIES AND POEMS, Edited by Bob Blaisdell. (0-486-48226-X)

THE DECAMERON: Selected Tales, Giovanni Boccaccio. Edited by Bob Blaisdell. (0-486-41113-3)

JANE EYRE, Charlotte Brontë. (0-486-42449-9)

WUTHERING HEIGHTS, Emily Brontë. (0-486-29256-8)

THE THIRTY-NINE STEPS, John Buchan. (0-486-28201-5)

ALICE'S ADVENTURES IN WONDERLAND, Lewis Carroll. (0-486-27543-4)

MY ÁNTONIA, Willa Cather. (0-486-28240-6)

THE AWAKENING, Kate Chopin. (0-486-27786-0)

HEART OF DARKNESS, Joseph Conrad. (0-486-26464-5)

LORD JIM, Joseph Conrad. (0-486-40650-4)

THE RED BADGE OF COURAGE, Stephen Crane. (0-486-26465-3)

THE WORLD'S GREATEST SHORT STORIES, Edited by James Daley. (0-486-44716-2)

A CHRISTMAS CAROL, Charles Dickens. (0-486-26865-9)

GREAT EXPECTATIONS, Charles Dickens. (0-486-41586-4)

A TALE OF TWO CITIES, Charles Dickens. (0-486-40651-2)

CRIME AND PUNISHMENT, Fyodor Dostoyevsky. Translated by Constance Garnett. (0-486-41587-2)

THE ADVENTURES OF SHERLOCK HOLMES, Sir Arthur Conan Doyle. (0-486-47491-7)

THE HOUND OF THE BASKERVILLES, Sir Arthur Conan Doyle. (0-486-28214-7)

BLAKE: PROPHET AGAINST EMPIRE, David V. Erdman. (0-486-26719-9)

WHERE ANGELS FEAR TO TREAD, E. M. Forster. (0-486-27791-7)

BEOWULF, Translated by R. K. Gordon. (0-486-27264-8)

THE RETURN OF THE NATIVE, Thomas Hardy. (0-486-43165-7)

THE SCARLET LETTER, Nathaniel Hawthorne. (0-486-28048-9)

SIDDHARTHA, Hermann Hesse. (0-486-40653-9)

THE ODYSSEY, Homer. (0-486-40654-7)

THE TURN OF THE SCREW, Henry James. (0-486-26684-2)

DUBLINERS, James Joyce. (0-486-26870-5)